1979

R. B- Stys

Night in Bombay

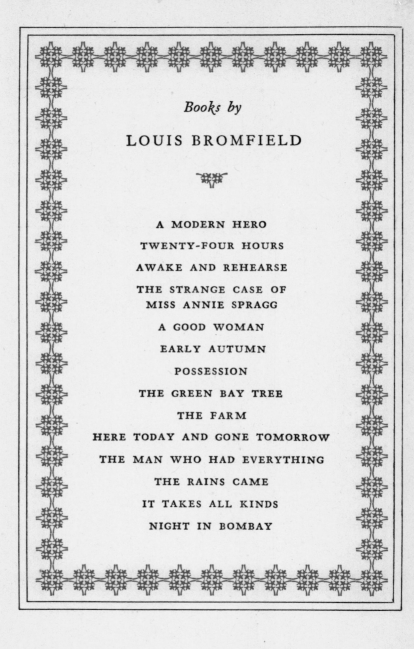

NIGHT
IN
BOMBAY

BY
LOUIS BROMFIELD

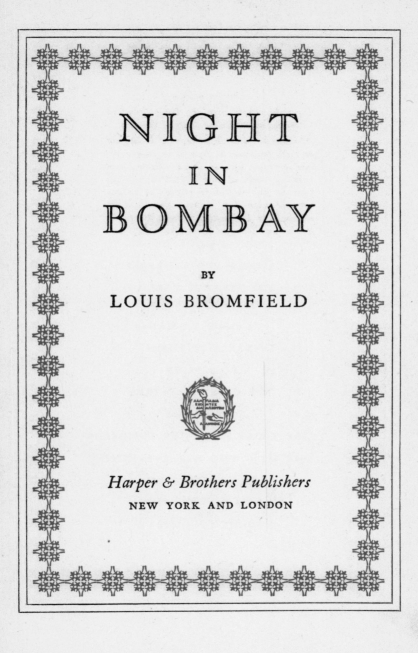

Harper & Brothers Publishers
NEW YORK AND LONDON

This story appeared serially under the title of BOMBAY NIGHTS

For

JEAN WHITE

WITH THE LOVE, GRATITUDE AND DEVOTION

OF ALL THE BROMFIELDS

FROM

LOUIS BROMFIELD

*

Night in Bombay

HIS luggage was all ready to be taken ashore, his cabin in order and now he stood on the upper deck just beneath the bridge watching the flying fish scud out of each jade green land swell of the Arabian Gulf like swift pencils of silver and disappear again in glittering jets of spray. He was a tall, good-looking fellow with square shoulders over which his Hanover Street tailor found no need to put any padding. His clothes said "London" in a discreet whisper, but you knew at once that he was an American. There was something in the blue eyes, the pitch of the chin, but more than anything in the generous, full curve of the lips and the tiny lines about the eyes which betrayed him. His face told you that he came of a people who were gamblers, who were sometimes reckless, and a people who knew how to laugh. He was the American who knew his way about the world, and so in many ways he was dangerous, to himself perhaps more than to others.

He didn't think of himself any longer as wild: he believed quite earnestly that he had settled down. In fact he was rather proud of himself that in his early thirties he had pulled himself together suddenly and made sense. That was the reason he had packed all his luggage carefully, even meticulously with his own hand, instead of asking the steward to do it; that was the reason he had carefully pulled out every drawer and left the door of the cupboard open to show that nothing had been left behind. He did things like that as an exercise, as a kind of discipline—to keep himself in order and prove to himself that he was a serious fellow, organized and efficient. It made him feel that he had developed something his father called "character," which he knew only meant counting ten before he acted: it meant not going off the deep end the moment the prospect of fun appeared on the horizon. Certainly, on this trip he meant to be good; it was a test. He meant to show his father that he had settled down.

So, at the moment, he felt virtuous and even proud, and fresh and cool and clean, although the heat was beginning to rise—the strange, dead, damp heat which hung over Bombay and the Arabian Gulf even in the winter season. No, he was being a sound business man, cool, shrewd, serious, on a tour through the Orient, visiting agencies of his father's company in Bombay, Singapore, Medan Deli, Sourabaya, Macassar and Tonkin.

'A voice beside him said, "Good morning," and he turned to find Mrs. Trollope standing beneath his elbow. She was a tiny woman but very tough, who came from Sydney. She was on her way from London to Bombay to stop off for a fortnight and then go on to Australia. That much she had told him and no more. He really didn't care very much what her plans were, but it annoyed him vaguely that she seemed to think that he was curious. He thought she must be about forty, but her dead brown hair and weathered skin made her perfectly ageless. She wore rather worn expensive clothes without knowing quite how to wear them. And she played excellent bridge and better poker.

"Good morning," he said. "Beautiful morning."

"Yes," said Mrs. Trollope. "But it's always fine here this time of the year."

"Funny things—flying fish."

"Yes," Mrs. Trollope wasn't much gifted in the appreciation of nature. She sniffed the air. "Ah!" she said. "Smell it? That Bombay smell."

He sniffed and became aware of a smell he knew at once—a curious mixed smell faintly dominated by the smell of drying fish.

"Bombay duck."

"Yes."

But there was more to the smell than that. There was in it the compounded odors of spice and wood smoke, of jasmine and marigold and of dust and copra and cow dung smoke. And for Wainwright there was much more in it—there was the strange excitement of memories—memories of parties, of drinking, of easy seductions, of extraordinary nights beneath a sky of blue velvet in which stars glittered like diamonds, of rides in gherries, down from some garden suspended on the side of Malabar Hill, to the Hotel Taj Mahal; memories of an immense, cool room of white marble high

[2]

above the bay. The man who a little while before had packed so meticulously and felt so virtuous, trembled a little with apprehension. It was, decidedly, a dangerous smell, but deliciously exciting. Even in the heat, a little shiver ran through his blood. There was no smell in the world quite like it.

"Have you seen the spy this morning?" asked Mrs. Trollope.

"No."

"I haven't either but I don't think she'll be looking for me after last night."

Bill chuckled, "No, I should think not."

He laughed now at the memory of the scene in the smoking room, although he hadn't laughed at the time because it had shocked him. The spy had forced her way into the poker game with himself and Mrs. Trollope and the little Maharajah of Jellapore, and Gibson, the trainer of the Maharajah's horses and Joey, the Maharajah's A.D.C. And then, sitting there, swarthy and covered with dirty diamonds and glowering, she had quarreled with everybody and even accused poor harmless, tipsy, little Joey of cheating. There wasn't any way of getting rid of her until Mrs. Trollope lost her temper and told her to get the hell out of the smoking room.

At the memory of the scene Bill laughed again—Mrs. Trollope like a small terrier worrying the Baroness who was like a fat elderly pug dog. And in the end the terrier had won, for the pug dog had become bewildered by the attack, and gathering up all her bags and cigarette cases and trinkets and bangles, she had gone off to her cabin. There was only one element in the whole scene which spoiled the complete absurdity of it. The figure of the Baroness, rattling, slinking and waddling away from the table across the smoking room had suddenly seemed, despite her offensiveness, pitifully defeated and broken, and, above all else, lonely. He had thought, "That sort of thing has been happening to her all her life. She must have been ugly and unattractive and hateful even as a baby."

And before she was well out of the door they had forgotten her and gone on with the poker game.

Mrs. Trollope was speaking again.

"Do you think she's really a spy?"

[3]

"No, she's too obviously made up like one."

Mrs. Trollope snorted, "I'd like to know what her history really is."

"She says she was born in Prague."

"I should think she came from Middle Europe."

"She's got a fine German accent for an Egyptian Baroness."

Mrs. Trollope laughed and lighted a cigarette. She did it efficiently, quickly, with an economy of movement, like a man. When she played bridge or poker she lighted one cigarette from another while the pile of butts grew into a small mountain beside her.

Puffing, she said, "It's very queer, her going to Bombay all alone —just for the ride."

"I should think she's been doing that all her life."

"Well, I've been in Egypt a good many times and I never heard of her."

"Cairo is a pretty complex town. You'd have to live there a lifetime to know all the intricacies of Cairo society."

"Anyway, there aren't any Barons among the Egyptians. Egyptians haven't got any titles."

"No, they buy them sometimes from needy Italians."

She was silent then, her attention caught by the spectacle on the foredeck below them. Lazily Bill thought how vindictively women could hate each other. The men at the poker party had forgotten the Baroness once her fat round-shouldered figure had disappeared through the door of the smoking room, but Mrs. Trollope had gone on hating her. She'd probably never forget the Baroness and when the opportunity arose, if it ever did, she would do her a dirty trick. It was just as well they were at the end of the voyage; people on the ship had begun to be bored and get on each other's nerves. They had begun to tell stories about one another.

On the foredeck below them everything was being put in readiness for landing, and Wainwright watched the spectacle with a faint sense of regret. So long as you were on a boat, life was simple and uncomplicated. People couldn't telephone you and you couldn't get involved in rendezvous you didn't want to keep, in escapades which really had no interest for you. He always behaved himself on a ship, perhaps because he had spent so much time on ships. He grinned and thought, "It's the one place to get away

[4]

from it all." As soon as he landed some sort of trouble would start again, some incredible complication he had never dreamed of.

It had never occurred to him that it was not only that he attracted preposterous adventures; he went out looking for them. That may have been the reason why long ago he had acquired the label of "black sheep."

The Goanese crew below them was coiling ropes and opening hatches, loosening winches and rattling chains. The third class passengers—Levantines, three or four thrifty Scots not wasting any money on their passage, a few rather scrawny bespectacled Indian students and a sprinkling of Moslems with beards dyed freshly red as a sign that they were returning from Mecca—had been thrust behind a barrier and stood there pressed together in the heat watching the hazy outlines of shore and islands emerging from the heat mist.

"Well," said Mrs. Trollope, "I won't have to listen to 'Alone' any more."

Wainwright laughed, "I'll miss little Jelly."

"Oh, you'll be seeing him."

Night after night they had gone to the cabin of the Maharajah of Jellapore for champagne, and night after night they had listened while the dark little man, with tears in his eyes, had played a sentimental tune called "Alone" over and over on his expensive electric gramophone. The nickname of "Jelly" suited him. It was a name known all over India and the Casinos, night clubs and race courses of Europe.

"It's not a bad tune if you don't run it into the ground."

"I found out why he wept when he played it. The tears were tears of self-pity."

"Why self-pity? He's got everything."

"No, he hasn't. He has a fixation for 'Alone' because he's been impotent for six months. He told me so."

Mrs. Trollope chuckled, "I get the point." It was a wicked, vindictive sound. Turning, she pointed with her cigarette. "Look, the palms of Juhu." And on the other side, "And there's Elephanta."

On the left out of the heat haze, the cocoanut palms swam above the muddy water of the bay as in a mirage, and on the right the

[5]

bulk of Elephanta Island arose. At sight of them Bill felt a shiver of anticipation run through his blood again.

"You know Bombay pretty well?" he asked over his shoulder.

A look of amusement illumined her face, as if she were going to tell him something remarkably interesting. He had already learned that when such a look came into the small bright eyes set in the weathered face, she was about to relate a shady story or a piece of scandal. This time it died almost at once and she said, dully, "Yes, I do."

For a time they watched the busy scene on the deck below them. Presently she said, "What do your friends call you?"

"Bill. You might as well call me that too. We'll be seeing each other in Bombay."

"Maybe."

"Why not? We can't miss each other—what with the Willingdon Club, the Taj bar and the races."

She turned sharply toward him. "I might as well tell you. If you're going around with the English much, you won't see me."

"I won't be. I don't go half around the world to spend my time with Englishmen I'd never see in England."

"Do you know many Indians?"

"Yes, I do."

"Like 'em?"

"Yes. They seem to me just like anybody else."

She turned back again looking at the muddy water of the bay. "I told you I was going to stay with my sister. Well, my sister married an Indian. She's an Australian to begin with, so we don't see much of the English . . . for both reasons."

"I see," said Bill. "What is he—a merchant or a professor?"

"He isn't anything anymore. He was a Rajah, but he's dead. She's got a palace on Malabar Hill next to the Nizam's palace."

"Is she . . . retired?"

"Yes. They've started her with a small pension."

Then through the heat and the laziness of his brain, his memory began to function, and he remembered a big, handsome, rather blowsy blonde woman—very blonde, the voluptuous peaches and cream type, with blue eyes, coming into Maxim's in Paris, marvel-

[6]

ously dressed and wearing wonderful jewels. That was the first time he had ever seen her.

He said, "But I know her. At least I've met her—Chandrapore . . . Chandragar."

"Chandragar. . . . Nelly is her name . . . Nelly Chandragar."

"She's not much like you."

"No, she's not. Nobody ever believes we're sisters. She's the Circassian houri type—right out of a Moslem paradise." She threw her cigarette into the muddy water of the bay and said, "I've got to go below and check up on my luggage before the harpies come aboard and seize it."

"You haven't told me your name," said Wainwright, "in case we do meet in Bombay."

"It's Stitch," said Mrs. Trollope, "Stitch Trollope. I got it as a little girl in my father's lumber camp in the bush. The lumberjacks used to call me that as a kid. It always stuck. Toodle-oo." And she disappeared around the corner of the smoking room.

For a moment he stood looking after her, grinning. He meant to look her up in Bombay whether she desired it or not. There was something hard about her and tough. He even liked her sexlessness—that she was neither a man nor woman, or if she had once been a woman, she had had enough of it and renounced it; that she had no coquetry and you could have a good laugh with her without becoming involved. He even liked her rather low mind and rough stories. "Who," he wondered, "was Mr. Trollope and what has become of him." He imagined that Mr. Trollope, whoever or wherever he was, had never counted for much in Stitch's life.

"Stitch," he said, half aloud. "A Stitch in time."

The deck about and below him began to fill with passengers who by now seemed old friends. They leaned over the rail looking at the city which had begun to appear out of the haze—the Taj Mahal Hotel, the Readymoney Building, the Yacht Club, the Gateway of India and the green eminence of Malabar Hill, dotted with bungalows and the palaces of the Maharajahs with the Towers of Silence at the foot of them all like the coffin which was carried among the guests at an Egyptian banquet. Life and death in India, more than anywhere else in the world, went hand in hand. He

[7]

sighed, "Here today and gone tomorrow." The state of life or the fact of death could not have much importance to millions of small dark people who owned no more than a loin cloth and lived and died without ever having enough to eat one day of their lives. Yes, Bombay was fantastic and romantic and extraordinary things happened there, if you didn't notice the coolies, the women and the children sleeping on sidewalks and in gutters as you drove home from a good party about sunrise.

Out of the corner of his eye he saw coming toward him the Indian woman they said was a dancer. She was a small woman, dressed in a black sari and wearing a great many silver bracelets. She walked superbly, scarcely seeming to walk at all, but to glide with the smooth easy motion of a cobra. She was neither very young nor very beautiful, but there was a perfection about the figure, the great dark eyes, and the camellia skin which held the glance of passers-by. All through the voyage Bill, like the other passengers, had noticed her, and it gave him a frank pleasure now to watch her coming along the deck toward him. It was not the attraction of a pretty woman; he was not conscious of her as a woman at all. The pleasure he experienced was more like the pleasure one finds in contemplating a fine picture or hearing superb music. She was a work of art. In a way she was India. They said she was a dancer and that her husband was a scientist in Bombay. That was all he could find out about her.

She was opposite him now and interrupted his staring with a scarcely perceptible smile, as if she were saying, "Good-bye. I hope you enjoy India." Then she was gone past him in all the serene dignity which had kept her aloof and apart from the other passengers throughout the long voyage.

The sight of her made him feel a sudden pang of self-reproach. "Maybe this time," he thought, "I really ought to find out something about India instead of just playing around Bombay." Bombay wasn't anything. It wasn't India, or East or West, but an extraordinary muddle of everything on earth.

A slap on the back roused him and a voice said, "Good-bye, laddie, and good luck." It was the Scotsman (he couldn't remember his name) who had a Shell agency in Burma—a tough, beefy man who looked singularly at home already.

[8]

"Don't say good-bye yet," said Bill, "I'll see you at the bar at the Taj Mahal."

"No, you won't. I'm going to pick up some kit at the Army and Navy Stores and be on my way. I'm only two-thirds of the way home. If you turn up in Rangoon, give me a buzz."

"Okay. Good luck."

The American missionary and his wife from the Punjab smiled and waved good-bye to him. They disapproved of his drinking and the endless poker games with Stitch and Jelly and Joey and Gibson but, now that the voyage was over and everyone was separating, they smiled and waved. That was sporting of them. They must be good sports to be working up there in the north among the hard-boiled Pathans. It was a lot easier to work among Hindus. When the woman—a little thin person in a black alpaca dress—smiled, it was a funny crooked smile and there was a look in the eyes, a twinkle that was infinitely human and personal. For a moment there was something in it oddly familiar. He could not say why. He had never seen her before he came aboard the boat and since then he had scarcely noticed the prim alpaca-clad figure. It wasn't only that the crooked smile was familiar, it was more than that. And it reminded him of something or someone. He looked toward her again but she had turned away and all he could see was the thin, tired, back leaning over the rail as a cutter came alongside the ship.

Looking down he could make out on the deck of the cutter, two or three port officers, a group of Indians in brocaded and embroidered ceremonial dress and two *chuprassies* in scarlet and gold, half buried beneath dozens of garlands of marigolds and jasmine, and in the midst of them a tall and good-looking young English officer, blonde and clad in spotless white with a white topi and a great deal of gold lace. He carried a sword and two or three large official envelopes in his hand. He stood taller than anyone on the deck and he had a kind of blonde personal radiance about him by which he outshone all the others—even the Indians in their brocade and jewels and scarlet turbans.

"Gosh," thought Bill. "The British Empire does itself well."

Then the cutter disappeared beneath the side of the ship and he became aware out of the corner of his eye that the Baroness was

[9]

coming toward him. It was too late to escape. He looked fixedly toward the advancing skyline, but these tactics gained him nothing and at once he understood that he should have known better. The Baroness had the hide of rhinoceros. Still he kept watching the dim and distant outline of the Taj Mahal Hotel—until he felt her standing there beside him, so close that her fat body pressed against his. In the heat she smelled of heavy scent and perspiration and the dead odor of smoked Egyptian tobacco.

"Good morning," she said. "Hot, aind't it?"

"Oh, good morning. Yes, it's hot in the bay."

"Not so much breeze."

"No, not much air."

He tried looking away from her but it did no good; anyway, he knew what she looked like. He knew her short fat body, the opaque oily skin, the dyed red hair that looked like an old tired wig but wasn't, the muddy greenish eyes and the bangles, rings, bracelets, brooches, earrings and the brocade bag with greasy stains mottling the design.

"Vere are you staying in Bombay?"

"The hotel, I suppose."

"The Taj Mahal?"

"Yes, the Taj Mahal."

"For long?"

"I don't know." He wanted to say, "None of your damned business," but he didn't.

Then she said with a clumsy coquetry, "Maybe ve could haf dinner togedder some time?"

"Yes, maybe. I'll be pretty busy. You see I'm here on business."

"Vat business?"

"Oil."

"Oh, oil! Fuel oil?"

"Yes, fuel oil and other things."

He thought, wanting to laugh, "If she's a spy, she's an awfully bad one."

"Vell, I expect ve'll be seeing each odder."

It should have been a parting remark but it wasn't. She still remained, and he noticed again the musky scent she used and thought, "I suppose that's patchouli—the scent opera singers and spies use in old-fashioned novels." And then he saw why she remained. The handsome young A.D.C. in white and gold with the sword was coming toward them. With him, just a little behind him, was Al, the radio officer, a wide grin on his humorous Irish face.

Al said something to the handsome young man and as he came up to Bill he saluted and said, "Mr. William Wainwright?"

"Yes," said Bill, thinking, "maybe they remember the old scandal. Maybe they're not going to let me land." And he wished that the Baroness would go away, although he knew that at that moment dynamite would not have moved her. She stood there, stricken with curiosity, all her vulgar soul bedazzled, fascinated.

"I'm Lieutenant Forsythe," said the young man. "The compliments of His Excellency, the Viceroy, sir." And he handed Bill a large envelope. "And the compliments of His Excellency, the Governor of the Bombay Presidency," and handed him a second envelope. "You can give me the answer to the Governor's note, sir."

"Thank you," said Bill, a little awed. Turning away a little, he tore open the envelope and read it.

His Excellency, the Governor of the Bombay Presidency would like him to come to lunch on Wednesday, the third.

"Will you tell His Excellency I should be delighted to lunch?"

"Thank you," said the handsome young man. "Is there anything I can do for you, sir?"

"No," said Bill, "thank you very much. I'll be all right. You see I know Bombay quite well."

"It's not a bad place," said the young man, "if you don't have to stay through the monsoon. If there's nothing I can do, I'll be off." Again he saluted.

"Thank you again," said Bill.

"Good day," said the British Empire and walked away.

The Baroness stood goggle-eyed. The grin on the face of Al, the radio operator, grew wider. "A toff, eh?" he said. "Getting letters from Viceroys and things."

"I don't know what it's all about," said Bill.

The Baroness said to Al, "No message for me?"

"No, nothing."

She shook her head from side to side and made a clucking noise. "Very fonny! Very fonny! I haf been expecting a message all de

[11]

vay from Aden." The shake of the head, the clucking sound, the look in the green eyes, were all full of implications—that Al had received a message and destroyed it, that he had been bribed to keep it from her, that he was in some colossal plot, a plot against her which embraced the whole world—Europeans, Americans, Africans, Indians, Malays. They were all against her. But there was also the defiant implication that she could defeat them all at their own game.

Al grinned and with a kind of satisfaction said, "It won't come now. The radio bureau is closed."

"It's fonny—very fonny!" And she suddenly turned and left him.

"We've had some funny ones," said Al, "but she's the top." The perpetual grin widened, "Get a load of what's coming."

Down the deck toward them came little Jelly. The rather loud checked racing clothes which he had worn throughout the voyage, were gone. The Maharajah and Joey, the A.D.C., were both in black *atchkans* and white *jodpores*. Jelly wore a *puggree* of scarlet and gold and Joey a plain one of scarlet. The Maharajah's dark little face and tiny, shrewd, black eyes, peeped out from among garland after garland of jasmine and marigold. As suited the difference in rank, Joey wore only three slim garlands. Still a little drunk, his face no longer was a fine copper color; it was the green of corroded copper. He hung his head like a child just punished. Gone were the two rulers of Longchamps and Epsom, of the Casinos of Deauville and Cannes. Behind them walked Gibson, the trainer, a big beefy man with a leathery face, clad in a loud checked suit and maroon necktie.

"Look," said Al. "The father and mother of the Universe is going back to work, and does he hate it. We've had him on board for ten trips and he's always tight from Aden on."

Al's grin widened and Bill wanted to laugh, and then thought better of it. There was something pathetic in the spectacle of Jelly, whom God had meant to be a bookmaker, returning to India to be a king.

Every year it happened. In the cold season the Maharajah returned to be hailed as the father and mother of his people. Because of them, he would stay at home in India for three or four months, bored, going over accounts, giving dinners which bored him in Bombay or Delhi or Jellapore, occasionally indulging in a first-class orgy. He had hung on to the life he loved to the very last minute, drinking champagne in his cabin, playing "Alone" over and over on the gramophone. And now the ship was docking and he had to emerge at last in full splendor, smothered in jasmine and marigold—the king of kings, the father and mother of his people, attended by tipsy Joey and his horse trainer.

Al and Bill leaned back on the rail. The Maharajah passed them and as he passed in all his splendor and majesty, the dark little face moved out of the garlands, a little like the head of a turtle, turned sidewise toward Al and Bill, and one dark eye closed. Then he and Joey passed on and as Gibson came up to them he said, "Come and look at the pier. Half of Jellapore is here—the Dewan, three wives and all the heirs and relatives. Come on."

The great ship was tying up now, close to the pier, still at last after the long voyage down the wintry channel, through the stormy Bay of Biscay, the gray-blue Mediterranean, the burning Red Sea and the sultry heat of the Arabian Gulf. The voyage was over and seven hundred passengers of all colors and races and creeds and nationalities were jammed together waiting to pour down the gangplank into the dusty, sun-baked city. On the pier and the pier-shed roof hundreds of faces peered up at the splendor of the ship, each face bright with a look of wonder and expectancy— faces which were brown and coffee-colored, yellow and sickly black tinged with malaria. They were clad in all colors and all fashions from the gleaming white of Hanover Square tailors to the dirty rags that scarcely preserved the modesty of the scrawny coolies. Here and there gleamed the scarlet and gold of the *chuprassies* and the brilliant poison green and candy pink *puggrees* of the Rajputs, the white stiff turbans from the north, fresh and glistening in the perpetual sunshine of winter. And a little to one side of the gang-plank, like a flower garden, gathered the party which had come down from the hot inland plateau to welcome home their father and mother, the Lord of Creation—little "Jelly."

This group stood apart in a little place cleared and reserved appropriately for the reception of a powerful and wealthy prince. In the little group there were a dozen Sikh bodyguards, twice the height of Jelly, clad in scarlet uniforms with gold turbans and ten foot bannered lances, and in front of them, a little cluster of shy and giggling women in brilliantly colored saris—the wives and their ladies-in-waiting, and at the side another group which included a pompous fellow, wide of girth who was probably the Dewan, a thin, worried man who was steward of the palace, and a chorus of small, quite black servants in azure blue and silver.

At sight of the bright spectacle on the quay, the tingling sensation of excitement swept over Bill once more, followed quickly by that feeling of delight which India always brought to him: all this was far away from the West and its drabness, its quarrels, its greediness, its depressions, its peculiar misery that was worse than the swarming misery of the East because it fed on the soul and the spirit instead of the body. Always at first sight of this absurd spectacle he thought, "I never want to leave it again. I never want to go back to the boring drabness of the West."

But this time a small voice answered him, "But it's different this time. You're settled down now. No nonsense, no adventures. You're making good. When your job is finished, you're going to take the first boat on your way back to steadiness and work."

A small thin voice beside him said, "It's always a pretty sight. I tried to describe it to the folks back home but it's hard. They didn't understand why I wanted to come back."

It was the little missionary woman again, drab as an alpaca sparrow, but for the bright blue in her eyes.

"I feel the same way," said Bill.

"Have you been out before?"

"Twice. Once I stayed a long time."

"The Pathan *puggrees* I like best. They always look so fresh and clean and smart . . . just like a wonderful new hat, fresh from the millinery store."

Surprised, he looked at her and saw her eyes were shining more brightly. From the look of her, you'd never have dreamed that anything as frivolous as millinery interested her. Then the expression in her eyes made him think again of someone—he could not think who—someone, a man or a woman whom he knew very well, who had the same bright, human, selfless look. Someone it was who was good but never a prig, someone whom he had loved and respected. The shadowy memory tormented him.

[14]

He heard her voice again, speaking with a note of apology, "Mebbe it's because the Pathans come from up north in my country."

Then suddenly she was gone, lost among the restless, pushing passengers and the coolies swarming up the gangplanks and all over the great, white ship, screaming and yelling in their soiled white uniforms, thrusting their ravenous dark faces into the faces of the passengers, yelling, "Luggage! Luggage! Baggage! Baggage! Sahib! Memsahib! Luggage! Luggage!"

The little woman in alpaca had slipped away but her face was still with him, very clear in all the heat and confusion.

Jelly and Joey, in all their finery and garlands, were now advancing with a tipsy semblance of majesty down the gangplank, and at sight of them, the waiting flower garden on the pier below shivered, trembled in the heat and became suddenly a scene of brilliant animation. The scarlet and gold Sikhs drew themselves up like brilliant red lilies; the black servants in azure and silver threw themselves into the dust and touched their foreheads to the ground like heavy-belled campanulas; the multicolored wives and their ladies-in-waiting, the fat Dewan and the palace steward bent over slightly, joined their palms together, like a whole garden swaying in the breeze. They were welcoming home from the gambling Casinos and the race courses their lord and master, their father and mother, the king of kings—the slightly tipsy Maharajah of Jellapore.

Jelly, still moving unsteadily, reached the foot of the gangplank and, with a faint inclination which sent all of the garlands swaying again, acknowledged the extraordinary animation with which the whole garden had been seized at sight of his majestic presence. Behind moved Joey, quite drunk, grinning and bowing with his palms joined together. And after him Gibson, the Cockney trainer, in his loud checked suit, his London hat tilted back on his head.

After a moment while greetings were exchanged, the flower garden began to create a new pattern. The red and gold Sikhs performed a military figure dividing themselves into two groups. The Maharajah and the Dewan took a position just behind them, followed closely by Joey and the palace steward, and after them all the women—the wives, the ladies-in-waiting, still giggling and

[15]

chattering, and their servants. The rear was closed by Sikhs and the flower garden started on its way into the shadows of the last customs house.

At about the same time, Bill heard a familiar voice saying, "Good day, Sahib! You are my father and mother, Sahib! I am always your servant, Sahib!"

It was Silas!

Silas was a tall, very thin and very black Tamil who had been converted to Christianity. He was almost handsome, with the look of a half-starved chicken hawk, and like most "boys" was ageless. On his head he wore a shabby black tarboosh with no tassel, and from the tattered filthy khaki suit he wore, one who did not know him would have said that he had been for months and years without work. But Bill knew better. This was only a "costume," the one Silas laid aside to wear when he came to greet old employers. It was designed deliberately to give the effect of starvation and extreme poverty.

The sight of his old bearer depressed him for a moment. He had meant to do without a bearer, although everyone said such a thing was impossible. Certainly he had meant to escape Silas because Silas was a liar, a thief, a hypocrite, a gossip and a petty blackmailer. Silas, who wrote twice a year to say that his enormous family of children and his wife and his parents and his wife's parents and all their grandparents who were dependent on him for food and shelter were starving. You couldn't take his stories of misfortune too literally because he himself seemed so uncertain as to the exact number of his offspring. Sometimes there were eleven, sometimes nine, sometimes seven. No, Bill wasn't pleased at seeing Silas. He had meant to escape from him this time—Silas who could become like the Old Man of the Sea.

"Where did you come from?" he asked the bearer.

"Bombay, Sahib."

"I thought you lived in Madras?"

"Yes, Sahib, all my family lives there . . . all my starving children and parents and grandparents." He would have gone on cataloguing them but Bill stopped him. "I know, I know," he said. "How did you know I was on this boat?"

"Have friend who works in big steamship office. Friend give me

[16]

lists of passengers. List comes by air mail from London. Saw Sahib's name. Came to welcome him. You are my father and mother, sahib, and the father and mother of my children, my wife, my parents. . . ." The cataloguing was beginning again.

"No, thanks. Come along. You can look after my baggage, anyway."

A gleam came into the solid black pupils of Silas' eyes. He had a job, the kind of job he liked, with a good-natured sahib, who didn't count annas or even rupees, or grumble over the *dhobi's* bill. He and his wife and children would be well off for another year. Silas, a lean Afghan hound, loped happily behind Bill to the cabin where Bill turned the luggage over to him.

"Don't let the coolies cheat you. I'll meet you on the dock."

"No cheat," said Silas. The dark face opened wide in a glitter of white teeth, and the bearer vanished in the crowd.

It wasn't a grin of gratitude, Bill knew; there wasn't much place for gratitude in the lives of people like Silas, living most of their lives without enough to eat, keeping a roof over the head and food in the mouths of a dozen relatives on less than ten cents a day. No, it was a grin of satisfaction, at having put something over— at having found out that business about the passenger list, over having caught Bill himself.

"Yes," he thought. "I'm a sap and he knows it. He knows damned well I'll keep him on after the luggage is taken care of." Grinning, he thought, "Well, I can afford it."

Then he saw Stitch coming toward him. She had changed her clothes at the last minute and appeared clad in an expensively cut but rather shabby suit of white. She was certainly a plain woman, and a somewhat weatherbeaten one, but she had a shadow of tired radiance about her which made you glad to see her. He had the impression that at some time in her life something terrible had happened to her, something which had extinguished all folly, all coquetry, all femininity; perhaps even warmth and humanity had been snuffed out.

She had a cigarette hanging from her lips and said, "Come on. Let's go ashore and get through this customs business."

They pushed their way through the crowd to the head of the gangway, and slipped, one after the other, like coins in a slot

[17]

machine, into the line going down the gangway to the pier. As they came from under the shadow of the deck, the sun struck their shoulders like liquid fire.

Below them the pier was crowded. The cranes of the ship were already working, swinging the cases and crates down from the high white ship. The Indian sun glared against the concrete and metal work of the pier and back into their aching eyes. The line of passengers coming down the gangway became jammed and from ahead of them came a warm whiff of that peculiar strong odor of the Baroness—a blend of mustiness, perspiration and patchouli. They heard her voice complaining, "That young man stepped on my foot."

Leaning out, Bill could see the young man, a very skinny Parsee with a muddy complexion, apologetic and embarrassed by the loudness of the Baroness' hoarse voice.

Behind them a gruff voice said, "Get on with it. Are we going to stay here all day in the sun?" And Bill felt a swift wave of irritation that comes to people in India, suddenly without warning, when something which is India seems to bare all the nerves.

"That bloody bitch!" said Stitch, and then the line began to move again.

They came to the end of the gangplank and Stitch, with an Australian lawlessness, stepped outside the barrier that kept the passengers in line and made as if to go directly into the shelter of the customs shed.

The voice of a Eurasian customs officer came out of the heat. The man was running toward her, crying out, "Look out, lady, there's a box. . . ."

It was the last word he ever spoke. The boom of the great crane swung round and somewhere a cable snapped. The man who had the fraction of a second earlier been running toward Stitch, shouting a warning to her, no longer existed, save as a hand, a single hand, reaching out from beneath the heavy crate which had fallen on him. Bill saw it all with a horrible clarity, the heavy crate with a truck inside it, the stenciled legend—"General Motors"—and the hand which moved convulsively for a second, then collapsed like a small animal that had been shot, and then was still and limp above a thin trickle of blood.

[18]

And he saw Stitch in her spotless white suit collapse into the dust and cinders of the pier, her skirt and jacket spotted with red.

The coolies began to crowd around, chattering and screaming, and Bill picked up Stitch and yelling, "God-damn it! Get out of the way, you bastards," carried her into the kind shade of the pier shed. And as he carried her he knew in a sudden flash, the face he had been searching for, the eyes that were like the bright eyes of the little missionary woman. It was the face and eyes of Homer Merrill, who once, long ago, had been his greatest friend.

He laid Stitch on one of the low tables among the baggage and bawled at the man near him, "Go get the quarantine doctor." Then he thought, pushing back his topee, "A lousy omen!" And again, "If she'd stayed in the line where she belonged that poor bastard wouldn't have been killed."

Between Madras and the Deccan in the middle of Hyderabad it rained suddenly with no warning at all out of heavy black clouds which had somehow found their way over the western ghats without dropping their burden of moisture on the narrow strip of land along the Arabian Gulf. It was that rare thing—a false monsoon—occurring in the middle of the dry season, and at first it brought a sense of relief, turning the thick dust into mud and gathering among the red rocks in pools which tomorrow would shrink and disappear beneath the brassy glare of an unrelenting sun. But for the moment while the rain fell in floods of rushing water, the trees, the scraggly thorny shrubs, picked bare of every leaf by wandering goats and cattle, the red soil and the rocks themselves, the coolies, the *ryots*, the untouchables, the rich merchants and their wives shut away in purdah rooms, all felt a profound sense of relief and satisfaction like that of a tired and thirsty traveler drinking from a spring of fresh clear water. The travelers on the Madras-Bombay express let down windows which had been kept closed to shut out the heat and allowed the rain to dash in a fine spray through the copper screening. What had been drifts of powder-fine dust across the floors of the compartments a little while before, turned to little rivulets of sticky red mud that was like blood.

And then when the flood stopped as suddenly as it had begun, the sun came out again and the feeling of relief was gone and in its place came a sensation of uneasiness and dread. All felt it— the coolies, the beasts, the shut-in purdah women in whose blood there flowed ten thousand years of India. Even the three European passengers on the Express grew restless and uncomfortable without knowing why. There was something unnatural about the sudden cloudburst in a season when there should have been no rain.

And the rain now seemed to have made the heat more intense. Before the rain the air had at least been dry and the perspiration evaporated and brought some relief, but now with the brassy sun striking full on the wet rocks and the bare muddy fields, the steam rose up, enveloping houses, cattle, laborers, even the moving train itself, until the whole of the vast Deccan plateau was like one gigantic Russian bath. In the train windows were closed again because the air which entered was more suffocating than the air inside. In the ditches along the tracks the flood water flowed blood red, diminishing almost as you watched it into a fine trickle, swallowed up altogether presently by the heat of the sun and the greedy thirst of the hot, red earth.

On the whole of the train there were only three westerners—a man, a boy and a woman of twenty-nine, all of them Americans. The man and the boy and a Moslem Indian child occupied a stuffy, uncomfortable second-class compartment, and one car off, the woman traveled in all the luxury which the Indian climate allowed. It was a car reserved for her alone, with extra fine copper screening to exclude the dust, with extra electric fans and a big silver basin filled with ice, replenished at every stop of the train to keep down the temperature. She had with her two bearers in the purple and gold livery of the Maharajah of Jellapore to wait upon her and serve her with fresh gin slings when she asked for them and juicy slices of pineapple cut from the heap of pineapple and melons and pomegranates which lay in the compartment at the end of the car.

She was a beautiful woman, blonde, with a fresh lovely complexion and superb figure which she made no attempt to hide from the Indian bearers who served her. She wore a dressing gown of heavy silk the color of *aubergine* with a monogram C.H. embroidered in scarlet silk, and lay on the divan, her eyes closed, her head against the pillows that were hard but comforting in the heat. All day, since early morning, she had lain there exhausted, suffocating in the heat, opening her eyes, turning her head a little now and then to look out of the window at the burning landscape or to lift the glass, perpetually filled, which stood in the little wooden rack at her side.

Late in the afternoon when the train had passed the burning plateau of the Deccan and began to weave in among the hills and valleys leading to Poona she began to feel a little better and sat up for a time to watch the noisy clamoring crowds at the stations and the flocks of dwarf black goats that fed here and there in the scrub and raised their heads to look at the passing train and then skipped away like antelopes among the burning red rocks.

Watching them, she thought, "This is the damndest country." And yet she liked it. Why else had she come back to it?

Underneath her, one of the wheels in the carriage began to make a clicking noise. "Click! Click! Click!" the wheel said, over and over again, "Click! Click! Click!" monotonously, irritatingly, "Click! Click! Click!" never failing, each time the wheel turned, "Click! Click! Click!" with a horrible inevitability, never once missing.

In the heat the sound took possession of her, driving out thought, its effect magnified with growing intensity, until it was like a hammer beating on bareness.

"It can't simply be a hang-over," she thought, "I never felt as bad as this before." And then after a little time during which the clicking sound took aching possession of her again, she thought, "Maybe there was something in Mrs. Goswami's story. Maybe they did get in their first licks. Maybe I did just get out in time."

Again she saw the fantastic open-air pavilion covered with bougainvillea and bignonia where the Maharajah's brother had given her a farewell party. She saw again the great pots of orchids, kicked over and shattered, one by one, by the English subalterns as a good "rag."

The whole party began to come back to her now, for the first time. Until now as the sun began to slip down the sky, she had lain there on the divan of the Jellapore royal car in a kind of coma, composed in equal parts of weariness, alcohol and discomfort. Now she saw again the dark jazz band, recruited from the

[21]

Sikh regiment, the long stairway, bordered by pots of flowers which led down to the pavilion. She saw the naked figures of the dancing boys, golden in the dim lights and beautiful in the decadent perfection, like the bodies of Krishna in the palace frescoes. She remembered crying out, "I want a dancing boy. I want to take one home with me." She remembered the scarlet coats of the subalterns and the tables filled with champagne bottles and the Maharajah's cousin dancing a rumba with one of the dancing boys, and the face of the boy, beautiful and evil, with the vice and knowledge of all time written on it. Funny how well she remembered the face. She remembered the furtive goings and comings to and from the moonlit garden outside. She remembered vaguely having fallen some time during the evening among the pots of flowers that bordered the high wide stairway.

"Yes," she thought. "They never had a party like that in New York even in the big days. I guess it must have been a real 'orgy,' " and in her thought she pronounced the g in orgy with a hard sound.

Then the clicking of the bloody wheel took possession of her again. "Click! Click! Click! Click!" It seemed louder now. She pushed the bell at her side and in a moment a dark servant in purple and gold livery came in.

"Krishna," she said, and the boy salaamed and said, "Yes, Memsahib."

"At the next station find the stationmaster and make him find out what is the matter with the wheel. Make him fix that noise. Do you hear it?"

The click, clack, click, clack, click, clack filled the silence between speeches and the boy said, "Yes, Memsahib, I hear it. I'll see the stationmaster." He would do what she asked. He worshiped her, she knew, not only because she was beautiful and always treated him as a friend, but because she had given him a bicycle.

Then he went away again and she fell into a half-sleep once more; in the heat, with the wheel making that damned racket, it was impossible to lose consciousness. And in her dreamy state, the memory of the party kept returning, ever more clearly. It was as if in the beauty and corruption of the night before, with all the noise and confusion and champagne, she had been only partly conscious, as if some part of her mind had marked down things which at the time she had scarcely noticed.

She saw the pots of orchids again flying through the air from the toe of a red-coated subaltern's boot, and with her eyes closed, the beautiful depravity on the face of the naked dancing boy appeared again clearly and came very close to her. There was something vaguely frightening about it.

Then she remembered very clearly Mrs. Goswami talking with her in the arbor of bignonias. She was a dark, thin little Bengali woman, an "intellectual" very nervous and anxious, in an unbecoming pale pink sari which gave her face a bilious cast. She spoke English which was very nearly perfect.

"No, Miss Halma," she was saying earnestly, "if you take my advice you will go away immediately, at once, as His Highness suggests."

And she remembered answering a little wildly and defiantly, having had too much champagne, "Why should I go away if I don't want to? I'm having a good time. I don't want to go back to Bombay."

Then Mrs. Goswami touched her arm, a rare thing for an Indian woman to do, as she knew now in comparative soberness. Mrs. Goswami said, "I'm thinking of your own good, my friend. Those spells you had were not just ordinary illness."

That had sobered her a little and she said, "It was just the heat."

"No," said Mrs. Goswami, "I've seen it happen before. I saw a woman die once."

It came back very clearly now, even above the click-clack of the wheel. She had said to Mrs. Goswami, "Why should anyone here want to poison me?"

And Mrs. Goswami, looking about her, had answered in a whisper, "The whole *zenana*."

The statement had terrified her for a moment, not because she really believed Mrs. Goswami but because of a kind of shadow which suddenly fell over her, the shadow of all those women who were shut away inside the palace, who never went out save in motors and carriages that were thickly curtained. You never saw

[23]

them in Jellapore, yet you were always aware of their presence. She was afraid because of all the piled-up sudden memories of little things—the strange, dark servant she had found one night by accident outside the door of her rooms in the guest house, the strange man who had been near her tonight while she sat in the garden with the captain, the *ayah* who had appeared as her servant coming from nowhere but who had insisted that she had been sent to care for her and who would not go away. And there was always that feeling of being spied upon, wherever you went, whatever you did. She was very suddenly afraid of all those women— the four Maharanees, the wives of Jellapore, the sisters and aunts, the young girls who were shut away whom she had never seen and never would see. All of them, it was certain, had seen her, from the grilled windows of the *zenana* or between the curtains of a passing bullock cart or Rolls Royce.

"You must remember," said Mrs. Goswami, "that they're savage. They're not like me. I've been to Europe. Most of them can't even read or write. They think they're in the right." The dark little Bengali woman was silent for a moment, and then as if moved by a great resolution, she said, "They know even about the ring and the necklace he gave you. That is what infuriated them."

She remembered being astonished that Mrs. Goswami knew about the ring and the bracelet. But if the *zenana* knew—how could they know? And yet they did. They knew everything. It was hard to believe when you thought of Jelly himself—with his horses, gambling at Deauville or dining in Maxims or the Savoy—hard to believe that behind him here in India he had this harem filled with half-savage, vengeful women.

"You see," Mrs. Goswami said, "they would be afraid if you were the Maharajah's guest, but with his brother it's different. The brother is more popular in the *zenana* than the Maharajah himself. They're more jealous of him, and he hasn't the same power to punish them."

"I get it," she had said, "I'll think about it." And then she had thanked Mrs. Goswami and the two of them had gone back into the pavilion but not before they had seen a servant slip away from the bushes near them into the tangle of bougainvillea.

And then with the champagne and the music, the dancing and the ragging, she had forgotten the scene with Mrs. Goswami. It was odd that the rest of the evening seemed to have faded out into nothing. She could not remember now, try as she would, how she had left the party, nor how she had come to be on this train in one of the Jellapore State cars with its silver fittings and gilded elephants. She had simply wakened here in the heat with a terrible hang-over long after the train had left Jellapore. The last thing she remembered were the subalterns in the red coats kicking over the orchids in the rising light of dawn. It couldn't have been simply the champagne. She had always been famous for being able to drink any amount and still keep her head, even long ago in the beginning with Bill. No, they must have given her a Mickey Finn just to get rid of her. One of those dark, hovering figures in the pay of the *zenana* women had done it. Or perhaps it was the Maharajah's brother himself, wanting to make sure that she left Jellapore before Jelly returned.

She was tempted to laugh. "Given the bum's rush! Mebbe that's what it was! Carol Halma being given the bum's rush! That's good!"

Lazily she opened her eyes and sat up, listening. The sound of the cracked wheel went in a slower rhythm now. It was saying, "click . . . clack! click . . . clack!" more and more slowly. They were coming to a station. Thank God!

She took a drink out of the tall glass of gin and fruit juice and felt better. The hair of the dog that bit you always worked. But champagne was always bad the next day—too acid, too full of headache. She looked at her fingers suddenly. The ring was still there, it's great square, deep shimmering green pierced by the long slanting rays of the lowering sun. A thought came to her and she pushed the bell.

In a moment Krishna appeared, "Yes, Memsahib."

"Is my jewel case with the luggage?"

"Yes, Memsahib."

"Bring it to me."

The boy vanished, and gathering the dressing gown about her, she sat up, swinging her long beautiful legs over the side of the divan. Opening her bag she took out a mirror and looked at her

[25]

face. She wasn't looking her best but much better than she had expected. It was extraordinary how much she could drink without losing her looks. That, she thought, must be her Swedish blood.

With a comb, she set the blonde hair in order. It was streaked now partly by the sun and partly by need of touching up. The listlessness, the dead feeling began to leave her, and she thought, "At the next station I'll get out and stretch my legs a bit."

The train was slowing down to a stop, but outside there was still only an endless expanse of red soil and rock with here and there an isolated farmhouse with walls of red clay.

The door opened and Krishna returned carrying her jewel case. She took it from him and opened it and dismissed him. She pulled out the little trays in turn. They were all there, the bracelets, the rings, the earrings, the clips—all glittering, red, blue, green, white and platinum. The necklace was there too, the rubies glowing like blood in their heavy, rather clumsy modern Indian setting. She could change that when she was back again in Paris. Ostertag would make her a wonderful new setting. She held up the necklace, turning it this way and that so that the rubies caught the light.

"Funny," she thought, looking at it, "that he should give me that and the ring—for nothing—after I told him in the beginning there was nothing doing. . . . Unless something happened to me last night." But that she dismissed as impossible. That she couldn't have forgotten!

Putting away the jewels, she sat quite still thinking. Maybe it was just because he liked to be seen with pretty women and blonde women. Maybe he couldn't do anything. He wouldn't be the first man who had given her jewels just to be seen with her, to make the world believe he was a great and active lady-killer when really there wasn't anything doing. It sure was funny, inviting her to Jellapore and giving her jewels like this for nothing. It was different in Bombay with the rich Parsees and Khojas. They gave her jewelry too, but they wanted to marry her. They wanted all Bombay, all India to believe that they alone owned her blondeness and beauty. Well, none of them did.

The train was really stopping now. Looking out of the window

[26]

she saw the funny little Indian houses and the pretentious State buildings rising above them like pompous fat priests moving among a kneeling crowd. Quickly she opened the valise left on the divan opposite by Krishna and took out a skirt, a jacket, a blouse and a pair of shoes. Slipping off the dressing gown she stood naked, superb, for a second before slipping on the blouse and skirt. Then the shoes and the jacket and she was dressed.

The click-clack of the cracked wheel ceased and the clamor of the station platform took its place—the chatter and uproar of an India which never seems to stop traveling, the wild alarming cries of the vendors of sweetmeats and Mohammedan and Hindu drinking water, the pounding of the gong which signaled the arrival of the train, the little bird-like cries of the women greeting friends and relatives, and over it all the scent of fading garlands of jasmine and marigold looped about the scrawny necks of departing or arriving voyagers by devoted friends and relatives.

Lazily she watched the spectacle through the copper gauze that covered the windows. An enormous crowd gathered about the purple royal carriage of the State of Jellapore. They pressed close to the car fingering the gilt elephants and peacocks which adorned the exterior, pressing their noses against the copper screen to discover the identity of the august personage inside. The odor of sweat and dust and withering flowers became overwhelming. It began to fill the royal carriage itself. She rang the bell, but no Krishna was there to answer. He had gone, no doubt accompanied by his subordinate, to find the stationmaster and complain about the cracked wheel. She tried herself to pull up the shutters to shut out the peering faces which somehow made her feel naked and ashamed, but in the heat she found the effort too great and abandoned the idea. She succeeded only in breaking one beautifully lacquered nail and said, "God-damn it!"

She would go outside on the platform. Anything was better than this goldfish existence. They might follow her about, staring at her milky skin and her blondeness, but she was used to that by now. She took up the topee that hung above the divan and at the same time, an uproar began among the crowd. They pushed and groaned and cried out and protested in Hindustani and Mahratta. Behind them appeared two tough little Mahratta policemen, lay·

ing out right and left with their *lathis,* shouting in guttural Mahratta. Suddenly the space beside the royal carriage was free, and in
peace she sat down and lighted a cigarette and took another swig
of the gin sling.

There was nothing to do but wait. If only the damned thing
would arrive in Bombay so she could go to the Taj Mahal Hotel
and have a bath and come down to the bar and see who was in
town. She was feeling much better now; all the old vitality was
surging back and with it an old impatience and restlessness which
attacked her on long journeys. If only Indian trains didn't spend
twenty minutes or half an hour in every station.

From beneath the car there came presently the sound of hammering. That would be the men examining the wheel. She hoped
to God they could fix it. If that click-clacking kept on all the way
to Bombay, she'd go crazy.

After a time the noise ceased. The crowd outside had retired
now to a decent distance behind the two policemen. They still
chattered and peered but they couldn't look in. Every time one
of them was thrust forward between the policemen he was whacked
over the shoulders with a *lathi.*

As the train drew into the station, the man in the second class
compartment stirred and looked out of the window. He saw the
station sign LEPTA and the sign just beneath *Junction for
Ranchipur.* All the hubbub, all the shouting, all· the confusion
on the platform was nothing new to him, and after a single glance
he turned to the small boy who sat turning the pages of an English child's story magazine.

"D'you want to get out and stretch your legs, Tom?"

"Sure, Dad."

The boy who was a little over nine jumped down from his seat,
and said, "Give me eight annas for some oranges," and his father
reached up to the pocket of the white jacket that hung by the
divan, took out a rupee and gave it to him.

"Don't get lost and don't miss the train."

"No, of course I won't."

The father was a man of about thirty-four or five with a wide
high forehead, blue eyes and a mouth which could have been

sensual save for the lines at the corners, lines which only come with years of self-denial. Yet there were lines of good humor in the face as well; it was not a forbidding face, nor the face of a disagreeable ascetic. There was too much humor in the blue eyes and too much sadness. It was a kindly face illumined by good humor. The lines, the set of the jaw and the firmness of the chin all gave it character.

In the heat he wore only a sarong, a habit he had picked up at the Malay states, and was naked from the waist up. It was a muscular body, a little too thin, but beautiful in its proportions, not tanned, but the ivory color of the body of a man who has long lived in the tropics. He lighted a cigarette and looked again out of the window at his son.

The boy was bargaining with a vendor of oranges, and enjoying the bargaining. The orange vendor said something violent in Hindustani and turned to go away. The boy stood his ground and waited and the vendor, after two or three steps, turned back. Then the boy said something in Hindustani and the vendor, a black, skinny man in a soiled white *dhoti*, threw up his arms and repeated the pantomime. Again the boy held his ground and this time he won out. The vendor in despair, gave him ten oranges and accepted the coin. The boy couldn't have given him the rupee because there wasn't any change and ten oranges on a station platform in the Deccan couldn't cost a rupee.

The father watching, grinned. His son hadn't been born and lived in the Orient for nothing. He had learned about bargaining. Maybe that would help him later on in the West where the bargaining was different but none the less vicious—not as straightforward or as amusing as the bargaining of the East.

The man thought, "I'll have him for another thirty-six hours and then I won't see him again for five years." The thought made him feel a little sick and he turned away, without thinking, to the Indian boy with the bandaged eyes who still sat cross-legged and very still on the divan opposite.

"Ali," he asked in Hindustani, "do you want to go out on the platform with Tom?"

The boy turned his head in the direction of the voice, "No, Sahib Buck, I couldn't see anything."

[29]

"Tom's gone for oranges. Do you want one?"

"Yes, Sahib Buck." Then he turned away his head a little and sat with it bent forward. He was listening. Merrill watched him, thinking, "He never had a chance at anything."

The boy was the son of a widow of a mahout and had grown up in the gutter of Jellapore City outside the elephant compound. Merrill had managed to keep him away from the missionaries. There wasn't anything for him to gain from Christianity. No Moslem ever had gained anything from it. A Hindu was different. Being converted could help them, socially and economically if not spiritually. He had had to unlearn a lot of things here in India in the villages. You didn't know India unless you knew the villages. That's where you got inside. . . .

The Indian boy suddenly spoke. "It's funny, Sahib, how you can see with your ears."

"Yes," said Merrill, watching the boy.

"Yes, I can see everything on the platform just by listening to the sounds."

Merrill didn't answer and presently the boy asked, "Do you think I'll ever get over being blind?"

"I should think so, Ali. The Doctor Sahib in Bombay is a great man. It's luck he's here. He comes from far away across the great black water."

The boy's head moved a little from side to side. "I'd like to see again because I want to be a mahout. I want to drive the Maharajah's elephant—his own great elephant Akbar. Hindus don't understand elephants. That's why all good mahouts are Moslems."

There wasn't any use kidding the boy into believing he would see if Colonel Moti's friend found there was nothing he could do. It would only be cruel in the end.

The door of the compartment opened and Merrill's son came in. He was holding the rupee in his hand. "I got ten oranges for four annas," he said.

"Give a couple to Ali," he said.

The American boy put two oranges in the empty, still hands of the blind Indian boy. "Can you peel them?" he asked.

"Yes," said Ali.

[30]

"I'll write to you when I get to America," said Tom. "I'll write to Dad and he can read it to you. It'll be exciting, I guess."

"Funny," thought Merrill, "wonder what he'll think of his own country." And again the sick feeling came to the pit of his stomach. It wasn't going to be easy giving up seeing the boy for five years . . . five years from nine to fourteen.

He looked at his watch and saw that the train had been in the station for more than half an hour. Twenty minutes was the usual time. He looked out of the window and saw that the crowd on the platform had gathered in a silence so unnatural for an Indian railway platform that he knew something of an extraordinary interest was taking place. They stood gaping and peering, and in the unnatural silence he heard two or three voices rising in a wild argument.

"Misery and desolation, Memsahib. There is nothing to do," said a vaguely familiar voice in Hindustani. That, he thought, would be the voice of Krishna, the head boy. There was a woman's voice—the gawdy woman's voice—saying something, and the voice of the stationmaster, in a sing-song Eurasian English. "The axle is cracked, my lady. It is unsafe for yourself more than for the others."

He thought, "Good Lord, that means she'll have to come in here." He was alarmed suddenly. What would he talk to her about? What would he say to the gawdy lady all the way to Bombay? He'd never known a woman like her. In the Biblical sense, he'd never known any woman but his dead wife. He sat up suddenly on the divan. The voices outside still went on, arguing interminably, but he didn't hear them. He was scared now. Standing up, he pulled on a cheap shirt of white silk, slipped off the sarong and drew on a pair of white shorts, stockings and a pair of shoes, terrified suddenly at the thought that she might have come into the compartment without warning to find them all half-naked in the heat.

His son looked up from the orange he was patiently dissecting and asked, "What are you putting on your clothes for, Dad?"

"Maybe we're being joined by a lady."

"Oh . . . that pretty lady in the Maharajah's carriage?"

"Yes."

[31]

"Oh," said the boy and went back to dividing his orange into neat segments.

There was nothing to be done. Her common sense told her that. You couldn't go on traveling in the car of a fast express with a broken axle. Krishna just kept murmuring "misery and desolation" and saying it wasn't his fault, but that didn't solve anything.

To the groveling, disgruntled stationmaster, she said, "Where am I going to go?"

"There's two purdah carriages, me lady."

"Empty?"

"No. There is two ladies in one and three in the other."

No, that was impossible. She couldn't spend the rest of the hot journey to Bombay shut up in a stuffy purdah carriage being stared at by a couple of women who had never been out of a harem. They would disapprove of her. They'd do worse, which was simply to sit and stare with enormous black eyes; and the compartment would be airless and hot and reeking with the sickly smell of musk and fading jasmine. The women, who had never been out of seclusion, had no manners at all. They'd simply stare and speculate in their cowlike way about what she was like and what kind of world she had come out of. They would stare for five hours . . . hour after hour, minute after minute.

A feeling of wild exasperation came over her. It was always like this in India. Just when you were beginning to enjoy yourself, the *zenana* women gave you a Mickey Finn or the train broke down or you got cholera. . . . The old complaint of Westerners attacked her. Why had she come back to India, anyway? When you were back again in the West it all seemed wonderful and romantic, and as soon as you returned the mirage was shattered by a million annoyances. It was the God-damndest country.

"Krishna," she said, "get all the baggage out on the platform and then go and . . . never mind. Just get the baggage out on the platform."

"Very good, Memsahib."

She had meant to order him to go and ask the strange man in the second-class compartment if she could share his compartment for the rest of the journey to Bombay and then in the middle of a sentence thought better of it. The man could refuse Krishna, but he couldn't refuse her under the circumstances. One thing encouraged her. The glimpse she had caught of her fellow traveler in the morning just after she had wakened. She had noticed a white man in a sarong and jacket talking to the stationmaster. She did not know what he looked like; she had been too drowsy and too ill to notice him very carefully. She only knew that he couldn't be the conventional English official. That sort of man would have been dressed in white drill and a topee, sitting bolt upright in the heat through the whole trip to Bombay. To that sort of man she might have preferred even the horrors of the purdah carriage. The man in the second-class compartment was, by British official standards, definitely nuts, or he wouldn't be dressed as he was, comfortably and sensibly for the heat. And she had always felt more at home with people who were a little crazy.

To the stationmaster she said, "How long is it going to be before we can go on?"

"Half an hour, me lady. We have to leave the carriage here."

She didn't answer him, but she was annoyed. She wanted to be in Bombay by eight o'clock in order to have a bath and change and come down to see who was in the bar of the Taj Mahal and find out which days there was racing, and pick up all the threads of that complicated unreal life where she had dropped them on going to Jellapore. Now, they wouldn't get there until nine or nine-thirty and everything was upset. She would have to miss the cocktail hour and dine late and alone. "Damn India," she said aloud and began to gather up her bag, her white felt hat, and her gloves. For a moment she thought, "Maybe I'd better put on some stockings." And then she rejected the idea. If the strange man wore a sarong he wouldn't mind her appearing stockingless.

Turning to the ostentatiously busy Krishna, she said, "Don't forget the gin and limes."

"No, Memsahib."

Then she did over her face and hair and set out for the second-class compartment and the stranger.

As she appeared on the platform of the railway carriage, a murmur, a kind of subdued "Ah . . . h . . . h" arose from the

[33]

crowd of Indians held back by the policemen. To them this sight of this tall, blonde woman was better than a circus to the citizens of a small town in the Middle West. At this obscure railway junction they had seen European women before, all of them, but never one like this one. Most of the women they had seen were of an uncertain age, dressed indifferently in dowdy clothes, withered and drained of youth and beauty and vitality by the cruelty of the Indian climate. This apparition on the platform was, in the heat and dust, golden and pink and white, with a body which underneath the thin white silk showed all the magnificence of her belly, buttocks and thighs. And she walked with grace and insolence like some animal goddess, with that slow measured tread learned years before on the stage of the New Amsterdam theatre. It was Freya appearing suddenly before the devotees of the dark Sita and the Evil Kali. Even though it was a slightly faded and hung-over Freya the effect of the blondeness and the voluptuous body was tremendous.

As she descended the steps and moved toward the second-class carriage with a gait which was like the low warm swells of the Persian Gulf—a gait which was calculated to arouse the weary lust of tired business men in far-off Manhattan—the crowd broke through the barrier of policemen, oblivious to kicks and blows of the *lathi*. They pressed closely around her, smelling of dust and oil and sweat, blocking her way until the tough little policemen clubbed open a pathway once more. Alarmed and a little disheveled, she managed, with the policemen at her back, to make the steps of the second-class carriage. She was less alarmed than she might have been, for she was used to such demonstrations. Wherever she went on foot, in the markets or the bazaars, a crowd collected and followed her, like small dark insects attracted to a light.

In the second-class compartment, Merrill had busied himself, like a housewife expecting a suddenly announced visit, putting the place in order. Even in the steaming heat, he experienced a sudden return of energy. The old indifference, born of long bouts of malaria which made even dressing seem a tremendous effort, appeared to have left him. Partly, the reason was good manners.

Because he had been well brought up long ago in the family of a clergyman in a small upper New York State valley, remote instinct told him that the house should look nice. But there was too another element—the faint knowledge, scarcely recognized, that the woman who was coming to join him came out of another world, a world of which he did not know and never had known anything at all, a world in which there were such things as luxury and utter freedom, license and drinking and wholesale fornification.

For he knew about this woman. Like every one of the six million residents of the State of Jellapore he knew of her presence in Jellapore City. The State officers, the *zenana*, the nobles, the rich merchants, the missionaries knew of it, but so too did the poor coolies and the *ryots* and their families. Even the shy, unseen aboriginal tribes in the mountain jungles had received vague intimations, already translated into legend, concerning a blonde goddess who had come to stay with the brother of the Maharajah. Lost among the remote villages, Merrill possessed information concerning the goddess which was scarcely more exact than that of the aborigines. And now suddenly this almost legendary creature, whom he had never expected to see, was projected suddenly into his life.

So, in a way, without his being aware of it, he prepared for the arrival of the strange woman as if he too were preparing to receive a goddess.

Her arrival was preceded by a murmur of the crowd on the platform and punctuated by the shouts and cursing of the policemen and the groans of those struck on the head or shoulders by blows of their *lathis*. Then there was a sudden silence as Merrill kicked the last of a pile of pineapples beneath the divan, and he looked up to find her standing there in the doorway of the compartment.

She was holding a jewel case and said, "Excuse me for barging in like this but my railway carriage has broken down and there's no place for me to go."

The words were English words rather than American, but the accent held an echo which came unmistakably from the Mississippi Basin. Out of his long experience with languages and dialects he had come to have a sharp ear for such things. The way she said "barging" with a broad r, brought him a sense of relief and dissipated a little the first frantic shyness which had attacked him at sight of her.

Tommy started up at sight of her and the blind Ali turned his head toward the sound of her voice. Merrill said, "Come in. I heard the row outside and thought you might be turning up here. Come in and make yourself at home. Better sit on this side. The boys have taken up that side of the carriage, and boys of that age are a little messy."

She sat down almost shyly on the edge of the divan, holding the jewel case awkwardly in her lap. He was aware suddenly not only that she too felt shy, but of the perfection of the body, now concealed, now exposed, beneath the white silk. She should have put on more clothes at least before walking along the platform in front of all that peering, lecherous mob. It wasn't safe for her and it wasn't fair to the crowd itself.

"I couldn't face the purdah carriage. You know what they're like?"

"Yes, I know."

The train suddenly jolted and began to move. She was alarmed. "The train's not leaving, is it? All my baggage is in the other car."

"No. They'll be taking off the car, that's all."

"Everything I've got with me is in there."

"You've got a bearer, haven't you?"

"Yes. Two of 'em."

The train jolted again and came to a stop.

"I'll take a look just to make sure."

"That's very good of you."

He went to the platform and leaning out saw that the train had moved backward a couple of hundred yards to a switch. Heads were poked out of every window, the length of the train, watching the operation. Voices shouted back and forth between carriages. With the patience and the good humor of the Indians, the accident had changed from what in the West would have been an annoyance into a hilarious party. Far down the platform he saw the figure of a Jellapore royal servant in purple and gold. He was standing beside an immense pile of luggage. Merrill thought, "All that can't belong to her." And then he decided to remain in the doorway until everything was settled. He didn't want to go back into the carriage with her now; he was not quite certain why, but he wanted to stay outside as long as possible.

Inside the carriage Tommy looked at the pretty lady and said, "What have you got in that box?"

She answered him at once. "A lot of pretty things. Would you like to see them?"

"Yes," said Tommy, coming over to her. "Let me look."

She opened the jewel case and the boy stood, looking down at it, his head bent a little on one side. Then one by one, out of each tray she lifted the jewels and laid them on the divan beside her—the necklace, the bracelets, the clips and the earrings—and the two of them, the Follies girl and the small boy, studied them. In the eyes of both of them was the same look, the expression of wonder and admiration in the poor for the mystery of small objects of beauty and immense value.

"Pretty, aren't they?" asked Carol.

The boy, his eyes shining, looked up at her. "Can I touch them?"

"Sure."

One by one he began picking them up. "Whee! They're like the Maharajah's. What are these?"

"Emeralds," said Carol, "and these are diamonds and the necklace is made of rubies."

"Could I let Ali touch them?"

"Yes."

She watched the boy take the jewels one by one and hand them to the blind boy. She watched the long sensitive thin Indian fingers feel and caress each one. The two boys, the son of the Mohammedan mahout and the son of the social worker, talked together in Hindustani. Then the American boy turned to her and said, "Ali wants to know if you're a queen."

At that the girl laughed, "No, not that kind of a queen anyway. Lots of women in America have jewelry like that."

The big blue eyes of the boy were still wide with wonder. "They're beautiful," he said.

"Haven't you ever been to America?" she asked.

"No, but I'm going to America to school. I'm sailing on a big boat in a couple of days with Mr. Snodgrass, the head of the Mission in Jellapore. I'm going to live in Minnesota with my uncle. Have you ever been to Minnesota?"

She laughed, "Sure I have. I was born there."

"Was your father a missionary?"

"No, he was a farmer."

"Gee. That must be fun living on a farm in America. I read a book about that. It's not like a farm in India, is it?"

"No, not much."

"Gee, it must be fun. I wish my uncle lived on a farm. He only lives in a city called Minni . . ." He couldn't quite say it, so she said it for him. "Minneapolis—it's an Indian name."

"Red Indian?"

"Yes."

"Yes, I read about them too in a book. Are there cowboys in Minnesota?"

Again she laughed, "I'm afraid not. But maybe your uncle will take you west to see cowboys."

"Gee, I'd like to be a cowboy. It must be fun."

The dark fingers of the Indian boy continued to caress the jewels. It was as if his hands took the place of his eyes, as if all his soul were concentrated in the tips of the slim fingers. She thought suddenly, "Orientals must feel differently about jewels. To us they're just something you wear and show off and have to get insured." To the fingers of the mahout's blind son, the jewels seemed to have life and soul. He stroked and caressed them as a child caresses a kitten.

Then the Indian boy said something to the other boy and the small American asked, "Ali wants to know if you're the daughter of a queen."

"No, my mother came from Sweden."

"Is that a nice country?"

"I don't know. I've never been there. I was born in Minnesota."

Again the blind boy spoke and again the tow-headed son of the missionary turned to her. This time he hesitated. "Ali is not very polite."

"What did he ask you?" And when the boy hesitated, she said, "Don't be afraid."

He said, "Did you steal them?" Quickly he added, "You mustn't mind that. You see Indians are kind of different from us."

She laughed, "No, I don't mind. You see, I had a rich husband. He gave me some of them and friends gave me the rest."

"Where is your husband now?"

"We're divorced."

"What does that mean?"

"It means that we don't like each other so we're not married any more."

"Oh." He was thoughtful for a time. Then he said, "Can you do that in America?"

"Yes. They do it quite often."

Again for a time he was thoughtful, fingering one of the earrings, but clearly his attention was not on it. At last in a small voice he said, "Maybe that's a good idea . . . if people don't like each other."

The observation interested her. She asked, "Why do you say that?"

"I don't know. I was just thinking."

Then a voice interrupted them both, a voice which said, "You'd better give those things back, Tommy, before you lose them—and I wouldn't ask so many questions."

She turned and saw the father standing in the doorway. How long he had been standing there she did not know, but she wondered quietly how much of the conversation he had overheard, and suddenly, for the first time, she found herself blushing. Wildly, she tried to control the blush, but even in the heat she felt the warmth in her face. Why she blushed she could not think, save that the things she had said to the child she realized swiftly would sound quite differently to a grown man, even to a missionary.

The father was smiling at her and saying, "You mustn't mind Tommy. In some ways he's half-savage from our point of view. He's been brought up among Tamil kids and in the elephant stables." She noticed for the first time the extraordinary blueness of the father's eyes and the tired lines about the lean mouth. She had scarcely noticed him before. Suddenly she saw he was handsome. More than that, more important than that, he was likable and sympathetic. All her life she had lived by instinct. Of preju-

[39]

dices she had few, if any. Reason did not cause her to stumble nor intellect to confuse an issue. This man she liked because her instinct told her there was a rare quality about him. In her lazy thoughts she gave to simplicity and goodness the label "being on the level."

The boy was collecting the jewels from Ali and giving them back to her. Clumsily, hurriedly, she put them back into the jewel case, willy-nilly, dumping them into the wrong trays, jamming the drawers in her haste when she tried to close them. She was aware of only one impulse, to get the jewels back into the case and put it out of sight. Because she was ashamed. Why she did not know, but it had something to do with the purity of the clear blue eyes. They made the jewels seem obscene.

Looking down at the box she said, "I thought they would amuse the kids."

The man grinned. "Pretty expensive toys." And she looked up at him wondering if what he had said was meant to be a crack. It wasn't. She could see by the expression in his face that it was made innocently, sincerely. She divined at the same instant that he wasn't the kind of man who made cracks. She was aware suddenly that there was a kind of innocence about him.

Something about him made her feel ill at ease and she thought, quickly. "I'm going to hate the rest of this trip. God-damn that axle! God-damn India!"

Then she heard the voice of Krishna and saw him standing there in his purple and gold. He asked, "Is there anything I can do for the Memsahib?" And she felt a sudden defiance and heard herself saying, "Bring me a gin sling." And to the man she said, "Won't you have something?"

He turned to Krishna, "Have you a gin and tonic, Krishna?"

"Yes, Sahib Merrill."

He went away and she asked, "Do you know Krishna?"

He grinned, "Yes, I know about everybody in Jellapore."

That too made her uneasy. She wished suddenly that after all she had gone in the purdah compartment. Even the staring eyes of all those Indian woman would have been better than this. It was too late to change now for the train had begun to move, on its

[40]

way to Bombay, leaving behind at Lepta the gaudy broken carriage of the Maharajah of Jellapore.

"Well, anyway," she thought angrily, "it's only for four or five more hours. After that I'll never see him again."

The heat was a little better now, although the sides of the railway carriage were still hot to the touch. Krishna brought the drinks and she drank the gin sling quickly in two or three gulps. The boy watched her with round eyes filled with curiosity. The headache was a little better now and she thought, "I've certainly made a big jump from the party last night. Me, traveling with missionaries."

It made her want to laugh—to think of the subalterns kicking over the pots of orchids and she thought, "Anyway, I don't see anything to be sore about. He hasn't said or done anything." But she ordered Krishna to bring her another gin sling, just so the missionary guy wouldn't make any mistake about what kind of a girl she was. But almost at once as she turned and saw again the honest blue eyes, she said, "It's been so hot all day. I just can't seem to get enough to drink."

Minute by minute, hour by hour, the train descended from the high burnt red plateau of the Deccan down through valleys and over passes, stopping now and then at clamorous stations; and in the second-class carriage the four passengers dozed or talked or stared out through the fine copper screening, meant to exclude dust which came through it like talc, settling over everything, piling up in little drifts on the floor, filling teeth and hair, and soiling the white clothing of Miss Carol Halma and Homer Merrill.

Outside the window the scenery grew less monotonous and more beautiful, the flat country breaking away into gorges and ravines where underground moisture fed the vegetation and tall lean betel palms leaned over tanks of water surrounded in the evening light by bathing holy men and *dhobis* and women in bright colored saris who had come in the cool of the day to do their washing. Sometimes a troupe of big gray, black-faced monkeys scuttled across the level ground and disappeared chattering into the mango trees. The best mangoes in the world came from this part of India.

Presently the blind son of the mahout lay on his sides with his

[41]

knees drawn up and fell asleep and the American boy in a little while lay down beside him and slept too. Outside, as if a curtain had fallen suddenly, the last rays of the sun vanished and the man and woman were left alone shut into the compartment together, the woman already a little drunk and the man tired and a little puzzled and uneasy. Both of them felt the aloneness; even through the haze of drink, the woman was aware of it. To the man it was painful.

She said suddenly, "You ought to drink more. It would cheer you up."

"I can't drink. I've been ill . . . a little gin and tonic . . . that helps keep off the return of malaria." He grinned, "But you have to think of the liver. The liver makes a lot of trouble out here. I'm caught between liver and malaria."

"I guess I haven't got a liver. Nobody's ever mentioned it." The train passed through a crossroad station without stopping and both of them turned to look out of the window. Then she said with a kind of tipsy elegance, "I don't want to intrude, but what was your illness?"

"The usual thing . . . malaria, liver, nerves . . . the old Indian disease." It was a lot more than that, but he didn't tell her. He could not have told anyone, because even when he thought of the last year he felt ill again and choked as if a lump had come in his throat to stifle his breathing. It was odd that in spite of everything he could do, the nerves of his whole body seemed to tighten. It was as if every nerve was an electric wire that was suddenly charged with current. He could feel the nerves in his legs, his arms, across his abdomen, through the muscles on his chest.

"I guess I've never been in India long enough," she said. "But I know what it means when India gets on your nerves. It was like that with me in Jellapore. I guess I got away just in time."

"Ever been here before?"

"Yes, I came here on my honeymoon."

"Is your husband with you on this trip?" He hoped she had a husband. It would somehow make him feel less strange. He liked her but he hated to think of her wandering about alone, visiting Maharajahs and doing things like that. In his heart he could only feel that it meant what he did not want to believe.

[42]

"No, he's not." Then the drink made her reckless and she thought, "What the hell! Even if he is a missionary, he can take it." And aloud she said, "You see, I'm divorced."

The expression on his face did not change and suddenly she wanted to justify herself. "You see, it was hardly a marriage really. I was young and so was he. He didn't have much sense and his family didn't like it. Neither of us tried to make much of a go of it."

"I see," said Merrill, gravely. "That happens sometimes."

The old regret attacked her. She called to Krishna and asked for another gin sling, and the man said, "Do you think you'll be all right if you have another?"

For a second she was angry. Then she said, "Don't worry about me. I've been at it for years. I'm a Swede. I know my capacity."

The man was silent. Krishna, with a dead face, brought the drink. She laughed and said, "I'm all right, aren't I, Krishna?"

"Yes, Memsahib."

"Krishna has seen me drink the Yuvarajah right under the table and all the others too."

"Indians can't drink," observed the man. "It's not in their blood."

"No, but Swedes can. They've been drinking hard liquor for thousands of years. Here's how. Sorry you won't join me."

She was feeling good now. Gay again. The headache was gone and with it that depression which always settled on her the moment she stopped drinking—and all the fears which sometimes attacked her, fear of losing her youth and her looks, terror of what was to become of her, and worst of all, the strange nameless terror of being lost. It was as if she were wandering in a desert or a forest, not knowing where she had come from or whither she was bound or why she was there at all. It was a sickening fear from which she always turned away.

She began presently to go to pieces. Carelessly, gayly she pushed back the light silk jacket, unaware, or at least heedless, of the fact that under the dim light she appeared half-naked. Her hair was in disorder and her cheeks a little flushed, but the disorder instead of making her appear sordid, only gave her the wild, charming look of a Bacchante.

Boldly she said, "What does it feel like to be a missionary?"

"I'm not a missionary really. I work in the villages."

"What kind of work?"

He grinned, thinking that it was a little futile to explain his work to her. "Well, I go among the farmers and villagers and teach them how to market their crops and improve the breed of their chickens and cattle and what to eat and how to avoid hookworm."

"Don't they mind your butting in?"

"Sometimes the Brahmins do," he grinned. "But the villagers don't . . . they're glad to have somebody help them. Nobody has paid much attention to them for about ten thousand years—except to collect taxes."

"And you don't try to convert them or talk about God or anything?"

"No, I'm just practical."

"D'you get a lot of money for it?"

"No, enough to live on."

"Well, I must say, it's a funny thing to want to do."

"I guess maybe it is . . . but I enjoy it."

She lifted the glass and drained the last drop. "Well, I always say, that's the thing that matters—that you like doing what you're doing."

Then suddenly a meaningless, unreasonable, aching silence separated them, as if everything which she was and all that he was had marshaled their forces and withdrawn into corners, facing each other, watchful and hostile. And with him, there was always his nerves and the particular nervousness of not knowing how to behave with women like this. The more she drank, the more changed she became, the more he was troubled. He looked away from her out of the window and closed his eyes. The long glare of the day had brought back the pain in the top of his head. With his eyes closed he could not see her lying back on the divan among the pillows. Yet when he closed his eyes the image of her was still there, the body only partly concealed by white silk, the gold-streaked hair, tousled and curly above the lovely friendly face and blue eyes.

Then he heard her voice asking, "Are you tired?"

"Yes."

"Is there anything I can do to help?" As he opened his eyes he saw her rising from the divan. "Come and lie down here. I'll sit in the chair. I'm feeling fine. Anyway, it was lousy of me to barge in here and take your place."

"No, I'm all right."

Through the mist of her tipsiness she saw how pale he was, how ill he looked. She said, "Don't be a damned fool. Get up and lie down on the divan."

"No. . . . I'm all right. It's nothing but a headache."

She was beside the armchair now, bending over him, tipsily insistent. "I'm nothing but a sow, I guess. Listen to me. Get up and go over there and lie down on the divan."

"No."

"Well, I'll stand up here in the corner until you do. And I mean it too . . . all the rest of the way to Bombay. Do as I tell you."

The pain grew thicker. It seemed to spread, pushing against the back of his eyes and the base of his skull. He didn't answer her because at the moment the effort was beyond his strength. She bent down and attempted to lift him to his feet, very nearly succeeding. It was astonishing how strong she was.

"Come on," she said, "help me."

Then he obeyed her, partly because he was suffering too much to do otherwise and partly because it was so pleasant to have someone caring for him. That was something he had never had from a woman since his mother died when he was ten in the parish house in a far-away New York State village.

With her help he managed to get as far as the divan and lie down. Weakly he said, "It'll go away after a little while. It never lasts."

"What do you do for it?"

"Nothing. There isn't anything to be done." And in spite of anything he could do his face grew white and contracted with pain.

She left him for a moment, passing the sleeping boys and opened the door at the end of the compartment. "Krishna!"

"Yes, Memsahib?"

"Make me a gimlet,—straight gin and lime juice—I can't drink any more water."

Then she returned again to the divan, where Merrill lay with his head pressed against the hard cushion at the end. His whole

[45]

body was rigid with pain. All his strength was concentrated in pressing the top of his head against the hard surface. That alone seemed to bring relief. For a moment she stood watching him, a little terrified. She had never known either illness or pain and the sight of so much concentrated agony bewildered her.

"There must be something a person can do," she thought, and aloud she asked: "Haven't you any dope? Haven't you got anything that would help?"

"No."

"That's foolish." Perhaps he thought you oughtn't to take stuff like that. There were nutty people who held such beliefs.

Then, as if she were unable to endure the sight any longer, she sat on the edge of the divan and shyly she put out one hand and began stroking, slowly and firmly, the back of his neck. . . . She did it instinctively but at the same time in her memory there came up the picture of her mother doing the same thing to her father, a little while before he died. He had had a tumor on the brain and the touch of her mother's hand firmly stroking his head had been the only thing which brought relief. She had left the show and gone back to Minnesota to be there when her father died from the terrible pain, and now in the railway carriage, sliding down the mountains into Bombay, she saw again the bedroom in Minnesota with its heavy furniture and the oil lamp beside her parents' great double bed and the Biblical texts in Swedish wreathed with garlands of flowers which hung against the ornate wallpaper. Was that what this man had? Was he going to die as her father had? He was too young and too good-looking and too nice.

Krishna brought the gimlet—a big one made of pure gin and lime juice and sugar with no water in it. She drank it down in a single swallow and suddenly she felt bolder and experienced a kind of tenderness for the suffering man. The stroking seemed to bring him relief. The muscular body, a moment before as taut as a tightly drawn wire, began slowly to relax.

Presently she asked, "Is it better?"

"Yes, much better."

The train stopped again. The stationmaster beat on the clanging railway iron. The crowd yelled and chattered. The vendors of water raised their harsh voices and at the sounds the man's body stiffened once more with the agony of all that raucous uproar hammering on his tired brain.

An hour or two from Bombay the pain left him altogether, and he sat up on the edge of the divan, white and trembling, his face damp with perspiration, suddenly old and tired. He looked at her and smiled.

"Sorry. I must have been an awful nuisance," he said.

"It wasn't anything. I hope you didn't mind my treatment."

'Again he grinned, "No, it was very pleasant. I'm very grateful. It goes away like that—suddenly."

"Now what you need is a drink. . . . Krishna! . . ." She clapped her hands, and at the sound the blind boy on the divan stirred in his sleep.

Krishna appeared and left again to fetch the drink.

Then she said, "Is that boy blind for always?"

He looked up at her and then at the boy and an odd look of tenderness came into his face, a look that she was unaccustomed to seeing in the faces of men she knew.

"I'm afraid so," he answered. "I'm taking him up to Bombay for an operation. There's a surgeon . . . a very famous one . . . in Bombay for a couple of weeks. He's visiting a friend of mine . . . an Indian. It was a piece of luck. I was bringing my own boy up to send him to America, so I brought Ali along. . . . There's about one chance in ten that he'll get his sight back. He wants it so much because he's got an ambition to drive the great elephant of the Maharajah when he grows up."

She had a sudden picture of Jelly—the king of kings, the father and mother of his people . . . in a checked suit at the races. Funny that this blind boy should want to drive his elephant, when Jelly never thought of his people. Jelly wouldn't have bothered to do anything for the boy; he'd only send him away because the sight of the boy would cause him pain and annoyance. Jelly would just turn away and order another bottle of champagne.

She raised her glass. She wasn't feeling giddy and excited now. She said, "Here's to Ali getting back his sight."

"That's a good thing to drink to."

Suddenly she felt very intimate and friendly with the man, as if

[47]

they had been through a great many things together. She lay back in the armchair and closed her eyes, aware again of the heat and the jolting of the train. She kept thinking, "I mustn't let it die on me now. I want some fun when I get to the Taj Mahal bar."

The train was two hours late by the time the first lights and smells of Bombay came into sight and hearing, lights already obscured by the low-hanging haze of cow dung smoke, and smells that seemed doubly strong and pungent in the heat which hung like a blanket over the low-lying city. She was feeling gay again and the familiar smell excited her. In a few minutes, in less than an hour, she would be back again where there were lights and dancing and people. The gin made her feel the old confidence. She would meet people—probably men she knew—in the vast bar of the Taj Mahal, and if there was no one there she could, she knew, easily strike up an acquaintance with a stranger and find herself a new circle of friends. Thank heaven she was friendly and that she could take care of herself. You were always hearing of girls led astray or deceived or swindled. Suddenly she laughed aloud. They must be bloody fools. Nothing had ever happened to her that she didn't want to happen.

She tried to rise and go into the washroom to powder her face and put her hair in order, but she felt suddenly dizzy and sat down again. "I can do that," she thought, "when I get to the hotel. Am *I* going to have a good time!"

The long journey across the burning, dusty plateau became suddenly a kind of nightmare, possessed only of the reality of dreams. It seemed now to belong to the remote past. Only the future existed. In her health and vitality, the aura of past experiences, however bad, never clung to her. The past had the power to depress you only if you were ill or tired. Hope, optimism, anticipation she knew, out of experience and instinct, were the rewards of health and vitality.

Her companion roused the blind boy and his son and told them to put themselves in order for the arrival. The blind boy asked him something in Hindustani; and when the man replied the boy grew suddenly agitated. He talked rapidly, wildly. She could understand not a word of the conversation, but she divined that the man was trying to calm the boy and explain something to him.

The discussion went on for a long time while the American boy disappeared into the lavatory. At last the blind boy seemed calmer, and the man said to her, "He slept through sundown without praying and he's frightened. I tried to tell him that God wouldn't mind. Even Allah couldn't be as tough as that—to hold that against him."

She laughed with unnatural loudness. "Some of them have the damndest ideas."

Then the man led the blind boy to the washroom and as they returned the train began to slow down for the station. She called Krishna and said, "You come to the hotel with me in the taxi. Let the other boy come behind us with the luggage. Bring the two small valises. I'll keep the jewel box."

"Very good, Memsahib." It was a task Krishna had had before—this guarding Memsahib and all her luggage, seeing that she got safely to her hotel.

To her traveling companion she said, "Well, I hope we'll meet again some time." But she said it without sincerity. At the moment she was scarcely thinking of him. She thought, "A nice enough guy, but just a missionary." She pulled on her hat and added, opening her bag, "Here's my card. I'll be at the Taj Mahal Hotel. I can never thank you enough."

Taking the card, he said, "It wasn't anything. I haven't got a card but my name is Merrill—Homer Merrill." (At the name Homer, she wanted to laugh. That was what Bill used to call a "barber shop name"—Homer, Ernest, Floyd, Leo, Albert, Clarence . . . he had a whole list of them.)

"I'm staying with a friend—Colonel Moti—you won't remember his name but he's a doctor and head of the Institute of Tropical Diseases. . . ." And then almost shyly he added, "In case you should want to reach me for anything I know Bombay pretty well."

The train had nearly stopped. She said, "I do too . . . very well." And hazily, she thought, "And how! But not the missionary's Bombay, old boy." (In half an hour she'd be in the bar and wouldn't have to worry about feeling tired or fussing about the future.)

[49]

Then the train stopped abruptly, in the way of Indian trains, nearly throwing them all to the floor. The din began outside and into the compartment came a small and handsome Indian, rather swarthy. At sight of him she thought, "That's the handsomest Indian I ever saw."

The impression came instantaneously. He was finely made like a steel spring, and wore Indian dress, white jodhpurs and black *atchkan* with a *puggree* of scarlet. When he looked at her she felt suddenly sobered and uncomfortable. It was the eyes which gave her the impression of his beauty. They were large and intensely black with a kind of fire behind them, not the eyes of the mystic or a dreamer, but of a fighter, the eyes that one sees rarely in India. Even through her tipsiness she had a quick impression of his looking through her, as if he saw her naked, not in the flesh, but in the soul.

For a moment the experience sobered her, as if suddenly someone had dashed cold water in her face. She stared back at him and then turning away, she shrugged her shoulders and spoke to Krishna, telling him to gather up the rest of her belongings, find porters and be off. She was in a hurry to be off to the Taj Mahal Bar. Time was flying past her. For a second, even above the clamor on the platform, it seemed to her that she could hear it—a wild rushing sound. She must be on her way to enjoy herself. She was twenty-eight. There was so little time left.

When she had gone, Colonel Moti stood for a moment watching Merrill with that same penetrating, all-seeing look in the burning black eyes. When at last he spoke, he said, "Who's your girl friend?"

Merrill looked at him wearily, "I don't know. She was visiting the Yuvarajah—Jellapore's brother. The axle of her carriage broke and she had no place to go except the purdah carriage."

"A *tart*," said the Colonel, and he made the word seem worse than it was.

"Oh, she's all right."

The Doctor didn't argue. "Come along," he said. "You ought to be in bed." And again he looked sharply at the American, noting everything, the color of his eyeballs, the lines in the weary face, the drooping shoulders. "You're not going back to Jellapore at once."

The shoulders straightened a little so that the powerful muscles stood out beneath the damp silk of his shirt. "I've got to go back. It's planting time."

"You're not going," said the Colonel.

In those days the Taj Mahal Hotel had the air of a vast middle western county jail. Built around two or three great wells which ran the full height of the building, the stairs were of stone and the railings of iron, and around the great wells ran galleries, likewise with stone floors and iron railings. Off these the rooms opened, each one more like a cell than a hotel room, each specially furnished with an iron bed covered with netting and with a single hard mattress, a washstand, and a couple of stiff uncomfortable chairs. Overhead there was a large old-fashioned electric *punkah*, and outside on the cool slate floors slept the bearers. They slept there not only at night, but all through the hot days, when they were not gossiping with other bearers. The jail-like corridors were as much an exchange place of gossip as any market place. The bearers from one end to the other of the vast hotel knew everything about every guest of the hotel, his vices, his peculiarities, his meannesses or generosities. It was as if each room were walled with glass for all the world to look inside.

And downstairs on the ground floor there was a vast hallway and a huge stairway which led up and up into the heights of the big hotel. Through the hallway and the bazaar which occupied half its area, came and went a procession of Arab horsedealers, British Governors and Civil Servants, Russian and German trollops, Indian princes, jewel merchants, Parsee millionaires, comic middle-aged tourists, gamblers, oil prospectors. The procession went on day and night, for in the heat of the city and with the fantastic character of many of the guests, the place was as alive at four in the morning as at midday.

Above the vast hallway there was another great room for dancing and drinking—a room with vast windows opening opposite the Readymoney Building against the heat, with a huge bar which ran across all one end of it where a score of bartenders, working on shifts, mixed gimlets and gin slings and *chota pegs* and served gin and tonic in quantities vast enough to float a ship. Around the edges of the dance floor, inside the tables, "advanced" Indian girls and Russian and German tarts danced odd versions of what they believed to be the latest American dances. In those days, Bombay was a wide open town. The Taj Mahal, like the Raffles Hotel in Singapore and the Hotel des Indes in Batavia, was a famous rendezvous for men and women from all over the East. They came from Sumatra and Macassar and the Malay States, from Medan Deli and Semarang and Borneo and Ceylon and Sourabaya. There is a legend that the hotel was designed to face the bay but that the Indian contractors who built it put it up wrong way around and that the English architect who designed it took one look at it on his arrival in Bombay and, seeing what they had done, hanged himself. Like the designer of Cologne Cathedral, rumored to have been the devil, his name has been lost.

As she came in through the great hall, followed by Krishna in his purple and gold, most of the people watching them knew her at once. The employees of the hotel knew her and the gamblers and the rich Parsees, the merchants and the poor down-at-the-heel Russian and German girls in whose tired eyes there gleamed for a moment a weary resentment that she had done so well and had all the luck while they worked so hard. And those who had not seen her before, coming and going to Indian States with the Taj Mahal always as a base, noticed her, because it was impossible not to have noticed the big handsome blonde girl with expensive clothes and an air of recklessness.

Among the newcomers to whom she was a stranger was the tired, hard greasy woman whom Stitch Trollope had called the spy. She sat in a wicker chair curiously alone in a room so filled with movement and noise and color, an island in the ocean of nationalities. She gave the impression of always having been alone. In her hands she carried the little string of beads which Persians and some Greeks carry with them to finger and count as they talk or sit silent; with them it is a kind of habit which takes the place of smoking cigarettes. She had been turning the beads around and around, over and over again, for a couple of hours, as she sat there, but at sight of the big, blonde girl her hands grew still and the faint clicking of the rosewood beads one against the other, ceased. The small, green eyes followed the figure of the girl as she spoke to the clerk, and the old woman thought, her lips even moving a little, "That is the girl I want. She's not too young or too old. She must know her way about. By the look of her she's American. She's a little bit drunk. That may be good or not so good. Maybe my luck is in again." American girls were what she needed. Russians were an old story in dying Europe. The French made too much trouble and wanted too much money. No, for a first class place it was an American girl that was needed. Everything that had to do with music and dancing was American now. This was just the one. She looked well and she wasn't too young and it was quite obvious that she was experienced.

The beads in her hands were still while she watched the girl leave and go into the lift followed by Krishna carrying a box which the Baroness divined must contain jewelry. When the lift door had closed, she left her chair and, trailing an aroma of patchouli behind her, went to the desk and asked, "Who is dat girl?"

The clerk, suspicious, said, "I can't give out the names of the guests. It is a rule here."

"D'you think I can't find oud from any vaiter?"

"Yes, Madame, but I can't tell you."

Unabashedly she asked, "Has she been here before?"

"Yes, often."

"Vat does she do?"

"Nothing."

"Vy is she here?"

"I can't tell you, Madame."

"All right. Keep your secret. I vasn't born yesterday."

But the clerk was polite and did not make the obvious answer. He turned away a little and she went back to her chair. In a little while the tiny rosewood beads in her fat hands began to rattle back and forth again and the dirty diamonds to glitter darkly. She was planning again. It was the only fun she had. It was better even than the sight of fat bank statements from Paris and Cairo, Budapest and London and Amsterdam.

Upstairs Carol moved uncertainly along the stone balcony following the boy who was showing her to her old room—the one at the corner which overlooked the gateway to India and the whole Bay of Bombay. Behind came Krishna with the jewel case and a small valise. As they passed each bedroom door the bearer lying there on the cool stone, rose and salaamed. One or two, asleep despite the sound of the jazz band and the clamor of the hotel which came up through the vast staircase well, snored on, oblivious to the passage of Krishna's regal gold and purple. The others, at sight of it, touched their foreheads to the stone, each one a particle of the vast and troubled India where life was a struggle not simply to get ahead but to live at all, to have enough to eat to exist from one day to the next. All night they spent in bobbing up and down to stand aside or to salaam, according to the importance of the guests returning to their rooms. That there were in the long all-night procession alcoholics and prostitutes and gamblers and swindlers made no difference; each bearer stirred himself sleepily and rose to his feet. Not only was this the rule of the hotel; it was a rule imposed upon each one of them by a grim and even more stony authority, the necessity of living. It was from these people going and coming all through the night, that each of them earned and begged and stole enough to provide rice and meat, scraps for undernourished families in the Punjab, in Bengal, in Goa, on the coasts of Malabar and Coromandel. They wakened, rose and salaamed and dozed again, a couple of hundred times a night, without complaint, patiently because that was their lot in life. In the next life, if they salaamed enough in this one, they might perhaps be among the alcoholics and gamblers and prostitutes who came and went—the salaamed instead of the salaaming, the fortunate instead of the starving.

Carol did not see the rising and falling of the soiled white-clad figures at all nor think of them. She had been born healthy and beautiful and blessed, and so she accepted life as she encountered it, leaving to God and Nature such things as justice and mercy and social conscience; and besides the gin was beginning to wear off again and the edge of her weariness beginning to show through the bright mantle of her high spirits. It was not only that her body itself was exhausted; the black eyes of the Indian doctor had some-

[54]

thing to do with it. She had been seeing them ever since she left the railway carriage.

She was glad to see the corner room again. It was as much home to her as any place in India, as much home indeed as any place she had lived in for a good many years. In India this was always the room she returned to, now from the North, now from the East, now from the South. It was in this room she could rest, sleeping all through the hot days to waken late in the afternoon in time to go to the races and gamble. It was in this room she could rest and be alone, walking about naked in the heat, shut away from all the world outside. Here in this room she could be herself. It was only lately that she had begun to feel the need of solitude, only lately that solitude had come to seem, without her thinking of it, a luxury.

And so when the porter opened the door and turned on the light, she flung herself down on the hard iron bed and said to Krishna, "Tell that boy to hurry up with the luggage—and get me a couple of gimlets right away. Hurry, Krishna!"

"Yes, Memsahib."

In the big bar which was so much like a Klondike saloon, Bill found a table for himself and Al, the radio officer and Sandy, the chief electrician of the *S. S. Sourabaya*, and Mrs. Trollope. For Bill the day had begun badly with the customs officer crushed by the packing case, and it had not gotten any better. When Stitch Trollope recovered herself, he sent Silas with his luggage to the Taj Mahal, and went with her to the palace of her sister. In the taxi she came out of her swoon almost immediately, without even asking, "Where am I?" She was the kind of woman who looked upon fainting as nonsense. One moment she opened her eyes and the next she was on her feet ready for a day's work. Indeed to Bill it seemed extraordinary that she should have fainted at all, even at the nasty sight of the poor man's messy death.

She hadn't wanted him to go with her; she had been so insistent about it that he thought there must be some reason more profound than simply that of inconveniencing him. But in the end, perhaps because she really did feel a little weak, she gave in, and together they set off in a rather rattletrap taxi, driven by a Sikh with long

[55]

hair and a long beard and the air of one of the more desperate of the forty thieves.

As they drove along the hot streets past the Maidan and the Juhu Beach station and the Towers of Silence where the vultures hovered, and Government House which was like a big English country house only with Sikhs in scarlet and gold at the gate, the old excitement returned again. There was nothing like this in the world, no city so fantastic. Baghdad in its heyday was no more absurd and mixed-up and fascinating. And it gave him a kick that he should still be able to feel that way about it. But of that he said nothing to Stitch.

He tried to make conversation, but nothing much came of the effort. Mrs. Trollope only sat there, hard and neat and controlled, the leathery tint of her face gone a waxen white and her rather thin lips set in a hard line. Although she said she was all right, this was obviously not true; she was controlling herself. He had the feeling that if she did not sit there rigid, every muscle taut, she would give way to hysterics. In all their brief acquaintance, it had never occurred to him until now that she had inside the tough, small body even the possibility of hysteria.

They drove for a time along the Nepean Sea Road past the great white wedding cake which was the Bombay palace of Jellapore, then sharply the taxi turned and with a rush and a rattle charged up a steep, narrow road bordered by big bungalows and hanging gardens filled with jacqueranda, bignonia and bougainvillea. The pepper trees hung so low that they brushed the top of the taxi; and as they drove Bill, silent now, wondered whether the extraordinary tenseness of Mrs. Trollope had more to do with the approaching meeting with her sister than with the accident itself. Certainly there was something odd about the whole thing.

Then suddenly the taxi came out of the flower-bordered lane and into an open square before a palace, made of pink marble. It was not an enormous palace, not so large as the great structures built by the rulers of Baroda and Hyderabad. It had not the pastry cake quality of Jellapore's shining white palace. It was feminine, rather boudoirish and a little gaudy, as if a French architect of the nineties, who had made his reputation building brothels, had been asked to dabble in the Saracen style.

[56]

"This is it," said Mrs. Trollope.

A pair of Ghurkas, small Mongolian men, in dark green and silver stood on guard at each side of the door just inside the pink marble *porte cochère*. The taxi stopped, the driver's long beard blowing backward on each side of his dark face in the hot wind that had come up from the Arabian Sea. A servant appeared and opened the door. Mrs. Trollope, still tense, said, "Well, good-bye. And thank you for coming with me. It wasn't necessary."

She didn't say, "Come in and have a drink." He was dying for a drink, and that would have been the conventional thing for anyone in the East to do under the circumstances. But she said nothing.

"How about going to the races with me some afternoon?" he asked.

"Maybe. I'll ring you up. Good-bye."

"Good-bye."

He turned to the taxi driver. "The Taj Mahal," he said, and then it occurred to him how odd it was that Mrs. Trollope's sister had not sent a purple Rolls Royce to the pier and a boy to look after her baggage. He himself would have to go back in the rising heat to check up on it. Funny, Mrs. Trollope had never even mentioned it.

He found that nobody had done anything about her luggage. It still lay on the pier, all marked with Vuitton's mark, spattered with labels from half the countries of the world, expensive once but worn now, and battered with much traveling. He sent it along to the palace of the Maharani of Chandragar, and at last, sweating and dying for a drink, he drove back to his hotel. But even then he found no peace. In the corridor outside the room assigned him he found in a line awaiting him a Parsee bookmaker, a Persian jewel merchant, a Koja jewel merchant, two dealers in curios, both Gujerati, a tailor and a Goanese looking for a post as cook. Before the porter had put the key in the lock, they crowded around him, each trying to outshout the others in pidgin English.

Heat, annoyance at the smell of his visitors broke his good nature and he shouted, "Go away! Get out! I don't want anything. Go away and leave me alone!"

[57]

But the shouting had no effect. When he entered the room, they all pushed and fought to get in the door first. Turning suddenly he gave one of the bookmakers a push backwards into the others and managed to slip the key in the lock and turn it.

In the corner of the room he found the real culprit. Silas was at work unpacking, benignly and all too consciously innocent of any connection with the mob outside the door. Under the ragged and dirty khaki suit his thin back was eloquent. It said, "Sahib, I know nothing of those low-born dogs." For a second Bill felt an impulse to fall upon the bearer and give him a thorough beating, because he knew very well that Silas had brought them all, hoping for sales and a commission for himself. Then the sight of the eloquent back of Silas made him want to laugh. He was so elaborately concerned with taking everything out of the bags and putting them conscientiously in the wrong combinations in the wrong drawers so that all the rest of the stay would be poisoned every time his master dressed himself.

All Bill said was, "Go and get me a gin sling, quick."

In any case there was no use arguing with Silas. He would deny everything and in the end you would only come out of it with a loss of face. Anyway, some of it was his own fault for the way he had lived when he was last in Bombay—buying things, betting, throwing money out of the window. They all remembered him. It was just possible that the vultures outside the door might forget a good customer but none of them would ever forget a sap.

"Well," he thought, "that's all over. This time I'm the sober business man."

As Silas opened the door he caught a glimpse of the crowd outside. They had not gone away. It seemed to him that their numbers had been augmented.

By now his clothing was wet from the heat and clung to him, making the heat seem all the worse. As quickly as possible, he took them off, turned on the *punkah* and lay down on the bed naked with a sheet over him. The *punkah* churned the damp, dead air but made the room no cooler. He thought, "This is certainly a bad beginning. Everything has gone wrong." The irritation which was so much a part of India had taken possession of him immediately.

That too was a bad sign. Perhaps, he thought, it would be better to finish up his business and leave by the first boat.

Closing his eyes he tried to imagine icebergs and electric refrigerators and glaciers, but none of it did any good. Then he heard the sound of a door opening softly and turning, he saw a lean dark face, and a pair of black eyes and behind it other pairs of black eyes peering at him. Jumping off the bed he ran naked to the door and slammed it, shouting, "Get out of here and stay out!"

Silas came a little later and after the drink, Bill felt a little better. While he drank, Silas plunged again into the task of throwing his belongings into utter confusion. For a moment Bill watched him, fascinated by his misdirected conscientiousness. Then he said, "Go away, Silas, for God's sake, and leave me in peace. Don't come back till five o'clock. Then you can go on with your work of destruction."

Silas grinned at him, "Very good, Sahib." And half-way to the door he said, "I sent away bad mans outside door but bad mans won't go."

"Go away. Leave me in peace and stop lying."

But Silas lingered. His glance fell reproachfully downward at his tattered costume of torn khaki. Bill waited and when this first pantomime made no impression, the boy lifted one ragged arm and examined the sleeve carefully. Again Bill had to laugh. Taking a ten rupee note from his pocket he gave it to the boy and said, "All right. Go and get yourself a new suit."

Certainly it was a bad day. But presently he fell asleep and slept soundly until he was roused by Silas pounding on the door. When he sat up he discovered that it was not yet five o'clock but only half past three and that he had a stiff neck from sleeping practically naked under the *punkah*. And it was still hotter, hotter than it had been when he went to sleep.

Once again he cursed Silas and was rewarded only by a wide white-toothed grin. Silas displayed a different costume, obviously not a new one but one he had had for a long time—"One perhaps," Bill thought, "that I bought him when I was here before."

The black face grinned as Silas asked, "Master pleased?"

"Yes, pleased as hell, you bloody embezzler."

He took a shower and spent ten minutes finding a complete

fresh costume from out of the confusion created by the bearer. Then when he opened the door he stepped full into the midst of the "bad mans." As one cluster of flies attracts other flies, their numbers had been increased by newcoming bookmakers and tailors and jewel salesmen. Cries assailed him on all sides.

"Remember Hakim, Sahib?"

"Doti, old friend. Doti make plenty money for Sahib last time."

"Sahib bought plenty rubies from Raschid, last visit."

Pushing his way through them, he hurried along the stone balcony followed by the whole tribe, still gesticulating and calling out, still unconvinced that the Sahib who had brought them so much profit on the last visit was not interested on this one.

Only at the vast stairway was he able to shake them off. They dared not follow him belowstairs for fear of being thrown out. Perspiring all over again, he reached the telephone and called Hinkle at the Amalgamated Oil office still wondering why Hinkle had not met him at the boat in response to his wireless. Even if you were the Bombay manager, you didn't altogether ignore the son of the boss.

The office gave him his answer, the last piece of bad luck during the day. Hinkle was in Burma on a holiday, shooting. The office didn't know exactly where. Even if they could get the message to him at once it would take him nearly a week to return, and it might even require a week to find him and deliver the message.

"I'm sorry, sir," said the groveling Birmingham voice of the clerk over the wire. "We'll do the best we can, but if I were you, I wouldn't count on seeing him before a fortnight."

"Thank you," said Bill, and slammed down the old-fashioned receiver. "To hell with it," he thought. "I've got to see him. I might as well enjoy myself in Bombay while I'm waiting." And then the thought struck him that maybe all those black-eyed "bad mans" who haunted the corridor outside his door were right, the way Indians for some strange reason nearly always were. Maybe he wasn't going to be the reformed young man after all, but just a sap as he had been the other time. A sap, a bloody sap! He had a sudden feeling of a vast, almost mystical pressure working against him and all his good resolutions, the combined forces of all those "bad mans" or fate, or maybe the Baroness had put a curse on him, or maybe it was just his own weak character.

"Good-time Charlie!" That was what Carol used to call him. He grinned. "That was it. 'Good-time Charlie'!"

Then as he stepped from the telephone box, a dark page boy said, "Mr. Wainwright, a call for you. Mrs. Trollope."

The familiar, hoarse whiskey voice came to him over the telephone. The tenseness was gone from it. "I want to go out tonight. Will you take me to Green's for dinner and then to the Taj bar?"

"Sure, I'll come and get you."

"No, I'll meet you at the hotel at seven-thirty. We can have a drink first."

"It's no trouble to come and get you."

For a moment the tension came into her voice again, "No. No. I'll be out playing bridge. I'll just come to the hotel."

"Okay."

And so she had come to the hotel, looking fresh again and restored and too neat and a little too mannish in her white tailored suit and a white felt hat pulled over one eye. Yet when he saw her sitting opposite him on the terrace at Green's, he experienced again that feeling of satisfaction at the sight of anyone so cool and neat and efficient among so many sweaty, blowsy, dowdy women. Her presence was, somehow, like that of a cool and able nurse in the midst of the confusion attending a disaster. What the disaster was, he could not divine very clearly, unless it was Bombay itself with its strange swarming assortment of people, all living together, most of them hungry, always on the verge of riot and disorder, a place where smallpox was endemic and superstition grew and flourished like fungus in a cave, where one race was divided from another and religions were perpetually at war.

The dinner went off pleasantly because the terrace at Green's Hotel made everything easy. You sat as you ate, overlooking the whole harbor with a fat, rich, hot moon overhead, and the food was good and around you the people were fantastic and the spectacle entertaining—sea-faring men who would have been embarrassed by the mid-Victorian imperial elegance of the Taj Mahal dining room, English officers and civil servants and clerks who were there because Green's was Bohemian and as wild a place as they dared frequent in a community where everything, every move one made, sooner or later became known; tired, plain girls shipped out from the British Isles to relatives in the East to find husbands; hard girls on the verge of middle-age from Hove and Cardiff and Liverpool and London whom some strange fate had dumped into Bombay as sleazy tap dancers and members of a ladies' orchestra. And here and there a stray Russian tart or an "advanced" Parsee or Khoja woman dining alone with a man.

Stitch asked him a great many questions about himself, so many that at one moment he laughed and asked, "Why am I being cross-examined?"

"Because I like to know about people."

She found out how rich his father was, and that he had been married and that his wife had been a show-girl, and that the marriage had come to an end, amiably on both sides, simply because they had both agreed that there wasn't any point in their staying married.

"Were you in love with her?" Stitch asked.

The question puzzled him for a moment. He hesitated, grinned and said, "I don't know. I was crazy for her for about three weeks, till I got enough of what I wanted. I guess I don't know what being in love means."

"It means plenty."

"Have you been?"

"Yes."

Half mischievously he asked, "What's it like?"

He asked the question humorously but she didn't take it that way. The small hard face became grim. "Well, if you'd been in love you'd know it. Just thank God you never have been and hope you never will be."

It was as if they were two men talking together, except that no man, unless he was a phony or a sentimentalist, would have been so grim about it. The grimness made him uneasy and in his nervousness, he said, "We were both kids. I had plenty of dough. I think we wanted to sleep with each other, and so we just ran off and got married. I was a junior at Cornell."

[62]

"What's Cornell?" Stitch asked.

"A University."

"I thought everybody who was rich in America went to Harvard or Yale."

He laughed, "Not quite. That's why my father sent me to Cornell. He thought Harvard or Yale would be a bad influence. He never thought much of my character. You see he was a missionary's son born in China. He made all his own money. He said he wanted me to go to an American school, not to a phony English one."

Stitch didn't answer him but sat looking out over the harbor. The boat from Karachi and the Kathiawar ports up the coast of the Persian Gulf was coming in, a low line of lights slipping across the moonlit water between them and the darkness of Elephanta. And for the first time in his life, on the terrace of Green's Hotel in Bombay he had a sudden comprehensive picture of his father—an extraordinarily clear picture of a heavy, humorless, rather grim man, whose every move was carefully weighed, whose smallest decision was a matter of ponderous responsibility. They had never understood each other, even for a moment, and there had never been any sympathy between them. To his father life was an affair of immense seriousness. And he was always right. That made it all very difficult—when someone so serious, so pompous, was always right.

A long time passed in which he wasn't in Bombay at all but back in America. And Stitch, it was clear, had gone off somewhere too, he did not know where. The cigarette dwindled away unnoticed until it burned her fingers. She crushed it out and said suddenly, with fierceness in her voice, "My father went to Australia because he had to."

He guessed what she meant and felt very shy suddenly about leading her into further confessions. He simply said, "My father is really a swell guy. I think that some day we may understand each other." And for the first time in his life he felt a kind of sympathy and understanding for the ageing man on the other side of the world.

"Living makes a lot of difference," Stitch said. "Sooner or later, I guess, you have to make sense in life or get the worst end of everything. Families are funny things." Then suddenly she rose and said, "Let's get out of here and go to the bar."

In the noise of the huge bar, the dark mood of the terrace left them. They both began to drink in earnest, and presently Al, the wireless officer and Sandy, the chief electrician of the big white *Souradaya* joined them. They were both a little drunk. Al was grinning. The more he drank the more he grinned. He was a man who worried and alcohol always made him stop worrying. And Sandy was always having trouble with his false teeth. That was always a sign when Sandy passed the safety mark. The false teeth kept getting out of place.

Stitch became unnaturally gay and wanted to dance, so in turn the three of them took her round the floor. She danced well although she was a little too short for any of them. While she danced with Sandy, Al said, "She's a good scout, Mrs. Trollope."

"She's no fool."

"Bombay is a hell of a town," said Al.

Bill had begun to feel pleasantly hazy. He asked "Why?" although he didn't much care.

"You can never find the kind of girl you like."

"You're too choosy." He knew what Al meant. He was a nice-minded fellow. He didn't like tarts. He wanted a girl from a nice respectable middle-class family who was a little wild and would go in for a roll behind the hedge with a man who had come from sea. Certainly that was hard to find in Bombay. So Al was getting drunk instead.

A troupe of sparrows suddenly swooped in through the big windows, flew about blinded by the glare of the lights and presently found their way out again.

"Even the birds don't go to bed here."

Then Stitch and the chief electrician came back to the table. The chief electrician mopped his ruddy face with a handkerchief. Stitch ordered another drink and something happened to the evening. It began to die, the gayety, the spirit, the effect of all the gin, going out like air out of a pricked balloon. More drinks didn't bring anything back. It just occurred to Bill that Mrs. Trollope hadn't been gay at all. It was just nerves and now she was sunk—plenty sunk.

[64]

It was time to call the party off and go home, but nobody had the energy to move. In the heat and noise they only sat and drank more and watched the crowd on the floor. The bewildered sparrows flew in and out of the big windows again, and then, his brain half-asleep, in the heat, Bill saw something he could not believe.

She was standing in the doorway, dressed in a red dress, watching the jiggling figures on the dance floor. His first impression was that she had not changed at all. The golden hair, the superb figure, the blooming look of enormous vitality were the same. Then as she leaned against the doorway, he saw that she had been drinking, and he thought at once, "She must be bored. She never drank too much unless she was bored and didn't know what to do with herself." And he knew why she was standing there in the doorway alone. She was hoping to find someone she knew who would take her on a party. He thought, "How in the name of God did she come to turn up here?" And at the same time he was aware of something lovely about the figure in the red dress; it was the same feeling he had had long ago, the first time he ever saw her. She had the old look of false innocence about her. No matter what happened to her she would always look innocent.

For a moment he thought, "I won't speak to her. I'll forget it and keep out of sight." But that, he knew, was impossible in a place like Bombay, unless he chose to shut himself up in his room in the hotel and lead the life of a man in a Turkish bath. And the sight of her roused a whole procession of memories, out of a life which he had been trying to make himself believe was dead. Then suddenly he knew that he could not help himself. In the past he had never been able to help himself, and it was no different now. In the heat his brain felt soggy, but with this emotion neither his brain nor his will power was involved. That much he had learned from experience. For a moment he was even a little afraid. But for the gin he had been drinking, he might have run away and then the whole story would have been different. Long afterward he knew that all the trouble began in that moment—when he knew that he *had* to speak to her.

She looked toward their table and for a moment, as her glance remained for a second fixed on them he thought that she recognized him, but she looked away again, perhaps not believing her own eyes.

He heard Mrs. Trollope say, "What are you staring at?"

"Someone I know. May I bring her over here?"

"Why not?" Mrs. Trollope grinned. "I was just about to go back to my sister's."

Al brightened a little, hopeful that the party might take on new life, "Sure, bring her!"

She did not notice him coming toward her until he was a few feet away. The change in the expression on her face was so sudden and so comic that he laughed. She came to meet him, saying, "Bill! For Gawd's sake, what are you doing here?" And then throwing both arms about him, she kissed him and said, "God, am I glad to see you!"

Then on his side there was a sudden awkwardness. He didn't quite know what to do next. It made him feel very silly. He said, "Come on over and join us."

"Sure," she said, "I thought I was going to have to go to bed. I was on the lookout for a party. I saw a couple of people but they weren't what I wanted."

"Where are you staying?"

"Here, of course, in the hotel."

"Gosh, that's funny. Who's with you?"

"Nobody."

That, he thought, was a little odd. His impulse was to ask, "What are you up to?" but it was too soon for that. He would have to find that out later, a little at a time. She had a bad temper, he knew, when she thought people were prying into her affairs.

"A coincidence—our both being here," she said, "it just shows what a small place the world is."

It had never been her mind that attracted him. On the contrary, it had been her mind which was the principal irritation. She was always saying things like that. The old reaction swiftly followed the old irritation.

"It's a coincidence," he said, "every time two people meet on the street."

She laughed, "Don't begin cracking at me already. I told you long ago it wasn't my brains that got me ahead in this world."

And then they were at the table and he saw in the eyes of Al,

[66]

the chief electrician and Mrs. Trollope that look which always came into the eyes of people seeing her for the first time. It was a look, which, when he was a little younger, had made him feel naïvely proud to be seen out with her. It was a look which bore witness to the fact that the human race was still pretty animal, to be so excited at the sight of so much beauty and health and good spirits. It was always the same—men, especially older men, seemed to acquire strength simply from the sight of her; younger men at sight of her threw out their chests and wisecracked and showed off. Sometimes women hated her on sight, but that was only if they thought themselves good-looking enough to compete. There was never anything in between. She was a girl you couldn't pass over with indifference.

The look in Al's Irish eyes asked him, "Where did you find this one?" for it was undeniable that she looked like a tart. Long ago he had reproached her with that and she told him that she liked to look like a tart because it burned up other women and she didn't like women anyway. Sometimes she behaved like a tart; that was what forever got her into trouble. That was what Al was thinking now, "Bill's got a hell of a good-looking woman, the best in Bombay."

When it came to introducing her, he hesitated for a second, and then said, "This is a friend of mine—Carol Halma." It was better not to say anything about their having been married once. It only led to a lot of explanations. But he always found it difficult to say the preposterous made-up name she had chosen for herself. It would have been much easier if he could have called her by the name her parents had given her—plain "Olga Janssen." Out of the corner of his eye he saw that she didn't mind. She minded very few things in life. And she nearly always understood what a man was up to.

The party came to life again almost at once.

Once the blonde woman was gone out of the railway carriage, the look in the eyes of Colonel Moti changed. The fierceness went out of them, as the rigidity went out of his small, erect figure, and in place of the fierceness there came a look of tenderness almost maternal. His nature was one of violence, and his mood could change as quickly as a cobra could strike. It wasn't that he had any

[67]

personal dislike for the woman he had found in the railway carriage of his friend Merrill; the thing which moved him so violently was his hatred of her as a symbol of a class which in his passionate philosophy he had long since labeled as useless and pernicious. He recognized the symbol at once by the lacquered nails, the expensive clothes, the jewel case. Nor was it the hatred of the man for a prostitute or of a symbol of the whole class of prostitutes. To him, prostitutes were unfortunate or misguided or the victims of a deranged glandular or economic system. His moral indignation never arose from any passion against sexual but against social immorality.

So when the woman left the car he took a deep breath as if the air had been suddenly purified, and said, "Did you have a bad journey, Homer?"

"No, not bad. Hot, but no worse than usual."

He said a word in English to Tommy, and shyly spoke in Hindustani to Ali, the blind Moslem boy. He was shy with children. He had never had any of his own.

Then he said, "Who was that woman?"

"I don't know anything about her. She's been staying with Jellapore's brother."

"Why?"

Merrill, although he was still suffering, laughed at the concentrated fury of that single word "Why?" and what lay behind it—Moti's unmitigated hatred of the whole Jellapore family as wasters and bad rulers. Then he said, "I don't know. How could I know? I never saw her before and will probably never see her again. I shouldn't think her very important one way or another."

"Maybe yes . . . maybe no." The Colonel had been helping collect the luggage, directing two coolies. He looked up saying, "Anyway, you'd better come along home as soon as possible and get to bed."

"Is it all right about Ali's operation?"

"Yes. Dr. Bliss was going to sail but I persuaded him to stay over till the next boat."

"I appreciate that. In a way Ali is almost like a brother to Tommy. He's been living with us since he went blind altogether."

The Indian boy, he knew, could not understand what they were saying. He had slipped down off the divan and was standing now, patiently. There was a strange stillness about him, the stillness of resignation which in a child so young had a quality of heartbreak.

"There were three other cases—two from Rajputana and one from Bhopal. He's operated one already."

Merrill looked at him. "Was it successful?"

"Yes," said Colonel Moti. Then suddenly he smiled and asked, "You love the boy, don't you?"

"Yes. He's a nice boy."

"That's why I love you," said the Colonel. "That's why you've got to have a rest."

"I've got to go back to Jellapore in ten days."

"You're not going back in ten days—not till I've fixed you up. Not unless you want to crack up altogether and be of no use to anyone."

"I'm all right."

"You're too valuable a man." The indignant look came again into Colonel Moti's eyes. "You're just being a God-damned fool!"

Merrill grinned and was silent. It was no use trying to argue with Moti because the hotter an argument became, the more dictatorial became Moti, the more he believed he was God. Anyway, it wasn't the first time that he (Merrill) had been ill, maybe not so ill as this time. He'd always pulled out of it before, and he would again. When Tommy had gone away and Ali's operation was over, he'd simply go back to Jellapore without arguing at all.

Two taxicabs were needed to take the party to Colonel Moti's house. The Colonel had no motor of his own, even though he could have claimed one, considering his position as head of the Institute of Tropical Diseases. He preferred to use the money for the Institute itself: God knew it was hard enough to get money for it. And the price of a motor went a long way in a country where labor was cheap and a workman could live on a little rice and curry once a day. So the Colonel, despite his rank and his renown in the world, rode on the crowded tramcars or if he went to an important government dinner, took a taxicab. He liked the smelly tramcars, overburdened with humanity. It kept him from forgetting what humanity, swarming Indian humanity, was like. And he heard a lot of things on tramcars which he couldn't have

[69]

heard elsewhere, what with his fame and distinction constantly operating to isolate him from the people.

On leaving the station, the taxis did not follow the course of Carol's taxi, in the direction of the Taj Mahal Hotel, the Bombay Yacht Club and Malabar Hill. Instead, the two taxis turned northwest past Crawford Market in the direction of the Mill district, and with each block the houses and tenements grew shabbier and more sordid, the streets more overcrowded. In the hot air every coolie, every mill worker, every low caste Hindu had come out of the tenements into the streets, crowding the sidewalks, jostling the vendors of sweetmeats, overflowing the gutters into the tramcar tracks where the cars, overladen with passengers seeking even the faintest stirring of air, moved at the pace of tortoises, clanging their bells. Here and there an ancient gramophone scratched out Indian music. Children swarmed under foot. As the taxis pushed their way through the mob, the Colonel forgot to speak, and while Merrill leaned back, his eyes closed, the pain drumming in the top of his head, he watched the swarming spectacle, a faint smile curling the corners of his hard mouth. These were his people. In a way he knew them all, all the thousands of them, with their ignorance and superstition and starvation and abysmal patience. It was for them he was fighting, to bring light to them and health and spirit and dignity. It was for them that he denied himself a motor and lived meagerly like the very sadhus he detested.

Presently the taxis left the slums and the Mill district and came into a district where the poor crowded into crumbling houses which once had sheltered the families of rich merchants. It was better here; there was at least a little space and air and a few ragged gardens where banyan and peepul and Java fig trees cast black shadows in the moonlight. And presently, at the Colonel's direction, they turned in a narrow street and came to the Institute of Tropical Diseases and the Colonel's bungalow.

It was a moderate-sized building with an open space covered with gravel surrounding it. Two great Java fig trees grew beside it and in the corners of the walled garden a few shrubs. In the house there was a single light and as they drew up to the door, the figure of a woman in a white and silver sari appeared at the top of the steps.

[70]

Merrill, opening his eyes, saw the dancer standing on the edge of the verandah all glistening and white in the moonlight, and the thought came to him that the small figure in its purity symbolized both herself and her husband. They were both too white, too pure, too fanatic to be of this world. They were not like himself, who, for all his absorption in his work, still had disturbing, sometimes torturing visions of the flesh and its pleasures. Even in the heat of the evening the still figure appeared clean and cool. With sudden envy he thought, "What peace she must have—what peace they must both know."

He said, "You didn't tell me Indira was at home."

"She only arrived this morning on the P and O boat," said Moti. "I forgot to tell you."

The inside of the bungalow had the quality of Moti and his wife. The big cool rooms were clean, the furniture bare and simple. The only ornaments were a collection of Persian jade and a dozen Mogul pictures. Those were Mrs. Moti's which she had bought with her own money, earned by dancing in half the capitals of the world. To her these were as necessary as all the shining equipment of a laboratory to Colonel Moti.

For Merrill, the house was an oasis in the heat and confusion and turmoil of India, and each time he left the hot squalid villages where he worked, he came straight here to refresh his soul. It was not only that he found peace, but he rediscovered faith, for there were times when the endless backsliding of the villages and the malarial apathy of the villagers themselves brought him near to the edge of despair. This bungalow had been, too, a kind of refuge from his wife, up to the very day of her death. When life at home became unbearable, he could come to the Motis', where he knew she would never follow him. She had hated them because when he was with them he escaped into a realm of the spirit where she could not follow.

Mrs. Moti led him to a big room and said, "This is for you and Tommy. Shall I put Ali in the compound?"

For a second he looked at her, surprised, and then he saw that what she proposed was the natural thing for an Indian to suggest.

She had believed that the blind son of the mahout would feel more comfortable among the servants.

"If you don't mind," he said, "I'll keep him in here with us. You see, he's been living with us. He's never been away from home before. I'll have the boys bring in an Indian bed."

Then she went away to give the order, and when she was gone, he sat down on the edge of his bed, feeling dizzy again and feverish, but even through the fever he kept seeing her in the white and silver sari. She was neither very young nor very beautiful but he too felt in her the perfection of art; it lay in the lacquered nails, the softly drawn hair, the perfect carving of the small oval face, and above all, in the stillness which seemed to envelop her. Wherever she went everything seemed to become cool and serene. Wearily he thought, "I would like to stay here forever to rest and rest and rest." For it was his spirit as much as his strong body which was ill and tired.

When she returned she said, "There is some dinner for you. When Moti told me you were coming I arranged it. There is some fresh goat's milk for the boys. It comes from the laboratory goats so you needn't be afraid of anything."

When they had dined, Merrill and the two boys returned to their room to sleep. Usually he liked to sit up half the night with the Colonel, talking about his discoveries and about his own work among the villages of Jellapore. But tonight he was too weary and ill, and the Colonel knew it. After he had undressed and had a shower Moti came in and gave him a sedative.

"That's what you need," he said, "sleep. Sleep late tomorrow. If the boys waken first, Indira will take them to see the birds and the animals at Crawford Market." He spoke as if little blind Ali would be able to see the brilliantly colored birds, but it may have been that he knew his wife would make him see them.

Presently Merrill fell asleep and during the night he dreamed wild, rather delirious dreams. Sometimes the central figure was Indira Moti, cool and sure and clean, in the white and silver sari, and sometimes they were of the woman he had seen on the train, beautiful, tempting, fleshly, of the earth, a kind of half-clad heathen goddess who had annihilated the frightful pain and brought him another kind of peace which the dancer could never bring him.

[72]

Because of the sedative, he did not waken until noon, and when he wakened the pain was still there pressing on the top of his head and his spirit was still unrefreshed.

Then he remembered that in the night, in the midst of his distorted dreams he had wakened and found his friend Moti standing there, looking down at him. What he did not know was that Moti, looking down at him, had thought, "We must not lose him. He is one of us. We need him and his spirit." And afterward when the fierce Colonel had gone back to his wife's room, the two of them had talked for a long time, planning how they would save him and bring him back to health. It was talk that would have astonished Merrill, because it was so removed from anything he had been taught or believed long ago in the house of his father in the Geneseo Valley on the other side of the world.

At about the hour that Merrill wakened to find his friend standing over him, Al, the wireless officer, and Sandy, the chief electrician (whose false teeth had now become completely uncontrollable), left the table in the bar on the other side of the hot city to return to their boat. They had a few hours more and then the big white boat would be off again past Cape Cormorin, and through the Malay Straits on its way to Sydney. Tipsily they said, good-bye and went their way, a little regretfully because they were a little drunk and feeling sentimental over the thought that very likely they would never again see either Bill or Mrs. Trollope. In the morning they would wake with a headache and Sandy would have to search for his false teeth before going on duty and then about eleven their great hotel of a ship would sail with a lot of new passengers and some of the old ones and they would find new friends to take the place of Bill and Mrs. Trollope, and presently they would forget them. Their life was like that. But at the moment they felt sentimental, and Al was sober enough to regret having gotten so far along with his drinking that he couldn't enjoy this gay and beautiful friend of Bill's who had turned up so suddenly out of nowhere.

So they took a long time with their farewells, leaning on the backs of their chairs to steady themselves. Sandy even wept a little, and all the time, in spite of his fondness for them, Bill wanted them to go so that he could talk to Carol; there were so many things he wanted to ask her.

But at last they went, weaving their way in their white clothes, through the pushing noisy crowd, and that left only Mrs. Trollope.

In the midst of the fun the old grimness had returned to her suddenly. It seemed to come over her at the moment Carol put her arm around Bill's neck in a friendly way and said, "My Gawd, it's good to see you again, honey."

Bill thought, "I suppose she thinks that's vulgar. Well, if she does—to hell with her."

She didn't go home. She just sat there, grim and silent most of the time. Sometimes she watched the crowd, turning her back ostentatiously, but now and then she turned to look at them, and once she said, "I'm going to give a party for you two. How long are you staying here, Miss Halma?"

Carol put down her drink. "Till my money gives out. I haven't got any plans."

And then a dark man, an Indian, rather plump and dressed in remarkably well-cut London clothes, came over to them from out of the crowd and said in perfect English, "Hello, Carol, when did you get back?"

"Tonight." She pushed back a chair and added, "Sit down and have a drink," and then introduced him. His name, it seemed, was Mr. Botlivala.

He didn't sit down. He only stood there, his hands on the back of the chair, saying, "No, I can't stay. I'm with some English people. What are you doing tomorrow?"

"I don't know. Ring me up."

"I'll ring you up."

"Not too early. Not before lunch time."

"All right." He bowed and the bow, in spite of his clothes and his perfect continental manner, was Oriental, a trifle too low, a trifle too exaggerated, like a salaam. Then he went away.

It was only when he had gone that it occurred to Bill that the stranger had scarcely looked at Carol at all, but had only stared at himself. And he remembered too Mr. Botlivala's hands—very long and thin and very collapsible, and very odd on a body so plump and sensual. They were repulsive hands, and cruel and incongruous. Bill couldn't remember the face at all—only the hands.

Mrs. Trollope lighted one cigarette from another and said, "I know who he is."

"He's stinking rich," said Carol.

"I'd keep clear of him, my dear," said Mrs. Trollope. "There was a scandal about some dancing girls."

"That's an old one," said Carol. "There wasn't anything in it. I know him awfully well."

Suddenly Mrs. Trollope stiffened. "How well?"

Carol laughed, "Not as well as that. I don't find him very attractive. But he's rich and he likes to spend his money. I'm never one to discourage a man like that."

It was Bill who said, "He's not very attractive."

Without any warning, Mrs. Trollope said sharply, "I don't see how a woman can have such a man come near her."

Bill wanted to say, "What the hell business is it of yours?" Mostly because he was a little sick of Mrs. Trollope and wished she would go home.

But Carol didn't seem to mind. "I'm not so particular," she said.

"Would you like to come to tea tomorrow?" Mrs. Trollope asked.

"I'd love to, if I get up in time. Where?"

"At my sister's. I'm staying with her. I'll come for you."

"Better ring me up first."

Then Mrs. Trollope turned to Bill. "I can't ask you. It'll be a *zenana* party. No men allowed."

"Okay," he said, but he wondered why she had lied, shamelessly, when she knew perfectly well that he was aware her sister lived like a European and did not keep purdah.

Then she rose and pulled the white felt hat further over her eyes and said, "Well, I'll run along, I guess."

"Can we drop you?"

"No, the car is waiting for me."

"We can, you know."

"No, I can take care of myself. Thanks for the party, Bill."

Then she smiled at Carol, "I'll ring you up."

"Okay," said Carol. "Not too early."

[75]

When she had gone, Bill said, "She was a pain in the neck most of the evening."

"Where did you find her?"

"On shipboard."

"She's not your type. Nothing very fluffy about her."

"No," he laughed. "Maybe I'm changing my type."

"Well, she's the kind that goes in for young boys."

"Nuts!" said Bill.

She said, "I want another drink."

"No, you don't."

"Why not?"

"I want to talk to you. We're just right now."

"Yes, but I may sink."

"No, you won't." Then after a moment, he added suddenly, "What are you up to?"

"Nothing. Just enjoying myself. Anyway, you needn't be so grim about it."

"How did you get here?"

"I came out with some people from London. You wouldn't know them. They went Goona-goona—off to Bali. I was having a good time so I stayed here."

"What are you doing?"

"Visiting Maharajahs, and going to the races and buying jewelry."

He thought, "She can't afford that. She hasn't enough money unless she's spending her capital or somebody is helping her."

"It's my turn now," she said. "What are you doing here?"

He told her and she said very seriously, "I'm glad you've settled down. The playboy stuff wasn't your type."

"Maybe. I've been good for a long time now—and respectable and hard-working. But I might go off the track."

She looked at him gravely. Then she said, "Not with me, you won't."

"Why?"

"Because I'm not going to get you started all over again."

"What are you going to do when you leave here?"

"Go back to Paris."

"What for?"

"I enjoy myself there."

[76]

"Are you ever going to marry again?"

"If I find the right guy. I'm engaged now, but I'm not going to marry him."

"Who is he?"

She didn't answer at once. Before she answered, she laughed. Then she said, "To that guy who came over to the table."

"The Indian?"

"He's a Parsee."

"How come?"

"He kept asking me and giving me presents. So I said 'Yes' I'd be engaged to him if it made him feel any better but I wouldn't promise anything."

"Nothing more."

"Not a damned thing. I don't allow him to touch me. You see, most of them are nuts for blondes."

"It seems kind of corny to me."

"Mebbe it is." She lighted a cigarette and said, "Let's have another drink."

"No, you've had enough. What do you want another for?"

"Because I need it after what I've been through the last week."

"What have you been through?"

She told him then of the visit to Jellapore, and as she talked her own natural high spirits began to take the place of the gin she had been drinking all day long. The story of the whole visit, made suddenly without any planning, now seemed funny to her, and as she talked and her spirits rose, she began to make of it an excellent story. The boycott of the Jellapore women, the party where the English boys kicked over the pots of orchids, even the story told her by Mrs. Goswami of the attempt to poison her became a joke. It was over now; it went under the head of experience. She was never one to live in the past, or the future either. The present, minute to minute, was everything.

This was how Bill liked her. This was why he had run off with her long ago to rouse a parson in Greenwich at two in the morning to marry them. It wasn't because either of them was much in love with the other; it was because they had fun together. Even their love-making had been punctuated by laughs. None of your Tristan and Isolde stuff.

[77]

When she was like this she became more beautiful. Drinking always subtracted something from her charm, for her charm was that of great health and high spirits which allowed her to stay up all night and appear the next day after two or three hours of sleep as fresh as a milkmaid.

And as he listened, laughing now and then at the absurd improbability of the whole story, a line of worry crept in between the blue eyes. "If only she could stay like this," he thought, "forever." He didn't like the drinking nor the shadow of weariness he had noticed earlier in the evening. And he didn't like that plump little man with the funny name and skinny hands.

Then she told of waking up on the train not knowing where she was or how she got there, and then about the axle cracking and about the choice she had made between traveling in a purdah carriage or with a missionary.

"Never a dull moment in India," she said. "There's always something going wrong. But the missionary was sort of nice—and good-looking. It wasn't as bad as I thought it was going to be. But he was awfully ill and I had to look after him. I felt awfully sorry for him. He said anyway he wasn't a real missionary. He did something in the villages—about crops and breeding stock and things like that."

Then Bill found a new interest. He listened a little longer and then asked suddenly, "What was his name?"

"He told me but I don't remember. It was . . . Homer, I think, a barber shop name . . . Homer something. I can't remember the rest."

"I think I know him. He went to school with me. Was his name Homer Merrill?"

"Merrill? Yes, that's it. Well, I'll be damned!"

"He was a swell football player—used to play halfback. He belonged to the same fraternity. He was my roommate for two years."

"You never brought him to New York."

"He didn't lead that kind of life. He wasn't a Christer, but he just went his own way. Couldn't afford it, for one thing, and wouldn't let anybody pay for him."

He saw Homer again suddenly, big and good-looking and clean. That was it—clean. He was the cleanest fellow he had ever known.

Sometimes, the sight of Homer used to make him feel ashamed, as if he needed a spiritual bath. It wasn't that Homer ever said anything; he was just a fact—honest and good and clean with a humorous twinkle in the clear blue eyes, working his way through school and always worrying about the good of mankind. He even grudged the time consumed by football, but he had a scholarship for that, which helped him through school. And now he was in Bombay after ten years of working among Indian villages. The good-humored, kindly eyes of the missionary woman on the boat returned for an instant—yes, that was it: they were eyes exactly like Homer's—the eyes of someone who wouldn't condemn you and always stood ready to help. Now he knew why they had seemed familiar.

"How was he sick?" Bill asked. "What was the matter with him?"

"Liver, he said, and climate. A lot of other things I should think."

"Where was he going in Bombay?"

"I don't know. He mentioned some doctor friend. That's all I know."

So he was lost again. It wasn't easy to find somebody in Bombay who was outside the circle—who didn't live on Malabar Hill and go to the Yacht Club, the Willingdon Club, the Taj Mahal and the races. The needle in the haystack was simple by comparison.

His mind, wandering away from Carol, began to speculate where he could find Homer. It might be that money would help him; at any rate it could get him proper doctors and maybe send him away for a rest.

"Haven't you any idea where he was going to stay?" he asked.

"No, I guess it was with some Indian. An Indian met him—a good-looking Indian about thirty-five or forty with big black eyes. He didn't like me much."

The crowd in the hot room had begun to thin a little. Bill looked about him and said, "You know, I think bed would do you more good than a drink."

"I couldn't sleep yet."

"That's a bad habit to get into."

She didn't answer him and he said, "You're not taking things, are you?"

[79]

"No, I'm not that much of a damned fool."

"You might go to bed and try to sleep."

"It's no good, but I'll go if you want to. Is there racing tomorrow?"

"No, not till Saturday."

"Will you take me?"

"Sure."

"What's running?"

"I don't know. I don't know anything about Bombay horses."

She was tired suddenly. Dark circles came under her eyes and little tired lines around the lovely mouth. He thought, "She's going to age quickly—all at once—if she keeps on. At thirty-five with luck she'll be a well-preserved blonde and nothing is harder than a well-preserved blonde." He felt a quick desire to help her, but could think of no way. It seemed to him that somewhere in the course of her destiny she had come on to the wrong track. It was like the spectacle of a good actress playing the wrong rôle. Something was wasted—energy, purpose, design—what it was he could not discover. He was a little tipsy now and all the shock and heat and bad luck of the whole day made itself felt, suddenly, all at once.

"I don't want to be rude, honey," he said, "but if I don't go to bed, I'm going to fall asleep."

"Getting middle-aged?"

"Mebbe. Anyway, aside from the fact that I've had a lousy day, my staying up days are finished. I began the day by seeing a man killed right by my side. My trousers were spotted with blood. I had to throw the suit away."

A faint look of interest came into her blue eyes. "What happened?" she asked. "Tell me and I'll go to bed."

He told her with apathy and weariness, for he was too tired now to recapture the sense of shock and horror. When he had finished she said, "That's a funny woman—your friend Mrs. Trollope."

"She's all right."

She rose suddenly, "We'd both better go to bed."

"I'll go with you as far as your room."

"You don't need to."

"I'd like to."

He paid the check and tipped the Eurasian waiter, and then as

[80]

they moved between the crowded tables, he felt someone staring at him and turning, he saw that it was the plump man with the skinny hands. He started to speak to him and then thought better of it and kept silent.

Outside they descended the stairs to the lift, and as they passed the clock he noticed that it was already three in the morning. Then as he looked up he saw the figure of the Baroness seated heavily in a wicker chair. She was watching the crowd, the beads of the wooden rosary slipping swiftly through her fat fingers. She did not see them, and he thought, "If only we can get to the lift without her noticing us."

But immediately, as if she felt their presence, she turned and saw them. That was enough. She was out of her chair and coming toward them, her face contorted in what was for her the nearest approach to a smile.

"Vell," she said, "I've been vondering vhere you vere all day."

"I've had a lot of business to get through."

"It vas horrible—the axident." She grinned faintly with sadistic enjoyment of the memory.

"Yes."

She looked at Carol and smiled. Bill knew she wanted to be introduced and for once in his life he was rude, but being rude to the Baroness was only like being rude to an inquisitive rhinoceros.

She said, holding out her hand, "I am Baroness Stefani. Ve come oud togedder on de boat—Mr. Vainwright and I."

"I'm sorry," said the routed Bill. "This is Miss Halma."

Carol said, "Glad to know you."

"You go to bed alreddy?" asked the Baroness. "I vould invite you to a drink."

"Thanks," said Bill. "Another time . . . tomorrow you have a drink with us."

"And tomorrow like today I not see you."

"We're tired," said Carol.

"Vell then, tomorrow I hold you to your promise."

"Good-night."

"Good-night."

They turned away to the lift and the Baroness went back to her wicker chair and the fingering of her beads. It was late but she was

[81]

enjoying herself watching the crowd. Her beady eyes saw every-thing; they were trained for that; loneliness and greed had trained them. And she was satisfied she had met the showy blonde girl who might be of use to her. She had already confirmed what her instinct and experience had told her—that the girl had been on the stage.

A little later, a small thin man, sinister in appearance with shifty eyes and rather shabbily dressed, came in and sat by her. They talked for a long time, earnestly, while the beads lay still in the wide lap of the Baroness, until even in the big hall of the Taj Mahal, very few people remained.

Upstairs Bill and Carol walked the long stone balcony past all the sleeping bearers and when they reached her room, she said, "Do you want to come in and talk?"

"No, I think we'll talk tomorrow."

For a moment she hesitated, then she said, "You could stay if you liked."

"No, I think it's better not . . . it's not because I don't want to, honey. Only it's no use beginning all over again. Get what I mean?"

She looked away from him. "Yes . . . maybe you're right. I only thought we'd get some laughs." Then she turned and looked at him—the girl he liked, the daughter of the big Swedish farmer from Minnesota. "Anyway," she said, "I'm glad you turned up. I needed somebody like you. You can chaperone me. Anyway," she added, "kiss me good-night."

She kissed him and it was a chaste and almost sisterly kiss. That was the odd thing about her—that despite everything, she had a kind of purity, a naïveté which nothing had ever destroyed. She was healthy and normal and nice. God had given her everything. And again Bill for an instant had the feeling of her having gotten on the wrong track somewhere early in life.

When he had gone back to his own room, the kiss troubled him, not because he desired her, but because he felt that somehow he had helped to change her destiny. If he had been a different sort of guy, the marriage might have been a success—a healthy, honest-to-God marriage. There was no reason why it shouldn't have been, except that there were too many people, too many parties, too many bright lights, too much nonsense.

When he was undressed and lying on the hard iron bed with the *punkah* churning the hot damp air above his head, he remained awake, troubled, for a long time, and at last, half-asleep he thought, "Maybe, after all, I am my old man's son. Maybe the old boy is beginning to claim me." And he remembered the old saying, "Nothing is more respectable than a reformed rake."

In her room, Carol did not sleep. She lay in the darkness, trying desperately to sleep but sleep would not come. Somehow, without her knowing it, her life had become strange and befuddled. She no longer slept at night but in the daytime. She did not know where she would be a year hence, or a month, or even tomorrow, and that, now that she was alone and her soul as naked as her body, troubled and frightened her. That was why she had asked him to stay with her, not because she was in love with him any longer, but because if he had been there beside her, she would not have been thinking of herself. They could have talked of old times and even laughed. He was a nice boy, she thought, nice as only American men can be, chivalrous and humorous and kind—too kind and good-humored perhaps. That had very nearly ruined him. And the old name for him returned to her—"Good-time Charlie"—and she felt a wave of warmth and affection for him.

But almost at once the night terrors assailed her again, creeping out from the shadows of the big room. Voices out of her own brain, beyond her control, kept talking to her. "You are afraid. You have made a mess of everything. You have nowhere to go. You are nearly broke. You have spent all the money Bill settled on you. You are beginning to drink in earnest. Soon you'll be taking drugs to sleep. You can't go back. You can't go home to your mother in a little house in Minneapolis. You know too much. You've gone too far. It wouldn't work. You know that better than anyone. Now, when you get up at noon your eyes aren't clear as they always used to be, in spite of everything. Your skin isn't clean and fresh any more. You have to drink to fight off the terrors. You'll get up even now and have another drink so you can sleep."

[83]

And aloud to the voices she said, "I won't! I won't! You can't make me."

But the voices kept on and at last when it was nearly dawn, she rose in the faint grey light and went to the drawer where she had hidden the gin bottle from the sight of Krishna and took a long drink, straight from the bottle.

When Mrs. Trollope left to find the big Rolls in the line outside the Taj, the driver was half-asleep and sulky and insolent. When she said, "Back to the palace," he only scowled at her without speaking at all and when she climbed in he slammed the door and Mrs. Trollope thought, "He knows too."

She knew that to the servants in the palace she was only a poor relation. She knew the East. She knew that even if she strained her purse to tip well, it would make no difference and give her no face. They *knew* by the state of her clothes and the shabby Vuitton luggage bought fifteen years ago when Jim Trollope was on the crest of the wave, by the look in her eye, even by the brazenness she had developed to give herself confidence. But the driver was a Ghurka too, so it might only be his evil temper. Why her sister had Ghurkas about her, she could never understand. They were treacherous, ill-tempered, stubborn, proud and contemptuous. She could not imagine why unless it was because the Maharajah had always had them and she hadn't the power or the courage to send them away. The small round Mongol faces always seemed to her full of evil and hatred for anyone—Hindu or Moslem or Burmese or European—simply because he was not a Ghurka.

Leaning back against the cushions, she felt limp now and utterly exhausted and on the verge of self-pity. At forty-two in the very midst of life she was defeated, with nothing before her but desolation and dreariness; and for the first time she experienced the awful exhaustion which is born of perpetually putting up a front, and the awful loneliness which the pretense created about you. She was weary of pretending to waiters, to fellow passengers, to that bullet-headed Ghurka on the driver's seat, even to her own sister, that she was not at the end of her resources. It destroyed even the pleasure she had once had in gambling; when you had to gamble for a living, to pay your passage and buy your dinner, it wasn't

[84]

fun any longer. And it wasn't even as if she could look forward to anything when Jim Trollope came out of jail. If he had anything hidden away out of the wreckage of the swindle, she wouldn't be likely to share in it. And at sixty when he came out, he would be a broken man, too old to begin over again. She didn't mind the disgrace; her hide was tough enough for that. (She hadn't even lived or traveled under a false name in all those years since the scandal.) But she did mind the prospect of the sordidness and the scrimping, the bitterness of having to calculate the price of a joint or a cheap cut, of eating always in a cheap restaurant. For she knew what that was; it wasn't as if she hadn't known. It was easier if you had never known poverty; then you might hope that perhaps it would be an adventure. But she *knew* there was nothing adventurous about poverty.

The big car turned off the road along the sea and rolled heavily up the flowering avenue. In one of the big bungalows there was a party under way; the jazz music filled the scented air and through the gateway she had a glimpse of the verandah and a garden hung with lanterns, of red and black coats and women in dowdy evening dress . . . And then in the sickening wave of loneliness which followed, she wished that she had not looked at all. She belonged to no community, to no life; she had no place anywhere. Once she had scorned people like the people at that party, small people absorbed in the life of their own small world, dull and unadventurous and smug. Now she envied them. Since the days she and Nelly left Melbourne to go to school in England on her father's ill-gotten gains, she had had no roots. Her father had hoped to make ladies out of Nelly and herself and look how the damned thing had ended—Nelly, a kind of luxurious prisoner in a pink marble palace with an allowance not much bigger than the pension of an Army officer, and herself the penniless wife of a jail-bird. All her life she had lived in hotels, wandering here and there, for a time when things were going well with Jim, in the greatest luxury. Of all that there remained only memories, and barren ones at that, hardly worth recalling. There wasn't any use asking Nelly to help her. Her sister would only say that she didn't have a cent over what she needed for her gambling, which was probably true despite all the soft female luxury in which she lived. Now that she was a

[85]

dowager Maharani they probably allowed her only pin money, because the Dewan and the State hadn't liked the marriage any better than the English had liked it. But Nelly didn't seem to mind; she hadn't that awful curse of restlessness on her; she was like a soft golden Persian cat, getting fatter and fatter, sitting all day like a houri playing bridge or mahjong, occasionally going to the races in a lace hat like a superannuated trollop, just to gamble. Nelly didn't even seem to mind no longer going to Paris, so long as she had champagne and bon-bons in Bombay.

Then she forgot about Nelly and began thinking of herself again. With forty-eight pounds in the bank and a small credit at Cook's and Jim in Brixton jail for another four years, there wasn't much ahead of her. She couldn't even get out of Bombay. There wasn't anything left to sell that anyone would buy. Nothing before her but board and lodging in her sister's pink, whorehouse palace, given grudgingly because after all Nelly really hated her; and the insolence of Oriental servants who knew that she was stony broke.

And then like light bursting into a dark room came the memory of the girl Bill had brought to the table. The health and radiance of her blondeness drove off the loneliness a little. She thought, "If only I had been born like that—tall and beautiful and full of vitality instead of dumpy and sallow and masculine."

Then an extraordinary thing happened to her. For a sudden brief and dazzling moment, she *became* the girl, radiant and reckless. It was as if her own skinny legs became long and beautiful, as if her own flat breasts had turned round and firm and voluptuous, as if her own sallow leathery skin had become clear and transparent, her own vague muddy green eyes had become blue and clear with a glint of good humor in them.

And then the moment passed quickly and left her shrunken and dry again, her life filled with an aching boredom and despair as if the experience had had a physical reality. Tipsily she thought, "I must see her again. I'll give her a ring tomorrow."

And then the big old-fashioned Rolls Royce was standing before the ornate *porte cochère* of the palace, and the Ghurka driver was holding the door open staring at her scornfully like a dog contemptuous of a drunken master. She tottered out of the car and up the steps. Until she reached the vulgar pink marble stairway she

[86]

managed to control herself, but as she started up the stairs she began to cry, sobbing hysterically until she reached her own room and threw herself down on the bed. In the morning she was still there, sleeping in the rumpled white suit.

Major Moti went with Merrill and his son to the boat. Merrill hadn't wanted him to go, but Moti insisted, although it ruined his whole day and took him away from his beloved laboratory. The Indian, with the over-acute sensibility and intuition which makes life a misery to so many of his race, knew that Merrill wasn't only a sick and suffering man but that the departure of the boy caused a slow keen agony in his heart and brain.

All the way to the pier in the heat of the rattling taxi, he watched the tired face of Merrill, cautiously, so that Merrill would not be put on his guard and withdraw into himself. Now, suffering, the man made no effort to conceal anything while Moti struggled to get beneath the surface and achieve an understanding of what went on inside the soul and mind of his friend. It was not the first time he had attempted it; but never once had he wholly succeeded. Something always remained hidden—that thing which somehow twisted the whole existence of Merrill, which harmed his work and ruined his health—that thing, so difficult for Moti to understand—which came out of the West, out of some small town in upper New York State, out of all that Merrill's childhood and early life had been—that something which Moti and no Indian would ever fully understand. It was something, Moti knew with his shrewd mind, which ran against nature, which was indeed a kind of perversion of nature. It was, he knew, something which would have to be plucked out before Merrill could be cured. An operation was necessary; the thing might have to be cut out, like a malignant tumor. But first, he knew, he must find out what it was.

They reached the pier at last and found Mr. Snodgrass, the missionary, waiting to take the small boy in charge for the rest of the long trip to Minneapolis. Snodgrass was a tall, thin, unsympathetic man. Moti disliked him at once and thought, "Luckily the boy isn't old enough to have his mind corrupted by that man's moral ideas." It was people like Snodgrass, Moti suspected, who long ago had planted in Merrill the seed of that disease which had thrown his whole life out of balance and helped to ruin his health.

It wasn't that Mr. Snodgrass was actively malignant. He was amiable enough in a tight-lipped almost professional way; it was the lips that Moti hated on sight, lips that were thin, smug and cold. It was almost as if the cadaverous man had no lips at all. The very sight of the missionary suddenly roused a fierce rage in the fiery-eyed Indian. This man, who had no warmth in him nor any fire, and knew nothing of love or even of charity, deemed himself worthy to set himself up to judge others scornfully. Watching the hairy hands that never moved but hung inertly by his side, listening to the cold, thin, precise voice while he talked with Merrill of arrangements for the boy, Moti thought, "That's what is in Merrill's background. It was something like that which has twisted his life."

The boy, excited by the ship and the prospect of the voyage, ran about the deck, unmoved by the prospect of the separation from his father. Coming out of the jungle, out of the villages, all this was to him a new and exciting world, far more wonderful than the Maharajah's elephants or the monsoon or the tigers which occasionally came down among the villages slaying cattle and sometimes men at night. And he had never seen water like this which seemed to go on and on further than the great flat plain of the high Deccan. He forgot too his friend Ali, left behind with Colonel Moti's serene wife. He forgot that Ali, sitting there alone in the bungalow trying to listen, was blind and could not see such wonders as this great ship. He forgot his father and the villages and the wild beauty and excitement of the upland country. Because he was going home—home to America, home to Minnesota where there would be other boys like himself and where everybody spoke American, where perhaps there were cowboys and coyotes and redskins.

While the boy ran about peering over the side, calling out and asking questions, Merrill watched him with hungry eyes, not hearing the commonplace conversation of Moti and Mr. Snodgrass. It was the terrible concentration on the boy that troubled Moti, as if Merrill were trying to capture and fix forever in his memory, each gesture and intonation, as if such small things were treasures to be locked away and carried back with him when he returned alone among the villages.

And Merrill, silent, his face gray with weariness and pain, trying to betray no emotion either to Snodgrass or his friend Moti, had his own thoughts.

Through his tired head, vague, disconnected thoughts and memories swept round and round. It seemed odd to him that he should feel so much love for a child born of a marriage so colorless, so cramped, so stifled as his had been. Now, in his illness, he no longer pretended to deceive himself as he had done while she was still alive. With his brain beaten by the heat and illness, all the deceiving, the pretense, the self-deceptions, which had made all those years endurable and lent to them the semblance of dignity, were gone. Maybe he loved the boy so much because the mother had given him no love, nor even permitted him to love her.

Whistles had begun to blow and there were cries of "all ashore." And the crowd all about him, dark and fair, European and Indian, garlanded and having their farewell drinks, began to dissolve, flowing in a little stream down the narrow gangplank.

Mr. Snodgrass was saying with an air of pompous authority, "Yes, I imagine it will be hot all the way to Port Said. But after that it will be cool, even cold perhaps. It is remarkable the sudden change that happens at Port Said."

And Merrill suddenly hated Mr. Snodgrass who, until now, had merely annoyed him. He hated him with a sudden sickening violence born of shredded nerves, for his pomposity, his unctuousness, his hypocrisy, the certainty that he was God's anointed and so, superior to other men.

He thought, "But maybe he can't help it. But for the grace of God, I might be Mr. Snodgrass."

He turned to the boy and suddenly picked him up in his arms, wondering at how chunky and healthy and heavy he was for a child brought up in India, how very like himself at the same age, with that chunkiness which later on would turn into hard muscle and make of him a fighter and a football player (all that seemed so long ago, hundreds of years ago). If he had taken Bill's father's offer of a job, it all might have been different. He might now be living in America with the boy growing up beside him. It was all those years, when that chunkiness was turning into muscle that he would miss—the years when he might be able to help the boy and steer him clear of the mistakes he himself had made, to help him to know how to live with joy, even with abandon, before it was too late to learn. When he saw him again—if he ever saw him again—Tommy would be almost a man who perhaps would be a stranger.

He gave the boy a hug and said, "Well, sonny, be a good boy and when you get home write to me. You might even write to me from the boat on the way home."

"Sure, Dad. Sure, I will."

The cries of "all ashore" grew louder. And Moti, watching with his brilliant black eyes, feeling everything with his own sensitive nerves said, "We'd better go, Homer."

Merrill put the boy down and shyly kissed the top of his head. When he saw him again he would be too big a fellow to kiss. Then Moti took his arm. He shook hands with Snodgrass. (Thank God, Snodgrass wouldn't be with the boy long enough to do him any harm.)

And then somehow in the heat and confusion of cries and sounds and smells, he was going down the gangplank with Moti behind him. He felt suddenly ill and filled with fears that he might collapse there on the pier among all these strange people. The pain in the top of his head was coming back again and he heard Moti saying, "Better go home and get to bed. You don't want to stay here and watch the boat sail. That will only make it worse." He turned to look for the boy but Tommy had gone from the rail somewhere inside the ship to discover new marvels.

Merrill said ruefully, "I guess he is pretty jungly. I suppose it's all wonderful to him—more wonderful than anything."

At two o'clock in the afternoon Bill telephoned to Carol. In spite of the heat which crept in everywhere, she sounded restored and quite fresh. It wasn't the somewhat nervy, hoarse voice he had heard on the night before in the bar, but the old rather golden, lush, fresh voice. His own head ached and his nerves jangled.

When she said, "Oh, hello, honey. How're you feeling?" a wave of irritation came over him. He thought, "Damn her good health and spirits!"

"Pretty good. What are you doing?"

"Nothing. Just lying here dressed like Eve reading Nash's magazine. It's too hot to do anything else."

"I've got to go out."

"Where?"

"The company office."

"What about the races?"

"I don't know when I'll get away. I might join you there."

The rather lush voice grew a little more lush, "Oh, come on. You've just arrived. Take the afternoon off."

It was the old story. It had always been like that. Business wasn't anything to her. All she wanted was a good time, a laugh and a spectacle and the sense of people around her.

"Listen, honey," he said, "I came all the way out here just to work."

"There won't be any races tomorrow."

"Okay, but when will I see you?"

"I'll turn up at the races or at the Willingdon Club."

"Don't be too late."

"No."

"You aren't sorry I turned up?"

"No, why should I be?"

"Well, I've never been a very good influence on a business man."

He laughed, "You're up against a tough guy now, honey. 'Good-time Charlie' is dead."

"It's a pity. Poor guy."

Then suddenly the conversation dried up. He was silent and in a moment her voice came back. "Are you still there?"

"Yes."

"I thought maybe you had hung up."

She would never be the one to hang up. She loved the telephone. She could lie in bed a whole morning doing nothing but talk on the telephone.

He said, "Tell me again about that guy on the train. Where did he say he was going to stay?"

"With some Indian—some kind of a doctor who was head of something."

"What did he look like?"

"He was a small fellow—very good-looking with wonderful black eyes."

"I don't mean the Indian."

"Oh, the American guy! Good-looking, sympathetic. Blonde hair and blue eyes. He was sweet really. A girl could fall for him."

"I guess that was him all right."

"Who?"

"Merrill—Homer Merrill."

"Yes, that was it. I remember now."

"It's a good thing you sober up once in a while."

"Don't make cracks."

"Well, I'll be seeing you."

"Yeah—at the races or at the Club."

"Do you belong?"

"Me—no. Botlivala fixes it up for me."

"Who's Botlivala—that Indian?"

"Yes."

"And Jelly and his brother are very important there."

"I prefer Jelly to your friend."

"Well, you can take your choice. Remember, you've got to get me disengaged from him."

"Sure. You can count on me."

"Good-bye."

"Good-bye."

He left the telephone and had a shower. Then he opened the door and called to Silas and told him to lay out his clothes. While he dressed, he thought about Merrill. Surely it must be Merrill she'd met in such a strange fashion on the train. The thought occurred to him again that Merrill might need money if he was ill. He knew you couldn't *give* him any money, unless he had changed a good deal since his college days. But he might be willing to accept a loan. He experienced a strong desire to see Merrill, a desire he had known before many times, when he was tired and felt soiled from dissipation. You always felt better after you'd been with him. Funny—you felt that way too after being with Carol—it had something to do with their health and vitality. They were the kind of people that others of less vitality, of less health, imposed upon, feeding off them. They both drew to themselves weaker, less attractive people, people who were in bad luck or had made a mess of their lives. Merrill was born to accept responsibilities and to help people and lead them. In a funny way that was true of her too, only somehow she had missed her destiny. He'd never thought of her in that way before. Maybe it was that beauty contest long ago that had started her off on the wrong foot. "Miss Minnesota!" That was it. And then Ziegfeld and all the rest of it. She had gotten on to the wrong track. And it was too late now to get her back on the right one.

He thought, grinning, "I guess that puts me in the vampire class, being a good friend of both of them." And then, in seriousness, he realized for the first time that they were the two persons who had been nearest to him. He had loved them both, in much the same way. Looking back on it now, he saw that there was never much desire mixed up in his feeling for Carol. He had felt more lecherous about a dozen other women he had known, almost any other woman he had ever known well, even about women who, aside from their sleek bodies, bored him.

Outside, the heat rose up off the streets like heat from the top of an oven. This was the kind of day you wanted to spend at the beach lying in the water up to your neck, only you couldn't do that here. If you went to Juhu the water, for all the beauty of the shore and the coconut palms, would be warm and muddy. It wasn't much better than the heat itself.

At the office, they hadn't expected him. The *chuprassi* returned after a moment followed by Mr. Smithers, the head man when Mr. Hinkle was away. Mr. Smithers was a rather plump middle-aged man with steel-rimmed spectacles and a shiny bald head, a new man since Bill had been here last. He kept smiling effusively and making little bows, and the moment he spoke Bill recognized him as the man who had talked to him over the telephone. It was the same Birmingham voice and the same rather groveling manner.

The servility of the English lower classes always embarrassed him, as the arrogance and bad manners of the upper classes irritated him. He wanted to say, "Listen, Mr. Smithers, we're both men. We don't belong to two different orders of the animal kingdom. I'm not going to fire you. Even if I am the son of the boss it doesn't make me God. You probably are a hell of a sight more important to the business than I am." This kind of thing always left him tongue-tied, but he knew that if he tried to force Mr. Smithers into behaving with some sort of human dignity as an equal, it would only upset Mr. Smithers and make him believe that the son of his overlord was simply vulgar and American.

They went into Mr. Smithers' office, a somewhat dingy, old-fashioned room with an antiquated electric fan, heavy teakwood furniture and half a dozen fly-specked maps adorning the liver-colored walls. He thought, "I see what Hinkle meant when he wrote for eighty thousand rupees to do over the whole office. This looks like something out of the Temple." It wasn't any office for a company as big as theirs—especially now that all the other American firms in Bombay had launched out into marble and *art moderne*.

He said, "I see what Hinkle meant about the offices. They ought to be brought up to date."

Mr. Smithers clapped his hands and said in a rather meek fashion, "I'm very comfortable, sir. I like my office. It's dignified, too."

"Yes," said Bill. "It's rather like the British Empire under a Tory government." Mr. Smithers looked shocked and tried painfully to smile at the same time with appreciation of the irreverent joke he did not understand.

In response to a clap of the hands a *chuprassie* appeared, and Mr. Smithers ordered hot tea.

Then he said, "I'm sorry Mr. Hinkle is away. I don't think he expected you until next month."

"Well, I finished everything in Alexandria and Istanbul sooner than I expected. I don't like either place, so I caught a boat two weeks earlier than I expected at Port Said."

"Well, you must let us do all we can to make your stay comfortable. I suppose you don't know Bombay very well."

Bill laughed, "On the contrary, I know it very well. You see, I've been here before. You weren't here then."

"No, I was transferred only a year ago from the Singapore office." He rubbed his hands together and beamed with satisfaction and good humor. "Anyway, you must come to lunch with me at the

[94]

Yacht Club." He seemed to swell suddenly, and added, "I've just been taken in."

Bill wasn't unkind or rude by nature, but now he struck. "I appreciate your kind invitation," he said, "but I never go to the Yacht Club. I've never been inside it."

Mr. Smithers looked alarmed. "Why not, Mr. Wainwright? Surely it's a fine club."

"It isn't that. Only you see I have a good many Indian friends— some of them very distinguished—and as you know, they are not allowed to enter the club. So I don't go either . . . it seems to me rather odd considering that India is *their* country."

The speech threw Mr. Smithers into such confusion that Bill regretted having made it. Mr. Smithers grew scarlet and said, "Yes, I know, it's unfortunate. You have to live out here to understand. It's absolutely necessary. We'd be over-run."

Thinking of a club filled with scores of Smithers, Bill thought, "It might be a good thing, too." But he held his tongue, and the unfortunate *impasse* was broken by the arrival of the *chuprassi* with the tea. He drank a cup out of politeness and promptly broke out into a violent sweat, thinking, "Now, damn it, I'll have to go back and change again before I go to the races."

Aloud he said, "There's a bit of information I want to ask you. I am trying to find a friend here. All I know is that he's staying with an Indian doctor, very well known. The doctor is the head of some kind of institution. I know it sounds very vague but I can't come any nearer to it than that. It's very important that I find him."

Mr. Smithers was clearly glad to be off the subject of the Bombay Yacht Club. He said, "I wouldn't know myself. I'll call the head *babu.*"

Again the *chuprassi* appeared and went to summon Mr. Das, the head *babu.*

Mr. Das was an elderly Bengali, very neatly dressed in European clothes, but his manner, like Mr. Smithers', was at once gushy and servile. When Bill described the man he was seeking, Mr. Das, rubbing his hands together, said, "Of course, that must be Colonel Moti." His Bunya face brightened and he added, "A great man—a very great man—a light in India!"

"Where can I find him?" asked Bill.

"At the Institute of Tropical Diseases." And Mr. Das described the way. "It is a bad section of the city—very full of mill workers and diseases."

Then with meticulous care, in Spencerian penmanship, Mr. Das wrote the name of Colonel Moti and the address of the Institute of Tropical Diseases. And all the time Mr. Smithers, Bill was aware, was watching them, a little bewildered by Bill's behavior and point of view, thinking no doubt that Americans were crazy and unpredictable and that their manners, rather than the stupidity and avarice of Tory politicians, would eventually wreck all white civilization; but at the same time Bill was the son of his boss, and he was American, and Mr. Smithers was paid a lot more for his job than any English firm would have paid him, and the Americans had a way of taking business from English corporations. So, Mr. Smithers, knowing which was the buttered side of his bread, took it all. He didn't even hate Bill; he tried to feel superior and contemptuous but only ended in feeling bewildered.

Mr. Das, still rubbing his hands, backed out of the room smiling and bowing, and when he had gone Bill said, "I wish he wouldn't treat a simple request for information as if it were a ceremony."

Mr. Smithers said, "They're all like that—Indians—always servile." And then when Bill asked for a bit of paper to write a note, Mr. Smithers produced it and laid it before him with the air of a grateful serf preparing a service for his feudal overlord.

Bill wrote a note to Colonel Moti and as he wrote, the figure of the small scientist became a little clearer to him, emerging dimly out of his memory—a tough, indignant little figure, which had appeared so incredibly out of place one evening ten years ago in the big bar of the Taj Mahal. He remembered the spirit in the fiery black eyes and the beauty of the Rajput slippers the Major wore. They were scarlet and gold.

He wrote:

My dear Colonel Moti:

I am writing to you for information regarding an old friend of mine, Homer Merrill, who, I understand, is also a friend of yours. I am in Bombay for a very short time and very eager to see him before leaving. If you could give me his address, I should be very grateful. You doubtless do not remember me—we met for one evening at the Taj Mahal nearly ten years ago. A note will reach me there.

With best wishes and apologies for troubling you, I am,

Yours faithfully,

William Wainwright

Then he asked Mr. Smithers to send a boy with the note and left. Outside the street was still like an oven. His clothes hung against his skin, sticky and miserable. It was after four o'clock. He thought, "I'll have to change before going to the races. It will be growing cooler now and by the time I've had a shower and changed, it won't be so bad."

But his instinct told him that he should go to the races, and as he drove back to the hotel, he began, for no special reason, to be troubled again about Carol. He had the feeling that if he did not keep his eye on her, and now and then pull her up short, she would get into trouble. He knew her, and he knew when her mood became dangerous. She was that way now, reckless and wild, and capable of any folly, and it was worse now because she seemed so disorganized and drifting. Miserable and depressed by the heat, it seemed to him as the ramshackle taxi approached the Taj Mahal, that she was headed straight for catastrophe—what catastrophe he did not know.

And he thought, "What the hell! I can't go on looking after her for the rest of my life!" Anyway, why should he? Simply because for a few months they had been married and had fun.

But the sense of trouble did not go away. It remained with him while he had a tepid shower and changed out of the clothes soaked by the reaction to Mr. Smithers' cup of hot tea. When he left he told Silas to return at eight o'clock to see whether he was needed. He did not know what he meant to do. It was a pleasant feeling— Mr. Smithers and the office were out of the way. Until Mr. Hinkle came back from Burma he could do as he pleased. He could have any sort of adventure. "Maybe," he thought, "it's the last chance I'll ever have."

At the race course Mr. Botlivala was suffering from an accession of pride. He walked as if treading on air and his plump little chest was thrown out like the breast of a pouter pigeon. Now and then when he passed an acquaintance or a friend, he bowed rather too elegantly, and a smug little smile curled the corners of the cruel and sensuous lips. He had good reason for feeling proud. Except for his liver, his health was good. He was rich. It was only one generation since his family name had been Bottlewallah, and only four or five since his family had any name at all. And now he had a big pink house on Malabar Hill and owned hundreds of acres of mill tenements and had money invested in foreign stocks that were booming and a string of race horses. But what made him prouder than any of those things was the knowledge that at his side, dressed in Paris clothes and wearing far too many jewels, was the most beautiful blonde in the whole of India. That she was a good deal taller than himself and made no concessions did not trouble him. It was enough that he created the impression that this radiant creature was his property. That this was not true did not trouble him; that even in his heart he knew there was little chance of its ever being true was at that moment of small importance to him. The mere sight of her at his side would start whispers that Botlivala had got possession of that big and wonderful American blonde; and Mr. Botlivala himself did nothing to destroy the impression. On the contrary, he managed by a curl of the lips and a sly look in the eye to say to passing friends and acquaintances, "Look what I got this time."

So, Mr. Botlivala, walking about, now in the paddock, now in the Racing Club enclosure, now having drinks in the enclosure of his own club, was stepping high, his Parsee blood circulating through the veins of his plump little body more quickly than usual, not because of desire but from pride.

And the whole spectacle of the races made him feel fine. It was the showiest race course in the world, better than Longchamps or Epsom, better than Peking or even St. Petersburg in the old days. Nowhere but in Bombay did you find all this color, moving against a background of tropical flowers—nowhere did you find Maharajahs and millionaires, Ranees and British governors, rich Americans and Arab horse dealers, visiting French and beautiful Indian women. The scene was not new to him but it was always fresh, and he was always proud of it. He liked showing it to all newcomers

[98]

as he was showing it now to Carol. He liked showing it to her even though she had seen it many times before. He liked showing it to her and telling her all about it, even if she was bored.

His horse Asoka III won the fourth race and Carol won money on it. He knew Asoka III was going to win, so it was easy enough to lend her a thousand rupees to bet on it. The only thing he didn't like was that when she had won and drawn twenty-one thousand rupees she promptly paid him back the thousand. She would accept jewelry, but she would never accept money. This, he divined after some weeks of experience with Miss Carol Halma, was a quaint American custom. Jewelry gave you the right to nothing. Money, it seemed, did. So he had never been quite able to get what he wanted, despite the fact that the jewelry had cost him several hundred thousand rupees. But at the moment his regrets were not too bitter; everybody at the races who knew him thought Miss Carol Halma belonged to him, even if she didn't, and except for the baser more depraved side of *l'amour* (as the cosmopolitan Mr. Botlivala always expressed it) that knowledge was half the satisfaction of any conquest. The other thing you could buy in quantity in Bombay with no trouble at all.

He was happy, too, because Carol seemed very good-natured today, and not tricky and quarrelsome as she could be at times. She was very amiable and did not even object to being walked about in the heat like a show filly so that people could see them together.

The race in which Asoka III ran was the big race and after Mr. Botlivala had discussed matters with the trainer and jockey and had a drink at his club enclosure, he began to feel restless again. Virtually everybody he knew had seen him by now with the beautiful blonde, and he experienced a sudden desire to show her to a new audience. The obvious place to go was to the Willingdon Club across the Road. All of Bombay that wasn't at the races would be turning up there for cocktails and a rubber of bridge, and although it was nearly five o'clock the race course was still a hot uncomfortable place. They would go to the Willingdon Club and then perhaps Carol would have a drink too many and he could take her to the Taj Mahal for dinner and show her off there.

But when he turned from talking to one of the race stewards, he found her speaking to an ugly little woman dressed in white whom she introduced as Mrs. Trollope. Mr. Botlivala bowed—one of his smaller bows reserved for inferiors—and his face took on the expression of someone in proximity to a bad smell. He recognized her vaguely as the woman he had seen the night before in the Taj Mahal bar, but of this he gave no sign. All his agitated little life he had spent in observing people—not profoundly—but only so far as he could judge their value and use to him in his worldly career. Very often because he only observed such superficial details as dress and speech, he had fallen into disastrous errors. (Once he made the awful mistake of taking a British Governor for an inferior civil servant because the Governor liked old clothes.)

So now, in a glance, he took in the worn and slightly yellowed costume and felt hat of Mrs. Trollope and dismissed her, not only as of no importance but actually an object with whom he did not care to be seen. He knew that Miss Carol Halma had a talent for collecting strange people, and he had found her on intimate terms with remittance men, blowsy English tap dancers and God knows what, but Mrs. Trollope was, he thought swiftly, the worst she had produced up to now. Why, she wasn't even a woman and she was ugly.

Like so many weak men, Mr. Botlivala was always talking about beautiful women and always wanting to be seen with them. The proximity of a woman as plain as Mrs. Trollope, even if she had been clothed in diamonds, seemed to him a reproach to the virility which was his greatest concern in life. What would people think? And it was none the easier that she appeared shabby and unimportant. He thought, "Well, we must get rid of her."

But Mrs. Trollope had no intention of being shaken off. She had come to the races, alone, to make money and augment the pitiful forty-eight pounds and three shillings she had left in Barclay's Bank. And she had lost. Her head ached from the drinking of the night before and the heat made her feel dizzy, and the loss of fifteen pounds had terrified her. And then suddenly like a blaze of light she had seen Miss Carol Halma, tall and beautiful in pale pink, covered with diamonds in broad daylight, coming down the steps from the owners' box. Again, this time in the heat and dirt, the queer sensation of becoming Miss Carol Halma swept over her and went away again, leaving her limp and exhausted. She thought, "She'll bring me luck. I must speak to her."

So she followed Miss Halma and Mr. Botlivala as far as the steward's enclosure and then while Mr. Botlivala was talking she managed to come face to face with Miss Halma and to be recognized.

When Mr. Botlivala, after being introduced said quickly to Carol, "We'll go and have a drink at the Willingdon Club," the response wasn't what he had expected. Surprisingly, Carol said, "No, I want to stay on for the next race. Mrs. Trollope wants to bet." And then Mr. Botlivala saw that Mrs. Trollope held in her hand a thousand rupee note and the awful suspicion came to him that it was one of the notes Carol had won with the thousand rupees he had loaned her.

It was. In the few moments while the two women talked much had been accomplished.

Carol had remembered Mrs. Trollope at once. It was not difficult to recall the small tough, weather-beaten face, and recognition was made all the easier by the fact that Mrs. Trollope was wearing the same costume, sponged and badly pressed by an *ayah*, that she had worn the night before in the Taj Mahal bar. Carol thought, "Maybe the only costume she has." She recognized all the signs of bad luck in Mrs. Trollope, even to the discouraged expression in the greenish eyes which did not vanish when the lips formed themselves into a meager smile. She had seen eyes and lips like that before, which did not function together when commanded to do so. And that Carol knew, out of her instinct and experience, indicated an inner desperation which was terrifying.

When Mrs. Trollope said nervously, "Do you remember me?" Carol, full of kindness and pity, answered almost with eagerness, "Of course I do. How are you?"

"Pretty good."

"Had any luck?"

"No," said Mrs. Trollope.

"I cleaned up."

"Well, I lost everything on every race."

Mrs. Trollope made the statement with such nonchalance and such fierce gayety that Carol divined at once that she *had* lost

[101]

everything. Her own bag was stuffed with thousand rupee notes. So she said again, "Well, I cleaned up." She opened the bag and took out a thousand rupee note. "Here, take this and have another try."

"Oh, I couldn't do that," said Mrs. Trollope.

"Go on. Don't be silly. I won a lot of them. If you win you can pay me back. If you don't, you can pay me back the next time you see me."

"I don't like to," said Mrs. Trollope weakly. It was preposterous —accepting money like this from a stranger she had seen but once before in her life. It was something she should never do; but she knew she was going to accept the money. At the pit of her stomach she experienced a sudden weakness at the very sight of it. That thousand rupee note might solve everything. Even if she only doubled it, it would give her a capital. If she won on a ten to one shot, it might solve everything. If she lost, there wasn't any way of paying it back. A little voice kept saying, "But the girl is lucky. She couldn't be anything else. It will bring you luck just to touch that thousand rupee note." It all happened very quickly, in a second, between speeches.

The small, remote voice won. She heard the big, handsome girl saying, "Take it. It'll bring you luck. I'm very lucky today. I can't lose."

She took the note and then said, "Give me a tip. I don't know anything about the horses. I only arrived yesterday."

"I don't either," said Carol. "We'll get a sure thing out of Teeny."

It was at this moment that Mr. Botlivala turned and discovered his blonde beauty talking to what appeared to be a charwoman on an outing in borrowed clothes, and his spine stiffened and a chill came over his effusive manner.

When he said nervously, "We'll go and have a drink at the Willingdon Club," Carol knew what was up and said immediately, "No, we won't—not until Mrs. Trollope bets. I feel lucky today. I'm going to stay until she wins."

He knew her well enough to know by her manner that she was in one of those moods when, if crossed, she would become difficult. He suspected—at times he even knew—that she was not very fond of him and that she had for him no respect whatever. He knew too that he could do things which would put her off altogether for long periods of time. Everything had gone so well today that almost anything seemed possible. It might even be, he thought wildly, that if her good humor continued, the impression he had labored all afternoon to create, might come to have some basis in reality. Bargaining was in Mr. Botlivala's blood and heritage, and he was prepared now to bargain, this time for something he wanted more than he had ever wanted anything.

So he said, "All right, if you like."

"But," said Carol, "you've got to give Mrs. Trollope a first rate tip, like the ones you've been giving me. Then we'll go after the next race. Go and get a tip. We'll meet you at the thousand rupee booth."

So Mr. Botlivala went off, grumbling a little and yet a little proud of being ordered about by so handsome and spectacular a girl. Anyway, it seemed the best and quickest way to be rid of that nobody in the shabby, expensively cut clothes. As he left them he had meant to go and find a tip that was a sure thing. Then Mrs. Trollope would win and go away satisfied quickly.

But Mr. Botlivala's intricate Oriental brain never functioned simply. He had not gone a dozen paces from his club enclosure before a new idea entered his head. It would be better if this Mrs. Trollope lost altogether. If she won, they might never be rid of her; she might want to celebrate or Carol might invite her to join them. If she lost she would be, from all signs, completely broke. Then they would be rid of her for good. So instead of going for a tip, Mr. Botlivala chatted with a friend or two and was rewarded by various questionable compliments regarding his relations with his companion at the races. After that he went to find Carol and Mrs. Trollope.

They seemed to be getting on very well—much too well for his pleasure. "Mrs. Trollope," he thought, "is the kind of bitch who tries to break up the love affairs of more attractive women. She's the kind of plain woman pretty women go to for advice."

Carol looked as if she were enjoying herself and the tired look of discouragement was gone from the face of Mrs. Trollope. Now there was in her eyes a bedazzled look of admiration which disturbed him and made him angry. Although he could not and did not attempt to fathom the reasons for his fierce resentment, he experienced all the sensations of fury that he might have felt at the sight of a man attempting to take Miss Halma away from him. The anger only heightened the pleasure he took in the plot to ruin Mrs. Trollope.

"I've got it," he said, "you can't lose and it's a twenty to one shot."

"What?" asked Mrs. Trollope.

"It's a horse called Tinker's Dam. They don't know much about her but she's a sure thing."

Mrs. Trollope's worn sallow face turned the color of a tallow candle. Her thin brown hands shook as if she had been seized by a chill. She turned and without a word went to the window marked "One thousand rupees." On the way she thought, "Maybe I'd better only bet half of it." But the small voice inside her—the voice which had always ruined her life—again said, "No. Bet it all and clean up." Yet putting the thousand rupee note across the board was like putting a part of her own heart in pawn.

They did not trouble to climb the stairs to the owner's box. The three of them stood on chairs. Tinker's Dam—Number seven—was a small sleek mare with a white forefoot. Beside the others in the race she looked no bigger than a small polo pony. At the sight of her, Mrs. Trollope who knew a good deal about horses, felt her heart contract and Carol who knew nothing about horses thought, "How can that little thing run against those other great big horses?" For a second the shadow of a suspicion crossed her mind and she glanced at Mr. Botlivala, but in the bland dark face there was nothing to be read. He was watching the horses with indifference.

Carol borrowed his glasses and then gave them to Mrs. Trollope.

There were two false starts and then they were off. The sleek little black mare was ahead and at the first turn she increased her lead by another length. Her jockey brought her inside next the fence. He was easy to follow with his scarlet and white jacket and cap. At the next turn she was still ahead. Then a big horse appeared to be gaining but the little mare, like a dryad pursued by a faun, increased her lead.

At this point Carol no longer paid any attention to the race. Unless she fell down, little Tinker's Dam with the white forefoot and pretty mane, couldn't lose. Carol took to watching Mr. Botlivala's face. She saw it contract slowly into a scowl and she heard the wild cries of "Tinker's Dam! Tinker's Dam!" and saw the scowl deepen. Then the race was over and Mrs. Trollope wasn't any longer standing on the chair. She had fallen off it and was sitting on it now, limp with the excitement, the worn white felt hat pushed far back on her head.

Before Carol got down from the chair, she addressed two words to Mr. Botlivala. Now she knew what he had done, and her voice was rich with contempt. She said, "You heel!" Mr. Botlivala cringed, pulled his face together and said, "You see, it wasn't any race at all. She couldn't lose."

Then Mrs. Trollope collected herself and, her face bright with excitement, she thanked Mr. Botlivala again and again, and Carol said, "Yes, something must have gone awfully wrong for her to win."

But Mrs. Trollope didn't hear her. She was already on her way to the paying booth.

"Now we can go to the club," said Mr. Botlivala. Frightened by the sudden ferocity of Miss Halma's contempt, he spoke wistfully, hopefully, pleadingly, but it was no good. Carol only said, "No, we'll wait for Mrs. Trollope and take her along. We'll have a drink to celebrate."

Sometimes Mr. Botlivala's temper betrayed his wiliness. It did so on this occasion. He threw his racing card violently to the ground and said, "What, that scarecrow!"

Carol remained dangerously calm, and he knew now that she meant to punish him for the shabby trick. She only said, "All right, you run along. We'll go back to the Taj Mahal. Anyway, Bill Wainwright was coming to meet us."

"Who's Bill Wainwright?" asked Mr. Botlivala, and into the opaque dark eyes came a sudden look of anger and suspicion.

When she said, "You saw him with me last night," the look changed to one of outright hatred—the hatred of a small, ill-favored, impotent male for one who was good-looking and virile and attractive. For a second Mr. Botlivala looked strikingly like one of the Russell vipers in the laboratory of Colonel Moti.

"Who is he?" asked Mr. Botlivala. "Where does he come from?"

Carol chose her words deliberately. She was getting a little weary of Mr. Botlivala and his moods, jealousies, vanity and pettiness. So she said quite casually, "He's an old boy friend of mine. His father is the Amalgamated Oil Companies. And he's plenty rich, honey. He could buy you and all your tenements and never notice it." She started through the crowd saying, "Come on, Mrs. Trollope won't know what has become of us."

Having been the first at the pay window, Mrs. Trollope had already drawn her winnings. They were stuffed away in the worn carry-all bag—twenty beautiful thousand rupee notes. The odd note she held in her hand and at sight of Carol she held it out, saying, "Thanks. You certainly are in luck today . . . a twenty to one shot. Whee!"

And at the same moment out of the crowd appeared the Maharajah of Jellapore and Joey. The garlands and *puggrees* of the landing were gone, and they were both back in their flamboyant European clothes. Jelly smoked an enormous cigar and Joey was a little tipsy—not drunk but just pleasantly dazed. His dark face wore a vacant and dreamy smile.

It was Carol the Maharajah noticed first. He said, "Well, sweetheart, how are you? You look fine."

Carol said she felt fine.

"I hear you've been in Jellapore with my disreputable brother."

"Yes, for three weeks."

"Have fun?"

"Up and down. You know Jellapore better than I do."

"A bloody dull hole."

Then he greeted his old poker companion Mrs. Trollope, warmly, and spoke to Mr. Botlivala. Mr. Botlivala pressed his hands together and gave one of his bows reserved for royalty, with an extra little bob for the kind of royalty that frequented Longchamps, Ascot and Epsom, and the more expensive night clubs and brothels of Paris.

Then the Maharajah said, "We've met just right. I'm giving a little cocktail party in the small palace—right now, after the races.

I'm going back there now. Can I give any of you a lift? Everybody's coming."

"Okay," said Carol. "We've got our own car."

She didn't consult Mr. Botlivala, but he had no objections. Things had turned out for the best—he could show off Carol at the cocktail party where Mrs. Trollope would doubtless be quickly lost in the crowd.

As for Mrs. Trollope, the world in less than an hour had turned into a different place. She had twenty thousand rupees in her bag and now she was going to a party, a good party, with the big beautiful blonde girl. Life was beginning all over again. Tomorrow she would have to go and spend a lot of the twenty thousand rupees on new clothes—now that she was back in the world and going around with Carol Halma. It wasn't only that Carol Halma was beautiful, thought Mrs. Trollope; she had sense. Mrs. Trollope, who had never cared much for men anyway, liked the way she bullied Mr. Botlivala. It was a pity that any man should ever approach anyone as lovely as Miss Carol Halma, except on his knees.

And so Bill missed them altogether. He met at the races two or three people who had seen Miss Halma but none of them knew where she had gone. At the Willingdon Club he found no trace of her nor anyone who had seen her there. He did discover the very handsome young Englishman, now in mufti, who had brought on board the letters from the Governor and Viceroy. Now that the beautiful white and gold uniform was gone and the young man no longer was a manifestation of the pomp of the British Empire, the stiffness had disappeared. He was simply Lieutenant Forsythe, a hell of a good fellow.

They had two or three drinks together and found a bridge four with Mr. Hazimboy, a rich Khoja cotton broker and an old acquaintance, and Mrs. Barroly, one of the Parsee fast set. It turned out that she was the owner of Tinker's Dam. The bridge wasn't very good and they talked, being racing people, much too long about Tinker's Dam. In the midst of the game restlessness began to take slow possession of Bill—the old restlessness which he had not experienced for a long time. Now that Hinkle wouldn't be back from Burma, there was no work to be done, and the prospect, if coupled with good behavior and respectability, augured boredom. He knew it as he sat there being bored by the talk of Tinker's Dam, by the plump, dull, rich face of Mr. Hazimboy and the somewhat affected horsey enthusiasm of Mrs. Barroly and the overcordial manner of the nice young A.D.C. of the Governor who was over-playing the rôle of an Englishman being at home with the darker races. Coldly he admired the motives of the boy and privately found him a very bad actor.

"No," he thought, trumping Mrs. Barroly's perfectly good nine of clubs, "this won't do. I can't go through a fortnight of this kind of thing. Life is what I've got to have—life with a capital L. It may be my last chance before middle age."

And as he played, very badly all the time, because his mind was elsewhere, he was aware too of the difficulties. What he meant by life was vaguely a "good time"—the kind of time you used to have in the big wide open days just after the War, which meant vaguely and confusedly, champagne, dancing, laughs, gayety, recklessness and now and then a quick and amusing love affair with some pretty entertaining girl. All this, he knew, was an order very diffi-cult to fill in Bombay—especially the last part. In the East there didn't seem to be anything between a sing-song girl and the dowdy respectable plain wives of the local European colony. Of course, if you stayed long enough in any colony, you presently got into the state where biological urge made even the plainest middle-aged wife of an oil agent seem entertaining and even pretty, but in a couple of weeks you couldn't quite work yourself up to that. And unless you were very young, sing-song girls didn't mean anything but boredom and a moment's sensual satisfaction. It was like drinking a whole bottle of whiskey at once to feel gay.

He heard Mrs. Barroly saying suddenly, "That's the second time you've trumped my trick." And this time her voice carried an acid edge of annoyance.

He apologized and said, "I'm playing like a fool, but I don't feel very well. I'll stop after this rubber and you can find another fourth."

He knew he must have been playing an even worse game than

[108]

he realized because nobody protested when he suggested dropping out.

He tried to pull himself together but it was too late now, with his mind wandering away on frivolous things. He and Mrs. Barroly, but for his mistakes, should have won long before, and now as if in punishment the rubber was going on interminably.

He looked at his watch and discovered that it was already eight o'clock. During a moment when Mrs. Barroly, with relief, took the bid and left him as dummy, he rose and left the table to stroll through the club to look for Carol. He found no sign of her and for the first time felt annoyed. He was used to her unpunctuality but now he felt as if she had deliberately let him down. Wherever she was there was always something going on—something fantastic and occasionally melodramatic. He guessed—he even knew—that she had not kept the rendezvous because she had found some fresh and unforeseen prospect of amusement, and so had ruthlessly forgotten all about him. "Damn her," he thought. It wasn't that he wanted to revive their brief experience of long ago. You couldn't warm over a thing like that; it was always cold porridge. He didn't want her in that way. He only wanted her as a companion. With Carol you always had a good time.

He returned to the table and at last the interminable rubber was finished. His fellow players bade him good-night without any show of regret and murmured politely enough about more bridge, and that was all. They didn't mind his going at all because with the restlessness inside him, he had never been there at all. He had been no more than a real dummy going through the gestures of playing a game.

Outside the night was almost cool with that false coolness of West Coast India. It seemed cool until you moved and then suffocation and perspiration took possession of you, and there were moments when it seemed impossible to breathe. The taxi followed Nepean Sea Road and for a time Bill, with his eyes closed, divined his progress by the sense of smell—the perfume of jasmine and jacqueranda; that would be the odor of the palace and bungalow gardens, hanging above the sea. The smell of spices and incense—that was the big Temple of Parvati on the edge of the harbor, with its great tank frequented night and day by worshipers. The smell

[109]

of wood and cow dung smoke— that would be the fires of pilgrims from deep India who had come to the crowded beach to purify themselves in the waters of the great sea. And the smell of the petrol lights of the sellers of sweetmeats. And there were sounds too —the clanging of the electric train that went to Juhu, and the ringing of the cinema bells announcing a new performance, and the music of the band at Government House where there must be a dance under way, and over it all the sound of the waters of the Arabian Sea, lapping on the flat beach, and the murmur of thousands and thousands of people, increasing as the taxi bore him toward the center of the city, and the whining music and cries of a religious procession as it crossed the road before the taxi on its way to the water. Once or twice he opened his eyes—once to see Jellapore's little pink pleasure palace, on the edge of the water, all its crystal chandeliers blazing with light—once as he passed Government House. As he passed the Jellapore pavilion, he thought, "Jelly must be giving a party," and leaned forward to ask the driver to stop there. But almost at once he thought better of it, and sat back again with his eyes closed.

The sounds and sights and smells swept over him, caressing his senses, raising lurid images, tempting him toward trouble—what sort of trouble he did not know; but he had no faith in himself. He only thought, "If I can find Carol, it will be all right. She'll entertain me and this craziness will go out of me." And there was only one way to find her and that was to go back to the Taj Mahal and begin all over again.

It wasn't Carol whom he found at the Taj Mahal and it wasn't Carol who saved him from folly. At the hotel he went directly to the desk and asked if she had left any message for him. There was none, and when he telephoned her room, there was no answer. Then the man at the desk said, "There is a gentleman waiting to see you, sir."

"Where?"

"He's in the reading room. He's been here for an hour."

"A jewelry salesman?"

"No, I shouldn't think so. It is an Indian gentleman. I wouldn't know what he is."

"I'll go and see for myself."

But on the way, he passed by the bar and had a look around. Carol wasn't there either and he thought, "Maybe she's lying to me about that damned Parsee. Maybe she's out with him and doesn't mean what she said." And suddenly he felt flat and depressed and tired.

When he arrived at the reading room, he entered it stealthily, determined to go away again if he did not like the appearance of the man who was waiting for him. It was easy to discover which was the man. The reading room was a place not much favored by the kind of people who made up the clientele of the Taj Mahal. It was empty save for a very comfortable looking old English woman who sat at the window knitting and watching the street outside, and a small dark man sitting at one of the tables writing in a notebook with a gold fountain pen.

For a long time he stood watching the man, trying to divine who he might be and what he might want, and then slowly out of his memory—a picture took form—a picture of a small dark man, wearing wonderful red and gold Rajput slippers. And he knew. The little man was Colonel Moti.

He sat leaning over the notebook, all his energy, his mind, the forces of his small wiry body pouring out through the tip of the gold fountain pen. Something about the figure of the scientist sobered Bill and steadied his nerves, and made him feel suddenly useless and unimportant. Then quietly he went over to the table and said, "I beg your pardon, were you waiting for me?"

Colonel Moti put down the pen, stood up, removed his glasses and asked, "Are you Mr. Wainwright?"

"Yes. You're Colonel Moti, aren't you?"

"Yes. I wanted to see you to talk about Merrill."

"I'm sorry I kept you waiting. If I'd known you were coming. . . ."

"It's all right," said Colonel Moti. "You see I was in the city and it's a long and slow way to and from the Institute. So I thought I'd take a chance."

"But you're a busy man."

The Colonel smiled, a curious smile of unexpected warmth. He said, "I haven't lost any time. I always carry my work with me. That way I don't lose any time. I've been writing an article for

New York on new discoveries we've made about the bubonic plague."

"Please sit down," said Bill. "Won't you have a drink of some kind?" He—Bill—who had never known shyness, felt suddenly shy, like a small boy.

Bill ordered drinks and they settled into comfortable chairs which were also cool, for the heat crept in from the street through the big windows like steam into a steam bath.

"I had meant to come out and see you," said Bill.

"It's all right," the Colonel said. "I came quickly because I had an idea and because the case is urgent. I spoke to Merrill. He's staying with me at the Institute. He wants to see you. . . . He wants to see you very much and as quickly as possible."

The man brought the drinks and the small fiery Colonel Moti launched into his story.

"I don't know," he said, "how much you've heard of the work Merrill has done. He didn't come here to convert Indians to Christianity. That rarely means anything. He came here to teach them how to live decently and well in the villages where for five thousand years they've lived in squalor and starvation. And now the British and every decent Prince or Dewan in India want him to come and help solve their problems. He is necessary to India, Mr. Wainwright—one of the most necessary living men—but there is a limit to one man's endurance—and he has already passed that!"

"I know him," said Bill politely. "I know how he works. He could have had anything he wanted in America and he chose to come out here and bury himself."

The black eyes of Colonel Moti flashed. "I wouldn't call it burying himself. Half of India knows him and thousands of Indian villages look on him as God—because he changed all their lives. No, Mr. Wainwright, I wouldn't call it burying himself. India is a great nation, stirring and awakening, after hundreds of years of sleeping. And Merrill is helping as much as any man."

He paused for a moment as if gathering his forces, and Bill knew that his own face was scarlet. Colonel Moti went on, saying, "You see, that's the trouble with the West now. It's always that same point of view—that one is buried if he isn't trying to make money or show off in politics." He crossed one slender leg over the other, and added, "That's beside the point. I came here to talk about how we can save Merrill from dying when we need him so badly."

"Is it as bad as that?"

"It is as bad as that. He has worked himself until his body is worn out and his brain is like a sponge. And he's been ill with malaria again and again and has had amœbic dysentery and enteric fever. Any man less strong and with less spirit would have been dead long ago. He has the strength of an ox and the spirit of an angel. Whatever happens he must have a long rest." The Colonel paused and lighted a cigarette. "But it is not only that which he needs. It will take more than that to save him." He looked sharply at Bill and asked, "Did you ever know his wife?"

"No," said Bill, "I never saw her."

"She's dead now. She died last year, thank God. She did her best to destroy him. And now that she's dead he reproaches himself for not having understood her, when the thing he should have done was to take her out and cut her throat." The fire blazed again in the dark eyes and then smoldered down and he went on. "She was the daughter of a missionary. He met her out here. She was pretty enough but she had some odd and very perverted ideas which passed under the head of Christianity. One of them was that no Christian woman should live with her husband except when they wanted children. You know Merrill?" Again he looked penetratingly at Bill. "You know that he was a strong and beautiful and vigorous young man. You know that he was meant by God to attract women, to live with women, to people the earth with offspring. God made him as he was for that purpose. God and Nature, Mr. Wainwright, are not fools, although priests and missionaries may very often be fools and evil and perverted as well."

He paused to take a drink of tonic water and then said, "Well, Nature won't be fooled. I know that better than most men. I have spent my life fighting Nature—fighting disease and germs and all the malice of Nature in India where Nature is more evil and powerful than elsewhere. What I am trying to say is this—that for ten years that woman perverted Merrill's whole life—his mind, his health, his body. She would not live with him and Merrill is too decent a fellow—and too much of a fool—to take an Indian woman into the house with his wife. And he was too kind to hurt her. For ten years—this boy, who was meant by God to breed—lived beside this monstrous woman in absolute chastity. That more than the typhus and the malaria has wrecked his health. It is that—a man-made evil born of religion—that and not a microbe which causes the hysterical pain in his head which sometimes makes him cry like a baby."

Until now the little scientist had spoken quietly but he began suddenly to turn Indian and become oratorical. The slender hand even beat the table as the eyes flashed. "That woman was a monster and as time went on she became more and more unsatisfied and dry and querulous. She hated living in the villages and did all she could to spoil his work. She blocked him and annoyed him, and even intrigued against him until, mercifully, she died. They said it was dysentery, but I should wager that the villagers who loved Merrill did away with her. There are more ways than one of accomplishing such things in India."

Bill, listening, wanted to say something but he could think of nothing to say. The feeling of his own insignificance paralyzed him. People like Moti—scientists or thinkers—always overawed him. He saw them rarely enough, but when he did encounter them he was reduced to shyness and utter intellectual impotence, like a small boy.

"I'm not boring you, I hope," said Moti. "I am gambling on the belief that you are a friend of Merrill and love him."

"That's true," said Bill.

"And that you're willing to help him."

"I'd do anything on earth I could do."

"Because if he isn't helped he will die . . . and before very long." The Colonel leaned forward toward Bill as if to emphasize what he was about to say, "He talked to me about you. I know a little about what kind of person you are, and now that I've seen you, I am encouraged. I think I know what sort of person you are and that you're the one person who can help him."

The remark made Bill suddenly uneasy. What could he do to help a man like Homer Merrill? What could there be between the two of them now after so many years in worlds as far apart as it was possible to be? For a second he was terrified even by the prospect of seeing Homer again. And a small selfish voice kept saying,

"Your whole stay will be spoiled—all the fun you might have—perhaps the last fun you'll ever have as a young man—will be ruined by taking charge of an invalid." Then he was ashamed of himself and said quickly, "Of course, I'll gladly do anything I can—if there is anything I can do."

He was aware that the black eyes had been watching him closely, testing him, with a cold and complete objectivity, as if he were a specimen in a laboratory. For a moment Colonel Moti was silent, and nervously Bill repeated, "I don't know what there is I *can* do."

The Colonel said abruptly, "You are a man who has enjoyed himself. You like to laugh. You like music. You like women—I don't say as an obsession—but because you like them around you. They make you feel well and happy. You have done all the things which Merrill has denied himself. . . ."

Bill opened his mouth to speak, in a half-conscious effort to check Colonel Moti's excellent analysis, but the Colonel checked him by holding up his hand.

"You are what Merrill needs. You were great friends, weren't you? Merrill says so."

"As great friends as two men can ever be."

"Then perhaps it is not too late to help him—even to cure him. I'm asking you to do this not only for the sake of Merrill whom we both love and admire, but for the sake of thousands—even millions of poor ignorant suffering people—because he is a man of immense value. And if we cannot cure him he will die." Then as if it had just occurred to him, he added, "You see his son, who is nine years old, has just sailed for America. He worships the boy. His going away was, for Merrill, worse than cutting off a part of his own body with his own hands. I saw the parting. I saw the look in Merrill's eyes. It was as if he would like to tear out his own heart and send it with the boy."

"What is it you want me to do?"

The doctor sat upright with the fine, sensitive hands clasped. He said, "When he is well enough I want you to come and see him. And then I want you to bring him here to the Taj Mahal with you. I want you to make him live for a little time the way you live. I want him to drink, to make love to women—any kind of women— I want him to gamble—to laugh—in short to live as such a man as he is should have lived." After a pause, the Colonel added, "It won't be easy—it'll be like teaching a paralytic to walk."

And while he spoke, Bill's mind wandered back to the days when he and Homer had shared a room—when Homer went to bed sober and he himself came in all too often drunk after a night in Maisie Dorsay's house. He remembered the time when he had done his best to get Homer to drink, to go on a party, to be for an hour or two wild and foolish and abandoned. And no argument could change his way of life. He had never persuaded him. The most Homer had ever said was, "Bill, it's your life and nobody's business but your own what you do with it, but sometimes I think you're kind of crazy."

Aloud Bill said, "No. It won't be easy. It wasn't long ago when he was younger."

"But it will be easier than you think. You see, he's very near the end of the physical and mental suffering which the human body can endure. There are moments when he is willing to do anything."

Then Colonel Moti stood and said, "I won't keep you any longer."

Bill murmured something but the Colonel did not wait for him to finish. He said, "We're both busy men and I have a long drive before me. If you do this thing—if you help Merrill to live as nature meant him to live—to relax those horribly knotted nerves— you will have saved him, and you will have done a great service to humanity for you will have saved a man capable of accomplishing an immeasurable amount of good for the human race. I cannot do it myself. I have not the temperament and I do not understand that thing in the background of so many Americans and Englishmen which so often deforms their lives and destroys them—that thing which was Merrill's wife."

He picked up the notebook in which he had been writing and took Bill's hand. "At present I am keeping him quiet with sedatives —sleeping most of the time. In a day or two he will be wanting to see you. I will send a boy to show you the way."

And then he was gone and Bill remained at the window near the old lady who had gone on knitting through the long talk. Like her, Bill looked down into the hot, swarming street but he saw nothing, not even the coolies who had removed their *puggrees* and wrapped them about their lean, starved bodies and lay down on the sidewalk to sleep.

In a little while he turned and went up the long stairs. On the way he met Krishna, Carol's servant, coming down, in all his purple and gold Jellapore glory, and when he questioned Krishna as to Carol's whereabouts, the boy said he knew nothing but that she had set out for the races about four o'clock.

He looked at his watch and discovered that it was already past ten o'clock. It wasn't any use setting out to find her in Bombay, and he was in no mood to face the stifling noisy bar or to go back again to the Willingdon Club. There seemed to be nothing to do but go to bed.

"Not a bad idea," he thought. "It'll do me no harm."

But the room, even with the *punkah* churning the hot air, was insufferably hot. The sheets clung to him and when he took them off he felt suddenly chilled and remembered the annoyance of the colic he had contracted many times before from sleeping naked under a *punkah*. But it was not only the heat which kept him awake but the old restlessness. He wanted to be up and about searching for something. Outside in the hot and swarming city things were happening, exciting things in which he himself, lying there sleepless in the hot room, had no part. If he rose and dressed and went out, some remarkable adventure might occur, something wild and exciting.

For a long time he lay tossing, trying to tell himself that he was so much safer here alone in the room. When he felt like this he invariably fell into trouble. The interview with the Colonel had sobered him a little; in the fierce black eyes there had been the light of wisdom and discipline and responsibility, all the virtues which, he thought ruefully, he himself had never known. The eyes, the presence of Colonel Moti had brought him peace for a little time and with peace, envy. And the story of Merrill had made him ashamed and even a little frightened. It was difficult, he found, even impossible, to picture a friend like Merrill after ten years, after the two of you had gone such different ways. He had loved Homer and been closer to him than he had ever been to any man, closer in a way than he had ever been to any woman because all his relations with women had been at once superficial and sensual.

[117]

Then the restlessness returned again, becoming this time unbearable, and presently almost without being conscious of what he was doing, he found himself dressing again to go out into the hot teeming city. He closed the door as he went out without knowing whither he was bound, but on the way through the jail-like corridor, he remembered the little pink pleasure palace on the edge of the water. That was where he would go—to Jelly's, where there was a party in progress.

The party which began with cocktails after the races was still going strong at two in the morning with the number of guests augmented rather than diminished. If you could stay up that late, the breeze changed when the tide was right and it grew a little cooler. It was a breeze at least, which came off the sea instead of from the hot baked dusty inland country.

The small pink pavilion was really a palace in miniature with a small ballroom, a great hall and a series of small rooms overlooking the garden on the side next the sea. Although the Maharajah of Jellapore had a huge state palace on the hill, it was here that he lived and entertained his friends. The great Jellapore palace he had not frequented for years save when it was necessary through reasons of state or to visit his wives in order to insure the succession; now that this was well accomplished he no longer spent any nights at the palace. The pleasure pavilion was more comfortable and more agreeable in its big garden, behind high walls, filled with flowering trees and shrubs. Here, below Malabar Hill, on the edge of the sea, there were none of the intrigues and jealousies and quarrels which made his life in the big palace take on from time to time the quality of a nightmare. And here, with Untouchable servants—the Maharajah did not care a hang about caste—he could live as he pleased. There was a good deal of gossip, particularly among the other rulers in the palaces on the hill, about what went on inside the pink pavilion, but no one really knew anything.

It was kept open night and day for the Maharajah's racing friends, both Indian and European, and so for a large part of every day it was more like a club than a house or the dwelling of a ruling prince. When he wanted privacy, which was rarely for he was a haunted and unhappy little man, he withdrew to the top floor

[118]

where there was a suite of rooms centering about one great room which, for the sake of coolness, were all built of white marble. One whole side of the great room overlooking the sea was left open to the sluggish breezes of the Arabian Sea.

Bill knew the house. He remembered even the grizzled porter who had seen so many strange and fantastic people pass through the doors and witnessed so many things which to the ordinary passer-by would have seemed improbable if not impossible. He acknowledged the salaam of the old man and walked straight through the great hallway into the round red and gold room where they were playing *chemin-de-fer*.

It was a big room with three great arches overlooking the garden that ran down to the sea—a room which the heat of the Indian climate and the salt dampness of the sea had corrupted into the likeness of a small and shabby casino on the Italian Riviera. Overhead, the old-fashioned electric *punkahs* churned slowly an atmosphere compounded of the smell of jasmine and patchouli, the scent of cigarette smoke and stale champagne, with overtones of salt water and drying fish. Above the murmured words of *"Banco"* and *"Suivi"* there rose the faint music of drums and flutes, and beyond the table through the arches Bill caught a glimpse of a Moslem dancing girl between two cross-legged musicians turning slowly against the faint line of phosphorescent foam where the warm and sluggish Arabian Sea broke over the rocks. The garden too was filled with people.

As he entered the room, those at the table absorbed in the play took no notice of him, and for a moment he stood quietly in the doorway watching the scene, his heart suddenly stirred in a way he did not understand. This—a scene like this—you would find only in the East. It was at once both tawdry and startling and beautiful, like the odd group of characters seated about the green baize table, their eyes fastened upon the shoe which held the cards. To all of them, money had no value in the sense that it had value to the middle class, suburban people the world over; all of them at the table were either too rich or too poor and reckless even to know what money really was. In that moment while he stood in the doorway of Jellapore's pleasure palace, Bill, whom Carol had always called "Good-time Charlie" felt a sudden wild desire to be a poet

[119]

so that he might communicate to others the odd emotional tempest which the scene roused in him. He thought, "This is where I belong. This is the life I love." But it was finished now. He was a sober and dignified oil man.

Then he began to recognize the figures about the table—Jellapore himself, a little drunk, looking at the same time dark and sallow in his pale ochre racing clothes at the head of the table. And Mrs. Trollope small and leathery in her soiled, expensively cut white costume, watching with a desperate look in her small green eyes the shoe out of which Jellapore was pulling cards. For the first time it occurred to him that she was broke. And that horrible little man Mr. Botlivala, neat and plump like a doll; and four or five strangers, two of them Indians, the others Europeans of indeterminate nationality. Then suddenly as she leaned back, he saw the Baroness and recognized her, realizing at the same time that he should have known she was there all the time by the faint penetrating scent of patchouli mingled with the other odors of the stuffy room.

She was dressed fantastically in an evening gown made of black sequins, looking, he thought, grinning, like the madame of a gambling house brothel in a cinema. In the wig-like red hair was thrust a single white orchid—its corrupt and expensive purity grotesque above the evil avaricious old face. She wore a mass of old-fashioned jewelry set with dirty diamonds and rubies, but herself looked rather cleaner than usual. He thought, "It's the first time she's ever been to a Maharajah's party and that's how she thinks she should dress."

Then he looked at Carol herself, of whose presence he had been aware all the time. He had known she was there; he had seen her without seeing her, and consciously avoided looking at her because in some way the sight would have been painful to him. But now he plunged and watched her without her knowing that he was in the room. She had thrown off her hat sometime in the course of the evening and the streaked golden hair in the heat and the damp sea air stood up in ringlets all over her head. The pink suit of *crêpe de chine* looked a little worn now, but the diamonds which had been ridiculous in the bright Indian sunlight were brilliant in the garish light of the gilt and red-plush room. Her face, a little flushed, was like the face of a child having a glorious time at a party. It was fantastic that she could look so young and so fresh, the only clean and radiant person in the whole room, perhaps in the whole party. She sat with her elbows resting on the table, the diamond bracelets slipped low on her arms. She smoked a cigarette. On the table before her there was a partly emptied glass of champagne, and a great heap of chips. Evidently she was doing well at the game.

For a moment longer he stood watching her, and slowly he became aware of an irritation which surprised him. It was that there was a mystery about her—that this woman whom he had always accepted so casually, he did not know at all. It was not because, sitting there with her champagne, with the pile of chips before her, she appeared different from the girl to whom he had once been married. It was something over and beyond that—a revelation which came from the room, and the garish disillusioned people surrounding her. He thought, "There is something there which I missed—which I have never known." It was odd to feel that this woman whose body he knew so well should suddenly seem to him a complete stranger. Then he saw Mr. Botlivala lean over her and, placing one thin soft hand on her shoulder, say something to her, and in the heat he felt his hair rising on his head in anger. She answered Mr. Botlivala without looking up, and Bill thought suddenly, "I must be going nuts—acting like this, thinking things, being jealous of someone who no longer has anything to do with me."

He started toward her and at the same time he saw suddenly for no reason at all, against the sea beyond and the sound of the flutes and drums, the dark burning eyes of Colonel Moti as he talked about his friend Merrill.

Carol was enjoying herself. It was cooler now and she was winning at *chemin-de-fer*, which she needed to do, and Mr. Botlivala was not troubling her too much—nothing beyond standing behind her chair to demonstrate to all the world his proprietary interest in her. That too might have annoyed her but for the fact that presently she came to believe that the dark oily little presence brought her luck. And she was enjoying herself too because her luck was helping Mrs. Trollope. Whenever Mrs. Trollope wanted to take the bank Carol shared the cost with her and out of ten times they had lost only once. Nobody seemed to mind her luck except a middle-aged Portuguese, who kept swearing under his breath, and the Baroness. Jellapore didn't care at all. He could lose all evening and never miss it. He did not even seem to know whether he was winning or losing.

She had arrived at the party to discover that the Baroness was already there at six in the evening in the sequin dress with a white orchid in her hair, as if ready for a court function. At sight of Carol, she had come out of the corner where she sat alone, and greeted her as an old friend and Carol thought, "Poor thing! Probably she doesn't know anybody here," because either the society of Bombay was hopelessly dull or it was made up of individualists, sometimes none too savory in character, who were neither hospitable nor friendly unless there was something they wanted of you. So Carol, out of good nature and not to embarrass the old lady, acted too as if she were an old friend, but when it came to the matter of introduction she was lost. She couldn't even remember whether she had heard the name.

It did not seem to upset the Baroness. She said, "Baroness Stefani," brightly and then the die was cast. The old friendship was established; there was, as Carol soon discovered, no turning back.

Mr. Botlivala recognized something odd about the Baroness, but he was never very good at "placing" Europeans and from the dirty diamonds he gathered that she must be rich and therefore important. So he gave one of his middle-length bows and let it go at that. Only Mrs. Trollope gave a tart nod of her head as her face turned hard, and she said, "Yes, I know Madame Stefani." And there was an echo of tartness in her voice, the shadow of the scene at the poker table on the P and O liner—and something over and beyond that as well.

And now Bill, standing quietly behind Jellapore while Carol drew the cards from the shoe, was aware that something was happening at the table, something which had nothing to do with the game itself. Three persons at the table were concentrating all their being, whatever they were, upon Carol. They were Mrs. Trollope and Mr. Botlivala and the Baroness. Each of them wanted to gain possession of her; each of them wanted something from her. In the eyes of all three there was the same greedy look. And Carol herself was unaware of the thing; or perhaps she was so used to it that it no longer troubled her.

Then suddenly she lost to Jellapore and he heard the Baroness saying greedily, *"Le main passe,"* as she snatched the shoe with the cards from Carol's possession. At the same time Carol looked up and saw him and said, "Hello, Bill, why didn't you show up at the races?"

He laughed and said, "I've only spent the last five hours looking for you. When are you going to lay off this game?"

"I don't know. I'm doing awfully well—so is Mrs. Trollope. If I go away I may take her luck too." In a whisper she added, "She needs it. Get a load of those clothes."

He glanced toward Mrs. Trollope and at the same time she looked up and her eyes met his. Caught off her guard, the green eyes had in them a look of weariness and desperation. It changed at once into a brittle forced look of gayety. Leaning toward her he asked, "Cleaning up?"

"Doing all right. It's Carol's luck."

"So it's 'Carol' already," he thought. "They must have made progress." Then to Carol he said, "When you're ready to go, let me know."

"Okay," and in the next breath, *"Banco."* And to Mrs. Trollope, "Do you want half of it?"

Mrs. Trollope held her breath and took the great leap, "Yes." Jellapore held the hand. In it, Bill thought, there must be fifty thousand rupees—probably more money than Mrs. Trollope had in the world. Jelly pulled the cards, his eyes swollen and half closed by champagne. Carol and Mrs. Trollope won.

Then Carol pushed back her chair and said to Bill, "Come on. We'll go home now." The Baroness and the middle-aged Portuguese glared at her, but the fierce looks left her unmoved. The orchid in the hair of the Baroness had wilted by now and hung low over one eye. Carol only said, "I'm scramming while Mrs. T. has her money." She leaned across the table and said, "Come on, honey. Scram while the scramming is good."

The Baroness began muttering words under her breath but Carol remained unmoved. Mr. Botlivala said suddenly, "I'll take you home." But Carol said abruptly, "I'll go home with Mr. Wainwright. We're both living at the Taj. We'll drop Mrs. Trollope on the way." Mr. Botlivala sulked, the plump little hands began to twitch and the pupil-less black eyes to glitter. Then in suppressed fury he said to her, "I spend all the money and you go home with somebody else." Carol heard him. She gave him a quick look of contempt, said "Nuts!" and called out to Joey, "Come on and change our chips."

Joey, who acted as banker for Jellapore, went to a cabinet, unlocked it and began counting out notes. He was a little drunk and gave Carol three thousand rupees too much. She gave it back to him and then helped him to count out Mrs. Trollope's winnings. Carol had won seventy-five thousand rupees, Mrs. Trollope thirty-one thousand. Carol grinned, "Well, honey, we cleaned up. And we took it away from a troupe of Harpies. One more glass of champagne to celebrate and then we'll go home."

Then, while they poured the champagne, a commotion arose in the garden and as they turned toward the marble stairway, they saw coming up it the Maharani of Chandragar. She was being supported by two servants, one on each side. Her blonde head lolled to one side, her fat voluptuous body collapsed, her legs moved mechanically, as if they were artificial. Carol chuckled, "The Queen has passed out."

Mrs. Trollope said, "Damn it, now I'll have to take her home," and went quickly to help the two servants while Carol and Bill followed in a vague desire to be of some help.

Outside the Ghurka driver of the old-fashioned Rolls Royce had disappeared, and they were forced to wait while the porter went off to find him. But the Maharani, limp and a dead weight, grew heavy and the two servants eased her gently to a place on the steps where she might rest. Something in the maneuver roused her out of the coma and propping herself unsteadily on her hands, she opened her eyes and looked about her tipsily. Presently her eyes focused on the figure of Mrs. Trollope and the sight of her sister in the rumpled white suit appeared to rouse in her a demon. She tried to rise but only sank back again. Her lips opened and the flabby, once beautiful face trembled, but for a moment no sound came out. Then she gained control of herself and in a drunken voice, she cried out, "Oh, there you are, Miss Prissy! The disgrace of the family always hanging around waiting for a handout, with a jail-bird for a husband." Turning to the others, she screamed, "Once I wasn't good enough for her because I married an Indian —but when she's broke she always turns up to kiss my arse. A fine bloody sister, she is! With her fancy ways!" Then suddenly she collapsed backward on the steps and the big hat covered with flowers fell over her face.

Opposite her, Mrs. Trollope stood very still and straight. She was trembling and her face had gone a horrid gray color. In a whisper, as if she had no control of her voice, she was saying over and over again, like a mechanical doll, "Don't mind her. She doesn't mean what she says. Don't mind her."

Then mercifully, the porter reappeared with the Ghurka driver, the old contemptuous look on his flat Mongolian face. The two servants, aided by Bill, hoisted the Maharani to her feet and pushed her into the Rolls Royce. Then Bill said to Mrs. Trollope, "Do you want me to go with you?"

Still in an hysterical whisper, she said, "No. It's all right. She's too drunk to do me any harm."

Then she stepped into the car where her sister lolled back on the purple cushions, her dyed blonde head on one side, and the Ghurka, upright, proud and contemptuous, drove off.

When they had gone the porter brought a taxi from the line of drivers who always appeared like vultures at the sight of bright lights in Jellapore's pleasure palace, and Bill said, "The Taj Mahal Hotel."

Inside, the two of them rode for a long time in silence. The land haze had come up again and it was hot with the dreadful unnatural quality of night heat. At last Bill said, "Nice people."

Carol didn't answer him, and he said, "Couldn't you do better?"

"Not in Bombay."

Again for a time they were silent. Then Bill asked, "Why do you stay here?"

"I might as well be here as anywhere else."

"That's a funny thing for you to say."

"Why? I've always been like that."

He lighted a cigarette and absent-mindedly regarded the little lights in front of the Parvati Temple. They were remote—those hundreds of tiny lights—a million miles away in another world.

"You sound depressed."

"I am. I don't like the luck I've had all day at gambling."

"I wouldn't complain about winning so much money."

"It isn't that. If I have luck at gambling, it always means I have bad luck somewhere else."

He chuckled, "In love?"

"Maybe. Only I'm not in love—I never have been."

"Not even with me?"

In the darkness she placed one hand over his. "No, honey. Honestly not even with you. You've always been like a little boy to me—a nice little boy who sometimes is naughty but never means to be."

The speech startled him and stirred again that strange feeling he had experienced a little while earlier as he stood in the doorway watching her—that there was a part of her he had never known at all because she had never permitted him to know it.

Her hand still rested on his and the touch made him happy in a curious fashion he had never experienced before. His fingers slowly intertwined with hers but there was nothing in the gesture of desire or excitement; nothing of the pretense of desire in those fingers which always, by habit, caressed the hand of a woman because it flattered her and made her happy. It was more as if by the contact a current of sympathy and understanding flowed between them. For a long time they were silent and by the sounds he knew that they were passing the open strip of beach opposite the Towers of Silence. He could hear the chatter and the clang of gongs and smell the heavy scent of smoking torches.

"We shouldn't be here—either of us," he said. "It's too dangerous for the beachcomber type."

He heard her laughing quietly. Then she said, "It's not time for me to leave here yet."

"Why? What do you mean by that?"

She was silent a moment as if thinking. Then she said, "I don't know. It's hard to explain. You see, honey, I'm not very good with words. I only went to school until I was sixteen. Then they made

[126]

me Miss Minnesota. I'm not very good at words, but I guess it's instinct I mean. I'm waiting for something—some new turn of things." The fingers pressed his. "Don't laugh at me. I know what I'm talking about. It's always been like that—each time anything important has happened to me."

Then abruptly the taxi pulled up under the *porte cochère* of the Taj Mahal Hotel. In silence Bill descended, helped her out and paid the driver.

"Do you want another drink before going to bed?" she asked.

"Not unless you do. Tired?"

"No."

"Well, I suppose there's nothing to do but go to bed—I could take a little sleep."

They walked to the lift and as they stepped in, he said, "I heard news of your friend on the train."

"What friend?"

"Merrill—the missionary fellow who was ill."

"How is he?"

"Pretty ill."

"It's a pity. He's such a nice man."

"Good-night."

"Good-night."

He kissed her on the cheek, and the lift took him swiftly out of sight, a little tipsy and utterly bewildered.

On the third morning after the Jellapore party, Bill was wakened by Silas pounding on the door. When he opened it, the bearer was standing outside with a small, skinny, very black boy.

"Excuse, Sahib," said Silas. "Boy come from Colonel Moti—take you his home. Boy no speak Englees."

"Good. Get me some coffee and tell him to wait. I'll come right along."

Silas and the boy went away and while he dressed and drank the coffee Silas brought him presently, the old nervousness at seeing Buck Merrill came over him again. It wasn't easy to talk to an old friend again after ten years. What if he looked so ill that you wouldn't know him? What could they have to talk about save old times which were dead to himself and would be even more dead to a man who had led a life as active as Homer's? But he thought, "This is where I can't run away from what is unpleasant. Anyway I don't want to in my heart. I love Buck—even if the Buck I loved may no longer exist." But in his heart he knew that it was not his own character but Colonel Moti's burning black eyes which left him no chance of running away even if he had wanted to.

The skinny little black boy was waiting outside with Silas, squatting against the wall of the jail-like corridor. He rose at once and salaamed and trotted along behind Bill down the cool stairway, like a well-trained dog, his bare feet making a slapping sound on the cool gray slate. As they neared the foot of the great stairway, the heat coming in from the street through the lobby struck them full in the face. He looked at the clock to correct his watch and saw that it was only seventeen minutes past nine. Then as he turned toward the porter to call a taxi, he saw coming out of the Maharani of Chandragar's Rolls Royce three familiar figures which made an extraordinary combination.

They were Carol, Mrs. Trollope and the Baroness. They were all in evening clothes. From a taxicab which followed, coolies were unloading luggage which he recognized as Mrs. Trollope's Vuitton bags. Then Carol saw him and came toward him, an odd light in her blue eyes. He knew the look; it meant she was enjoying herself. She came across at once to join him.

He said, "For God's sake, what's going on?"

"We've been gambling at the Maharani's. Stitch is coming to live at the Taj. Her sister got drunk and tried to kill her with a pearl-handled revolver."

He grinned and said, "Never a dull moment. So it's 'Stitch.' You seem to be getting on."

"Don't speak of it to her."

"Of course not."

"Haven't you even been to bed?"

"No—not even the Baroness. Get a load of her if you want a good scare."

He looked at the Baroness who was, as usual, hounding the porter for telegrams which never came. She wore the same black sequin dress but the orchid was gone from her hair. The rouge on her cheeks and the violet shadows below her eyes, the long velvety artificial eyelashes made her appear a walking corpse in the day-light—a corpse made up and mascara-ed by an undertaker with theatrical ideas. He laughed and said to Carol, "How do you do it? I went to a business dinner last night and I'm licked."

"It's all mental. Where are you going at this ungodly hour?"

"I'm going to see your friend the missionary."

The statement appeared to sober her suddenly. "He's not dying?" she asked.

"No. I think I must have been sent for because he's better."

She sighed. "I'm glad. I wouldn't want anything to happen to him."

He laughed and said, "I didn't know you cared."

"Well, I do. He's nice and nice people are scarce."

"I'll tell him."

"Go ahead. I'll never see him again."

Then the Baroness and Stitch Trollope joined them and said, "Good morning," and he fled, depressed suddenly by the thought that in a few more years if she went on as she was going, Carol would be as terrifying a sight as the other two.

The little black boy showed a precocious knowledge of the intricacies of Bombay. It was he who, sitting by the Sikh driver, directed him to the Institute where Colonel Moti lived. Once beyond the Victorian Gothic Post Office, the city through which they passed was a Bombay new to Bill—a Bombay which for him, as for most foreigners, was beyond the pale, a world into which they never penetrated, a world full of smells and sweat and dust whose only sign in the world of Malabar Hill was an occasional noisy procession passing through on its way to the beach to bathe some smallpox victim in the Arabian Sea or to perform some religious rite older than the city itself.

The taxicab rattled over cobblestones and slithered along the tram tracks, always at top speed, now dodging a pedestrian, or skidding aside to avoid a group of children. Through the bazaar district past the great and beautiful Crawford Market, it dashed as the city grew steadily hotter and filthier. Bill thought, "Thank God, I don't have to go often through this part of town!" But a little further on he found that the heat and dirt through which he had just passed was nothing to what lay just ahead. The district grew shabbier, the houses a little taller, the burning streets more filled with sweating people, the smells of garlic and cow dung and filth became overpowering. He thought, "How do people manage to keep alive in such a world? How do children ever survive?" And then he was overcome by a sudden nausea and for a brief second was afraid that he would be sick out of the taxicab window. It wasn't, he knew, the nausea of the morning after but something born of the heat and smell and the horror of the life all about him. The life of any animal was decent and clean by comparison.

Then the taxicab halted suddenly, caught by a procession which passed the corner a dozen feet away. In the front an ugly old woman rode in a wheelbarrow pushed by a thin old man. In the burning sun, she writhed and moaned and tossed as the barrow bumped over the cobblestones. Her face was livid with disease and heat. Behind the pair came a scramble of poverty-stricken coolies and women, the men clad only in a bit of cotton, the women in cheap cotton saris, once white but long since stained and discolored. They were all wailing and moaning in the cloud of dust that arose from the flopping bare feet. Everybody, black to coffee-colored, was gray with dirt and dust. Four of the men carried gongs which they kept beating violently in time to their wailing.

It took ten minutes for the procession to pass and as the men with the gongs came opposite the window of the taxicab, Bill leaned forward and said to the Sikh driver, "What is it?" and the man said, "Smallpox, Sahib. Woman has smallpox. Driving out demon!" This time Bill leaned out of the window and was sick. No one noticed it. What had happened made very little difference in the filth of the district.

As the last gong beater passed, Bill leaned forward and yelled, "Get on! Let's get out of here!" But there was no escape from the filth and heat and smell. For another twenty minutes, with his eyes closed, his handkerchief pressed to his nose he rode through the Mill district. It wasn't that he was frightened of germs or infection; that was something to which he paid very little attention. It was only that he wanted to avoid the shame of being sick all over again, not for itself, but because in an odd way he was humiliated that he should be made to vomit by the horror of a world in

[130]

which millions of fellow men and children lived year in and year out, all their lives, without ever knowing any other.

After twenty minutes the taxi came into a district of old houses, some of them like small palaces, but mildewed and shabby, their once bright-colored walls discolored by damp, with the plaster falling away in patches. In and out of them swarmed hundreds of men, women and children, for the houses had long since reached the estate of makeshift tenements, a little better than those in the district through which they had just passed only because they were surrounded by small gardens, filled with filth and rubbish and shaded by dusty, withered peepul and banyon trees. These were the houses where the ancestors of Mr. Botlivala and the rich Khojas and Parsees who owned the mills had once lived, all those whose parents and ancestors had moved long ago to the splendor of the Race Course and the Willingdon Club and Malabar Hill.

At last the Sikh driver turned and said, "There it is!" Ahead of them Bill saw a big austere building rising above a gray stone wall and a second wall of sheltering trees. It was Colonel Moti's Institute.

The porter at the gate admitted them at a word from the little black boy and at the boy's direction the driver took Bill through a courtyard into a walled garden, cool with the shade of three great Java fig trees whose branches, like the umbrellas raised above the holy men at Benares, sheltered a small low bungalow. The driver tooted his horn and at the sound the small slim figure of a woman in a snow-white sari appeared in the doorway. She led by the hand a small, dark boy with a bandage over his eyes. As he opened the door of the taxi Bill recognized her as the serene strange woman he had seen on the ship coming out, the woman they said was a famous Hindu dancer.

"You are Mr. Wainwright," she said, smiling. The smile was like the opening of a magnolia flower.

"Yes."

"I am Colonel Moti's wife. He's at the laboratory. If he can get away he means to come over. In any case, Mr. Merrill is expecting you. He's better this morning. He was better yesterday. I'll take you to him."

Bill thanked her, and still holding the boy with the bandaged

[131]

eyes by the hand, she led him through two rooms to a verandah overlooking a garden and an open court. The rooms were cool and clean and almost empty save for some scarlet flowers, flamboyant against the gray wall. It was an odd sensation—coming from the horrible crowded streets and the smallpox procession into the clean serenity of Colonel Moti's house. Here was peace. Here was intelligence. Here was accomplishment and civilization.

As he stepped through the doorway, he heard a voice saying, "Hello Bill!"—a voice which took him back a long way into the youth which he had spent so recklessly. At the sound, he turned and saw Homer Merrill, lying on a bench of rattan, a light blanket thrown over him in spite of the heat. He said, "Hello, Buck," and went toward him, knowing him at once and yet not knowing him. The eyes were the same clear blue and the voice he had known at once. But the face had changed. The wholesome health and high color, which had always made Homer Merrill seem like a healthy young bull, were gone. The skin was saffron-colored and the face was thin—not wasted, but the warm look of health was gone. It was finer, more chiseled, beautiful, where before it had been merely handsome and healthy. The high cheekbones were there and the big generous mouth, but the sensuous look was gone from the lips; they were tight and drawn with fine lines at the corners. It was the face of one who had suffered, not only from illness, but from some illness that came from the spirit.

They shook hands and Bill thought, "It's the same big hand, only thinner and harder." Aloud he said with false heartiness, "Well, and how are you doing?"

Buck laughed, "Night before last I nearly popped off. But now I feel better. I've been feeling better for two days." Then suddenly the blue eyes were wet, whether from emotion or weakness, Bill did not know. Perhaps for both reasons.

Mrs. Moti stood for a moment, watching them, smiling quietly. Then she said, "I'll leave you two together. If my husband comes over I'll send him out to you." And Bill was aware suddenly of a goodness and intelligence shining from inside the woman. It wasn't that she said anything but simply that quietly she wished them both well—as very likely she wished the whole world. Then with the blind boy at her side she was gone like a shadow.

As she disappeared an odd tension sprang up between the two men—the strain of two old friends trying to come together after years of separation.

"What have you been doing?" asked Merrill.

"Working—I'm a reformed character. I'd have looked you up but I was only here for a little while and didn't know where to find you."

Merrill laughed, "It wouldn't be easy—in fact impossible if I'd been in Jellapore. You might have spent a month looking for me in the jungle or among the villages.

"How's it going—your work?"

"All right. Only there's so much of it." He sighed. "It's a little like an ant attacking a mountain." He looked at Bill and grinned. "You saw the district just before you got here—or maybe you didn't notice it."

"I noticed it all right. We ran into a smallpox procession and I threw up."

The grin on Merrill's face widened, "Well, that district is the real India. It isn't Malabar Hill. That's what you're up against."

"A stiff job."

"Yes, it's something to wrestle with for the rest of a man's life."

"Could I help?"

"You could give a little dough—that always comes in handy. It's not easy to raise money in India—even from the Princes and the millionaires. They've never had the habit. And the Government is always economizing with the excuse that it mustn't step on the toes of Indian superstitions."

"No sooner said than done. I'll send you a check."

Then the nervousness between them began to abate a little, and something of the old sympathy began to show itself. A curious sympathy it was, in which two men, very different, found themselves complemented.

"My looks didn't frighten you?" asked Merrill.

"No. You look different but I'd have known you anywhere. After all, we are ten years older. You can't go on forever looking like an adolescent football star."

It was easier now and when Mrs. Moti herself brought them gin and tonics the sense of strain disappeared altogether. It was almost as if her wise serene presence were a catalytic agent. She said to Buck, "I can't stay. Dr. Bliss has come to operate on Ali's eyes. I took them over to the laboratory. Ali didn't want to go without you but I persuaded him. I don't think he was frightened. It's just that he looks on you as a father."

Merrill threw back the blanket and stood up quickly. "I'll go over," he said. "You should have told me."

"It isn't necessary but I thought you'd want to know."

"Do you mind?" asked Merrill. "Why don't you come along? The laboratory is a hell of an interesting place."

"Sure," said Bill.

Together, with Colonel Moti's wife, they crossed the patch of scalding sunlight which was the courtyard between the cool bungalow and the laboratory. Merrill's walk was that of a man who had been very ill—uncertain, vacillating. Bill noticed that Mrs. Moti watched him without his being aware of it. The big dark eyes of the dancer, he decided, saw everything.

They went through a cool corridor and up a flight of stairs to a room which was Colonel Moti's office. It was a place of infinite order in which he himself stood, shining and white in his laboratory uniform. He greeted Bill and then said, "I'm acting as Dr. Bliss' assistant."

"Can I speak to Ali?" asked Merrill.

"If you're quick about it. He's in there," said Colonel Moti. "They're about to give him the anesthetic."

Merrill left them and when he had gone, the Colonel said, "Have you spoken to him yet?"

"No," said Bill, "I was leading up to it. I thought if I began too abruptly, he might refuse."

"That's true." The Colonel frowned and his black eyes looked serious. "I think he'll agree. He's been so ill. There was a crisis night before last. It's as if he had passed into a new phase. I think he understands how near he was to death. I think he's reached the stage where he would do anything to get stronger and be able to go on with his work. I think after what he has been through the idea of sin doesn't mean much. You need to be near to death to understand what a vicious old fool John Calvin was."

When Merrill came in again, he looked happy. He said, "I'm

glad I came over. The boy *is* frightened but won't admit it. He's a Moslem and the son of a head mahout, and his pride wouldn't let him whimper." He turned to Colonel Moti. "What does Dr. Bliss think? I couldn't ask with Ali in the room. He smells what he doesn't see."

"He's hopeful," said the Colonel. "But he won't really know for a couple of weeks at least. I'll go in now." To his wife he said, "Come in, Indira, you might be useful."

When Merrill and Bill were left alone in the cool office, Merrill sat down weakly and said, "That is a very great man."

"The Colonel?"

"Yes."

"He scares the bejeezus out of me. He doesn't say anything, but he always makes me feel a louse."

"He doesn't mean to. It's just that humanity means so much to him—humanity and science. He's one of the new sort—what you might call a human scientist."

Then while they waited they fell back into the old talk and presently they were both happy because they had found their way back to the room they had shared long ago when they were boys. Bill knew it and thinking, "Now is the time," he said, "The Colonel and I have a plan for you."

Merrill grinned, "Talking about me behind my back."

"Yes."

"What is it?"

"It's not very complicated. You're to come and live with me at the Taj Mahal Hotel. You're going to forget work for a little while and enjoy yourself. You're never going this side of the Post Office. It's going to be the races and the Willingdon Club and the Taj Mahal bar and Jellapore's pink palace. We're going to deprave you, willy-nilly."

For a second Merrill was silent. Then, grinning, he made the most astounding answer. He said, almost shyly, "But I haven't the right clothes."

Bill laughed, "That's nothing very difficult. I thought you'd have other reasons and balk like a mule."

"No, I decided the other night that I had a fling coming to me. I've never had one in my life. I thought I was going to die and in

[135]

the moment when I wasn't delirious I said to myself, 'Buck, you're a damned fool. Maybe you've gotten to be a prig. There's no one in the way now. You might try just once relaxing and yielding to temptation.' But honestly when I suddenly faced the fact that I might pop off during the night, what upset me most was the thought of the things I hadn't done—things you had done and seemed to enjoy." He grinned again. "So here I am—ready to be taught—if an old dog can be taught new tricks. Moti thinks it might do me good."

Listening, Bill saw slowly the sadness that lay behind the speech. There was even a certain enviousness which Bill had never suspected in Merrill among all people. It was as if he said, "What the hell! My past life has added up to nothing, I'd better try another, if it'll do any good. Anyway I'm not good for much longer." And the speech raised a certain alarm in Bill. What if Buck went off the deep end altogether? Sometimes that happened if a man tried too late in life to capture what had evaded him in early youth. Buck wasn't an old man—thirty-two—but for ten years he had led a hell of a hard self-denying life and before that he had never known what it was to be wild. Bill felt a sudden necessity to think and rising, walked over to the window to look out. The window gave on a courtyard filled with cages. In them were mongooses, white rats and mice, rabbits and monkeys and on the far side four or five glass cases in which slept an assortment of sluggish cobras, Russell's vipers and nasty little kraits.

Turning from the window he said, "What's the menagerie?"

"Moti's experimental animals," said Buck. "The snakes are for snake bite serum."

At the window Bill laughed and Buck asked, "What's funny?"

"Only you and me sitting here in blackest India surrounded by cages of animals and serums and what not—it's so damned unlikely. And Carol—" He turned and added, "By the way, I have a message for you. Remember the girl who came down on the train with you?"

"The big blonde girl."

"Yes. She sent you her best. You seem to have made an impression. That's how I knew you were in Bombay—through her."

Buck looked grave. "She seemed a good sort," he said. "She was very kind to me. I must have seemed a bloody nuisance."

"Yeah," said Bill, "she's a good girl." He was about to say more, even perhaps to tell Buck that once she had been his wife, but the door of the laboratory opened and Colonel Moti came out.

"It's over," he said.

Merrill turned quickly with an air of anxiety. "Successful?"

"Dr. Bliss thinks it ought to be. It's a question of time."

"Good."

Bill saw the sudden relief in the tired face and understood then for the first time the anxiety which had lain hidden all the time during their talk together.

"When will he be out from under?" Buck asked.

"Half an hour, perhaps," said Moti. "They're taking him back to the bungalow now."

"I want to be there when he wakes. Then he won't be so scared." To Bill, he said, "He's only a kid and he doesn't know anything about hospitals and operations. He'd never been out of the elephant stables till he came to live with us." He smiled as if he were talking to himself. "It all must seem awfully funny and frightening to a kid like Ali. He's like a puppy dog who loves and trusts you . . . he wants to get well and see again so when he grows up he can take his father's place as head mahout to Jellapore's elephants."

Bill thought, "He's thinking of his own kid too." And then almost at once came into his mind the picture of Jellapore himself —a little extravagant, dissolute Jelly, good-natured but useless, at the head of the *chemin-de-fer* table, gray-faced and sick with champagne. It was a long way from Colonel Moti and Buck Merrill to Jelly. Then the fantastic thought came into his head that he might be able to get money out of Jelly for Buck's work—just the money which Jelly lost in one evening of gambling would carry on Buck's work for a year.

The door opened and Dr. Bliss came in. He was a lean man with a rosy face and bright blue eyes, dressed in a makeshift surgeon's outfit.

"This is Dr. Bliss," said Colonel Moti, "Mr. Wainwright."

They shook hands and Colonel Moti continued, "He's on a holiday but because he is a friend, he operated on Ali. It was very good of him. Probably nobody else in the world could have done the operation."

[137]

"That's not altogether true," said Dr. Bliss.

"Oh, but it is," the Colonel said. "Anyway, when you're back in America, if you get tired and discouraged, you can always remember that you changed the whole life of one small Indian boy. You brought light to him." He chuckled, "And maybe you gave a head mahout to the Maharajah of Jellapore, Child of the Sun and Father and Mother of eight million people."

Buck interrupted him, "If you don't mind, I'm going back to the bungalow. I want to be there when Ali comes out."

"I'll say good-bye," said Dr. Bliss. "I'm going straight from here to the dock. My boat sails at two for Singapore."

Merrill thanked him again and Bliss said, "And good luck to you in your work. I'll get some money for you when I reach home. The way the world is today we've got to pull together."

Bill left him sitting beside the boy Ali, waiting for him to waken, and set out in the same taxicab for the Taj Mahal. On the steps Mrs. Moti stood to speed him on his way. As he left she said, "You've done Mr. Merrill a great deal of good. I think he needed more than anything some bond with the old life. You see he's been away so long, among us and the English—and then sending his boy back to school in America upset him. He's lonely and homesick and there isn't much we can do about that."

When he had gone she went back to Merrill, walking very erect and gracefully, like the women who bring the milk from the villages every morning a little after dawn. Merrill watching her as she came through the big cool rooms to the verandah where he sat beside Ali thought, "She dances even when she walks."

She only said, "If you need me when he wakes, call me. I think it will be all right to leave him with us if you want to go away for a few days. He's used to us now. He isn't so jungly as when he first came."

Then she went away and Merrill waited for the boy to stir and waken. He took the small dark hand in his, knowing that to a Moslem this was a gesture which meant more than mere friendship; it would mean to Ali that he was a man and the brother of Sahib Merrill.

And while he waited his thoughts were not of the boy but of

[138]

Bill. What Mrs. Moti said was true; the sight of Bill had done something which nothing else could have done. It made him feel young again and less tired; it took him back to the hills and lakes and waterfalls and cool woods of northern New York State, and that in turn gave him a kind of strength which was not to be found in all India; for in his heart he belonged always to a northern country where there was rain and the winters were fierce and the heat of summer violent, though different and less terrible than the eternal unrelenting heat of India. He was not one of those northerners who seem at heart to belong to the tropics and to establish themselves with no difficulty in a hot and exotic climate. And there was in him nothing of the beachcomber. This had made it all the more difficult for him, during all the years of heat and dust and monsoon among the villages. If there was any experience beyond the satisfaction of his work it lay in the mortification of the flesh, in forcing a body which revolted against heat and dust and filth to accept it without complaint. For at heart, and he knew it better than anyone, he was a Puritan.

It was not that he believed in the Puritan doctrine or even respected it; for any such acceptance he was too intelligent, and in his heart he was too sharply, even agonizingly, aware of all the beauty and color and sensual delight in the world about him. Now sitting there beside the unconscious son of Jellapore's chief mahout, he knew for the first time that since the moment he had met Bill Wainwright in a tap room in New York State, he had envied him. He had envied him during the years they shared a room together, during all the years he had lived in the jungle and among the villages. And never had he envied him more than during those few minutes they had been together in Colonel Moti's office while Dr. Bliss operated on Ali's eyes. It was not that he had ever envied Bill his money or the freedom it brought him; it was something else, much more profound than that. As near as he could discover, it was Bill's good-natured acceptance of life and the perfection of his adjustment to it. For Bill there was never any problem, no complicated and puzzling sense of values and standards to confuse and in a way to complicate everything he did. Bill was, in his way, a happy animal, whom everybody liked and many people loved. And Bill had never been hurt or wounded in any encounter. Thinking of it, it seemed to him that Bill was a child of the sun, to whom the Gods had given everything—good looks and charm and intelligence and physique and worldly wealth. It was probable that Bill had broken again and again half the moral laws which had been hammered into himself from childhood; he had even broken them again and again without suffering or retribution. He himself had observed the same laws only to go down with illness and despair.

In his thinking now there was neither self-pity nor self-indulgence; he had survived too much suffering, too much hardship to turn soft now. He regarded himself as dispassionately as he regarded Bill; they were two individuals who had lived long enough to serve as specimens possessed of a certain research value, and the two specimens, set side by side and examined carefully, led one to doubt many of the teachings of the Christian church and turn to Hindu beliefs in reincarnation. It was as if Bill had lived so many lives already that he had reached the stage of reward, while he himself had many lives to live before he could be free from the stupidities and prejudices which burdened the human race.

"Or maybe," he thought, "there is a curse upon one brought up in a religious and Puritanical family."

He knew now that he had always envied Bill. Long ago, on those nights when he had lain awake tormented with envy while he waited sleepless for Bill to return from his girls and drinking and gaiety, he had not told him of the envy because, priggishly, he had believed it would be bad for Bill and lead him into fresh dissipation. And now it was too late to tell him. The most he could do would be to take a fling at Bill's way of living, if such a thing were any longer possible.

Because in his heart it was the last forlorn hope—that perhaps Moti was right; perhaps if he lived more wildly—or as Moti said, "more like a decent normal human creature"—his health and strength might be saved to go on with his work. For that he was prepared to sacrifice anything—his morals, his deeply rooted standards of decency, even his immortal soul. For in his heart, that was the only thing that mattered—his body, his very soul were only instruments.

Then suddenly the current of thought which had carried him

far from the cool bungalow, and the Motis, and the boy at his side, was checked by the stirring of the small brown hand he held in his. Ali moved and sighed—the slow heartbreaking sigh of a child, the sigh burdened with the child's foreknowledge of misery and suffering that lies beyond its consciousness. And the sigh did an extraordinary thing to Buck's heart; it brought him closer to the boy than he had ever been. It roused to consciousness the old instinct, so profound in him since the very beginning, for protecting the weak and the less fortunate. Because at the core of his soul it was this which sustained and drove him onward in the face of everything. For a second, mystically, the small boy at his side became all of India, that ugly, tragic, swarming India which Bill had never seen save for a moment as he drove through the mill district.

He heard the voice of the boy saying, "Sahib Buck."

"Yes, Ali."

Then the boy sighed again, saying nothing, and Merrill said, "You see, everything is all right. There wasn't anything to be frightened of."

At first the boy was silent and presently he said, "I wasn't frightened, Sahib. I was lonely." And after a little pause, "Will I be able to see again—the sunlight and the elephants?"

"I hope so, Ali. We must be patient and trust God and his Prophet Mohammed." That, he knew, would help the boy, for to him Mohammed was not a mystical figure, but a reality, a human like himself and his dead father, the head mahout.

On the way back to the Taj the heat and filth and misery of the mill district disturbed Bill less than on the journey out. It was as if he saw it in a new way—not merely as an offense and a horrible spectacle to avoid, but as something else, which he could not explain to himself, but which had something to do with that cool and ordered oasis where he had left Buck sitting beside the mahout's son. It was a feeling which had something to do with shame. The experience with the two men and the woman at the Institute left him feeling uneasy and disturbed, why, he could not say. The mere circumstance that he thought about himself at all, left him puzzled. Until lately his own ego was something which had never troubled him at all.

Seeing Merrill again, after so many years, at once cheered and saddened him. He knew now that what Colonel Moti said was true; something had to be done about Buck and quickly, and very likely the Colonel was right in his belief that making him a human man was the only cure. When he thought of it, he chuckled—that after all these years he might succeed in those efforts which had begun as boys when they shared a room, to "corrupt" Buck and induce him to enjoy those things which had been put into the world for enjoyment—women, and wine and laughter.

Leaning back in the taxi, he took off his topee and with his handkerchief mopped it dry. The heat was that of a steam bath, the smells were overpowering. And then he thought of Dr. Bliss, so clean and pink and healthy with the clear blue eyes, saying, "We've got to pull together nowadays." The remark was such a pitiful, almost comical, understatement considering the state of the world, coming, too, from a man as great, as famous as the eye surgeon. He, too, had that peace and certainty which enveloped Moti and his wife—a kind of physical, tangible peace which seemed to annihilate all else, even the heat.

It was after one when he arrived at last at the Taj. The Lloyd-Triestino boat *Victoria* was in, and the passengers and their luggage cluttered the whole lobby. They were a different lot from those who came on the P and O; they weren't respectable, hard-working rather dull people simply using up in India forty years of their existence between the suburban and small town England where they were born and the dubious Paradise of Cheltenham where they would die; these passengers were of every nationality, shrewd business men, rich widows, fading middle-aged women with their gigolos, crooks and swindlers, Indian Princes and politicians, and all manner of adventurers; but they were all rich. One saw that at once by their manners and their luggage. Bill's eye, always on the lookout for adventure, regarded them one by one quickly, and discovered here and there fresh prospects. They were certainly a better lot than the outfit with which he came out to India. There was a pretty blonde not more, he thought, than twenty-two or three who appeared to be traveling with a dark woman a little older.

They would, he thought, be working the Maharajah racket—maybe chorus girls or girls who had gotten their start in Hollywood and were now hunting, on the make before it was too late. And there was a handsome woman of thirty-eight or forty who spoke Italian to her maid. Looking twice at her because the voluptuousness of her beauty and the whiteness of her skin demanded a second look, Bill thought that she was perhaps past her first youth—like a full-blown magnolia flower.

If it hadn't been so hot he would have been more interested. Now his only feeling was that the women could wait; he wanted a couple of cold drinks and some cold lunch. After that he could look for trouble. In the meanwhile, he wanted someone to lunch with him, for he hated eating alone, and the obvious person was Carol if she hadn't a dozen other engagements.

He pushed his way through the crowd to the telephone. Almost at once Carol's voice came back over the wire. She said, "Come on up."

"I want you to come down for lunch."

"It's too hot."

"Oh, come on down. There's a lot of new people come in on the *Victoria*. They'll make you laugh."

"All right—all right. If you'll come up and entertain me while I dress."

"Okay."

The sound of her voice made him feel less depressed. Above-stairs in her room he found her clad only in a pale pink and lace affair, sitting before the mirror brushing the streaked hair.

She said, "I've just had a shower and damn it, I only feel hotter." And before he could speak, she said, "I'm letting my hair go back to it's own color. Think it's a good idea?"

"I do. You'll look less like a strip-tease artist."

"Get yourself a drink and order me a gin sling."

He opened the door and told Krishna to fetch the drinks and as he came back, she stood up and he saw again, with a kind of pang, the perfection of the figure which belonged to Olga Janssen, Miss Minnesota, Carol Halma. There wasn't another like it in the world.

"That," he said, "is what has always gotten you into trouble."

[143]

"What?"

"That figure."

"You're telling me." She pulled a white skirt over her head, and asked, "What have you been doing with yourself?"

Krishna brought the drinks and Carol put hers on the dressing table. She did not seem to mind the presence of the Indian bearer in the purple and gold. Bill said, "I'm going to put out a picket line carrying signs 'Miss Carol Halma is unfair to Indian bearers.'"

"Oh, he's used to it. It doesn't seem to stir you much."

"After all, honey, there are no mysteries about it for me."

"Why, you dirty dog."

"You wouldn't like to begin all over again, by any chance?"

She pulled the blouse over her head and said, "Well, sometimes I've thought of it. I might if a certain party rushed me off my feet . . . only I've got big Swedish feet and it's pretty hard to rush me off 'em." Then her face grew serious. "Anyway, that's not what I'm looking for."

"What is Miss Carol Halma née Olga Janssen looking for?"

She laughed, "I'll be God-damned if Miss Carol Halma knows, only it's got to be something new." She put on her hat and two or three diamond bracelets.

He said, "Do you *have* to wear those in the daytime?"

"I've got 'em—why not wear 'em? I never pretended to be re-fined, did I?"

"God knows you never have."

"Anyway, I don't know why you're dragging me downstairs to that lousy dining room. Once upon a time you'd have given plenty to lunch up here with me alone."

"Maybe I would again."

It was true. He had come upstairs, without any such thought in his mind, but while he sat there, drinking and watching her dress, the old thing—that odd indefinable thing which had set him off long ago—began stirring with life. The thing which attracted him was an odd mixture of her beauty, her flat-footed honesty and her good humor. Being in love with Carol was always grand fun, like a successful party at Coney Island.

"Oh, no!" she said, "Oh, no. After I've taken the trouble to put on all my clothes I'm not going to take them all off again. Finish

[144]

your drink!" She finished her drink and said, "Come on, I'm hungry."

In the vast dining room with windows looking out over the hot bay toward Elephanta, they sat at a table near the door. One of the elements which had always drawn them together was the interest in a spectacle, in people, in all the hub-bub of living; it was this which had lured her downstairs, this love of life itself which these new people were satisfying. It was a good show—all the new people from the Lloyd-Triestino liner mixed in with the more or less permanent Bombay spectacle.

When they were settled at the table Bill said, "What's this about Stitch Trollope?"

"Well, her sister got a little stinking on champagne and tried to shoot her. It seems the two girls don't care for each other."

"I gathered that after the scene on Jelly's front steps. Where did it happen?"

"At the Maharani's palace. We went up there to play *chemin-de-fer*. Stitch and the Baroness kept winning and that seemed to burn up her sister. So suddenly without any warning, she pulls out a pearl-handled revolver and fires it. The Baroness knocked it out of her hand. It might have hit any of us."

"The people you know!"

She laughed, "They were your friends first, honey. You introduced them to me."

The handsome woman whom Bill had seen speaking Italian with her maid came in and sat near them. The maid was still with her. Bill noticed her at once, and Carol asked, "Who's that one?"

"Don't know. She came in on the *Victoria*."

"She looks like someone."

"Yes."

"By the way, the Baroness isn't so bad."

"She's about the worst thing I've run across in a good many years."

"She managed Stitch's sister—the only one who could."

She looked at him for a moment, "I've just discovered something about you."

"Yes. What?"

"You said my figure was the source of all my troubles. Well, you've got a worse source of troubles than just your figure. The trouble with you is that you've got to have everybody like you. You start off as everybody's best friend and it doesn't mean a damned thing, and then when they make demands on you, you just aren't there."

"Good-time Charlie!" he laughed.

"Yes, honey, that's it. If you don't like the Baroness, kick her in the pants but don't act as if you were crazy about her when you're with her."

"She amuses me and by nature I'm kind."

"Yes, part of that may be true—the kind part. But you're damned lazy too. You can't always be amused just at the moment it suits you."

"I'm a heel. Okay, I'm a heel."

She did not protest. She made no attempt to deny it. "Yes, honey, you are. One of the worst. Everybody thinks you a dream—so attractive, so pleasant, so amusing, so kind, and by God, inside there isn't a damned thing."

Slowly the banter had become serious. In the beautiful face there came a look which he had never seen there before. Somehow it was related to that Carol he did not know, the stranger he had divined as he stood watching her in the doorway. Now she was looking out of the window across the hot harbor toward Elephanta. Quickly he studied the face, and the idea came to him that she was changing, that before very long the Carol he had married, the Carol he had loved briefly as much as he had ever loved any woman, was slipping away. It was as if the old face were fading and a new one taking its place.

Then a new thought came to her and she said, "That's what was the matter with our marriage. I got charmed and fell for your front. I thought I'd find something behind it—but when I opened the door there wasn't anything there—just a false front."

"Lay off me." Inside he was squirming. His soul was suddenly like a worm with a pin thrust through it. He was annoyed, but he was not suffering. He was irritated, but he was not touched very deeply. In an odd way, he was afraid, or at least uneasy—why he could not say.

She laughed. "Okay, I'll lay off you. Let's talk about something else."

It was the first time they had ever come near to a quarrel, now when a quarrel no longer meant anything as lovers or as man and wife. Then he knew suddenly why he was so uneasy and afraid. She had never seemed to him so attractive, so lovable as she was in that moment as she sat turned away from him a little, looking across the hot bay toward the island of Elephanta. He thought, "My God! What's going on here?" And at the same time he heard her saying, "What's the news of your friend, Merrill? You haven't said anything about him."

He prodded his spirit and said, "He's better. We talked about you. He's coming to live at the Taj."

"What did he say?"

"He said you were a fine big handsome girl."

"Nuts!"

He grinned, "Well, that's what he said." He was having his turn now. He knew he had hurt her vanity. She did not care whether people thought she was beautiful. She wanted admiration for other qualities which perhaps she had never had. He felt a sudden impulse to go on being disagreeable, simply to get back at her.

"Well, what I told you was true. Your figure is your own worst enemy. Nobody can ever see past it."

"You bastard."

He laughed and after a little silence she asked, "When is he coming?"

"I don't know."

And then an extraordinary thought came to him, a solution to all the worry and responsibility for Buck Merrill. Carol was just the one to take care of him, to show him a good time. Her spirit, her health could carry anyone through. People were always feeding off her, usually scrubby, defeated people like Stitch Trollope and Mr. Botlivala and the Baroness. Buck would be a real job for her, and he'd be worth the effort. Carol was better equipped than himself to teach Buck to enjoy himself. The thought left him delighted and filled with a sensation of relief.

"I'll let you know the moment he appears. We'll go on a party." And almost at once he was sorry that he had spoken. It was an old trick and an old habit—to speak without first counting ten. Usually it did not matter, but this time it seemed an error, an important error.

Then he saw the Baroness coming in, dressed in a preposterous costume of white china silk and wearing a topee with a white scarf hanging down the back. It was extraordinary how much thought and effort went in the elaborate clothes which covered the fat mis-shapen body. Carol saw her at the same time and together they watched her make her way to the table where the Italian woman was seated with her maid. The two women greeted each other with a certain stiffness and the Baroness sat down. The table was too far away for Carol or Bill to hear what was said, but they were both listening.

"Now we can find out who she is," said Bill.

"Who wants to know?"

"I do. Why shouldn't I?"

"You mean—'Now I'll get a knock-down to her.' Well, good luck, Charlie. Only I wouldn't get too mixed up with that outfit."

"Why?"

"It smells bad."

At the same moment, they saw Mrs. Trollope come in and join the women at the table. They saw Mrs. Trollope being introduced to the Italian woman and her maid and saw the quick bright look of admiration in her tired green eyes for the warm smoldering beauty of the woman. Stitch had a whole new costume, a rather mannish and very smart suit of heavy oyster white Chinese silk, with a panama hat ornamented with a pert, dark green feather. At the moment all the weariness seemed gone out of her. She seemed ten years younger.

Bill said, "Stitch is all dressed up. Looks like a different woman."

"It's money, honey," said Carol. "All the money she's made since she took up with me that day at the races. Money and getting away from that tart sister of hers." She sighed, finished her coffee and lit a cigarette. "But it won't last. I can't go on bringing her luck forever and no matter how much she makes she'll always spend more than she's got. She's like that—born under the wrong sign. There's nothing to do about it."

Bill looked at her, troubled again. Funny that he had always thought her dumb. He looked out of the window. In the haze of heat from the bay, the sacred island of Elephanta had turned misty and unsubstantial as a mirage. Bill thought, "Something very queer is happening to me or to somebody around here."

It was true that Mrs. Trollope was riding on the crest of the wave. It had all begun with that chance meeting at the race course and gone on from there. It was as if Miss Carol Halma had brought her inexhaustible luck. She had won money at the races, more money the same night at Jelly's and finally more money at the party her sister gave in the gaudy pink palace on Malabar Hill —a party adorned dubiously by the same set which had gone to Jellapore's all night cocktail party.

About twice a year the Maharani of Chandragar "threw" a party, once in the autumn when she came back from Ootacamund and once just before the rainy season began and she left for the hills. She no longer spent even a day in the State of Chandragar itself. It had always bored her as an Australian of wild, uncertain parentage, to live in semi-purdah surrounded by a *zenana* of women who could barely read and write and spent their time eating or being massaged and oiled; and for a long time now she had had no choice in the matter. From the very beginning she had been a source of trouble to the State and now that she was a widow, the Dewan quietly made it impossible for her to return. So nowadays she lived between Malabar Hill and a bungalow in Ootacamund which, luckily, she owned outright.

The party she gave this time was an "extra" party, given not in honor of the sister who was visiting her but in the hope of winning back some of the money she had lost at Jellapore's pleasure house before she became too tipsy to play any longer. The gamble turned out to be a failure, for in her own shabby palace she had simply gone on losing. She couldn't afford to lose and when she saw most of her losings going to her sister, something like a brainstorm occurred inside the blonde head that was filled mostly with champagne, bon-bons and caviar. At five o'clock in the morning, she calmly, if unsteadily, opened her gold bag, took out a tiny pearl-handled pistol and aimed it at Mrs. Trollope. There were no very complicated motives behind the act. The sisters had always hated

[149]

each other. Champagne and the disaster of losing twenty thousand rupees moved Nellie Chandragar to achieve peace of mind in the simplest way she could think of—by shooting her sister.

Luckily, she was drunk and the Baroness, with a bar-room agility, had the quickness of mind to push the muzzle of the pistol upward so that the bullet only chipped a couple of rock crystal pendants off the chandelier above the *chemin-de-fer* table and harmlessly pierced the pink and gilt ceiling. And then the Baroness, with a strength remarkable in so elderly a woman, disarmed her and ordered the servants to put her to bed. The Maharani went away like a punished child, crying hysterically that she was sorry and ashamed. Then the game went on and when it was finished, a little after the sky over Malabar Hill was bright pink with the reflected glow of sunrise, Mrs. Trollope rose from the table, another thirty-nine thousand rupees richer.

It was the Baroness who suggested that she return with her spoils to the barren grandeur of the Taj Mahal Hotel. She said, "You can't go on leeving in de same house vit a voman who vants to keel you."

Mrs. Trollope said not to be alarmed because this attempt wasn't the first. It had happened several times, first when she was a little girl and Nelly tried to drown her by pushing her under a waterfall in New South Wales.

And then Carol had urged her to leave and go to the Taj Mahal. "You have plenty of money now," she said, "it'll last a long time if you take care of it." And immediately Mrs. Trollope thought it an excellent idea.

So the Baroness and Carol helped her to pack her belongings in the worn Vuitton bags—and sent a boy for the Maharani's Rolls Royce. They had more champagne to celebrate the migration and about nine o'clock they set out for the hotel.

The champagne had done its work and whatever barriers of pride or breeding or prejudice had separated the three were now gone. The Baroness no longer seemed a fat and preposterous and exotic insect. She had saved the life of Mrs. Trollope and the feud between them was dead, at least temporarily. Mrs. Trollope was escaping and everyone was enjoying the lark.

The Baroness, taking Mrs. Trollope's hand in her fat, be-ringed one, said, "Und now, dear, everyting is going to be vunderful. Dis Carol, she brings luck, hein? She change everyting. Never you vorry, you girls. De Baroness vill look oud for you." Her voice was hoarse with champagne. Carol's head was clear enough to think, "She's exactly like a bull-frog."

"You see, girls," the Baroness continued, "if you ever ged into trouble, I can geeve you a job. I've god a whole string of night clubs in Budapest and Cairo and Paris and Milano. Dey make de Baroness plenty money, ha! ha!"

"That's swell," said Carol. "We'll count on you, won't we, Stitch?"

The old woman, wagging her head, said, "You can gount on de Baroness. She never led ennybody down."

"Sure," said Carol, "I'll be the hostess and Stitch can run the cash register in the bar."

The Baroness thought this a good idea. "Sure," she said, "a great team. Ask Jellapore. He knows my places. He's spent plenty money dere. We godda dress up Mrs. Trollope. She's god style. I know how ve dress her—very smart—vit a sort of vemale dinner jacket vit a monocle."

"Sure," said Mrs. Trollope, "that's it." She was listening, but her mind was elsewhere, considering all the things she was going to do with the money which Fate had taken so ironically from the sister she hated because she had been once, a long time ago, very beautiful, like a lovely Jersey cow. She would get a lot of new clothes and write to London and see about getting some of her jewelry out of pawn, and if she went on winning with the capital she already had, she and Carol would go back to America by way of Singapore, Saigon, Sydney and Hawaii; maybe by that time, Carol might want to go to Hollywood and then something might turn up. Now that she was free of Nelly and had money in her bag, anything could happen. She couldn't look at Carol without wanting to cry. She was like a goddess, not only in beauty, but because since she had come into her life at that table in the Taj Mahal bar, everything had changed. To hell with Jim Trollope now. He could rot in Brixton jail. She thought, "I've entered a new cycle of life. The stars have changed. I knew it was coming." The first thing on the list of new plans was to go to a fortuneteller.

Beside her the Baroness was happy, for she was enjoying one of the rare moments in her gaudy, bedraggled life when she did not feel alone. She had first become conscious of her ugly face and dumpy body as a child of four, long ago in Prague, when she had been knocked about, snubbed, mistreated. Long ago as a young woman she had crystallized out of a dull unhappy existence a simple and direct philosophy—that she must have money because money gave you the power which otherwise had been denied her. It was an excellent substitute for beauty and charm and culture. For nearly forty years she had gone ahead ruthlessly—organizing, acquiring money, achieving power, in any way her shrewd, unscrupulous head could invent. Even the War hadn't knocked her business on the head, for during the four years she had earned a fine return as head of a small net-work of female spies. She was rich now, and powerful. But all her life she had wanted only one thing, and that was that people should be nice to her. And this, for which at times she would have given all her money and her power, had been denied her, save for a half dozen times like this moment when she sat between Carol and Stitch Trollope, riding back from Malabar Hill to the Taj Mahal.

And so the trio, still gay and full of champagne, had arrived at last to encounter Bill in the big lobby of the hotel on his way to visit Buck Merrill. The Baroness saw him slip away quickly and thought shrewdly, "He's worse than Mrs. Trollope. She calls names, but he smiles and is kind and then gets out from under." A hard life had taught her a great deal about people.

When he had gone, Carol went with Stitch to the desk and arranged for a room with a view not of the bay and the sacred islands, but on the city side with a view of the Readymoney building; it would make her money last a little longer. Mrs. Trollope didn't mind. She had escaped from Nelly and was near to her touchstone Carol.

Carol and the Baroness, still under the impetus of the champagne, went up to the room and, to celebrate the event, offered to help her unpack, but Mrs. Trollope, conscious of the shabbiness of her clothing, refused, saying that they all needed sleep and that it was already too hot to make such an effort.

When they had gone, she had a shower, took out another shabby tropical suit, donned it and quickly went out straight to the Army and Navy Stores. There she found a new costume and a suit which pleased her (she was easy to fit; she had the figure of an undeveloped young girl of sixteen). Then she was measured and ordered eight day dresses and four more suits. She selected seven hats that suited her and bought two dozen pairs of silk stockings, five pairs of shoes, five dozen expensive handkerchiefs and several outfits of imported French underwear. From the Army and Navy Stores she went straight to a decaying old house in Calaba on the bay.

It was a big house surrounded by an imposing garden and had been made over by Mr. Botlivala, who owned it together with about one-tenth of Bombay, into flats. She went through the garden gate and straight up the stairs to the third floor where she knocked on a door which bore the sign "Rama and Paravati— Astrologers and Fortunetellers." The door was opened by a lean middle-aged man with gray eyes set oddly in a very dark skin, the eyes of some Cockney sergeant who, a generation or two before, had spent a night with a sweeper girl in a cantonment in the Central Provinces. He was Rama. He remembered her at once as the sister of the Maharani of Chandragar, who also came to see him. He was a man who forgot very little.

Leading her into a dark, curtained room smelling of incense, he sat down at a teakwood table, took out a ball of crystal and went to work.

It was very successful. He was a wonderful fortuneteller. He told her everything she wanted to hear—that she had entered a new cycle, that there was a person near her whose influence was of the greatest importance because he or she (he could not quite divine which) was a bringer of luck. There were, however, two influences which were bad, both of them male, one a little dark man (Mr. Botlivala, said Mrs. Trollope to herself), and the other a good-looking blonde man, very plausible and charming, but not to be trusted. ("That," she thought, "would be Bill Wainwright.") She paid him out of the shrinking roll of rupee notes and went away to the taxicab which she had kept waiting.

It seemed to her that as she left her feet did not strike the garden path beneath the pepper trees. It was as if she floated out of the house. In the assurance and satisfaction provided by the conference with Mr. Rama, the weariness of twenty-four sleepless hours utterly vanished. She felt young again and even gay as she had been long ago in the lumber camp in the bush, before she was sent to London to school to be made into a lady and met Jim who was now in Brixton, and before she discovered how cruel and bitter life might be. God was rewarding her, after all, for all her sufferings. She had even escaped that awful and bitter loneliness that had possessed her for so long. All on account of Carol Halma.

"Carol!" her heart sang, "Carol! Carol!" And for a second she again went through the strange experience of feeling that she *was* Carol Halma, that somehow her own skinny, mannish figure had been transformed into the lovely body of the girl, that body which Bill had said was the source of all her troubles.

All the way back to the hotel, her heart sang, and when she arrived in her room, she found a note from the Baroness. It was written in French, very bad French; even Mrs. Trollope out of her boarding school teaching was aware of how bad it was. The Baroness asked her to lunch to meet the Marchesa Carviglia. "The Marchesa," the Baroness wrote (with the wrong accent), "is an old friend of mine. She worked for me once. I think you will find her very sympathetic."

And so she found herself at lunch in her new clothes with the Baroness, the Marchesa and her maid. Having been brought up in the Australian Bush and having had a share pusher for a husband, Mrs. Trollope had encountered in her time a good many unsavory characters, and so at the lunch she began to suspect a great many things. She discovered that the Marchesa had once been a very beautiful woman, and that she had also been, and still was, very stupid. She discovered also that the Baroness had some mysterious power over her, and that, with a look of slyness in the green eyes, she kept reminding the Marchesa of the power. It was a cat and mouse game. But most important of all, Mrs. Trollope began to suspect what the profession of the Baroness really was. It certainly was not spying.

The next day Bill went to lunch at Government House. He had no desire to go but there was no way out. Some friend in England, who he did not know, had written to arrange that he be asked to lunch, and so the business had to be gone through; it did not matter that the Governor of the Bombay Presidency had never heard of him and was not the least interested, and it did not matter that Bill himself hated the idea of putting on his best clothes and spending two good hours out of his life making conversation between two strange women whom he would very likely find dull and whom he would never meet again. It was one of the things which had to be done.

On arriving he found the party exactly as he expected—the Governor's wife and a congregation of middle-class English tourists and Bombay business men and their wives. He found it very difficult to tell one from another except for one strange female dressed in the robes of a Buddhist monk and a very sprightly old lady of eighty-seven traveling with a companion, who kept telling everyone her great age and leading them up to the observation that she was a remarkable woman to be making a trip round the world at her age. And then at the same moment from one door the Governor came in, a small, cold little man, with a preoccupied air —at that time the terrorists were after him—and from the other the handsome Italian woman who was presented to the Governor by his wife as the Marchese Generalissimo Carviglia's wife. "You remember, John, General-Commander Carviglia who visited Malta while we were there."

"Of course," said the Governor, who did not remember at all. And then past the tall Sikh guards in red and gold, they went in to lunch.

It was hot, for Government House lay on the edge of the muggy bay just at the foot of Malabar Hill. Bill found himself between the strangely costumed female and the Marchesa Carviglia. Hoping to save the best for the last, he turned to the female lama.

She presented a remarkable appearance. Her face was long and lean, with protruding teeth and very thin hair, and she was dressed loosely in what might have been called an adaptation of a Buddhist monk's robe. It had long sleeves and was belted by a yellow cord. On top of this she wore an extraordinary amount of Indian art jewelry which made a clanking noise every time she moved.

She turned out to be the sister of a Duke and lived most of the time in a cell in a Buddhist monastery in Bengal. There seemed

[155]

to be no impropriety in the arrangement, although all the other occupants were monks. When she traveled, she told him, she always lay down and slept on the station platforms along with the coolies and sweeper women. This, she said, was very good for the soul. Within a few years she would, she said, be entirely above discomfort and so very near to Nirvana. As a young woman she had, she told him, lived a very worldly life, frequenting balls and Bohemian studios. Then a disappointment in love turned her thoughts in a more spiritual direction and on a visit to her dear cousin Lord Curzon, at the time he was Viceroy, she had embraced the Buddhist faith. Since then she had been completely happy.

"Like a cow," thought Bill, who aloud, said, "All this is very interesting."

Then she opened her robe and from some place inside brought out several rather greasy tracts published by the All World Buddhist Society and presented him with them. He thanked her and thrust them into his coat pocket. When the whole table turned as if at a given signal, he found himself talking to the Marchesa.

Almost at once he became aware of two things—first, that her beauty, only a little faded, was of an extraordinary, voluptuous sort. She had enormous black eyes with fantastically long lashes, an ivory white skin and very beautiful hands with nails done in a curious acid shade of magenta-scarlet. The aura was one of mingled viciousness and stupidity. The attraction was one of mingled excitement and repulsion. She was, he thought, rather like an unhealthy tropical plant, like the legendary Upas tree which poisoned you as you lay sleeping in the shelter of its branches. The second discovery was that she spoke only Italian and French and her French was as bad as his own.

After they had struggled for a time over the bumps of countless misunderstandings arising from the lack of a common language, he mentioned the Baroness and almost at once a change came over the woman. For the first time she displayed animation and interest. A dull fire smoldered in the black eyes and a faint color appeared beneath the water-lily skin. In bad French she said, "The Baroness is no friend of mine. I knew her once in Paris—not very well."

"I know what you mean," said Bill. "She is everybody's most intimate friend." He supposed that she had forced herself on the

Marchesa as she had upon himself and Carol and Mrs. Trollope and Jellapore. She had, of course, the hide of a rhinoceros.

The Marchesa grew more vehement. "You must not believe anything she says. She is a wicked woman who makes up stories about people—evil, malicious stories."

That Bill could not doubt. One needed only to glance to discover that she was evil. Still, it was odd that only yesterday the Marchesa and the Baroness had been lunching together apparently in perfect amity.

"She is a witch," said the Marchesa Carviglia. "But let's not talk about her. She upsets one's digestion."

And then he was made aware by the tinkling of the jewelry on the Duke's Buddhist sister that they were rising from the table. The Governor having finished one of the most odious of the tasks required by his position—that of entertaining people who brought letters—excused himself on the pretext that he had a terribly busy afternoon before him (overshadowed always by the possibility of being shot or blown up) and left the room, relinquishing the task of entertaining the strange assortment of guests to the long-suffering wife who had largely made his career by being patient with bores.

Then came the part of the official luncheon which Bill designated as the "hanging around." This consisted of making dull conversation with people who bored you and whom you would never see again, who stayed as long as possible in order to have a good story for the suburban bridge parties when they returned home. For Bill there wasn't much choice. It was necessary to remain for at least fifteen minutes, and for that period he found himself again with the Marchesa. The conversation wasn't very interesting and he found himself wishing that he knew Italian well enough to divine a little of her background and origin. It was extraordinary how much accent and grammar and the turn of phrases could reveal of people's background and character. Speaking badly another language was like wearing a domino and mask.

After exactly fifteen minutes he said good-bye to the Governor's wife, who was beginning to look pale and shaken. As he said good-bye to the Marchesa, the long white fingers with the magenta nails held his hand for a long time, and a soft look came into the opaque eyes.

"You must look me up at the Taj," she said. "Very soon."

"Of course," said Bill and to himself he said, "Whee! That's progress."

The garden of Government House, pitched toward the sun at the foot of Malabar Hill, seemed to trap the heat. The red cannas which filled the beds in front of the verandah and the red tunics of the tall Sikh guards looked hot. Going out to lunch in Bombay was always a horror because it meant that you had to return in the heat between two and three in the afternoon. His white costume began to wilt and shrivel but at the moment he did not mind. He suspected that things were beginning to happen, the way they happened in the East, where the heat seemed to speed up and exaggerate every process of life, even to human contacts. What was happening he did not quite know, but the set-up looked very promising—the Baroness, the Marchesa, Carol, Mrs. Trollope, perhaps now even Buck. For the first time he was not sorry that Hinkle was off shooting in Burma. Business could go to the devil when life was so much more entertaining. The strange inviting handclasp of the Marchesa had produced a kind of excitement he had not experienced in a long time, if indeed he had ever experienced it. He knew by now that she was made for one thing and that was certainly not conversation. But it was Carol he wanted to see. For twenty-four hours, since their slightly acid lunch, he had neither seen her nor heard from her. When he was with her life seemed to take on a new savor, even when she was disagreeable.

He had meant to go at once to his room and have a shower and sleep until the heat had abated a little, but when he stopped at the desk to ask for mail or messages, the clerk said, "A Mr. Merrill who said he was a friend of yours has come in. I gave him the room next to yours. I hope I haven't done wrong."

"No, you were perfectly right."

He took the letters which had come in on the *Victoria* and glanced through them. There were three from London and two from New York and one, a message by hand, from the Company's office. He didn't trouble to open them. It was extraordinary how remote the western world had suddenly become. It was no longer of any importance. It had become hazy like Elephanta in the heat of the mid-afternoon. That, he knew by experience, was what you might call the second stage.

The great jail-like corridors were cool after the heat of the streets. Wearily and with unselfishness he passed the door of his own room and went to the room which Merrill had taken. He knocked on the door and a voice which he recognized with a sudden start of astonishment said, "Come in."

It was Carol's voice and as he opened the door he saw her bending over a suitcase taking out articles of clothing. She looked hot and uncomfortable. The streaked hair was all in disorder and as she turned toward him, he saw that her face was covered with small beads of perspiration. Lying on the bed was Buck Merrill, his face white and shaken. He was just recovering from one of his attacks.

For a moment the spectacle left Bill stranded—Carol, who never rose if she could help it until the cool of the evening, working in the suffocating heat of mid-afternoon for a man she had seen but once before in her life.

Buck nodded at him and tried to grin. He was dressed in a shabby suit of white duck that had turned yellow from years of punishment by the *dhobi*. The suitcase out of which Carol was removing a nondescript set of clothes, was a cheap paper affair, badly worn, of the sort the villagers carried when they went on a journey.

Bill asked, shyly, "How are you feeling?"

"Better, thanks," said Buck. "The last day or two it hasn't lasted as long."

Carol looked up from the drawer she was filling with Buck's clothes. "I found him in the hall leaning against the railing. Somebody had to look after him, so I came along."

So that was it. Bill felt suddenly angry. It wasn't jealousy. It was anger, and injured vanity. She had never taken any trouble over himself, and now she was looking after Buck as if he were a baby. Very likely she'd waited there in the hall for him to come along. But that was too absurd. She couldn't have known when Bill was coming to the hotel. Then suddenly he was ashamed of himself.

[159]

Carol closed one of the drawers with a bang. "Where have you been all day?"

"Working . . . and I went to the Government House for lunch."

"Who was there?"

"Nobody . . . except the Italian woman who lunched with Stitch and the Baroness."

"Snob!" She pushed her hair back from her blue eyes and asked, "What was she like?"

He told her frankly, caddishly, everything about the Marchesa, even to the prolonged handclasp at their parting. "She's a very handsome woman," he said, "I could go for her." He said it to annoy Carol.

He failed. She only laughed and said, "I know the camellia type—cool and vicious and a little too ripe. Getting to be an old lecher. It isn't time yet. You're too young."

That he failed to annoy her made him angry again.

Buck sat up suddenly, "What about a drink?" he asked.

"It's on me," said Carol. "I want to give you boys a party."

"No," said Bill, "the first drink of the new life is on me."

"Okay," said Carol.

Bill opened the door and called to Silas who sat cross-legged outside the door of his own room and told him to bring the drinks. He had barely closed the door when there was a knock and to Carol's, "Come in," the door opened and Mrs. Trollope appeared.

"My servant said you were all in here. May I come in?"

"Sure," said Carol. "We're having a drink. Do you know Mr. Merrill—Mrs. Trollope. You're both friends of Bill's."

Mrs. Trollope smiled but it was a pinched barren smile. Something came into the room with her, something at once indefinable, unnameable, but none the less acute. She smiled, but it was as if the smile were wrenched out of the depths of her soul. With the quickness of a serpent she took in the scene—Buck sitting on the bed, Bill leaning against the old-fashioned washstand and Carol standing between the bureau and the half-unpacked suitcase. In her pursuit she had blundered into an atmosphere, a world in which she had no part, a world which was in a way beyond her understanding. It was as if a wall of glass or crystal separated her from the other three. She was in the same room with them; she could

[160]

reach out and touch them, yet for the moment there was no means of communication. Something new had come into her relationship with Carol, and she herself, with her odd abnormal brain knew what it was, without knowing. She knew then, long before any of the others divined anything.

Carol too was aware of the thing which came into the room, changing and complicating the whole atmosphere. She stiffened and turned cold without quite knowing why, except that in her brain a voice said, "She's been following me. Spying on me. Fun is fun, but that's something I won't tolerate."

For Mrs. Trollope, her face now leathery and gray, an eternity passed in that second of understanding. During that second as she stood with her back to the door, her heart missed a beat or two.

Dryly she said, "I'd love a drink."

"I'll send for it as soon as Silas comes back," said Bill.

Buck Merrill gave her a cigarette and lighted it for her, and then suddenly there seemed no place for them to go. Carol went on with the unpacking, but that did nothing to help the silence. It was Mrs. Trollope who broke it by saying, "The Marchesa's husband, it seems, is a big boy in the Fascist organization. She's been to Government House and she's going to Delhi to stay with the Viceroy."

"I sat next to her at lunch today," said Bill. "I should say that she's not quite bright."

Carol looked up from her nearly finished task. "But sexy, according to Bill, the cad."

"She's not so bad," said Mrs. Trollope. "She's good-natured, anyway."

Then Bill explained to Buck about the Baroness. Silas brought in the drinks and departed to bring another for Mrs. Trollope.

"What is the Marchesa?" asked Bill. "Is she Italian?"

"No," said Mrs. Trollope, "she's Levantine. . . ."

"And lush," added Carol, putting away the last of Buck's sarongs and closing the drawer. Then she turned toward them and said, "And now what do we do?" It was necessary to do something. They all knew it. The atmosphere had become intolerable.

"There's always the races," said Bill, and at the suggestion Mrs.

Trollope relaxed and brightened perceptibly. "We could all go to the bar and have a drink and then go."

"All but Mr. Merrill," said Carol, "maybe he doesn't feel well enough."

Buck grinned, "I could stand it," he said. "I'm all right as soon as it's over. I'm usually good for another day or two."

As if by a common plan, they finished their drinks and went downstairs. Once outside of the four walls of the barely furnished room, the tension disappeared and a kind of hysterical gayety took its place. The bar was crowded with the passengers from the *Victoria* and swarms of tourists from a cruise ship which had just come in, mostly middle-aged and elderly spinsters and widows who sat for a long time over one dangerous gin fizz, watching the wicked life of the East.

"Tomorrow morning," said Bill to Buck, "we're going to the Army and Navy Stores and buy you an elegant trousseau. You can't lead a fast life in those sickly dungarees. And the trousseau is going to be paid for out of the funds of the Amalgamated Oil Companies."

"No," said Buck.

"Yes," said Bill, "it'll go in my expense account. Nothing will please my old man more than to know that a little of his crooked money was going to so good a cause. He's already beginning to give away millions to appease his bad Methodist conscience." He ordered another gin sling and added, "It's wonderful how rich men grow pious as the grave draws near."

Because of the heat, they took two taxicabs to the races; Carol and Buck went in one and Bill and Mrs. Trollope in the other. It was not what Bill had wanted or planned, but somehow it had happened, he did not quite know how. If Carol had arranged it, she did it with great deftness. It wasn't only that he himself wanted to be with Carol, but the arrangement put Mrs. Trollope, who had had the same idea, into a nasty mood. He had seen her depressed and elated, he had seen her angry with the Baroness, but he had never yet seen her sulky, and it was not a pretty spectacle. She was petty, like a spoiled child, and curiously enough, more feminine than he had ever known her to be. On the way she complained of the heat, of the way the taxi driver drove, of the smells from the beach and presently she said, "I don't know why in hell I ever came here anyway. I hate the East."

She did know why she came—because broke and with her life in ruins, she was homing for Australia. And she was in Bombay because she hadn't money enough for her fare the whole way to Sydney and she had stopped off hoping to get it from her sister. And now that she had the money, not from her sister but from gambling, she did not want to leave Bombay because Carol was there, and suddenly she couldn't imagine a life, however luxurious, which did not include Carol. It would be no life at all.

She varied her complaints only to ask, "Who is this Mr. Merrill?"

Bill, hot and annoyed by her mood, told her as briefly as possible about Buck, and when he had finished, she said with a curl of the lip, "Oh, a missionary."

"No," said Bill, and tried to explain to her that he was a kind of combination of doctor, educator and agricultural agent. But this made no impression. She only said, "A missionary is a missionary—I know the kind."

Then Bill, who was always polite, always good-natured, said abruptly, "It isn't just the same and to hell with you." To which Mrs. Trollope replied, "Shut your mouth. I won't be sworn at."

"You will," said Bill lighting a cigarette, "unless you change your disposition."

"There's nothing the matter with my disposition."

And after that they did not speak again and she sat, her lips set in a hard line, looking out of the window at the bay. At the race course she got out first and without speaking to him walked to the gate while he paid the taxi, impatient because he took so long to have a fifty rupee note changed.

Inside, Carol and Buck were waiting for them in the shade of a jacqueranda tree. They were laughing at something and it struck Bill suddenly that Merrill seemed a different man from the ill, gray-faced fellow he had seen lying on the bed in the hotel a little more than an hour before. The worn, shabby yellow clothes were the same but the man inside them was changed. He seemed to stand a little more erect and in the pale cheeks a faint color—the merest shadow of the old ruddiness—had appeared. As Bill and

Mrs. Trollope approached the pair—Mrs. Trollope hurrying and walking ahead as though she were not with him—two thoughts occurred to him, one, an old thought, that it was remarkable the effect Carol had upon men, and the other, that she was taking Buck over and showing him a good time, without even being asked to do it. It had just happened. It was as if the whole affair had been taken out of his hands, and now that it had happened he did not like it.

They were laughing, it seemed, because Carol had just shown him the Baroness and Mr. Botlivala who, Carol said, looked like a pair of beetles equipped with racing glasses. The Baroness had added to her white costume and topee a shooting stick, which she had discovered was a smart bit of equipment carried by most of the Government people and their wives. And Carol too was amused, although she said nothing of it, by the astonishment of Mr. Botlivala at the sight of her in the company of a man so shabbily dressed as Merrill, so shabbily dressed that Mr. Botlivala had not even considered him a menace and so showed no interest. It was the Baroness who displayed shrewdness and curiosity. No sooner had she been introduced than she began asking direct questions of Merrill. Where did he come from? How long did he mean to stay in Bombay? Where was he living? What did he do?

Buck had answered her as quietly and directly as possible, a little astonished by her hostile cross-examination. It was as if she were a detective examining a suspicious character. When she was gone, he asked, "Who is she? Where does she come from?"

Carol laughed. "I really don't know. She says she lives in Cairo but I guess she doesn't live anywhere in particular. She says she owns restaurants and night clubs. Mr. Botlivala thinks she's pretty important or he wouldn't be going about with her."

But they were gone now, over to the paddock among the owners and the Arab horse traders.

Mrs. Trollope was nervous. She said, "Let's go and place our bets on the second race. There's just time." The ill-humor was partly gone, overshadowed by her desire for more money.

"Okay," said Carol, "but I'm not betting today."

Mrs. Trollope suffered a start. "What do you mean?"

"Nothing," said Carol, "I've got a hunch. It's not the day for me."

"Why?"

"I can't tell you why," said Carol, and then added, "because I don't know. But I'll go along. You can touch me for luck if you like."

It wasn't what Mrs. Trollope wanted but it was better than nothing. Together the four of them went to the betting booth, the two men walking behind.

Buck was a little like a small boy seeing Coney Island for the first time. In all the years he had been in India, he had been twice inside the Taj Mahal and never to the races. He kept asking questions, about the club enclosures, the betting systems, the Arab horse traders.

Mrs. Trollope bet a thousand franc note on what a Eurasian tipster in the Taj Mahal had told her was a sure thing. The horse came in fifth, and Carol said, "I wouldn't bet today. I've got a feeling in my bones. The stars are wrong." The last phrase she had used because by now she was aware that it was the most convincing argument which could be employed. By now she knew Mrs. Trollope's dependence upon superstition and fortunetellers. It was the dependence of someone who was frightened.

So on the next race, Mrs. Trollope refrained from betting, although her fingers itched to put money across the board this time. But it was not through strength of will but because she had hoped it would please Carol. The gesture appeared, however, to pass unnoticed, for Carol was busy pointing out people and sights to Mr. Merrill. What she saw in him Mrs. Trollope could not discover. To her he seemed a commonplace man, rather dull and naïve. It was not in her nature to feel his charm or to be aware of his worn good looks, nor to divine the thing which lay beneath the surface. Out of irritation Mrs. Trollope began to have a "splitting" headache.

Meanwhile Mr. Botlivala and the Baroness had been following the others, at a distance, it is true, but keeping them in sight most of the time. At that moment, indeed for the whole afternoon, the two of them were suffering from a "left-out" feeling, like little girls who have been excluded by the whispering of other little girls in a corner. For the Baroness it was a familiar sensation, so familiar that she had long ago come to accept it as the normal state of affairs, but with Mr. Botlivala, it was different. In the first place, he was a man and therefore had a better right to force his way in where he was not wanted, and in the second place, he had always been accustomed to buying his way. He might have bought his way with Mrs. Trollope, but his only desire was to avoid her, especially since he had learned that she was Mrs. Jim Trollope, wife of the share pusher now resting in Brixton jail. With the others he knew it was hopeless. Hadn't he tried it with Carol?

So as they walked about, the Baroness now and then pausing to rest her enormous behind on the inadequate shooting-stick as she had seen others doing, they sulked, neither of them wanting to be with the other. They would be silent or talk semi-polite banalities for a while, but inevitably they would return to talk of the other party, and in the other party it was Carol they both wanted.

The Baroness showed her hand first by saying, "I haf a fine position for dat girl—a position vit a great future. I haf a club in Paris. She vould be vonderful as a hostess—such looks—such personality!"

Mr. Botlivala's eyebrows lifted a little. He had divined the Baroness' unusual interest, but he had not understood it until now. A second before, he had meant to boast to her that Carol was secretly his fiancée, but now he held his peace, thinking it better not to show his hand. So he told another secret, partly to make himself seem more important and interesting.

He said, "You know Carol and that Wainwright were married once."

He was rewarded by the Baroness' astonishment, "Vat you mean?" she asked.

"They were married and divorced. She told me herself."

"So," said the Baroness and fell into a silence, brooding.

The news explained many things that troubled her. In fact it explained everything—the curious quality of their relationship, that they were so intimate and still (so the bearers in the hotel corridor reported through her *ayah*) were not living together. Until now she had spent a good many wakeful hours trying to divine just how much of a menace Bill Wainwright was to her plan. She had found out a good many things—that Carol was very nearly broke, that she wasn't simply a tart, and that no man could buy her. To her middle-European mentality all this was puzzling. Anywhere but in America a girl living as Carol did would be a tart —an expensive one, but a tart nevertheless. It seemed to her that Carol lived more like a man than a woman, going her own way, taking care of herself admirably. The odd thing was that all the puzzling habits and qualities made her all the more desirable from the Baroness' point of view. This was exactly what she wanted—a beautiful and attractive woman who did not lose her head and could not be bought. That was exactly what the Paris house needed. She hadn't been able to find such a woman since Violette married the Senator and went to live in the Charente.

When Botlivala turned to speak to her, she was studying the other group through her lorgnette. She seemed hynotized and said to him, "Dere's one vay to ged dot girl to tink like you vant her to tink—if she geds broke and alone—I mean me, not you."

At the same moment the Maharajah of Jellapore and Joey emerged from the crowd. The Maharajah was in a good mood. He said, "Hello, Botlivala," and to the Baroness he said, "Hello, Irma. I see you're well fitted out for the races."

Her face darkened. The eyelids lowered halfway over the bulging eyes so that for a moment she looked exactly like a turtle. "Don't call me Irma, Your Highness. You know my name is Colette."

"Sorry, Baroness," said Jellapore, his bright little eyes dancing at her alarm and indignation. "Any luck?"

"I haf not bed today," she said, soberly.

"No," said the Maharajah. "It is not a good day. Have you seen the Marchesa?"

Again the turtle lids lowered over the greenish eyes and she said, "You know her?"

"I've known her for fifteen years."

This time the expression in the eyes of the Baroness did not change. They were like flint. "Dot," she said, "is a very long time."

"Yes," said Jelly, suddenly overcome by Hindu sadness over his memories. "It is a very long time. I hear the Marchesa is practically an official person here. She's been to Government House and she's going to stay at the Viceroy's house in Delhi."

The Baroness grinned, "You know everyting."

"It's easy in Bombay. It's nothing but a big cluster of villages." Thoughtfully, he said, "The Marchesa was a good girl." And then seeing the turtle lids closing again and aware that he had accomplished what he meant to do, he said, "Come over and have a drink with me."

"Vit pleasure," said the Baroness.

As they started away the Maharajah turned to Botlivala, "Where's your blonde friend today?"

Mr. Botlivala murmured, "She's here today . . . somewhere."

"She's a very busy girl."

He had meant simply to let Mr. Botlivala know that he, for one, knew she didn't belong to him. By Mr. Botlivala's tortured expression he knew that he had succeeded. The Maharajah hadn't had a drink all day. His wits were alive. He was enjoying himself. In the old days he would have had in criminals to be tortured in his presence, but that wasn't any longer respectable. And since impotence had overtaken him he found an urgent need of new ways to amuse himself.

In all Bombay he was one of two people who really knew what the business of the Baroness was. The other was the Marchesa. While he sat drinking in his club enclosure with the Baroness and Mr. Botlivala, he permitted a part of his complex mind to wander languorously back to the happy times when the Marchesa was always reserved for him during his stay in Paris. And with another part of the intricate mind he was laughing at poor Botlivala who, in his snobbery, thought that when he was out with the Baroness he was accompanying an important titled European woman to the races.

He laughed and when the Baroness looked at him with curiosity, he said, "I was just thinking. Maybe after all, you *are* important."

About the fifth race, the faint look of health went out of Buck's face. It turned yellowish white again and the perspiration began to wilt the shabby suit. Bill was the first to notice it and thought, "Better not let him run till he's learned to walk." And to Carol, he said, "We'd better get him back to the hotel," and as an afterthought, he said, "and for God's sake shake Mrs. Trollope."

Carol laughed, "That's your job, honey. She's with you."

"She is like hell."

"Okay."

But when they looked about Mrs. Trollope wasn't there.

"Shall we scram?" suggested Bill.

"We can't do that. I'll find her. Put Buck on a chair in the shade. She's probably at the betting booth."

It was there Carol found her, shame-faced at being caught in the act of betting after Carol had warned her against it. Carol thought, "The damned fool, instead of hanging on to the money she has, will go on betting until she loses it all." And it occurred to her at the same time that Mrs. Trollope was on the way to becoming a pest. In the beginning she had been puzzled by her, but now she was beginning to understand. Mrs. Trollope was the sort of woman who gave you on first sight the impression that she was utterly independent and self-reliant like some men, and then slowly you discovered that she wasn't like that at all. She was the sort who was always in some sort of scrape, the kind who simply sat down and let somebody else get her out of it. "She's really the leach type," thought Carol, rather pleased at the discovery of her own unexpected perspicacity.

She began to understand a little why the Maharani of Chandragar had pulled out a gun and tried to shoot her. If you had a sister who always kept turning up broke, with her life in a mess. . . .

"What did you bet on?" she asked, although she had no interest.

"Number six and number two," said Mrs. Trollope.

"Tips?"

"No," said Mrs. Trollope, "but according to my horoscope they're my lucky numbers all this week."

"I'm going home. We're all going home," said Carol, "Mr. Merrill isn't feeling well."

"Wait till this race is over and I'll go with you." The bright, happy look had come back into her face. She was sure now that the old luck would return with Carol there beside her.

"No, we've got to get him home. I'm not feeling so well myself" —a statement which in view of her radiant appearance, was an obvious lie. She saw that Mrs. Trollope meant to cling. The bell announcing the race began to ring, and Mrs. Trollope to show signs of being torn between a desire to watch the race and remain with her.

"Come on," said Mrs. Trollope, "just this once, stay for the race. Then I'll go."

Perhaps the only thing Carol hated in all life was groveling and pleading. When Mr. Botlivala did it she banished him from her company for two or three days. And now Mrs. Trollope was groveling and pleading in a fashion that far outdid Mr. Botlivala. There was a desperate intensity in her manner which was a little terrifying—much worse than Mr. Botlivala's pouting and teasing. Somehow it infuriated Carol.

Firmly she said, "I'm going."

"Don't go," said Mrs. Trollope, taking her hand. "Let the boys go back alone."

Violently Carol freed her hand. "I'm scramming," she said, "see you tomorrow."

"What are you doing tonight?"

"I'm going straight to bed." The bell announcing the race was clamoring now. "Go on or you'll miss the race."

"How am I going to get home?"

The question made Carol want to laugh—the very picture of tough, leathery Mrs. Trollope being unable to find her way back to the hotel. Quickly she thought, "I've got to get away before I sock her!" So she said, "Go and join up with Botlivala and the Baroness. And now go on and watch the race." She was aware suddenly that Mrs. Trollope's unnatural intensity was endowing their conversation with a sensational quality. Two or three people were watching them. All she wanted now was to get away. So quickly she said, "Ring me up when you come in."

The sop worked, "All right," said Mrs. Trollope.

As Carol turned away she said, "Jeez-us!"

She found the boys sitting under the jacqueranda tree by the gate when she arrived after a hot journey the length of the enclosure. The cheering at the finish of the race died away. Buck was smoking but he still looked ill and white.

She said, "Your friend Mrs. Trollope is getting to be a load."

"She's not my friend, honey," said Bill, "since you brought her all that luck she's forgotten about me."

[170]

"Let's scram and get a drink."

In the taxicab the three of them settled back with a sense of relief. Now that Mrs. Trollope was gone, the uneasiness which had troubled the surface of the whole afternoon slipped away. As they left, Carol turned back to have a look at the board. Numbers three, five and seven were placed. Mrs. Trollope's numbers weren't even in the running. She thought, "Hell, in two more days she'll be broke."

Buck in his corner of the cab felt tired and a little dizzy and the tension and the kind of talk he had been listening to all the afternoon left him a little bewildered. It was a kind of conversation he had never known, even before he came to India, and it left him with the feeling of being an outsider at a party. It seemed to him that he was always two or three jumps behind. Never during the whole afternoon had he been quite aware of what was happening or had he understood until he had pondered over it, what was really being said. The conversation he had been used to for ten years was that of Indians or of English officials. With the first, because very often English was a difficult tongue for them, all conversations had to be simple, slow and explicit. With the second the same rule held true because by nature they were slower-witted than himself and very often their minds had been rendered muggy by long residence in the tropics. The conversation between Bill and Carol was so rapid-fire that it left his tired brain exhausted by the effort of trying to understand it. Most of what passed between them was not said at all; it was simply hiatus. And each phrase was compact and vivid like the speech of a primitive people. He thought, "I guess I've been out of the world too long. I'll catch up in a few days." It was really the struggle to keep abreast which had exhausted him far more than the heat or the excitement of the races.

"She's going to ring me up," he heard Carol saying, "how are we going to get out of that?"

"Don't answer the telephone."

"She'll come to my room."

"Don't answer the knock."

"I wouldn't put it past her to knock down the door."

"We can all go out to dine."

"Where?"

"Some Indian restaurant."

"No Indian food for me tonight."

"Then Green's."

"She'll guess that."

"Well, what do you want to do—jump in the bay?"

"No, Green's. Only it's got to be quick and early."

For a little while Buck tried to follow. Then he gave it up and closed his eyes, thinking only of the shower that would be waiting at the hotel.

They managed to escape to Green's without Mrs. Trollope, for in the end she returned to Jellapore's pleasure palace with the Baroness, Botlivala and three or four other gamblers to play poker.

On the terrace at Green's, the three of them—Bill, Carol and Buck—sat for a long time after dinner at a table just at the edge of the roof terrace, overlooking the bay. It was a hot, steamy night and the haze hid Elephanta and dimmed the lights of the *dhows* and the coastwise boats slipping in and out to and from the Arabian Sea. At about nine o'clock, above the distant Mill district behind the bay, a late full moon rose like a disk of hot copper.

It was a still peaceful evening with no breeze either from the land or the sea and as they sat there peace began slowly to descend upon the three of them, the first peace either Carol or Bill had known since coming to Bombay. It was one of those evenings when talk seemed unnecessary, when for a long time they were content simply to sit quietly watching the bay and the lights and listening to the music. And while they sat there, the tired look went out of Buck's face again and when they began asking him questions, he talked, shyly at first, about the life he had known for the past ten years. It was not only shyness which hampered him but the sensitiveness which afflicted all his habits and instincts of human communication. It wasn't only that sometimes the shorthand quality in the conversation of Bill and Carol left him bewildered, but that he felt "jungly."

But after a little time his intuitions, sharpened by long contact with Indians, told him that both Carol and Bill were interested in what he was telling them of all that world of jungles and villagers and poverty-ridden *ryotes*. "Perhaps," he thought, "what is everyday life to me is interesting to them because it is so different. It's all new to them."

And so he went on, roused by their questions and the look of interest in Carol's blue eyes, telling them of how he had built up from one small poverty-ridden village a movement that was spreading over the whole of India, how in three or four years he had changed the appearance of whole villages and the character and physique of people in them. And to his astonishment he found the two of them listening utterly absorbed by his accounts of village co-operatives which shipped eggs to Bombay and Madras and Calcutta, of Karachi bulls and Senegal goats and white leghorn cocks and Italian bees brought into remote villages to change the whole economic life of a countryside. He told them how hookworm had been eliminated and malaria, the curse of India, checked. And he told them how all these things, occurring before the eyes of the villagers themselves, had weakened superstition and the power of the lazy swindling priests.

As he talked, the old love and admiration for Buck returned to Bill in all its richness, and presently with half his mind listening and half lost in the past, he thought, "Maybe without Buck I would have gone completely to the dogs long ago when I was a kid." He was aware, as he listened, that a remarkable change had come over Buck—that the blueness of his eyes had become more intense, that beneath the waxen skin there appeared again a hint of color; and he understood after a time that nothing on earth would ever draw Buck away from his villages and farmers, that he would go on to the very end, whether it was soon or late, working and fighting for them. In his eyes was the look of a great artist; this change in India was a thing which he was creating as a painter painted a picture or a composer wrote a symphony. It was a new and better world that he created. And Bill saw now and *believed* what Colonel Moti had said—that Buck must regain his health and live, that nothing else mattered. And he saw too that all this thing Buck was talking of meant so much to him that he himself would sacrifice anything to get back his strength, even the old stern ideas of morality, even his immortal soul. That thought suddenly frightened Bill, because it could be so dangerous a course for a man like Buck to whom everything mattered so profoundly.

He saw too that there were moments when Buck seemed to be talking to Carol alone as if he, Bill, were not there at all; and then suddenly Buck himself would become aware of what he was doing and turn to address his old friend. It was natural that he should talk to Carol, not only because she was a woman and beautiful (which in itself was dangerous for a man like Buck) but because she knew about farms. It was astonishing how much she remembered out of that remote Minnesota childhood. And she could ask questions which were intelligent and to the point. It was astonishing, too, that out of one or two encounters she and Buck had become old friends—that in so short a time they seemed to understand each other better than he and Carol had ever understood each other. And as he watched them he re-discovered that mysterious Carol of whom he had never been aware until that curious moment in the doorway of Jellapore's gaudy gambling room.

For the moment again Buck was talking to Carol as if they were alone, and Bill watched Carol, her face flushed with interest, even with excitement, her eyes shining, and an odd thought occurred to him. He thought, "Buck as he talks, is making love to her, and he is too innocent to know what he is doing." But Carol knew, and she would never let Buck discover it until he found out for himself. She was happy. Bill thought, "It's the first time anyone has made love to her talking about chickens and goats instead of her figure." And again he was afraid suddenly for both of them, and a little jealous because he had never seen her like this before.

Then in a blast of brassy music, the floor show began destroying the whole mood of the evening. There was an opening chorus—a number done by six girls with very odd legs—some bandy, some thin, some as muscular as those of the bottom man in a strong act. Their faces were scarcely less extraordinary—worn, raddled and not too well made up. They sang in a variety of English dialects ranging from Manchester to Liverpool. When they had finished there was a juggler whose act was embellished by some very bad jokes, and then a tired trio of adagio dancers and then the sleazy chorus again. Although the sailors seemed to like it and applauded and cheered, it was a depressing show, and when it was over, the mood of the evening was entirely gone.

Bill said suddenly to Carol, "Why didn't you gamble today?"

"I didn't want to."

"A hunch about bad luck?"

"No, I was afraid my luck might be too good."

And then he remembered what she had said about being frightened when she had too much luck at gambling. So that was it. He looked at her again. Yes, he saw by the look in her eyes—that was it.

He reached into his pocket for a cigarette and found the letters he had picked up during the afternoon at the hotel desk. He had carried them all the afternoon and transferred them from one coat to another when he changed without ever reading them. The message from the office was among them.

He said, "Do you mind if I look over these? I forgot all about them—and I'm trying to be a good business man."

He opened the note from the office and read:

Dear Mr. Wainwright:

We have just had distressing news of Hinkle. A message came today from Saigon saying that Hinkle was there in a serious condition in the French hospital. It seems that he was pursuing a wounded tiger on foot. It turned and mauled him badly. Further details are lacking, but the office will keep you informed of developments. We have telegraphed for more news. The office called the hotel several times today but you were out so we have sent this message and would appreciate it if you would let me know when I might come to see you. The accident has occurred at a singularly unfortunate time in view of the planned improvements and reorganization. We are unwilling to go ahead without the approval of Mr. Hinkle or yourself.

I am,

Yours sincerely,
Albert K. Smithers

His first reaction was sympathy for Hinkle. The poor hard-working guy had gone off on a holiday and then been messed up

[175]

by a tiger. After that the full significance of the note in relation to himself became apparent. It meant that he wouldn't leave in a couple of weeks. It meant that he would be kept here until Hinkle recovered or a new man was sent out to take his place. Smithers was no good. He was wonderful when it came to details and keeping books and disciplining the horde of *babu* clerks, but when it came to initiative or making a decision, the poor little fellow was terrified of the responsibility. Anyway, buried always among books and clerks, he couldn't know anything of oil wars and rate cutting and such things. No, unless they sent somebody quickly from some other post in the East, the note itself meant that he was stuck in Bombay for at least another month or two.

At the moment he did not know whether he was glad or sorry. Until now he had always evaded responsibilities very neatly and now there was dumped on his shoulders, out of the blue, responsibilities which he could not evade. His hunch was to leave Bombay as quickly as possible not because he wanted to run away from his responsibilities but because he was uneasy. It hadn't been the same this time; it was all muddled and unsatisfactory, and except for one or two rare moments, perfectly commonplace and dull. And back of all that lay a curious feeling of dread and presentiment which he recognized now had begun in the moment when the man had been crushed to death at his feet as he stepped off the ship. It wasn't that he was very superstitious; it was only that this sudden death might be an omen. And then there was Hinkle, a respectable oil executive, being mauled in the most unlikely fashion in the remote upper Burmese jungle.

"Things like that always go in threes," he thought wildly, and immediately said to himself, "That's rubbish."

Turning over the letter of Mr. Smithers, he drafted a cablegram on the back to his father in New York. He found himself writing, "Hinkle badly hurt by tiger on vacation stop Suggest you transfer Downes Singapore or Hellman Batavia carry on reorganization stop All well Best regards. Bill."

As he read it he knew suddenly that he didn't want to stay in India. Looking up, he glanced at Carol and Buck. They were laughing. Carol was telling stories of life on the farm in Minnesota.

[176]

He heard her saying, "And the old maid said, 'We've been the whole damned morning trying to get that cow on her back.' "

He didn't know what the story was but he saw an odd startled look in Buck's eye as he laughed, and thought, "I hope she's not opening up on some of her stories. They'll scare him to death." Not because they would shock him but because in all his experience he'd never known a woman who talked in that free and easy way.

With a rueful grin he saw that they weren't missing him at all. So quietly he took out the letters from his pocket and read them. Only two were of any importance or interest. One was from his father congratulating him on the reports which had come back on the work he had done in Istanbul and Alexandria. He wrote, "I always knew that you had it in you. Now you've settled down, stick to it. Achievement is the only enduring satisfaction in life."

The letter was written in longhand in his father's old-fashioned Spencerian writing and the sight of it brought him a sudden twinge of affection for the old man, not of a paternal quality but the affection one might have for a "character" who was no relation to you. He was a hard old bastard but he had been as hard on himself as he had been on others about him. He'd never had any fun unless building up all that power was fun; anyway it wasn't Bill's idea of fun. He hadn't even married until he was over forty so that when Bill came along, he belonged to a generation once removed from the old man. The father was the old side-whiskered politician, swindler, industrialist, and the son a play-boy. "Shirtsleeves to shirtsleeves," thought Bill, "in two generations." There was one generation missing. Bill thought, "He's always been like my grandfather," as if his own father had died without his ever knowing him. The copy-book phrase, "Achievement is the only enduring satisfaction in life," went over and over through his head, as if he had been ordered to write it five hundred times as a punishment.

The other letter was from a woman in London. He'd been fond of her and had fun with her, but he hadn't thought of her since leaving Marseilles where she came to see him off, all the way from Paris, in a cold mistral. She wrote, "There isn't any fun with you gone. I've been to Paris twice but it's as dull as London without you there, darling. For God's sake write to me. I'm depressed because Hugh is suspicious. The other night he threw one of his

[177]

scenes and said he knew all about us. He must have known something because he knew about the Hotel Lotti. He said he'd divorce me and name you as corespondent. Don't be alarmed, I'm only writing what he said. He won't so long as I have the money. But you'd better not write me here. Write care of my Aunt, Lady Burnham—York Terrace, Regent's Park. She's a Theosophist and never suspects anyone or anything because suspicion might ruin her spiritual state. I hope the Governor and the Viceroy do right by you. I wrote both of them to invite you to lunch. Forgive me, but I thought you ought to have official recognition. The Governor is my cousin—a tiddly, pompous, little man."

Quickly he tore up the letter, placed it in a little heap in the ash tray and set fire to it, thinking, "My God, that's all I need—just when I'm making good—to be named in a London divorce trial."

Then Carol turned to him and said, "What's the bonfire?"

"A letter from a girl friend."

He pushed the communication of Smithers over to them and they both read it as he watched them. Carol saw the point at once, "Does it mean you have to stay here in Bombay?"

"Don't know yet. Do you want me to go?"

"Yes and no," said Carol.

"Meaning what?"

"Nothing at all, except I like having you around."

"Thanks."

She stood up. "I think it's time to go to bed."

"Okay. What about you, Buck?"

"I'm ready."

"We've had a lot of luck this evening."

"How?" asked Bill.

"Mrs. Trollope didn't show up."

"Oh, that." He grinned. "Yes, having an evening off has been fun."

Bill paid the check and they walked slowly under the hot moon as far as the Gateway to India and back before going into the Taj. Inside Bill asked, "D'you want a night-cap?"

"Not me," said Carol.

"Or me," said Buck. "I feel as if I could sleep. I don't want to muff the chance."

"Okay. I've got to send a cable."

Then out of the corner of his eye, he saw the Baroness coming toward him. With her was a small, shabby looking man with a wall-eyed expression which gave him a singularly sinister appearance. She said something to him and he turned away suddenly and became interested in a bookstall filled with travel books. Bill thought he didn't look the sort who would be very interested in reading.

The Baroness, it appeared, was on the crest of the wave. She told them that she and Botlivala and Mrs. Trollope had gone again to Jellapore's little palace for cocktails and stayed to gamble. This time she and Botlivala had won.

"And Mrs. Trollope?" asked Carol.

"Ve left her dere."

"Winning?"

"No," said the Baroness, with an odd grin like the smile of a turtle. "She vas losing."

"Much?"

"Lots."

That, then, was why she hadn't turned up.

The Baroness had an idea, "Vy not all go back to de Maharajah's palace?"

But Bill said "No" and the others backed him. They said goodnight to her and Bill went to send his cablegram while Carol and Buck went upstairs. As Bill returned to the elevator, he saw that the Baroness had rejoined the shabby little man. "He's a Eurasian," thought Bill, "and not the kind you'd expect to find her with." As the lift disappeared, he grinned, thinking, "Maybe Trollope is right. Maybe she is a spy." And it struck him suddenly that the Baroness had been singularly happy at the news that Mrs. Trollope was losing.

In his own room he dismissed Silas, knowing that Silas would spend the night on the floor outside the door and wondering what the sex life or even the domestic life of a bearer must be, since they seemed to be on duty twenty-four hours a day. At some time or other Silas must have had time to beget that large family he was always whining about. Or maybe he begot them only in his imagination.

[179]

He felt tired tonight and uneasy, he did not know why, unless it was the prospect of having to stay in Bombay. There could be, he told himself honestly, but one other reason—and that was Carol. It wasn't as if the thing was beginning all over again—that thing which once satisfied, had died so quickly. It was something new which he had never experienced before, and it put his nerves on edge, making him jumpy and irritable over such simple things as the way she spoke to someone else or the look in her eyes. He thought, "What the hell has come over me?" and tried almost at once to dismiss the whole thing as an attack of "Indian nerves." She had never irritated him before and now, lately, she made him lose his temper suddenly in flashes that passed quickly. When he tried to discover the reason it seemed to him as if she had changed and there were moments when she treated him as a grown-up treats a child, as if, a little annoyed, she was saying to him, "This is something you don't understand. Children should be seen and not heard." As if she knew a great deal which he did not know, as if she had a secret of some sort and mocked him by keeping it from him.

"After all," he thought as he undressed, "she needn't be so damned superior. Whatever else I am, I wasn't born yesterday."

He threw all the clothing he had taken off into a corner of the room for Silas to pick up and send to the *dhobi* in the morning. Then he put on pajamas and going to the door of Buck's room knocked softly. He didn't want to waken Buck but he felt like talking and for the first time he felt toward Buck as he had felt long ago. All the strangeness, the shyness was gone.

He was about to turn back to bed when Buck's voice said, "Come in."

"Do you want to sleep?" asked Bill.

"No, I don't go to sleep easily."

"How are you feeling?"

"A lot better, thanks."

Bill grinned. "The cure working?"

"All right, so far."

"You've got to let yourself go. That's the whole trick."

"That's what I'm trying to do."

"How does it feel?"

"Fine so far. I'm a bit bewildered."

Bill sat down on a chair by the side of the bed. "Why?" he asked.

"By all of the people I've met. I've never seen anything like 'em before."

"Luckily, there aren't many of 'em—like the Baroness and Botlivala."

"I like Carol."

"Yes, she's a good girl. I've known her a long time."

"But I've never met any woman quite like her either."

In the darkness Bill laughed, "No, I don't suppose you have."

"All the women I've known seem to be one kind or the other. Either they're too easy to get acquainted with or too hard."

"That's true," said Bill, "Carol is different that way. She just likes people and likes them to have a good time."

Then Buck was silent for a time, and in the darkness Bill felt suddenly peaceful. In the back of his mind a curious thought occurred—that Carol and Buck were both simple people and that he himself was by comparison, complex, wanting complications and then running away from them, liking people but keeping them always at a distance in reality. "Maybe," he thought, "Carol was right about me," because what she had said to him at lunch still had the power of annoying him.

"I've got to go and see Ali tomorrow," said Buck suddenly. "Do you want to go along?"

"You've got to order some clothes first. You can't go on leading the high life dressed like a poverty-stricken Methodist missionary."

"Okay," said Buck. "Do you think she'd like to go with me?"

"Who?"

"Carol—Miss Halma."

Bill laughed. "You don't need to be so damned formal—not with Carol."

He knew that in the darkness Buck was blushing and added, "Sure, she'd like to go if you can get her out of bed. She's not an early riser."

"Will you ask her?"

Again Bill chuckled. "Ask her yourself. You're of age."

[181]

"I don't want her to think I'm rushing things and I don't want to bore her."

After a little silence Bill said, "You won't bore her. Haven't you got eyes? Don't you know anything about women?"

"No," said Buck, "I don't—not a damned thing."

"You can ask her but I don't think you'll get her out of bed."

Bill stood up in the darkness and touched Buck's shoulder. His friend's hand reached out and took his own.

"Anyway," said Bill, "I'm glad we met up again. Let's not lose track of each other again."

"Okay," said Buck, "and thanks."

"For what?"

"For bothering about me."

"Don't be a damned fool. Good-night. Try to get some sleep."

He went into his own room, closed the door and turned out the light. But he did not sleep. The hard bed seemed lumpy. The heat was like a weight. The turning *punkah* squeaked, with a small tiresome squeak like the sound made by a bat. And be began to worry—Good-time Charlie who never worried—about Hinkle, about being kept in Bombay, about that letter from England now perhaps ashes in the dust bin at Green's Hotel. And the copy-book phrase in his father's letter seemed to be written in fire on the wall of the room—"Achievement is the only lasting satisfaction in life."

Then he tried various methods of putting himself to sleep, but none of them were of any avail. Along about three in the morning, he faced what was the trouble and acknowledged it. He was afraid.

In the huge hotel there were at least three other people who were afraid.

On the fourth floor the Baroness in her room undressed slowly, heavily, down to the stays which when removed allowed her vast figure to expand and her breasts and stomach to hang like withered gourds. In the harsh light of the one electric bulb she stood naked for a moment and faced her image in the mirror—the image of an ancient turtle, its face fantastically made up, its body gone soft and protuberant.

"There you are," she said, speaking to herself in Czech, "ugly as sin. All you've got is a brain. But they can't beat that—none

[182]

of 'em can. There's more ways than one to cut the throat of a hog."

It was a trick she had learned long ago to give her strength when she felt tired or frightened. Only two things in the world could frighten her. Unlike some women, she had never had any looks to lose. Death she did not fear. And never for a day had she been ill. She feared only losing her money and prison. In prison she could not use her wits nor weave plots. In prison she would suffocate. Once long ago, before she was powerful and rich, she had spent three months in jail in Vienna. The jail was clean and decent. It was not that which mattered to her but the awful horror of being behind a locked door. Sometimes, at night, she wakened to lie for hours thinking of that peculiar horror of all the horrors, when it seemed to her that she was slowly suffocating.

And now she was afraid again, driven by the only two terrors which had the power to move her. There was bad news from Europe, news which each day seemed to grow more frightening. To her shrewd mind with its occasional vague overtones of wisdom, it seemed to her that Europe had fallen into the hands of madmen—that a whole continent was reverting to a kind of primitive savagery. For to her, a civilization which no longer respected money was a civilization degenerate and doomed. For ten years now, she had been shifting her money from here to there and back again, round and round the endless circle—Amsterdam, Berlin, Frankfort, Paris, Rome, Vienna, Stockholm. And now Vienna, Berlin, Rome and Frankfort were eliminated. In those places they simply took your money if they wanted it, and now in England and France taxes were beginning to amount to confiscation. Before long there wouldn't be any place left but America, and people said that America too was beginning to put socialistic ideas into practice.

She felt a sudden desire to weep with self-pity, but in the turtle eyes there were no tears, even for herself. There had been none for thirty years. All that good and wonderful money she had worked for and hoarded for forty years, all the power which it meant, the only power she could ever know! And now the whole world seemed in a conspiracy to take it from her!

And the other terror had to do with the shabby little man who came to see her. He had brought bad news—that a strange man had spoken to him in an Indian restaurant and put embarrassing questions as to his occupation and his friendship with the Baroness. It might mean nothing at all, or it might mean—she avoided the words—arrest and prison. She thought, "Who in Bombay could know? Who could have tipped them off?" Only the Maharajah and the Marchesa knew anything, and the Maharajah knew nothing which could get her into trouble—nothing save that she had once been proprietress of the house in the Square Chaussée d'Antin, and in that there was no harm. Besides he was much too lazy and good-natured to make trouble. Only the Marchesa knew anything which could really cause trouble.

The turtle eyes grew hard as steel. The Marchesa was an ungrateful bitch, after all she had done for her. Never would she have caught that doddering old Fascist nincompoop of a husband but for all she had done to help her. It only went to show you that you could never trust a whore. So, frightened, the old woman looked again at the reflection of her hideous face and body in the cheap mirror and said to herself, "You are ugly as sin, but you have a brain. None of them is going to defeat you."

Then she put out the light and went to bed but not to sleep. She was tired and she felt old and never in all her wolfish life had she felt so alone.

On the floor above a few doors away, Flora Trollope came in a couple of hours after the Baroness had gone to bed. She had had too much champagne and was feeling sorry for herself. She had meant to keep her wits about her and not have any champagne at all, but she had taken a glass or two to cheer herself up and then rapidly she had gone from bad to worse. And, once started, she went on drinking to drown her uneasiness over where Carol was and what she was doing. Doubts, fears, dread kept getting in the way of her gambling; she lost two large pots because she was thinking about Carol instead of the poker game. She had gone to Jellapore's to win back what she had lost at the races, and at Jellapore's she had done nothing but lose more.

But worst of all, about midnight she had looked up from the table and discovered that her sister, the Maharani—that omen of bad luck—was standing beside Jellapore watching the game. It was

[184]

a big pot and in it Mrs. Trollope already had thirty-four hundred rupees as well as three queens in her hand. She called the raise of the Baroness and saw the old woman with a triumphant glitter in her green eyes lay down three aces. And then she heard her sister laugh, and something in her own slightly befuddled brain gave way; the strained nerves in her tired thin body seemed to explode and she heard herself shouting, "Shut your dirty mouth!"

It was exactly what the Maharani wanted. Of the two sisters, Flora Trollope had always been quicker-witted than Nelly Chandragar and now Nelly knew that she had the advantage. Flora was befuddled, and she herself, aside from the customary sluggishness born of auto-intoxication, was quite sober. For once she had the advantage she had been waiting for for years.

So she said, with a wicked quietness, "Keep a sober tongue in your head."

Mrs. Trollope said, "I'm sober three days to your one."

"That's a God-damned lie. And never come into my house again —after sneaking out without even a word of thanks."

"Thanks for what?"

Then the Baroness, eager to continue playing her good luck, said, "Come, come. Let's play."

But Jellapore didn't want to go on. He was enjoying the quarrel more than the game. He said, "No, let them have it out. They've been snapping at each other for years. Let's get it settled."

"Maybe I should thank you for trying to shoot me," said Mrs. Trollope.

"I wasn't trying to shoot you. I was only trying to scare some sense into your head. Always coming to me when you're in scrapes —you and your bloody swindling husband."

In Mrs. Trollope's befuddled head, the room began to revolve in the most extraordinary fashion, the Baroness, the Maharajah, her sister Nelly, and the great chandeliers all muddled together, in a vast and monstrous maelstrom of blazing sound and color. She felt herself bursting; tears streamed from the tired burning eyes and she heard herself screaming, "Shut your bloody mouth!" Then abruptly her body took possession of her muddled will; she rose up from the table and ran out of the room crying. She did not stop running until she had reached the *porte cochère* and asked

[185]

the porter to call her a taxi from the line of vultures which had gathered at the sight of lights in Jellapore's pleasure palace.

All the way back to the hotel she wept hysterically and once there, she thrust a ten rupee note into the hands of the vulture and, still sobbing, ran through the noisy hallway to the lift. At last in the safety of her own room she gained possession of herself and sat down in a chair by a window overlooking the street. The outburst of weeping sobered her so that her tired mind began again to work with a little clarity.

Now it seemed to her that she had been drunk all day long, beginning hours before she had even touched the champagne. She had risen in the morning to go to Barclay's Bank and leave there some of the rupees which she had carried day after day stuffed willy-nilly into the worn handbag. She had risen telling herself that the time had come to make sense, and she had been on her way through the lobby when she saw Carol meet "that missionary" and go with him into the lift.

That was the moment, she knew now with extraordinary clarity, when the drunkenness began. She watched the lift swallow them up and from that moment on something above and beyond her common sense and her will power seized possession of her. She had struggled for nearly an hour—belowstairs, trying not to follow Carol and the missionary, trying to go on with what she had meant to do, but in the end she had gone upstairs.

The moment she entered the room and saw Carol and Bill and Buck she knew that she was not wanted there. They were polite to her but they had shut her out. And again she had meant to go away, but again she was powerless. She had stayed on, gone with them to the races and quarreled on the way with Bill who had always seemed to be her friend. And then she had gambled against the advice of Carol and lost and then gambled again and lost and then gone to Jellapore's palace and lost more and drunk too much champagne and quarreled with Nelly. And now she was back again alone in her room, staring down at the street.

It wasn't the first time she had sat alone by a window looking down into the streets. It had happened to her a hundred times; now in London, now in Paris, here, there, almost everywhere in the world; it was always the same. Everything would start off well

[186]

and then just as she was making new friends in a new world where they didn't know her, and didn't know about Jim Trollope—just when her life began to show signs of order and decency, everything would go wrong and her life would grow disorderly and again she would be alone. She was a little more alone each time it happened.

She thought, "There is a curse on me. It isn't much I want— only to be friends with Carol, only to be allowed to worship her." And suddenly she understood what the drunkenness was—that in a very little time Carol had become necessary to her. It wasn't only that Carol had cheered her up and brought her luck; it was more than that. When Carol wasn't there a grayness enveloped the whole world that surrounded her. The people in it bored her until she hated them. In a way, rapidly, mysteriously, Carol and the thing which Carol was had become her whole existence. She had drunk too much champagne and lost at poker all that precious money only because she hated the whole evening and all the people about her and could only think of how wonderful it had been on the other evening when she and Carol shared the banks at *chemin-de-fer* and won everything. And all the time instead of keeping her mind on the game she had been wondering about Carol and what she was doing with Bill Wainwright and that missionary in the little world which they had suddenly closed to her. Where were they dining? What were they saying? In a moment of clarity she saw why she had experienced, two or three times, the sensation of *being* Carol—it was because Carol was everything she was not, all that she wanted to be more than anything in life.

And she remembered then what the fortuneteller had told her— that there were two men, one blond and one dark, who stood between her and her luck. Mr. Botlivala, she knew, was the dark man but he was a poor thing who, her instinct told her, was no menace. It was the blond man who had come between her and her touchstone Carol, but whether it was Bill Wainwright or the missionary bloke she did not know. After thinking about it tipsily for a long time she decided that it must be Bill; her instinct, she told herself, had revealed the truth when she quarreled with him in the taxicab. She knew it now, especially after the bit of gossip she had heard at the races—that once he and Carol had been married. And she knew, too, because there was a part of her which was like a man, that he was in love with her. In a way Bill was her rival. In the haunted darkness, the room, the hotel, the whole of Bombay presently became a trap, a prison from which there was no escape. When she was afraid, the superstitions clamored for satisfaction. Now she had a feeling of doom, of some awful end from which there was no escape. She had been fighting it for a long time now, for years, ever since her father had sent her to school in England to learn to be a "lydy." She had been fighting it even for longer than that—even since she was a little girl. And now she was tired—too tired to fight it off any longer.

Above Flora Trollope on the opposite side of the hotel Carol undressed slowly and thoughtfully, feeling curiously quiet and sober at this hour of the night. Years had passed, it seemed to her, since she had gone quietly to bed like this, before two in the morning. The odd thing was that she did not seem to mind the experience. She felt very still and peaceful, the restlessness all gone from her. It was a nice feeling—one in which there was a sense of security, although she could not divine why, and calm and relaxation. She thought, "I actually feel as if I could go to bed before two and sleep."

Taking off her make-up before the mirror, she thought, looking at her own lovely face, "Well, honey, that guy Merrill is the nicest guy you've ever met. But don't be too nice to him or you'll get yourself into complications. Nice fellows like that are tough to shake off when the time comes to give them the air. They're a lot tougher than the Botlivalas and the old lechers. So watch yourself, honey."

He wasn't, she decided, like any man she had ever met, at least since she had left Minnesota. All the others, it seemed to her, were too complicated. They were on the make or they weren't; it never made any difference. In one case they needed handling, and in the other, the relationship was all the same—just a series of wisecracks all a little mauve in color. Bill was the only man she'd ever known who was a mixture of the two. That was why she had married him. That was why she had a special feeling for him which wasn't love, perhaps, but different just the same from any feeling she had had for other men.

"He's a honey," she thought, "if he'll only stay the way he is."

But the funny thing was that lately he didn't seem to be satisfied with being what he was. He was jumpy and quarrelsome. There were even astonishing moments when for a second he behaved as if he were jealous. A thought came to her suddenly out of the blue.

"Gawd!" she thought. "It couldn't be that. It couldn't be that after all these years I'm going to have trouble with him." And the thought was so funny that she laughed aloud.

At last she rose from the dressing table feeling extremely virtuous, because in the morning she would waken for the first time in many weeks with her face washed and covered with grease instead of powder and rouge.

Before turning out the light and climbing into bed, she locked the door lest Mrs. Trollope come in late feeling in a mood to confide in her. She knew that Mrs. Trollope was ripe for confiding. She displayed all the signs and if there was one thing which Carol found insupportable, it was hearing the troubles and self-pity of another female. In fact she was beginning to discover a great many things about Mrs. Trollope—things which made her more interesting as a character but less desirable as a friend.

And after the lights were out and she was lying in bed, she did what for her was an extraordinary thing. Closing her eyes she went back suddenly to that remote Lutheran childhood and said aloud, in a low voice, "Oh God, thank you for all the good times I've had out of life and help me to get things sorted out." She prayed not out of fear but out of gratitude because she felt extraordinarily well and happy.

When Bill wakened, slowly, uncomfortably, in the heat, he rose and went to knock on Buck's door. When there was no answer, he was afraid suddenly that when he pushed open the door he might find Buck was lying there dead. But when he opened the door, the room was empty. And then he remembered that Buck had said he was going off early to see Ali and Colonel Moti. And he thought, too, "Why didn't he waken me?" And almost immediately, "I wonder if he took Carol with him?" The thought made him suddenly suspicious and uneasy again, almost as if the two had a plot against him. They might have taken him, the dirty dogs; the expedition would have been fun with the three of them.

Then all at once he was ashamed of himself, thinking that he was behaving like an adolescent schoolboy rather than a grown man who, anybody would have said, certainly knew his way about the world. But the uneasiness would not be dismissed; it hung over him as he dressed and gave orders to Silas for the day.

He did not like the way Silas looked at him, with sidelong, rather secret glances, as if he were aware that inside Bill there was some sort of disturbance. He thought, "Damn these Indians, they always smell everything." For a moment he felt a wild desire to tell Silas to mind his own business, but at once knew that such a course would only make him seem ridiculous. Silas simply would pretend he didn't know what he was talking about. He would put on a meek and humble manner and a pious expression on his black face —all but the black eyes. They would go on mocking you; that was the way a worm like a bearer could get back at you, mocking you, tormenting you, not because he hated you but because the race from which he came was infinitely older than your own, so that out of the black eyes of an Untouchable Christian boy there glimmered from time to time a look of scorn and superiority. He knew suddenly why the Indian got beneath the skin of the stolid Englishmen, why it was that always the Indian won out. You could beat him or shout him down or even shoot him but still he knew all the answers and had the jump on you. That was the secret of Gandhi.

He hurried through his dressing to be rid of Silas' black accusing eyes—eyes which said, "You're being a damned silly fool." And no sooner was Silas gone from the room than he went to the telephone and called Carol's room.

She wasn't there. When he called the office desk, the clerk said she had gone out early, about half-past eight, and he heard himself against his will asking, "Alone?"

"No," said the impersonal voice, "she went out with Mr. Merrill."

He hung up, thinking, "Left out in the cold," and because already the intolerable heat was making him irritable, he said, "To hell with both of them! I'll go to work."

He called Smithers and Smithers offered to come up to the hotel, but he refused that. It wouldn't be like working to sit here like a big shot and have the groveling Smithers wait upon him.

"No," he said, "I'll come down to the office."

When he went downstairs there was a cablegram just arrived for him. As he opened it he saw that his hand was shaking and thought, "That just shows it's no good reforming. The one night I didn't drink, I have the jitters."

The cablegram read:

"Order you take over Hinkle job until recovery stop Contact Calcutta and Madras offices at once stop Fine opportunity to make good possibly Eastern managership Regards

Anson W. Wainwright.

As he tore up the cable he said, "Oh, hell!" It was like his father to sign himself not "Father" or "Dad" but "Anson W. Wainwright." That was business. No sentiment or feeling in business. So the old man thought he would like the job of Eastern manager. To hell with the East! To hell with everything!

When he arrived at the office, Mr. Smithers came out of his liver-colored sanctum wearing a lugubrious expression. He had just had a telegram from Saigon. Hinkle was dead.

"Too bad. Poor guy," Bill said automatically, but at the moment he wasn't thinking of Hinkle. As soon as he heard the news he knew that it was settled. He'd have to stay. His instinct told him to flee, but he knew that if he chucked now, he'd never have another chance. He'd have to stay in India and lick this job or he was through except for the gradual easy descent into the gutter.

He mopped his head and face and to Smithers he said, "Let's get to work." And then, "Was he married?"

"No," said Smithers.

"That's good. There won't be any widow for us to console."

In the bungalow at the Institute, Indira Moti wakened knowing that she would see Merrill before the day was finished. She knew well enough that he would return to visit Ali. The boy knew it too. When she went in to waken him, she found that he was already awake, feeling his way about the bare room toward the door which led to the verandah. She knew where he was going. He would sit there in the shadow all morning seeing with his ears, listening to the sounds of the birds in the garden until he heard the crunch of tires on the gravel and heard the step which he knew was Merrill's.

She spoke to him in Hindustani and at the sound of her voice, the brown face parted in a smile to show a row of white teeth. He was happy and that pleased her, but she knew that beside the boy's worship for Merrill neither her husband nor herself was of any importance.

The boy asked, "Is Sahib Buck coming today?"

"Yes, Ali," she answered, not knowing except by her inner self.

"I knew he was." The smile stayed on the small dark face.

Then quietly she took the boy by the hand and together they crossed the hot courtyard between the laboratory and the bungalow, and once inside the laboratory yard she led him to the cages of rabbits and guinea pigs where in turn she took out three or four animals and let him hold them. While he stood caressing them she watched the slim dark hands, fascinated by their sensitiveness and by the story which they told of the child's close feeling and love for animals. It was as if the two hands were each one an artist in pantomime. It was one of the things which interested her passionately—which had always interested her since the days long ago when as a child wakening in the *zenana* in far-off Bengal she had become aware of all the exquisite beauty of the small things, a beauty which, to her astonishment as she grew older, lay hidden from most people, as if like poor Ali, they were blind. It was the beauty of all these things which she had put into her dancing through all the years she had danced in the East and West, a beauty transmitted to the less gifted and fortunate through the art of dancing stylized by ten thousand years of practice. She was middle-aged, soon she would be old, but still she could dance, still her body would remain supple, obedient, and still she would have that precious secret, that other sight which now revealed the loveliness of the two small brown hands of a blind boy caressing a guinea pig—a blind boy whose hands were dancing the dance of "seeing"; for that was what he was doing—seeing with his hands.

As she watched the boy she divined why it was he loved animals.

[192]

It was because he had lived with them all his life, close to them, as if they were persons who were his friends. He had lived most of his life in the elephant stables with those great animals which more than any others were like people you loved. And lately there had been all the animals of Merrill's farmyard in far-off Jellapore—the animals which, Indian fashion, lived close to the house, sometimes going in and out, but always there, breeding, living, dying, as part of a family.

She thought suddenly, "Merrill knows all that." He was one of those who held this secret. It was that which gave him his irresistible simplicity, his lack of guile or envy or indecency. It was that which gave him the strength to endure and to survive all he had endured. It was that which made everything he did in life pure and lovely and touched by kindness and nobility. Because in the animals and in the earth was the source of all serenity and strength. It was odd, she thought, that knowing what he knew, his personal life should have been so twisted and complex and unhappy.

So lost did she become in her own thoughts and in the spectacle of the childish hands that she did not notice the opening of the gate of the enclosure. It was Ali who heard it first and then the sound of footsteps on the gravel. Raising his head a little like a gazelle startled while feeding, he said, "There! It is Sahib Buck."

Looking toward the gate Indira Moti saw Merrill coming toward them. He wasn't alone. He had with him a European woman, tall and blonde and very beautiful, with the direct beauty of a lovely animal. The clothes and even the make-up, Indira saw at once, could do nothing to dim that beauty. It was there for all the world to see. All the world would be aware of it, but only a few people like Indira Moti understood its quality and its power and what it was.

She thought, as she moved toward them smiling, "Something has happened to him."

He had gone away, only a little while before, a friend whom she loved, but a friend dimmed and weary as if there were a veil between him and herself. And now he returned changed, as if the veil had been withdrawn. And she thought, "Perhaps this woman has done it." With the wisdom of her ancient race she knew that such things were possible. She knew the effect of people like this woman. She was the sort from whom others, ill, less strong, less happy, drew strength. Indira Moti knew Europe, and she thought, "She looks like a tart but she isn't. She never could be."

The blind boy moved swiftly toward the sound of Merrill's voice as he spoke and in a moment the small brown hand was lost in Merrill's big one.

"I've been looking at the guinea pigs," said the boy in Hindustani.

"Good," said Merrill, "why don't you take one back to the bungalow with you?"

"Would Memsahib Moti let me?" he asked.

"Of course," said Indira Moti. "Why not? I'll get you one." And while she lifted a young guinea pig out of the cage to give the boy, she said to Merrill, "I knew you'd be coming."

"I brought Miss Halma with me." And for the first time it struck him that the fancy name was ridiculous. The sound of it on his tongue made him want to laugh.

The two women smiled at each other and Carol said, "I hope you don't mind."

Indira smiled, "A friend of Merrill's is a friend of mine."

The boy held the small still guinea pig quietly in his cupped hands but his head was tilted a little to one side as he listened. In a low voice he said to Merrill, "Is it the pretty lady from the train? The Princess with all the jewels?"

Indira and Merrill both laughed and Merrill translated for Carol what Ali had said. It pleased her, she laughed and put one hand on the small turbaned head.

"Tell him," she said, "that I'm glad to see him again."

Merrill translated what she had said and told her that Ali said he too was glad to see her because she had a beautiful voice that was like music.

"Come," said Indira, "it's growing very hot here. We'll go to the bungalow." And to the sweeper who took care of the laboratory animals she said, "Bring a box for Ali's guinea pig."

They moved back again across the blazing courtyard into the shelter of the big Java fig trees which covered the bungalow like two vast umbrellas, and there on the verandah Merrill and Carol and the boy sat while Indira went to give orders for cold drinks.

"It is a nice place," said Carol. "Peaceful."

She wasn't good with words and what she meant was far more profound and full of meaning. Here in the house it was cool not only because it was shaded and hidden away; it was something more than that. It was the serenity which touched her. After the Taj Mahal and the races and Malabar Hill, above all, after the nightmarish drive through the filth and clamor of the Mill district, this was another world, like Paradise.

Indira came back and they sat peacefully talking while Ali played with his guinea pig. It was a comic little beast. Wherever he put his hand the guinea pig would run under it for shelter.

Indira asked how Merrill felt and when he answered her, she said with a quiet smile, "I knew you were feeling better."

"He needed some fun," said Carol.

Then she listened while Indira and Merrill talked of Moti's work and the progress he was making and about Merrill's work in the villages and about her own tour of Europe, perhaps the last one she would be able to make in a long time if things went on there as they were going. And while Carol sat there, lazily watching the antics of Ali and the guinea pig, with half her mind, an odd thing happened to her. She knew suddenly that she was tired. It wasn't a physical weariness but a weariness and boredom of the spirit, as if her life had become intolerable to her.

Presently Buck suggested that she might like to go through the laboratory of the Institute and have a look at the snakes. It was, he said shyly, all very interesting. He thought Carol might like it.

"I'd love to see them," said Carol. "I've never seen any real venomous snakes—only the kind the snake charmers have on the streets."

So the four of them went off to the laboratory, Ali carrying his guinea pig and still holding, Moslem fashion, to Buck's big hand. They saw how the serums were made and met the odd old man who extracted the snake venom and had been bitten twenty-seven times by the cobras and Russell's vipers and had his life saved twenty-seven times by Moti's serums. Grinning proudly, he displayed his tough old brown arms spotted with tiny scars.

"His arms must be like sieves," said Carol. "Doesn't he mind?"

"No," said Indira, "he seems to like it. If you spoke Gujerati or

Hindustani he'd tell you about each snake and each bite. He's very proud of his record."

Then they visited the snake cages and watched the cobras rise up behind the glass and weave back and forth to strike futilely at them, and the heavy Russell's vipers which hissed like sluggish steam engines. And then Ali said something to Mrs. Moti and Buck laughed aloud.

"What did he say?" asked Carol.

A faint color came into Buck's cheeks and he said, "Ali asked would Mrs. Moti hold his guinea pig so that he could take the hand of the pretty lady."

Mrs. Moti took the guinea pig and Ali stretched out his hand in a vague groping gesture for Carol to take. And then the two of them—Carol and Buck—walked back to the bungalow linked by the small son of the mahout.

On the verandah they sat for a little while longer until Buck looking at his watch said, "We'd better go. I promised Bill I'd go with him this morning to buy some clothes. He doesn't think that I'm enough of a swell."

Indira smiled, "You must come and see me then. I'd like to see you dressed up for once."

They said good-bye and Indira and Ali walked to the taxicab with them. Indira said to Carol, "You must come back often."

"I will . . . every time Buck will bring me."

In the taxicab as they drove back through the awful Mill district Buck did all the talking. She answered his questions now and then but otherwise she was silent, thinking. It seemed to her that this simple morning had been the happiest one she had known in a long time.

When Buck and Carol arrived at the hotel, he said, to her surprise, "Let's go to the bar and have a drink?"

"Okay!" She looked at him and added, "You told me it wasn't good for you to drink too much."

He only laughed and said, "It's different here. In the heat alcohol doesn't stay with you. It's all gone almost before you drink it. Anyway, I'm feeling fine."

"You're the doctor. I can always take it."

[196]

Then the moment they entered the door they were caught. At the very front big table there was a party going on, an odd and raffish party which caused Carol to think as she saw it, "I've seen some pretty hot collections but this one wins the prize."

At one table were the Baroness, Mrs. Trollope, Jellapore and Joey, Botlivala, Bill and the Marchesa. As if at a signal they all said, "Come and join us." There was something strained about the invitation, as if the whole group were a party stranded in the middle of the Red Sea calling for help. Carol thought, "Damn it! There's no getting away now." She had wanted to have a drink alone with Buck, sitting there talking peacefully and comfortably, watching the crowd. She wanted to keep the pleasantness of the morning, hugging it to her, carrying it on and on.

So they sat down, separated from each other, to Carol's regret. Chance in the opening of the chairs brought her between Jellapore and Bill; it placed Buck between the Baroness, to whom he gave a single look of startled alarm, and Mrs. Trollope.

They hadn't been doing very well. That was why as one person they had put up the flag of distress at sight of Buck and Carol in the doorway. Only two persons had not cried for help—the Baroness, who was insensible to the intricate feelings of people and parties, and Jellapore, who flourished in a sour and disagreeable atmosphere.

He was already bored with Bombay and wished he was back in Paris. And he knew that before him was not Paris but the worse boredom of the tiny confined life of Jellapore State. When he was bored he was dangerous, not only to himself because boredom betrayed him into follies and scandals, but to others because in order to entertain himself he indulged in intrigues, spread insinuations and led people to make fools of themselves. He had already been at work, and as if a devil had seized him, he would continue.

There were a great many things going on around the table, things which enslaved them all in a web of ego and intrigue and desire, all but Joey, who was already pleasantly oblivious and ginny and simply sat there smiling pleasantly at one after the other without ever saying a word.

They all had drinks and made conversation and cracks, but underneath the surface things were going on. For example, Mr.

[197]

Botlivala was on the make for the Marchesa until Carol appeared in the door. The Marchesa was exactly Mr. Botlivala's type. She was good-looking and expensively dressed; she had a title and managed an air of distinction, bogus to those who *knew*, but impressive to Mr. Botlivala who was the sort which thinks that overacting is genius. So until Carol appeared he had been engaged in impressing the Marchesa. He had a great many ways of doing this. He did not attack by making believe that he was overwhelmingly smitten; in an odd way he knew his limitations—that he was small and unattractive and not very potent. He began by attempting to create an air of wealth and importance. So he laid his platinum cigarette case, a very feminine one inset with a border of emeralds and diamonds, on the table beside his drink, and then went into a conversation about racing stables at Deauville and Cannes. Oddly enough, the Marchesa, who had told Bill that she only spoke French and Italian, spoke English with Mr. Botlivala, a good deal better than she had spoken French with Bill at Government House.

Her opaque black eyes noted the cigarette case and into them came the look of a greedy concierge at the sight of a fat tip. While they talked her eye kept returning to it as if something about the diamonds and emeralds hypnotized her. She, like Mr. Botlivala, was not too good at the appraisal of people, and so, just as he had been taken in by her bad performance, she was convinced by his. But in spite of the attention exercised by the case and the conversation, her mind occasionally wandered elsewhere, frequently enough to make Mr. Botlivala aware that there were moments when she was not actually listening and moments when he was not being as fascinating as he meant to be.

Actually, although Mr. Botlivala had neither the experience nor the perspicacity in his plump brown little body to understand it, the Marchesa was suffering at the moment from an acute division of urges—one toward Mr. Botlivala's cigarette case and the other toward the body of Mr. Wainwright, the American gentleman seated on the other side of her.

Such a division of urges had in fact dominated her whole existence since its very beginning as a pretty, dark ox-eyed child of mixed Greek and Syrian blood born in Adrianople.

Mr. Wainwright, the American, had made an impression upon

her from the moment she entered the room at Government House, and the memory of him had been with her pretty steadily since the moment when, in a sort of vague, gambling hope, she had clung a little too long to his hand as he bade her good-bye. For more than a week now she had tried to find an opportunity for another meeting. She had succeeded only in seeing him once or twice in the distance without even a chance of speaking to him. And then this morning as, chaperoned by her maid, she stopped for a moment in the doorway of the bar, Jellapore had seen her and invited her to join the table where he was sitting with the Baroness and Mr. Wainwright. The presence of the Baroness, normally, would have driven her away, but the presence of Mr. Wainwright more than overbalanced that unpleasant fact.

Mr. Wainwright attracted her as a new type. Although she had had a good deal of experience, she had known very few American men, and never one like this one. When she tried to remember, she could think of only two or three rather beefy, clumsy, stupid, middle-aged men who, terrified inside, had tried to make her believe that they were experienced at love.

Mr. Wainwright, clearly, was different. In the first place he wasn't beefy or stupid, and certainly he was neither terrified nor unexperienced; that much she had divined from the meeting at Government House. She knew as well as if the meeting had happened in the old days when the Baroness opened the door of the little sitting room in the Square Chausée d'Antin and said in bad French, "Girls, a couple of gentlemen want to be entertained," that she was being looked over. That she sat at the table of the Governor of the Madras Presidency as the Marchesa Carviglia, wife of the Generalissimo Carviglia, made no difference. She had, she knew, been looked over, and while she had not been actually rejected, she had been card-indexed for future reference.

It was not intelligence or even instinct which told her all this, but simple deduction from a very long and varied experience. She divined the card-index theory from the way in which he had looked at her as they talked, from the way in which his hand had responded ever so slightly to the unabashed inviting pressure of her own. His hand had said to her, "Not right off, but perhaps a little later." At the same time, knowing the signs, she did not abandon hope. She knew that he had not held back through any moral scruple, nor because he did not think her a possibility. More than likely there was another woman somewhere who, at the moment, had possession of him.

So she had waited, not without impatience, for a second meeting, and as the impatience grew, the object of her interest—Mr. Bill Wainwright—became steadily more attractive to her. She knew, without seeing him, the way his curly blond hair grew and exactly the angle of the squarish jaw and the look of the large rather sensual mouth; but most of all she remembered and saw again and again the mocking twinkle in the blue eyes. It had disconcerted her at first because the eyes seemed to be jeering, but by now that no longer troubled her. There was behind the look a kind of devilishness which made her want to know him better. In her handsome voluptuous body there was an element of masochism. In the distant past the Baroness, aware of this, had thrown some generous clients with odd tastes in her direction.

And the Marchesa was pressed for time in both the long and the short run. The Levantine tendency toward fat, which up to now she had managed by nearly starving herself to keep in control, would, she knew, claim her altogether before many more years. That was the long run. In the short run she had only another month or two for adventure. After that she would have to go back again to Italy, back to the elderly Generalissimo and the nunnery existence which he demanded of her in order to preserve his own honor and his own reputation as a lady-killer. She was, in fact, on her annual holiday. He knew exactly how she employed it, and did not mind so long as she enjoyed herself in out of the way places.

Up to date she had had no success, either on the way out to Bombay or in Bombay, and the time was flying. Six weeks or two months was short enough with the years piling up on you. It wouldn't be very long until she wouldn't have any charm whatever for an attractive man. So she went to work in earnest. As she wasn't a clever woman who could get what she wanted in an intelligent way, she went to work in the oldest, most vulgar way she knew. That was why, ignoring all the etiquette which the Baroness and, after her, the Generalissimo, had taught her with such infinite care, she had plumped herself down next to Bill Wainwright instead of on the opposite side of the table next to the Maharajah.

The first time Bill felt her foot creeping up his instep, he drew his foot away and turning toward her he said, "I'm sorry." She was talking to Botlivala and apparently noticed nothing, not even his apology. Without even turning she continued her conversation. Then in a little while as his leg grew cramped and he extended his foot once more, the foot of the Marchesa touched his again. This time he did not trouble to move his foot or apologize. He only thought, "She means it. I guess she's in earnest all right. Well, I've done worse."

In an odd way he wished that he could feel more excited about the Marchesa, principally because he was still irritated by Carol and Buck having gone off together leaving him alone. He had gone on being irritated all the morning, all through Smithers' sanctimonious examination of the deceased Hinkle's desk and papers, all through Smithers' groveling explanation of the plans for reorganization and the tough job he had before him. And he was still irritated. He would have liked being interested enough in the Marchesa just to have a fling and show Carol.

But he wasn't. So he just sat there indifferently wiggling his foot now and then to communicate to the Marchesa that he was aware of what she was up to, and because out of long habit he always wiggled back in order to be polite and avoid hurt feelings. Then presently she abandoned Mr. Botlivala and his cigarette case and turned to him, and as she turned the knee went into action.

"Why did you tell me," Bill asked her, "that you didn't speak English?"

The full red lips parted in a smile and the long, false eyelashes fluttered for a moment over the ox-eyes.

"Because I thought eet would make me more eenteresting."

He returned the mammy-palaver saying, "You don't have to make yourself more interesting." And at the same time, he thought, "My God, she's stupider than I thought," and suddenly he divined what it was she was and where she came from. He thought, "She ought to be dressed in a chemise and black silk stockings sitting on a red plush and gilt sofa." And at the same time he had intimations of her connections in the past with the Baroness. The old woman, he saw, had been watching them. And at the same moment Carol and Buck appeared in the doorway and he forgot about the Marchesa altogether. At the same time he knew that he was in love with Carol. It wasn't any use kidding himself any longer. The astonishing thing was that he knew too that he had never before been in love with her. He'd never before been in love with anyone.

His voice was saying to the Marchesa, "Yes, I'll be leaving for Calcutta tomorrow night," but inwardly he was saying, "Jeez-us! I'll have to sell myself all over with Carol and this time it'll be tough." Because she knew him so well he would have to persuade her, even deceive her about himself.

Then with a sudden feeling of delight he saw her come over and sit beside him. Quickly he turned and said, "Well, did you enjoy yourself?"

Joey, at the Maharajah's orders, roused himself to ask them what they would drink and after they had ordered, Carol said, "Yes, I had a swell time. I want to go back there again."

"A pretty dirty part of town."

"I didn't notice it."

"You must have been blind."

"No, I was thinking hard most of the time."

He grinned. "What about?"

"None of your damned business."

(There she was again—shutting him out.)

"You might have taken me with you."

"Buck said you were sleeping so hard he didn't want to waken you."

"Nuts to Buck."

She looked at him with surprise. "You needn't be so earnest about it. Buck is the best guy you'll ever know."

"Oh!" said Bill.

He had forgotten entirely about the Marchesa, but she had not forgotten him. Nearly a bottle of champagne had made her bolder. Even though his back was turned to her, the knee was close against his, pressing, hard at work. It was easier now that the table was crowded. She meant to get what she wanted. Bill wanted to turn and say suddenly, "Oh, all right, but later when I'm not so busy." But you couldn't quite say that.

Across the table the Baroness was still watching. She knew what was up because, after all, she knew the Marchesa very well. The green eyes peered out of the raddled old face between the chenille eyelashes. She thought, "All right, I'll fix her before she gets out of India. She never was anything but a second-rate whore. You can't make a silk purse of a sow's ear."

After a moment Carol forgot her disappointment and began to enjoy herself. After all, she liked parties and people, the odder and funnier the better. That was one of the reasons why she loved India better than any place she had ever been. That was the reason she stayed on in spite of heat, of discomfort, of nerves, of nearly being broke. She was happy presently, without knowing why, without troubling to understand that the moment she came to the table the spirits of all these tired and hard and jaded people suddenly rose as if something magical had occurred, because she was beautiful and happy and because she really liked or loved them all.

Only the Maharajah understood pretty well what was going on around the table because he alone of them all, with his talent for intrigue, possessed the detachment to watch them and to be fascinated by all the currents and complications which crossed back and forth like an intricate web. Joey, sitting back, had an indifference toward them all, and he was too drunk and anyway he wasn't very bright. But Jelly, impotent, bored, malicious and jeering, saw it all. He saw the face of Mrs. Trollope light up like an electric bulb at the sight of Carol. He saw the Baroness hating the Marchesa. He watched the game of the Marchesa, her heavily beautiful face intent upon Botlivala and his cigarette case while her knee worked on Bill Wainwright. He saw Bill turn from her to Carol the moment Carol sat down, his body leaning toward her as if drawn like a bit of iron toward a magnet. He saw too the silly groveling emptiness of Botlivala and the way the newcomer they called Buck looked at Carol. There was very little that he missed and as he sat there leaning back, his long, thin, cruel fingers stroking the icy glass which held his drink, the dark and intricate mind ceased presently to be bored, because it was occupied again, this time by the greatest passion he knew, a passion even greater than women or gambling—the fabrication of mischief and intrigue. He began rearranging the lives and personalities of the people at the table, changing them about, moving them here and there, placing them side by side, like pieces in a puzzle which, when complete, made an ugly, indecent picture. For weeks now, ever since women had become something beyond his attainment, he had been considering secretly the prospects of abdicating and putting his oldest son on the throne with his own dissolute brother as regent, to retire into a saintly life of atonement and contemplation. But that idea was forgotten now. The world and the people in it remained too fascinating to abandon. As he watched them, planning, shifting the pieces about, he took on suddenly a kind of evil beauty and dignity, for the only time Jelly was not merely silly was when he was creating mischief and sometimes tragedy.

In the afternoon Bill took Buck to the Army and Navy Stores to buy the trousseau. The trip wasn't at all what Bill had expected it to be. In the first place Buck displayed an interest in what he was buying, an interest which Bill found astonishing considering Buck's indifference to clothes in the past. From the time he had come to college to work his way through, he had never been able to afford good clothes and so he had ignored them, dressing himself in incredibly ill-fitting and shabby garments which had never seemed to make much difference since they could not dim his own natural health and good looks. Now, as the two of them went from department to department of the big store, Buck was fussy about shoes, about materials, about neckties, about handkerchiefs. He was like a long sober citizen going on a spree, and the spree occasionally led him into choices which upset Bill's more conservative tastes.

Once he said, protesting, "You don't want that tie and handkerchief. You'll look like a Eurasian stationmaster on an outing."

But Buck had them just the same. Grinning, he said, "This is the first chance I've ever had to *express* myself in clothes. Let me have my fun."

"It's your funeral," said Bill. "If you're planning to attract crowds, you're doing fine." A little later he looked quizzically at

Buck and said, "What's come over you? You never used to be so fussy about clothes."

"I'm doing what you want, ain't I?" said Buck. "What you and Moti wanted me to do. I'm cutting loose. Don't get in my way."

A little ruefully Bill answered, "Okay! But we didn't expect you to get yourself up as a 'con' man. That wasn't part of the plan."

There was a grin on Buck's face and a twinkle in his eye which Bill didn't like. It was as if Buck had a secret joke of some kind up his sleeve, as if he were saying, "You and Moti got me into this. Now watch me!"

It was all a part of the odd feeling which had come between them since they sat at the table in the bar with all those nightmarish people, something which was intangible yet separated them, marring the old relationship precariously restored only a little while before. It was like sand in smoothly functioning machinery. In the heat and bustle of the shop the aggravation grew steadily worse and worse. Bill felt hotter and hotter and wearier and more irritated as the shopping continued. And then at last it was finished and Buck said, surprisingly, "I'm paying for all this."

"That wasn't the agreement," said Bill. "It was to be part of the cure contributed by me."

"If your father wants to give some money, let him give it to the work I'm doing. I can handle this. I've got a little money my grandfather left me. I'd kind of like to spend it this way." He grinned sheepishly, "He was a pious old fraud. He darkened my whole childhood. It would be getting back at him—if he knew how I was spending that dough."

Again Bill thought, "What the hell has come over him?" But he only said aloud, "It seems to me you're making a lightning recovery."

Buck laughed, "Moti said it would be quick."

Then Bill felt sour and said, "Well, take my advice and don't go ahead too fast. There's nothing worse than a middle-aged man trying to make up for lost time—unless it's an old lecher."

"You ain't seen anything yet," said Buck.

Bill didn't answer him. He only grinned and thought, "My God! What have we let loose!" And again he felt an inward alarm, even

[205]

above the faint irritation, lest Buck should get completely out of hand and go to hell.

Sourly he said, "What you need is a date with the Marchesa."

On the way back from the Army and Navy Stores, Buck said, "Let's get Carol and go to the races."

"I can't. I've got to work. You may be on a spree but I'm not. Anyway she very likely won't be there. She's probably gone already."

"Who with?"

"Oh, Botlivala and Mrs. Trollope probably."

There was a little silence and Buck said, "I don't like either of them very much. I wish she wouldn't go around with them."

"If you think you can tell her who she's to go around with, you're crazy. I've never been able to and I've known her a hell of a long time. She likes disreputable people."

"Botlivala especially is bad news. I've been around India long enough to know his kind. They ought to be shot."

"You don't have to be around India to discover that." And he heard himself saying, "Anyway, she's engaged to him."

Buck sat up straight, "I don't believe it," he said. "Who told you that?"

Bill grinned, not without malice. "She did. She asked me to get her out of it."

The reaction was unexpected. He felt Buck draw away from him into the far corner of the taxi seat, not physically so much as psychologically. And he knew that half-willfully, half-unwittingly he had poured more sand into the bearings of the relationship between them. For a long time Buck didn't say anything. When at last he spoke, he said, "I don't believe it."

"I'm only telling you what she told me."

"I don't believe she ever meant it."

"Well, I don't either, for that matter. At any rate, Botlivala thinks so. It's supposed to be a secret engagement, but I wouldn't trust Botlivala to keep his mouth shut."

Then as if talking to himself, Buck said, "The dirty little rat!"

Bill couldn't resist baiting him, so he said, "Who?"

"Botlivala."

"Oh, he's harmless enough. She's managed a lot worse than him."

[206]

And presently he said, "Anyway, I wouldn't let it worry you. She's able to take care of herself. The thing most people don't give her credit for is brains. She doesn't know herself how smart she is or else she's ashamed of it. That's a smart girl—I *know*."

Buck suddenly turned and looked at him but didn't say anything. And Bill was silent too, a little amazed at his own speech about Carol's brains. He'd never thought it out before. It just seemed to come out of his mouth. The important thing was that he knew that what he had said was true.

Then the taxi drew up at the door of the hotel and Bill felt suddenly that the best thing for him to do was to clear out, so he said he was having a shower and going to the office and would see Buck at cocktail time.

When he was gone Buck called Carol's room and got no answer. At the desk they said she had gone out with Mrs. Trollope, where the clerk did not know, but he supposed it was the races. There wasn't anywhere else to go.

Then all at once Buck felt tired with that utter feeling of collapse which malaria victims experience, and he knew that it would be better to go upstairs to his room for a rest, but he knew too that he could not do it. The high spirits had melted away in the heat and conversation of the taxi, and he felt a little ill now and confused, like a boy of sixteen in love for the first time. He did not know what to think or what he should think. He was only aware that suddenly he had found himself on the fringe of a world which was beyond his experience and understanding. It wasn't only that what he had heard of Carol was puzzling, but that Bill should have told it so cynically, as if what he said was of no importance but only a subject of mirth. For a moment, as he turned away from the desk and stood looking at the crowd but not seeing it, he was afraid. He thought, "Maybe I'm too dumb to go on with it. Maybe what Bill hinted is true—that it's too late for me to make up for lost time. Maybe I was born a sap and will always be one."

But there was only one thing which he had to do and that was to find Carol. Maybe he'd speak to her about what Bill had told him or maybe he wouldn't have the courage. It wasn't, perhaps, any of his business and maybe she would only laugh at him. But he had to see her.

And so with his head aching and the heat pressing down on him, suffocating him, he set out again through the burning streets for the race course. What had started out at the table in the bar as fun had changed into something else. The heat did nothing to ease or clarify his bewilderment.

At the race course it seemed hotter than ever, hotter even than in the city. There was a great crowd, churning about under the jacqueranda and peepul trees, going and coming to and from the paddock, the stands, the club enclosure. Paying off the taxi at the gate, Buck plunged into the crowd as he had often long ago plunged into a football game, feeling groggy and confused and ill. Only now it was not the ball he had to find and rescue but Carol. His brain no longer seemed to function properly. There was no reason in it but only the growing power of obsession, a gnawing, driving power which forced him into places where he had no right to go. He jostled Arab horse traders, Parsee beauties, bold Khoja women, British officials, Princes. He entered sacred club enclosures and even the owner's box. It was a world in which he was a stranger, knowing no one. He did not even find any of the little group he had met that morning at the bar. There was no one whom he could ask, and after a while the search took on a night-marish quality in which it seemed to him that he was rushed, now from this side, now from that, by hundreds of strange people intent on crushing him. Two or three times when his head became con-fused he sat down on a chair in the shade until he again gained some control of himself. He was aware that people stared at him with curiosity but it did not matter to him. And at last in one of those moments of clarity he thought, "She is not here. If I don't go back now I won't be able to make it alone. I'll make a fool of myself by fainting." And the shyness which was always there deep inside him seized him and, staggering as he walked, he made his way to the gate and climbed into a taxi.

In the heat of the drive back, the noises of the streets pounded in his ears and there were moments when he seemed to slip into unconsciousness and then out again like a bird flying through clouds. The drive seemed endless and in the moments when his brain functioned properly, one phrase kept going through his head over and over again, "Walking before you can run! Walking before you can run!"

How he paid the driver and managed to enter the hotel and find his room he was never able to remember. In the end the obsession left him and he could not remember where he had been nor why he had gone. But at last on the bed, after tossing restlessly for a long time, he slipped into unconsciousness, and just before the room faded into a blur, it seemed to him that he was back again in the compartment of the train crossing the burning Deccan and Carol was there stroking his head to ease the pain.

It was Jellapore's idea that they go to Juhu Beach for a swim. He had there a small house where in the old days as a young man he had kept from time to time a nautch girl who held his fancy. It was a pleasant house, he said, with a garden overlooking the beach surrounded by a high wall. It was too hot to go to the races. They could go to Juhu and play bridge for a while, enjoy the cool of the beach in the evening and if anyone felt like it, he could go for a swim. He asked Carol and Mrs. Trollope, Botlivala, the Marchesa and a couple of Parsee friends. He had not meant to ask the Baroness but she got wind of it somehow and while Joey was arranging about the food and the champagne she ran him to earth and told him enthusiastically what a wonderful plan it was, so there wasn't anything to be done.

Before Carol left the hotel, she wrote a note to Bill saying where they had gone and asking him and Buck to join them. The house at Juhu, she thought, would be easy to find. It was, she said, the fifth house beyond the signal station.

She wasn't enthusiastic about the expedition. She didn't really care whether she went or not, except that she had never been to Juhu and felt a desire to see it. She thought too that as long as Buck and Bill were busy all the afternoon there wasn't any reason for her to hang about in the sweltering heat of the city. And anyway it would make Mrs. Trollope and Botlivala happy. You could see that the moment the expedition was proposed and the faces of both of them lighted up.

[209]

And so she had not gone to the races and Bill didn't find her note and Buck looked for her in the burning heat at the race course until illness drove him back to the hotel. At the last moment the Marchesa, learning that Mr. Wainwright would not be in the party, stayed behind, sending word that she was suffering from a migraine.

It was a lovely house. When Carol stepped through the gate she knew that it was worth going all the way to Juhu to see it. It stood in a walled garden between the road and the sea, hidden by a grove of cocoanut and betel palms so that until you had passed through the gate you did not see the house at all. It was only when you walked through the grove past a tank ornamented with small Shiva bulls in white marble that you came upon the lacy structure. It was small and built with a wide jutting roof and windows carved in the Mogul style in filigrees of marble. Just below the eaves there was painted a slightly indecent frieze running round the whole pavilion which depicted on the four sides of the house the pleasures of drinking, love, the table and the chase. All round the house in a wide border there was a wide terrace ornamented with flowering plants, in pots, changed each week to alter the design and give variety. On the side facing the bay there was a marble terrace with a singing fountain and white marble steps which ran down through the cocoanut palms to a grilled gateway overlooking the sea.

Inside there were four rooms on each floor—belowstairs a banqueting room, a gaming room and two lounging rooms and abovestairs two bedrooms in the Indian style and two furnished in the most luxurious and vulgar French fashion with gilded beds and bed covers of heavy brocade. The carved sandalwood walls were adorned by French engravings of an intimate and bawdy nature.

The heat and the smell of the city were gone and in their place was the heavy damp atmosphere of the sea and the lush smell of growing plants and trees. The little party, all save Botlivala, who had been there before, moved about under the trees and through the house. Joey set the two servants to work preparing the champagne and presently Carol said, "I don't want to play bridge. I want to lie here on the terrace and be lazy," and so Jellapore and

Joey and the Baroness and one of the Parsees made up a four with the fifth Parsee cutting in.

Mrs. Trollope pulled up a deck chair and lay down in it next to Carol. She was happy now. She had Carol all to herself. That was all that she asked. She began almost at once to talk about the Marchesa, not very interestingly and with a great deal of hostility, why, Carol could not divine since long ago she had dismissed the Marchesa as not worth the exertion of conversation. Evidently Mrs. Trollope hated her, and slowly it began to dawn on Carol that perhaps inside her bitter twisted self she hated very nearly everybody. It did not occur to her that Mrs. Trollope hated anyone who came near Carol herself, that she was jealous of everyone who even spoke to her.

"She's just a common Levantine woman. I don't know anything about her title or that phony old husband," said Mrs. Trollope. She went on and on, her voice a dim buzzing in Carol's ears, but after a time, like the buzzing of a fly, the sound of her voice began to become unendurable. She was hot and uncomfortable and bored, because there was something on her mind that she wanted to work out, and Mrs. Trollope kept annoying her.

So presently she said, "Listen, Stitch, do you mind going away or just sitting there without talking? I don't often think but I'm trying to think right now." Mrs. Trollope looked hurt again, with that dreadful collapsed look, as if she had been kicked in the face. So Carol leaned toward her and laying one hand on her arm said, "Listen, honey, it's just because I'm worried about something."

At the touch of the hand on her arm, the hurt look in Mrs. Trollope's face was supplanted by one of delight.

"Of course, my dear, I understand. If there is anything I can do call on me. I've worried myself. I'll go in and play some bridge."

As she left Carol said over her shoulder, "Tell the boy to bring me some champagne." That too made Mrs. Trollope happy.

Carol thought, "I hope she doesn't begin gambling again." And rolling over lazily in the heat, she thought too, "Well, being kind to her didn't cost anything and it made her happy." But with Mrs. Trollope gone, the strain imposed by her tense and tortured presence disappeared and she applied herself to her thinking.

There were a lot of things she had to "think out" and this

seemed the perfect place for it, with the sound of the singing fountain and the faint rustle of the cocoanut palm fronds deadening the edge of nerves and heat. The boy brought the champagne in a tall glass, spiced the way Jellapore liked it, a strange aphrodisiac beverage, with the gaiety of Paris and the sensuality of India, half-East, half-West, all in one drink. She had hated it in the beginning when Jellapore's brother had first given it to her, but since then she had acquired a taste for it. It made you feel terribly well and the spices somehow took the headache out of it. Idly, she thought, not really caring very much, "Another sign of going to pieces."

It was that which troubled her. It was "going to pieces" which she had to think out. Just how she was going to prevent it, or how to pull herself up and change the whole line of her existence, she did not know. What puzzled others about her and what confused her own life was the fact that whenever she arrived at a certain stage of disintegration, something Swedish, something even Swedenborgian, rose up out of her childhood and made her both afraid and ashamed. It was as if a voice came out of the very blood saying "You are a Swede and Swedes never go to pieces. They can drink and be dissolute and still cope with wild living." There were moments when she was passionately proud of being a Swede, prouder than of anything on earth. This was one of those moments.

She was nearly broke. Lying there in the garden of the little marble house called Jai Mahal, she didn't push the thought away from her. All she had left was the few thousand rupees she had made gambling, and that, considering her extravagance, wouldn't last very long. She thought, "Tomorrow I will invest in a ticket as far as Paris. Then I can get away when I want to go. Once in Paris I can make out somehow."

She had spent all the money Bill had forced her to take when they were divorced. Where it had gone she did not know, but she did not regret its going, since it had made her for a little time completely independent, and out of spending it she had had a wonderful time. She was not going to accept another penny from him, no matter how desperate she became; she was not even going to let him know that in five years she had succeeded in throwing it all out of the window.

She opened her eyes and for a moment, attracted by its raucous cries, she watched the Minah bird which hung in a big red lacquer cage at the end of the terrace. It would scream and then say what appeared to be a long and complicated sentence. She tried to make out what it was saying and at last gave it up, thinking, "It's probably talking Hindustani anyway." And with that she went back to her thinking.

She considered the question of making a living. There wasn't a chance of going back to the stage. Ziegfeld was dead and the market for show-girls was glutted with girls younger and perhaps more beautiful than herself. And as for acting—she didn't deceive herself —she wasn't interested and she had about as much talent as you could stick in your eye. So that was out.

She might marry, but at the moment she couldn't imagine whom. Certainly she was not going to remarry Bill just when he was getting on his feet. She knew, with a vague but iron-clad certainty, that very likely she could do it any time she wanted; but she knew too that no good would come of it. They were bad for each other, because they had too good a time together. That was all right when you were young but it wasn't any good later in life. Bill had to settle down and make sense. If they married again, they'd just begin staying up late and leading a rollicking life and Bill would end up a penniless bum. She was fond of Bill and if he stuck to his knitting he'd have plenty of money, but she wasn't going to marry him all over again just because she was too fond of him. What Bill needed was a good, conventional American wife to read him the riot act every so often. He'd hate it at first but after a time he'd like it and come home late at night asking for it. It would keep him going along the narrow path and make him think that it was his own strength of character instead of some wife's iron hand which accomplished the miracle. He was already headed in that direction. He was showing every sign of it. In another five or ten years Bill would be the perfect American husband or he'd be lying in the gutter, and she wasn't going to be the one to help him lie down.

There was always, of course, the proposition of the Baroness, made over champagne, half in jest and half in earnest. She didn't mind the Baroness as much as other people seemed to mind her.

The poor old thing had probably never had a break. She looked like a turtle and had the manners of a rhinoceros, but neither thing bothered Carol particularly. Except when gambling the Baroness was gentle as a dove with her. In fact she was rather fond of the old girl, tough and evil as she was.

She had suspicions as to just what the business of the Baroness was. Still, if the job she offered was only that of being hostess in a Cairo or Paris night club, she could manage that. It would give her enough to live on and she might even find new openings. She wouldn't take the job, though, without a guarantee and a percentage all in writing. The Baroness, she knew, would steal the pennies off a dead man's eyes.

And then there was Mr. Botlivala. But Mr. Botlivala was out from the word go. She knew now how foolish she had been to say to him, simply to end his persecution and be rid of him, "All right, all right, if you want to be engaged *secretly*, I don't mind." Because she couldn't get rid of him now. He was always on the telephone, always wanting her to go places with him. And she knew too that there wasn't any longer any *secret* about the engagement. He had managed to convey the news and intimations of worse things to the whole of Bombay. And she knew that all this had made her lose caste and put her in a false position, so that all the European population of Bombay was inclined to look the other way when she appeared anywhere. The snobs didn't bother her because she had no desire to go about either in Government or business circles, but it was all messy and disorderly. The Swede, rising up in her, protested now. She had to straighten things out. And always she was a little alarmed by Mr. Botlivala. He was the kind who might do treacherous and unexpected things—especially when his incredible vanity had suffered.

And Mrs. Trollope was getting to be unendurable, hanging on like a limpet to a rock.

She took another sip of Jellapore's fantastic champagne concoction and thought, "No, honey, you've got to do something. You've got your foot in your ear plenty. You've got to get straightened out." Out of all the world which surrounded her there seemed no security except in one direction—the Colonel Moti and his wife, whom she scarcely knew, and Buck.

[214]

Her thoughts wandered away from the tangle of her silly existence to Buck, and thinking of him, she relaxed suddenly and closing her eyes again, she saw him in her imagination with a startling clarity. She saw things about him which she had been unaware of noticing—not things like the blueness of his honest eyes and the squareness of his jaw and the beauty of his big capable hands, not obvious things like that, but the way he threw his head back when he laughed, his simple uncomplicated friendliness, the way he enjoyed himself. In some ways he was extraordinarily like Bill. All the nice things in Bill were in Buck and none of the nasty things, none of the weakness or boredom, none of the too-quick feminine quality of mind which could annoy and even torment you, none of that air of "What the hell does anything matter?" That was the dangerous almost evil thing about Bill. In a way he corrupted everybody about him with his plausible philosophy that nothing mattered but the fun of the moment. "Good-time Charlie!" She loved him, though, even when he was impossible.

But she forgot him quickly and thought only of Buck, wishing he were here with her and that the white marble pavilion behind her was empty. All those tired, raddled defeated people gambling in the cool marble room seemed to desecrate and corrupt the extraordinary beauty of the place. She wished they could be alone together in some remote place like this. Except for the drive in the taxi, they had never had a chance to talk together, alone, without others about them who altered the atmosphere and made it somehow like a scene, a conversation, that was taking place on a stage or in a cinema. She was aware presently that something had happened during the visit to the Moti's which had changed the quality of her existence, how, she could not say, except that the savor seemed to be gone out of all which before then had been fun. She saw suddenly that that was why she was lying alone here on the terrace instead of being in with the others, gambling. That was why she had to drink. It occurred to her that all this might be a part of the change she had been waiting for. And again the thought occurred to her that Mrs. Trollope and all her fortune-telling nonsense might not be so lousy after all. Things, circumstances, atmosphere at times seem to take hold of you and sweep you along, willy-nilly, whether you wanted to go or not. That was what had happened to Mrs. Trollope; maybe that was why she believed in fortunetelling.

Then her thoughts wandered back again to Buck and the afternoon of that first day on the train when she had seen him in a physical agony that terrified her. It occurred to her that she might be the one to help him. And suddenly opening her eyes and smiling, she thought, "It wouldn't be, honey, that you've fallen in love. That would be the pay-off, because what could you do about it—you as the wife of a missionary!"

Then through her thoughts and the sound of the running water and the rustling of palm fronds, she heard another sound from the inside of the pavilion. It was the rattle of poker chips being shifted from one player to another. Sitting up, she thought, "She's off again. She got them to give up bridge and play poker. She'll probably lose her shirt." And finishing the spiced champagne she rose and went into the pavilion to save Mrs. Trollope from herself and from the end which the fortuneteller had chosen not to mention.

In the small room with the marble grilles, she saw at once from the white, desperate face, that Mrs. Trollope had been losing again. She gave Carol one quick glance of appeal and Carol thought, "She'll lose everything and then what will become of her? She'll be around my neck and I'm broke too."

It wasn't the first time she had had people around her neck. It had happened again and again. How, she never quite knew. She only knew that most of her money had gone to people she found hanging around her neck.

She sat down and took from Joey a stack of chips and her mere presence appeared to raise Mrs. Trollope's spirits and give her confidence.

But nothing came of it. Mrs. Trollope went on losing and Carol herself had no luck. She could not discover how much Mrs. Trollope had lost, but she knew from her face that it must have been a great deal. She herself lost over four thousand rupees which was far more than she could afford. Most of it went to the Baroness, who sat like a turtle-headed spider collecting the only thing she loved in the world.

[216]

But there was something wrong about the whole party. They had come out to the pavilion to escape the heat of the city and amuse themselves, but the party wasn't going well. There was something tired and grim and flat about it. Instead of staying on and sending Joey for a picnic supper, they all went back to Bombay. Nobody protested. As they left, Carol said to Jellapore, "It's a lovely place, this house." And grinning, he said, "Yes, but not for this kind of a party. It's made for *l'amour*. When you have a second honeymoon, I'll lend it to you."

She laughed, a kind of empty, prop laugh, and said, "There ain't going to be any second honeymoon."

The heat increased as they drove into the city and with it the depression which had settled over the whole party. Mrs. Trollope rode back in the same car with Carol. When she said, "Let's have dinner together," Carol said, "No, I'm tired. I'm going to have dinner in bed and get some sleep."

At the hotel, Mr. Botlivala was persistent about taking her to dinner and Carol had to insult him to be rid of him. He said, "I don't see any use in going on being engaged." To which Carol replied quickly, "I don't either. We'll call it off."

That frightened Mr. Botlivala, who said, "You know I didn't mean that."

"Well, I do, and I'm not going to discuss it." In a funny way, Mr. Botlivala suddenly seemed a complete stranger to her, as if she had never seen him before. He wasn't simply a persistent, vain little man whom she humored. Tonight there was something hateful and menacing about him.

The door of the lift opened and she stepped in and was carried up out of sight at the very moment Mr. Botlivala was beginning to bluster and make a scene.

On the way up she changed her mind suddenly and asked the boy to stop at Bill's floor. She didn't want to be alone. She had lied to Mrs. Trollope about having dinner in bed. She couldn't sleep now anyway, because the persistence of Mrs. Trollope and Botlivala had put her nerves on edge. She thought, out of nowhere, "Maybe they're both bad-luck bringers. Stitch acts and looks like Calamity Jane." Bill, she thought, would make her laugh and put her in a

[217]

good humor. So she walked to Bill's door and knocked. His voice answered, "Come in," and she pushed open the door.

He had just come from the shower and was standing in his shorts pulling an undershirt over his head. At sight of him, she thought, "He is attractive, damn him. If there was only something behind it all."

He said, "Have a chair, honey. I'll be dressed in a minute."

"Okay."

She sat down, already feeling better at the sight of Bill's grin.

"May I ask what brought a lady calling on me at this hour?"

"Hadn't anything to do. I had to get away from Trollope and Botlivala."

"Where have you been?"

"Didn't you get my note?"

"What note?"

"I left it for you at the desk."

"Oh." He buttoned his shirt and turned serious. "I didn't ask for letters at the desk. I've had a hell of a day."

"How?"

"Well, wrestling with Hinkle's affairs. He died."

"Oh, I didn't know that."

"And the old man has given me his job with a lot of other business attached."

"Did you accept it?"

Fastening his tie, he turned away from the mirror, "There isn't any question of acceptance with my old man. It's either accept or else. You ought to know that."

"That means you're going to stay here?"

"Yes. Damn it!"

"I thought you liked it."

"So did I."

"Where's Buck?"

"That's the rest of the story." He nodded toward the door of Buck's room. "He's in there. I came home and found him in bed and couldn't waken him. It's kind of a coma. Moti's been here. He said he's been like that before. It's a kind of super-exhaustion."

He watched her face and found there what he was afraid of finding.

She said, "Oughtn't he to have a nurse or something?"

"Moti says there isn't a good one to be had. There's only a handful in all Bombay and there's a lot of typhoid."

"You weren't going out and leave him?"

"Moti said it wouldn't matter. He said Buck would probably wake up in the morning all the better for it. It's the only time he really sleeps properly."

She got up and went over and stood looking out of the window over the harbor. The sun was setting and the *dhows* and one or two trading boats were black against the blaze of red light. Without turning, she said, "I'll stay with him."

"You don't need to."

"I think somebody ought to."

This time he was silent. Then he said, "Well, we can both stay. We can have dinner up here. It's a bit sordid—dining in a bedroom—but it might be a relief."

"Okay. That's a good idea. We might have a drink first."

"Sure. I'll tell Silas."

Silas came in and took the order for gimlets, his black eyes full of knowledge and mockery. When he went out, Bill said, "Some day I'm going to wring his neck."

"Why?"

"If you understood eye language, he was making a long, indecent and razzing speech."

"It's probably the only fun he has."

"Do you want to use the bathroom? It's probably in a mess."

"I don't mind. I'll prink up."

When she had gone, closing the door behind her, Bill went to the door between his room and Buck's. It stood open a little way. He closed it quickly and softly.

Silas returned with the drinks, showing a speed in carrying out orders that was sensational. Bill thought, "He doesn't want to miss anything." He said, "Now go and tell the waiter we want dinner here and bring me a menu card."

The black eyes glittered, "Sahib," he said, "no can serve dinner here."

"Why not?"

"Rules not allow."

Nerves and the heat made Bill's face turn red with anger. "Go and do as I tell you. I want dinner for myself and Memsahib here. Tell them to go out and buy tables and chairs and hire servants. I'll pay for it all, but I'm going to eat here."

"Okay," said Silas. A look of delight came over his black face. Now he could go down and bully and threaten the management. As the servant of a "beeg shot" he suddenly had power. He knew all along that his master was a "beeg shot" but he felt only scorn because he never acted like one. In his long experience with "beeg shots" Silas knew that they were bullies, that they cursed and swore and sometimes kicked him, that they boasted of their money and what it could buy. For weeks now he had had to go about meek and ashamed before the other bearers because his master didn't behave like a "beeg shot," like a burra sahib, but only like a gentleman.

Now Silas was happy. He could raise his head again.

When Carol came out of the bathroom the first thing she noticed was the closed door.

"Why did you close it?" she asked.

"I thought our talking might disturb him."

"If anything went wrong, we wouldn't know it."

He looked at her sharply, "I'll open the door now and then and have a look." He took up the drinks. "This'll make you feel better," he said.

"I'm feeling all right."

In a little while, the head waiter himself appeared at the door accompanied by a triumphant Silas. The rules of the hotel were being broken and he had given the order. The head waiter was subdued, but his black eyes at sight of Carol became as mocking and eloquent as those of Silas himself.

Bill ordered a silly dinner—the kind of dinner he had ordered long ago for Carol when she was a show-girl, and he took her out to supper after the performance at the New Amsterdam was finished. There was *bisque* of *Surat écrivisse*, and fish and guinea fowl and sherbet and champagne and *friandises*. As she listened to the order, Carol smiled. When Bill turned to her and asked, "Does that suit you?"

She said, "It all sounds a little gay."

"Why not?"

"Sure, why not?"

Now that Bill had come into the open as a "beeg shot" the service was miraculous. A table and chairs were whisked in, flowers appeared and a white tablecloth. The waiter bowed and asked, "Would you like a radio?"

Bill said, "No, thanks."

Suddenly Carol said, "Yes."

"You can't get anything on it but Indian music."

"I want it. It would be gayer."

So the waiter brought a radio. It was an old-fashioned affair and came from the manager's room. When Carol saw it she laughed and then grew serious, "Will it disturb Buck?"

"No, Moti says when he's like this nothing disturbs him."

Bill had been right. The only music was Indian music. He didn't understand it and he didn't like it, any more than he understood the voice of the announcer speaking Hindustani with a finicky diction. But Carol said, "I like it. It's the nearest to India I've been in a long time—since I left Jellapore."

But it was like everything else. When the dinner came, Bill complained of the soup, although Carol couldn't find anything wrong with it. The whole atmosphere seemed sour and wrong, like the atmosphere at Jelly's failure of an excursion to the lovely house called Jai Mahal. Carol felt it at once and she knew that Bill sensed it too, but it only made him rather disagreeable. He wouldn't trouble to ask himself why everything was wrong. He never did. She thought, "Maybe it's me. Or maybe the stars are wrong."

Bill ordered a second bottle of champagne, and toward the end of dinner he said, bluntly, "What's the matter with you?"

She had been looking out of the window at the flamboyant sunset beyond Elephanta and for a moment she did not hear him. Then she said, "Nothing's the matter. Why?"

"You're funny and depressed . . . not like yourself."

"I'm bored."

"Thanks."

"Oh, not with you. With nothing in particular. Just with everything. It isn't any good any more."

[221]

"What?"

"Everything. All this kind of life. It's disorderly."

Bill grinned. "I can't deny that."

She drank a full glass of champagne and then said, "Shouldn't we take a look at Buck?"

He rose quickly, "I'll look."

She had wanted to look too but he was too quick for her. So she waited until he came out of Buck's room and said, "He's all right. Sleeping like a log."

He sat down and looked at her, still puzzled by the new remoteness which at moments completely isolated her.

Then abruptly he said, "Are you broke?"

She answered him quickly, "No, what makes you think that?"

"Nothing. I only thought if I asked you quickly I might get the truth."

"Smart guy."

"I'm glad we had dinner alone together. I wanted to talk to you about a lot of things."

"Fire away."

"You don't make it very easy."

"I'm sorry." She realized that she was listening with half her mind to Bill but that she was really thinking about Buck.

"I'm going away tomorrow night for a swing around India and Burma. I don't know when I'll be back. There were a couple of things I wanted to settle."

"All right."

"I want to marry you again."

Quickly she said, "No." Then she smiled, "That was certainly a lightning proposition."

"I'm in love with you. I wasn't before."

"I know that."

"It would be all right this time."

"No. It would be just the same."

"I've changed."

"No, you haven't—really."

"So have you."

"No, I haven't either."

"Yes, you have, or I shouldn't have fallen in love with you."

"How do you know the difference?"

"There's plenty of difference and don't ask me how I know."

She didn't answer him and he said, "And wipe that grin off your face."

"I'm not laughing at you. Only you're always so optimistic. You'll never grow up."

"You said that was why you liked me."

"It was. But after a certain age, Peter Pan gets to be simply a case of arrested development."

He was half-angry, half-moved to laugh. "Damn you and your cracks!" At the same time the new emotion which troubled him asserted itself again. She had never seemed so beautiful or so desirable to him as at this moment, but it was the thing over and above that which made the emotion dangerous, a desire to have her with him for the rest of his life, to protect her, to make life easy for her. If he did not have her he would be lonely all the rest of his life. He knew this with a curious disturbing certainty. No matter what happened to him, no matter whom he married, he would always be alone, wanting her.

He put out both hands and took her hand in his, looking squarely into her blue eyes. "I'm serious," he said, "I mean every word I'm saying. If you marry me I'll be a model husband. I'll be faithful. I'll work like a dog. I'll be a great success. I'm not a dumbbell, you know. If you'll marry me, I'll do all that. I swear to God, I will."

She smiled, "No, it wouldn't be any good, Bill. If you got to be like that you wouldn't be Bill any longer—not my Bill. I wouldn't like you. You'd bore me. . . . And if you didn't change, we'd both end in the gutter."

She spoke truly, earnestly, but it was her heart speaking, and not her head. Her head was tempted. It would be so easy, having Bill always there to look after her, to have all that money, to know what the future was to be, never to be tired and worried again. But her heart kept saying, "No, it wouldn't be any good. Don't be a fool." And she knew that her heart had always been right.

He had freed her hand and was lighting a cigarette. "I never *could* talk to you."

She rose and said, "I'm going to have a look at Buck."

[223]

This time she had outwitted him. She was at the door before he could prevent her. He only lighted a cigarette and watched her disappear into Buck's room, never taking his eyes off the doorway. The forehead frowned and the eyes were full of concentration as if he were searching for something.

Inside the room the only light was the glow which came through the door from Bill's room and from the lights in the street. For a moment she was blinded and then slowly out of the dim light emerged the figure of Buck.

He was lying on his side, one arm thrown up over his head, sleeping quietly. The first thing she thought was how much he looked like his own son Tommy. Asleep he was oddly like the small boy she had seen sleeping on the train. The thought made her see Ali, the blind boy, and the odd touching brotherly relationship between him and Buck. It was like nothing she had ever seen. And then she thought, "How good he looks. How kind." And then what Bill himself had always thought, "How clean." Then she noticed the beauty of his face and the line of his throat where it left the square jaw and disappeared into the shadows. It disturbed her, making her want to cry suddenly, and she remembered with pleasure the trip down on the train and how she had helped the pain by stroking the rough, curly blond head. At the time she had felt no emotion; the emotion only came to her now, long afterward. She stood there for a long time, how long she did not know. She was happier than she had ever been.

At last quickly she turned and left, closing the door behind her, thinking at the same time, "How silly! I'm going to blush at sight of Bill, and I mustn't."

She saw that he was watching her with extraordinary concentration and she thought, "Bill, who has never been jealous, is jealous."

She tried to walk to the table as if nothing had happened to her, as if her heart were not beating overtime, as if she did not feel weak at the pit of her stomach.

Bill said, "He's okay, isn't he?"

She sat down and took up her champagne glass. "Yes. He's sleeping."

Quickly he said, "It isn't Buck, is it?"

[224]

She knew what he meant but she evaded answering, as if she wanted to keep all the emotion to herself. "What do you mean—it isn't Buck?"

"I mean he hasn't come between you and me."

"That's a funny way to put it."

"You know what I mean. You must have felt it yourself—as if the two of you clicked. I've felt it."

"I don't know. I really don't think so."

He grinned maliciously, "My God! Love at first sight."

"No, it isn't that."

"You'd make a hell of a missionary's wife."

"Maybe I've thought of that too."

"So it is that far along?"

"No, it isn't, but I've got an imagination."

"Like a cheap serial."

She stood up. "I think I'm going to bed. Will you stay here with Buck?"

"I may go down to the bar for a drink. I can't go to sleep this early and I'm not very good at sitting alone with my thoughts."

"If you want to go out, I'll stay."

"I wouldn't go away for more than ten minutes."

"And then you'll meet someone down there and begin enjoying yourself and forget all about Buck."

"He's all right, I tell you."

"If you want to go out for the night, I'll stay until you come back."

"No, I'll stay. I'll go down and get something to read and come right back and go to bed. I promise you."

"All right."

He rose and went to open the door for her. "I'm sorry the party wasn't more of a success. It was my fault."

"I enjoyed myself."

"I can't say I have. It isn't the same any more. We used to have fun together."

She smiled, "Maybe it's because you're in love—if you're speaking the truth—and I'm not."

He shrugged his shoulders. "Maybe you'll come round."

"Maybe—a girl never really knows—but I wouldn't count on it."

He took her hand. "Kiss me good-night."

"If you like."

He kissed her, holding her for a long time in his arms as if by doing so he could change her. While he still held her, she began to laugh. Quickly he freed her and stepped away from her.

"God-damn you! What's so funny?"

"I think you're trying to kid yourself. I think you're in love with some idea you have about me."

"That's too damned complicated."

"I'm not in love with you, Bill. I didn't feel a thing."

"If you weren't so damned honest, life would be a lot more pleasant."

"If you're going away tomorrow, I think we might give you a going-away party. I might be gone by the time you come back."

"I don't think I'd enjoy it much."

"We can get a fourth."

"Who?"

"Who do you want?"

"Anybody."

"It might cheer up Stitch. She's been losing again."

"All right, only I think she's bad luck."

Carol laughed, "So do I." She reached out for the handle of the door, "Good-night, honey. Thanks for the dinner. Anyway the food was like old times."

"I'll look out for Buck," said Bill.

Just outside the door Silas sprang up and salaamed. She went quickly away and climbed the two stairways that led through the jail-like corridors to her own room. She wanted to be alone now. She felt all funny inside and knew she must get herself sorted out. She was sorry for Bill; there had even been for a moment, a sudden brief moment, when she was tempted out of pity to stay behind with him all the night. She no longer doubted his sincerity; she knew now that what he felt for her was new and astonishing, not only to him but to herself. The odd thing was that it made him seem less attractive to her—that he should ask her to love him, that he should almost plead with her. The fun of Bill had always been that everything was give and take.

And she was happy inside with a perfectly unreasonable happiness which came from the moment she had stood there in the half-dark room looking at Buck. That, she knew, was not enough to make a girl happy. There wasn't any sense to it. Nevertheless she was happy. But she was afraid too.

On the way upstairs she planned to go to bed, turn out the lights and go on "thinking" again, but when she opened the door, she found that the plan had been ruined. The lonely figure of Mrs. Trollope was standing by the window looking out into the street.

She would have closed the door and gone away but Mrs. Trollope had already seen her. As she turned from the window toward the light Carol saw at once that she had been crying. In the sallow face the eyes were swollen nearly shut, with great dark pouches beneath them. She looked hideous, almost sinister. Carol thought, "I'm in for it. Here comes the story of her life."

But briskly she said, "Hello. How did you get in?"

"Your bearer let me in. I shouldn't have done it, but I couldn't stay alone any longer—not in that horrible room. I was going crazy. It was nice just being here. It made me feel a lot better."

"Sit down. I'll get some drinks. What do you want?"

She opened the door and told Krishna what to bring, and then closing the door behind her, she said to him, "What did you let her in for? You're not to let anyone in my room." She was angry—the first time Krishna had ever seen her angry—and he rolled his great liquid black eyes in alarm, salaaming and saying, "Didn't know, Memsahib, didn't know."

"Well, run along and get the drinks."

Inside the room again she found Mrs. Trollope sitting down on one of the stiff chairs, her whole body collapsed. Carol sat on the bed and at once Mrs. Trollope asked, "Can I stay here tonight?"

The question caught Carol off balance, and she answered it quickly, directly, "No, I can't bear sharing a room with another person—not a woman at any rate. It's a complex with me—I'm sorry."

"All right," said Mrs. Trollope, "it's only because I've got the horrors. I'm afraid of myself tonight."

"Nonsense. You'll be all right when you get a drink."

"I had to talk to somebody. I don't mean just anybody."

[227]

"There's always Bill," Carol thought, "if only I could steer her back on to Bill!" And then almost at once she was ashamed of herself. She wanted to help Mrs. Trollope if she could but at the same time she had her own troubles to "think out" and she wanted to hug her happiness to her. And now Mrs. Trollope was spoiling everything.

Mrs. Trollope was saying, "A man is no good . . . not even Bill." She began to cry and said suddenly, "I'm broke. I've lost everything . . . all that money. I can't even pay my hotel bill. I can't pay for my clothes. And I can't go back to that bitch of a sister."

Rising from the bed, Carol thought, "Oh, my God!"

"I don't know what I'm going to do. Oh, my God, what can I do?"

Going over to her, Carol put one arm about her shoulder and said, "Come on, buck up. We'll find some way out." But Mrs. Trollope began to scream suddenly and cry out, "Don't touch me! Don't touch me! I think I'm going crazy. Nobody can save me but you."

Then the door opened and Krishna came in with the drinks at the very moment Mrs. Trollope was screaming her worst. Carol exchanged quick looks with the humbled Krishna. It wasn't the first time in his life with the Maharajah and his friends that the boy had been witness to a fantastic scene. The screaming of Mrs. Trollope he accepted as a matter of course. Out of his experience he had come to conclude that all Europeans were a little mad. So quietly he put down the drinks and went out as if nothing in the least unusual were happening.

When the door was closed, Carol shook Mrs. Trollope saying, "Stop that screaming! There's nothing the matter. We'll fix it up." She brought a drink to Mrs. Trollope and then thought of her own sleeping medicine. Pouring a dose, she gave it to her saying, "This will quiet you. There's no use carrying on like this."

The shaking appeared both to please and to quiet Mrs. Trollope. It was as if she found some curious masochistic satisfaction in it. Obediently, like a well-behaved child, she drank the sleeping medicine and then suddenly quiet, she said, "I'm sorry. I shouldn't have come here like this. I promise to behave. Only sometimes I get so lonely."

To herself Carol said, "Hold your hats, boys, here we go again!" And aloud she said, "Go on. Talk to me. It'll make you feel better."

Then suddenly Mrs. Trollope began to talk. The words poured out of her like a torrent released by the breaking of a dam. She told everything from as far back as she could remember, of her life as a child in an Australian lumber camp, of being sent to London to become a lady, of always being an outcast in school, of marrying the flashy Jim Trollope who wanted her money, of the wild unreal life she had led in expensive hotels while he played his game as swindler and share pusher, of his arrest and imprisonment and all the disgrace and the discovery that she had only a husband in jail and no money left, of her sudden flight toward Australia because there seemed to be nothing else left to do, of stopping off in Bombay, and now of losing everything. She was stuck, stranded in Bombay, alone and friendless save for the people she had picked up since her arrival.

It was a long, detailed and sordid story which would have been tragic save that there was in Mrs. Trollope herself none of the stuff of tragedy. It was all small and mean. She blamed all her troubles on others. During the long saga of disaster Carol sometimes listened and sometimes her mind wandered off to Bill and to Buck. Once, listening, she thought, "There's a curse on her. Everything is wrong and perverse and tangled. Even if you helped her now, it would be the same all over again." And then she knew why Mrs. Trollope was afraid. Once Carol interrupted the story to send Krishna for two more double drinks.

The story after a long time simply trailed off into irrelevancies with a final chapter devoted to how Mrs. Trollope had hoped to increase her winnings so that she could go on to Australia. And now she was broke, with no prospects of any kind. For a moment Carol had a feeling that there was really nothing you could do to help anyone in this world since their fate was always in themselves.

Then Mrs. Trollope said, "Please be kind to me. Lately you've run away from me. You've tried to avoid me."

"No, I haven't."

"Yes, you have. I've felt it. You've been like everybody else always is. I don't know what I've ever done to be treated the way I always am. I never harmed anybody."

Carol could think of no answer to that one, so she only said, "Don't work yourself up again. I think the best thing would be for you to go to bed."

"No," Mrs. Trollope said. "No, I couldn't do that. I couldn't sleep. I couldn't be alone!" And then immediately she grew calm again and for a long time sat staring at her heavy, masculine hands. Presently, she said, "If only you would be kind to me. You brought me luck. Ever since you've avoided me, everything has gone wrong."

"That's your imagination," said Carol, "I've been losing, too."

Then she looked at Carol and said, "If only we could get out of here, out of this hole of a Bombay, everything would be all right. Why don't we go to America? You and I, together. I know I could get a job there and everything would be all right. If only I had some money—if only someone would lend me some, I'd get out and get on my feet again."

"I haven't any myself," said Carol bluntly, "I'm practically broke."

Mrs. Trollope's eyes mirrored her incredulity, "With all that jewelry?" Her eyes turned hard, hostile. There came into them suddenly a hard, vicious glint.

"That's not cash," said Carol, and suddenly without knowing quite why, she heard herself saying, "Anyway, a lot of it doesn't belong to me."

"What do you mean?"

"It's just loaned."

Mrs. Trollope rose and went to the window where she stood looking out. The confidences exhausted, she was alone again. Her back was eloquent. It said, "The world is against me. You're like everybody else. You won't be kind. You're lying to me. You won't even put out a hand to help me."

Carol thought, "What in the name of God am I to do with her?" And then came a knock at the door. Quickly she went to open it.

Bill stood outside and she knew at once that something was

[230]

wrong. He said, "Buck's having an attack. It's awful. He asked for you."

Quickly she said, "I'll go down right away, only you'll have to look after Mrs. Trollope. She's carrying on like a lunatic. Take her downstairs and give her a drink."

"Okay, only hurry up. He says you're the only one who knows what to do."

"All right."

A look almost of horror came into Bill's eyes. "If you can do anything, for God's sake do it. I never saw anything like it." And she thought, "Yes, you're one of the lucky ones. You and I. You've never had anything worse than a hang-over."

She didn't even trouble to explain to Mrs. Trollope but left her with a bewildered Bill.

With Carol gone he quickly told her what had happened. She said, "Oh, that dumb missionary!"

"Yes." He had a sudden panic at the thought of being alone with her, and said quickly, "Let's go downstairs and have a drink."

She was disagreeable, suddenly, and angry. "All right. Whatever you like." It wasn't Bill she wanted for company. With Carol gone it didn't make a damned bit of difference what she did.

Carol didn't wait for the lift. She ran along the stone corridors and down the stairs, leaping over the prostrate figures of the bearers who hadn't time to waken, spring up and salaam to the rich lady. There was terror in her heart and happiness too, because he had asked for her to come to him. And she was glad, too, though ashamed, because Bill was out of the way now. It was funny what mixed up emotions you could have.

She went in by the door to Bill's room and then through the communicating door into the dim light where Buck lay on the bed.

In the heat and the pain he had pushed off the sheet and lay now on his face, pressing his head against the end of the iron bed. One hand clutched the bedpost and the other was extended at his side, the fist contracted with pain. He was silent but in the haze of pain he did not hear her come in. He did not know she was there until she sat on the edge of the bed and touched his head with her hand. The blond curly hair was damp with sweat.

[231]

At the touch his whole body relaxed a little and he managed to ask, "Is it you, Carol?" in an odd distant voice which frightened her.

"Yes, honey," she said, "What can I do to help?"

"Do what you did on the train."

In the train the attack had passed quickly, more quickly than ever before, as if there was something hypnotic and healing in the touch of her hand. Half an hour earlier when the pain had wakened him out of a sleep of utter exhaustion, he had thought wildly, "If she were here, it would help." But for a long time he hadn't cried out. He hadn't even called to Bill in the next room. In his shyness he had gone on enduring the pain until Bill, bored, hot, unable to fix his attention on the detective story he had brought from belowstairs, came in to look at him and found him barely able to speak. Even then Buck hadn't asked for Carol at once. It wasn't only that he was shy about asking for her, but even through the pain he was aware of that something—that sand in the bearings—which had come into the relationship between himself and Bill.

When Bill said, "I'll send for Moti," Buck only answered, "Don't bother. He can't do anything."

It was only when Bill, after watching the spasms of pain running through Buck's strong body, could bear it no longer and cried out, "God-damn it! Somebody's got to help!" that Buck said, weakly, "Where's Carol?"

"In her room, I think. What can she do?"

Buck started to speak and then was silent as a new paroxysm made him press his head against the cold iron and stopped all speech. When it passed he said, "She helped me on the train. It is like a laying on of hands."

"I'll get her," said Bill, "if she's there."

And so he had gone away, leaving Buck alone, and between the attacks which returned every two or three minutes, he thought, "Maybe it's better that I die. Maybe I'm used up and only a nuisance." He knew well enough that he couldn't go on enduring attacks like this. No physical organism could survive the experience. But again he thought, "I can't die. There's Ali and a thousand others like him. And there's Tommy. I've got to live to help him. I can't die." And then a fresh attack blurred all his consciousness

[232]

until he felt the touch of a hand on his head and knew at once that she was there, beside him.

It was extraordinary, the effect of the mere touch of her fingers. It was as if the nerves of his whole body, stretched and taut beyond endurance, had been released. The pain was still there but over it, softening and deadening it, was a kind of curious physical peace. The fingers began slowly but firmly stroking his head, finishing at the nape of his neck where the pain was worst. The pain kept returning in waves, each time diminishing a little like the recession of some monstrous tide on a beach. Each time the wave blurred his consciousness. Each time it passed he returned hazily from a great distance, to know that she was there beside him as she had been on the train. And he was aware too that this time it was different. She was not tipsy and wild, and somehow, in some intangible way, they were no longer strangers but friends.

As the waves of pain diminished beneath her touch, he managed to say, "I'm sorry to have bothered you." And he heard her voice saying, "It didn't bother me at all. It made me very happy if I could make any difference."

"It made a great difference. I didn't mean to be a coward, but sometimes I can't bear it."

"Listen, honey, anytime you want me for anything, just call on me. I'm not much damned good to the world anyway."

It was true that she was happy. More than that, she knew, sitting there on the bed beside him, a kind of peace she had never known before, a peace for which she had never had time before in all her disorderly life. It was a peace which had something to do simply with the physical contact with suffering, and the knowledge that somehow, in some almost magical fashion, she was destroying pain and helping someone whom she loved. It was for her like entering another world where until now the doors had been closed to her. They opened a little way on the morning they had gone to visit Ali and Mrs. Moti—only a little way, but enough for her to glimpse something which delighted and astonished her and brought her peace. And now as she sat there beside him the door was opened wide, but she had not yet entered. It might be that she would never be able to enter—that because of what had been in the past she would not know the secret which Buck and Colonel Moti's wife knew, the secret which in an odd way had to do with the small blind orphan son of the mahout.

She went on stroking the tired head, quietly, but with a kind of concentration as if she willed all her strength, all her radiant health to pass from herself through her lacquered finger tips into the tired ill body. Once she thought, as she felt the pain going from him, "Maybe I'm a healer. Maybe this is what being a healer means."

On the train she had tried to help a stranger, to kill suffering which frightened her because she had never known it. She had tried the only way she knew, as she had seen her mother ease the pain which in the end had destroyed her father. But this was different. Now, sitting there, she poured all her spirit into an effort to help someone she loved, for she knew now that she loved him in a way she had never before loved anyone. Why, she did not know, except that it had something to do with the lovableness of the round curly head, the blue eyes and the goodness and simplicity which looked out of them, small things which to her in that moment were like manna in the desert. Yet she was afraid too because, for all the physical contact, he seemed to her unattainable, shining and bright behind those opened doors through which she could see but could not enter.

But oddest of all, she, who in all her life had never known shyness, was shy.

She thought, "I must remember that to him everything is different—that he does not understand things as I do." What you had been through in this world, all the compromises you had made, changed everything.

Presently the body beside her grew less tense. One hand released the iron at the top of the bed. The other unclenched and after a time she was aware that Buck lay quite still, so still that for a moment she was frightened and bent over him to see if he still breathed. Then she realized that he had slipped back again into the sleep of exhaustion. But her hand went on stroking his head lest if she stopped he would waken, and because it made her happy. She felt a desire to go on thus forever.

Now and then she was aware of noises from the hot night outside. Her own mind no longer functioned but fell into a kind of vague dreamy state in which she was aware only that the body of the man on the bed beside her was no longer tortured but still, all the pain gone. And so she did not hear the knock on the door of Bill's room when Colonel Moti arrived, nor the sound of the door opening when no one answered the knock. She did not know he had come in until she saw him suddenly watching her with the enormous black burning eyes which saw and knew everything. On the train their gaze had angered her; now it did not seem to matter.

He said nothing at all, but only stood watching her. Nervously, she said, in a low voice, "It's all right. He's asleep." And at the same time she thought, "He's trying to find out something." What it was she did not know. Slowly, she moved away from the bed, fearful lest Buck should waken, but in the sleep of utter exhaustion following pain, he did not move.

Nervously she said, "We can talk in the next room unless you want to wake him and talk to him."

"No," said the little dark man, "sleep is what he needs more than anything. For three years he has scarcely slept at all."

So she went into Bill's room followed by the Colonel and as she went through the door she experienced an extraordinary physical sense of his presence behind her, almost as if she could see with the back of her head. Turning quickly she sat at the table where a little while before she had had dinner with Bill. She thought, "I'll let him do all the talking. It's not my job." But almost at once she heard herself saying, as if to justify her presence, "He sent for me, you know."

"I know," said Moti, sitting down opposite her. "He told me you had helped him on the train." The intelligent eyes laughed but the mouth was still. "It seems you have a power of laying on hands." She knew he was mocking her, but did not know how or why. It was extraordinary how disturbing this small, wiry man could be.

"I needn't have come at all. There is nothing I can do. That's your job. I wouldn't have come but Wainwright was hysterical on the telephone."

"Oh, Bill . . . he can't stand looking at any suffering. He always runs away." She had spoken to Moti as an intimate friend—Moti whom she scarcely knew and she had cast a slur on Bill which she had not meant to do. Quickly, she added, "Bill's one of the best fellows in the world but he's like most men who aren't doctors. Pain and suffering make him panicky."

"It doesn't you?"

"No, it doesn't."

There was an awkward silence. Colonel Moti lighted a cigarette and then looked at her sharply. "What do you want of him?"

"Nothing. Why? What do you mean?"

Moti smiled and for a moment the wise smile almost made her like him. He said, "Well, most women always want something . . . marriage or money or position or martyrdom or something. Buck couldn't give you much . . . not even martyrdom. I don't imagine that's what you want. I don't know you very well and what I've seen of you puzzles me. You appear to be one kind of woman and you behave like another kind, and you behave as if you were ashamed of what you are."

The speech confused her for a moment, but when she thought it out, quickly, instinctively, as her brain always worked, she was angry and asked, "Is it any of your business?"

"Yes," said Moti. "It is for at least three reasons—one because I am always intensely interested in the behavior of people; two, because Buck, despite differences of color, or race, or religious background, is the man I love best in the world; three, because he is immensely important."

She wanted to say quickly with all her heart, "I know what you mean. I love him too. I don't know why. You and I could be friends but that is going a little too fast," but she only said, "Yes, that does give you a reason."

She took out a cigarette, opened her bag and took out her lighter but it would not work. The Colonel leaned across and held his own cigarette for her to take a light. It was a curious thing to have done, because she knew he had paper matches in his pocket. But the gesture relaxed the tension a little and made the talk seem a little friendlier. A little while later she knew he had done it for this reason.

He said, "I have a very remarkable wife. You know her, I think?"

"Yes. I've met her."

[236]

"She too loves Buck. I might add she almost loves you for making him happy."

"I made him happy?"

"He was quite changed when he came to the Institute with you the other day. She saw it at once."

She felt suddenly happy. Why, she could not say. At the same time she saw Buck's head on the pillow with remarkable clarity. She heard Colonel Moti saying, "I am asking an extraordinary thing of you." He paused and she said, "What is it? If I can help Buck, I will."

"It's not very simple or easy."

"Tell me anyway."

He did not answer at once. For a long time he regarded the end of his cigarette. Then he looked at her directly with a curious light shining in his eyes, "What I want," he said, "is this. I want you to go away with Buck . . . somewhere away from Bombay and the silly people who infest the race course and the Taj and Malabar Hill. I don't mean simply the wicked people are silly. The stupid, respectable ones are just as bad or worse, because they're smug and they aren't very entertaining." He crushed out his cigarette and a look of humor came into the great black eyes. "If I wasn't such a busy man I might enjoy their company—the company of the wicked ones, I mean. I have always felt more at home with bad people. I only say they're silly because very often they have very good brains and great energy which they waste in silly ways."

She knew that what he was saying was aimed at her, subtly. "If the shoe fits . . . ," she thought, and carefully she made her face a blank.

"I want you to go away somewhere . . . it does not matter much where . . . Udaipur, Traavancore, Cochin . . . any romantic, beautiful place where the two of you will be alone. Oh, you don't know the beauty of India—the incredible, splendorous beauty of authentic India which is like nothing else in the world. It is the kind of beauty which makes anything possible and wonderful." A fire came into the black eyes. "I want you to go away with him and change his life."

"How can I do that? I haven't anything to offer him."

Moti smiled, "Even you," he said, "aren't free. I thought you

[237]

might be, but always in the background of every Westerner there lurks evidence of the mean, unnatural spirit of Zwingli, of Calvin, of John Knox."

The three names meant nothing to her, but she was ashamed to ask what he meant. He looked at her directly again and said, "I want you to cure a sick soul and body. I want you to take him away and make him happy. I want you to be the courtesan—Cleopatra, Helen of Troy, Thais, Aspasia."

She recognized the names of Cleopatra and Helen of Troy and supposed that the other two possessed similar characteristics. She said, "That's a very big order."

"I want you to make him happy and untwist that knot inside him. I want you to make him forget work. I want you to teach him what a woman can be if she chooses—how wonderful, how divine a complement to man. He has an odd idea about women. He's not bitter or cynical. He's too good a chap for that. He's simply innocent. He thinks all women were like that damned monster—his wife."

"What makes you think I could do all that?"

"I don't know for certain. I only hope. You seem to be the best candidate on the horizon. And something must be done quickly."

He looked very grim and suddenly she was afraid. He couldn't mean that Buck might die . . . not Buck. He couldn't die. He mustn't die. Not now. She strove to pull herself back from panic. She tried to hide her fright, but the shrewd little man had already seen it. She knew at once, again by her instinct, when he spoke.

"And hardest of all," he said, "you must go away when he is well and never see him again."

She knew that she had already thought of that, without knowing she had thought of it, because she faced the idea at once without reservations as an obvious condition. She heard Bill's mocking voice saying, "Is it Buck? A fine missionary's wife you'd make!" No, she knew that one day she'd have to face that.

Colonel Moti was still talking. "You couldn't marry him. You couldn't help him when he came back to his work. You couldn't stand the filth and heat and disease and long hours. You couldn't give him the moral support he'd need. . . . Pardon me if I speak frankly. . . . You could scarcely go back to Jellapore as the wife of

Buck after the way you have been there before. Everybody in Jellapore, even the aborigines in the jungle, know you. I may seem hard but I'm talking to you intelligently. My wife, whose judgment I trust, says you are intelligent."

She smiled and there was a little hardness in the smile, "Maybe I am. Maybe I'm not. But I usually know what I want."

Abruptly he said, "Will you do it?"

She grinned, "I can't kidnap him."

"You'll have to make him want it. You can."

"What makes you think that?"

"Where did all your jewels come from? Ali told me about them."

"They didn't come from men like Buck."

It was odd, she thought, that she wasn't angry or insulted. There was something admirable about Moti's directness, his honesty, his straight talking, that cut away all nonsense. She had never talked with anyone like him before. She had never before had such a conversation. She was aware that he was showing a great respect for her honesty and intelligence. He had even hinted that she was both necessary and useful to the world. She was beginning to like this man. "There is," she thought, "no hog-wash about him."

He stood up and said, "And now I am going home. I am a very busy man. I hope you are going to help. You will not regret it. You will have done a great thing, not only for Buck but for thousands, maybe millions, of poor wretched human beings." After a second he added, "And for you yourself it may be a great experience—different from anything you have ever known."

She covered her eyes with her hand. Desperately she was "thinking things out" again, and the effort made her feel a little dizzy and confused. Even with her eyes covered—blind like Ali—she saw Moti's handsome face and burning black eyes. It was as if they hypnotized and compelled her to do what, she knew suddenly, was the thing she wanted most to do in all her life. She knew suddenly what it was she had been waiting for, why some instinct, some intuition had kept her there in Bombay which slowly she was coming to hate.

Moti took her hand, and uncovering her eyes she looked at him, "Will you?"

"I don't know."

"You must. There is no one like Buck—no other such man. Believe me, I know."

Then he said good-night quickly and went away, leaving her alone in the room with the table where she had had supper with Bill, empty now but for a half-bottle of champagne in a bucket of tepid water which once had been ice.

Going over to the window she stood there for a moment looking out over the black harbor. She thought, "It doesn't matter anyway what happens to me. Maybe he's right. Maybe I can help. Anyway I'm on the skids."

The lights of a Red Sea *dhow* moved slowly across toward Elephanta—the only moving light in the whole of the harbor. She watched it for a little while, feeling lonely for the first time in her life, as lonely as poor Mrs. Trollope. Like Mrs. Trollope she belonged nowhere at all. She had no roots. She belonged in Bombay as much as a small town in Minnesota. For the first time she understood how terrible a thing that could be, how it lay at the very base of all the folly and the recklessness of her life, how it was because of what she was and all she had been, of all the waste of everything which had been given her, that Moti had been able to talk to her as he had talked. Her strength, although she did not know it then, lay in her acceptance of all that the fierce dark little man had to say, that it was all true, that she did not fall a victim of self-pity, nor of egotism nor a desire for martyrdom.

After a little while she turned away from the window. Sighing, she thought, "Well, where do we go from here?" and walked across the room to the door of Buck's room.

Opening it she went in and crossed to the bed where she stood for a long time looking down at him. In his sleep he had turned on his side once more, with one arm thrown over his head, the side of the face with the lean strong jaw exposed to the dim light which came in through the doorway. Looking down at him, she thought, "Maybe there is something that is bringing us together, something stronger and fiercer even than the will of Colonel Moti, something neither of us can beat." And quite suddenly she was happy again, because in her mood of recklessness, she felt sure of herself once more, confident that no matter what she did, what folly she undertook, it would turn out well as it had always turned out in the past. The feeling of uncertainty, of waiting for something, which she had described to Bill in the taxi coming home from Jelly's party, was gone now. She knew what she meant to do. It might be the last reckless thing to succeed, the last folly of her first youth. In her heart she believed that it would be worth whatever price it cost.

So she sat down on the edge of the bed, confident in what Bill and Moti had both told her, that when Buck was like this, nothing could disturb him. She sat there for a long time, quite still and happy, unaware of the passing of time, and presently, almost without her knowledge or will, in a kind of blurred and dreamy semi-consciousness, the hand with the great diamond and lacquered nails began to stroke the blond head. The state of dreamy peace continued and she thought, "If only this could go on forever I would be happy." For in the gesture there was something which satisfied a part of her that for long years, ever since she could remember, had gone hungry and unsatisfied. After a long time, out of a fog, she heard a voice which vaguely she remembered.

It said, "Is it you, Carol?" The body on the bed did not stir. He did not even turn his head to look at her.

"Yes, honey."

"It was good of you to come back." She knew then that he had been awake for a long time, long enough to know that she had gone away and returned.

"Are you all right now?"

"Yes, it's all right."

"I'm glad."

There was a silence and presently he said, "You'd better go and get some sleep."

"I don't need sleep. I never do. I like sitting here much better."

"You're a wonderful girl . . . to bother about me."

She didn't answer him but after a little while a curious thing happened. His hand stole up quietly and took her hand. Then slowly he turned his head and holding tightly to her hand, he kissed it. For a moment she felt faint. Then he said, "I didn't know there could be anyone like you."

Again she was silent because she could think of nothing to say, and after a little while he said, "I mean, I didn't know anyone could be so kind, so cosy." He paused for a moment searching for words. Words were not his medium and when he was moved he fell silent and unhappy like a dumb man trying desperately to communicate. "I mean . . . anyone so natural . . . so simple."

Quietly she said, "Thanks, Buck." Then they remained silent for a long time, but content.

Presently, in the darkness, she said, "Colonel Moti was here."

"Why did he come?"

"Bill sent for him. He got panicky."

"Poor Bill. I'm sorry he was upset."

"Buck."

"Yes."

"Colonel Moti propositioned me."

For a moment he was silent, puzzled, as if she had fallen again into that strange double talk which she and Bill used when they were together. He asked, "What does that mean?"

"He didn't proposition me for himself but for you."

"What kind of a proposition?"

She pulled herself together to gain strength for the effort. It was the most difficult thing she had ever tried to do, not only because something about Buck made her feel terribly shy but because she was frightened of what lay far ahead, somewhere in the future. It required all her will-power to say, "He thought it would be a wonderful idea if we went away somewhere together . . . alone, where you could rest and I could look after you until you were all well again."

He did not answer her at once, and in the darkness, anguish took possession of her. She felt a sudden swift tension in the hand which still held hers, and she thought, "I've shocked him. I should have known better. We're too far apart ever to understand each other." And again summoning all her strength and thinking, "Now everything is lost or won," she said, "What do you think?"

In an odd voice he said, "I think it would be wonderful." And after a moment she heard a faint sound in the darkness and panic seized her again. Frightened, as if she had been a Piccadilly tart mocked by the man she had solicited, she said, "Don't laugh, Buck . . . what are you laughing at?"

"I'm laughing at Moti. It's just like him to think up a thing like that."

"Oh!" She felt suddenly ill from relief and when that sensation had passed, she was bewildered because she could not make out what was going on in Buck's tired head.

"Where shall we go?"

"Would you like to do it . . . Buck, really?"

"Yes." There was a sudden gravity in his voice as if he had been thinking.

"Moti spoke of two or three places . . . I don't remember the names. One of them was Udaipur."

"I've never been there. They say it's beautiful."

Then all at once she knew where they must go . . . neither to Udaipur nor to the other places. They were both unknown to her and might be disappointing and tragically wrong. The place where they must go was to Jai Mahal, that lovely house of Jellapore's on the beach at Juhu. She heard Jelly saying, "You can spend your second honeymoon here," and herself answering, "There ain't going to be a second honeymoon." It seemed weeks and months ago. And then she knew that the conversation had only happened in the afternoon.

"I know a place. It's a lovely spot." And she told him about the house. He listened, and when she had finished he only said, "I don't like the Maharajah."

"Once you see the place you'll love it." The talk seemed easier now; until he said, "It's funny how we get on. I was scared of you in the taxi."

"So was I."

"I'm not any longer."

And then she heard the door of Bill's room open and the sound of uncertain footsteps. Tense, she listened, aware that Buck was listening too. Then came the crash of a falling chair, and she drew her hand out of his and stood up quickly. "I'll go in there. I think he's drunk." Her brain was working now with lightning quickness. She said, "Don't say anything to Bill."

"All right."

Quietly she went into the next room and standing in the doorway, she saw that she had interpreted all the sounds correctly. Bill was

[243]

bending over with a curious tipsy dignity, supporting himself with one hand by holding to the table, while he tried to pick up the overturned chair.

After a struggle he succeeded in raising the chair which he put back at the table with the over-elaborate care of a bad waiter. Then he turned and saw her.

"Why didn't you say something? I hate being spied on."

She laughed and said, "I wasn't spying." She saw now that he was really drunk. She had seen him gay and she had seen him tipsy often enough, but she had never seen him like this, stupefied. It hurt her in an odd way, because it made him seem like all the others in the long procession of drunks who at one time or another had passed quickly through her life. No one but a stupid man or a despairing one ever became soddenly drunk.

She said, "You must have given Mrs. Trollope a swell time."

"It was a dirty trick—unloading her on me."

"What else could I do?"

"She got a thorough crying jag." He frowned as if trying to collect his thoughts. "You know, I think she's nuts. I'm afraid of her."

"She's harmless."

"No, she isn't. Some day she's going to do something awful."

"What makes you think that?"

"The way she talked. She's got a grudge against the whole world. She thinks it owes her everything and won't pay its debts." He was steadying himself by holding to the back of the chair. "Do you mind if I sit down?"

"No, I think it's safer."

"How's Buck?"

Deliberately she lied. "He's all right. He's asleep."

He started to get up. "Better go and see him." But she pushed him back into the chair.

"No. Let him sleep."

He looked at her with dull suspicion in his eyes. Then his head dropped and he said, "Do you know, I think you're nuts for him."

She didn't answer at once. She knew she had to keep Bill in ignorance till tomorrow night when he went away. She was afraid that if he discovered the truth he would laugh at them.

So she said, "I'm not. Why should I be?"

[244]

"God knows. But I've never seen you like this before."

"Like what?"

"Sort of secretive . . . and . . . ," he groped for a long time for the word, "and radiant."

She couldn't help laughing. "You used to tell me that long ago—that I was always radiant."

He looked up at her. "You aren't as young as you once were, sweetheart." Then he added, "You'd better think that one over."

He wasn't being nasty, she knew. He was just drunk and speaking the truth. "I have thought it over," she said.

"Buck's really a very dull fellow, you know. I'm not trying to run him down, but I've got to think of you both because I'm really very fond of you. And that's from the heart too. He's the sweetest guy in the world, but he's dumb."

"You mean he isn't a wisecracker like us."

She could have given him a better answer. She could have said that at the moment Buck filled the order perfectly. That Buck was the only thing she wanted in the world. She was aware that Bill, drunk, was speaking truths he would never have spoken sober. Bill, in his way, was the nicest, sweetest guy in the world too, only he didn't have anything to steer by.

"You're kidding yourself," he said suddenly, and poured himself a glass of champagne from the bottle in the cooler filled with melted ice.

"That's lukewarm dishwater," she said, "it'll only make you sick."

"I don't get sick and I've got to have a drink."

"Suit yourself." The talk was depressing her, perhaps because Bill was saying too many truths. All the happiness deep inside her was collapsing slowly. "What time is it?" she asked. "I'm going to bed. Are you sober enough to keep an eye on Buck?"

"I'm all right."

She put her hand on his head, affectionately, and surprisingly he said, "Please don't do that."

"All right. I'm going to bed. I don't think the farewell party tomorrow night would be a good idea."

A thought came to her. "Did Mrs. Trollope make a touch?"

"Yes."

"How much?"

[245]

"It's none of your business." Then he said quickly, "I paid her hotel bill and the bill for her clothes."

Carol smiled, "Good-time Charlie."

"She seemed so damned hard up and depressed. I can afford it." He took another drink and said, "Why did you tell her most of your jewelry didn't belong to you?"

"Because it's true. I got it under false pretenses . . . from Botlivala and Jelly's brother. I'm sending it back to them." She knew she couldn't go to Buck still owning all that jewelry. She hadn't known what she meant to do with it until now when, with a sense of surprise, she heard herself announcing the intention to Bill.

Bill grinned, "Missionary reforms gold-digger!"

"That's a dirty thing to say."

"Yes, it is. I'm sorry. But every now and then the thought of you and Buck makes me laugh."

He was right, she knew. If she hadn't cared so much, so profoundly, if she hadn't been aware that it was something that went to the very core of her being, which would change her whole life, she would have laughed too. But even though she saw the humor, she did not feel like laughing. It was something, she thought, that Bill wouldn't understand.

She said, "I can see it's funny."

"Anyway, I advise you to keep away from Mrs. T."

"That's what I mean to do. Don't go downstairs again."

"I won't. See you tomorrow."

"Maybe I'll come to the train."

"Okay."

She went out and as soon as she closed the door, the surging, unreasonable happiness returned to her. All the intimations of disaster, which Bill's drunken talk had wakened, died now. She only thought, "It doesn't matter. If we're happy only for a little while, that's enough. If I can make him well again, that's all that matters." But at the bottom of her happiness there was a small maggot of uneasiness which concerned Bill. His being drunk troubled her, because it might not be simply an isolated "bender," but the beginning of something worse, something for which she herself might be responsible in spite of the fact that over it she had no control. It wasn't only that; unwittingly, unwillingly she had come between two friends, both of whom she loved in different ways, for she was aware now that the old bond between Bill and Buck was broken, that they had become hostile and suspicious of each other. As she slowly climbed the stone stairway she thought, "God-damn this sex business. Why does it have to be so complicated?"

To hell with it all! Day after tomorrow she would take Buck to Jai Mahal. And they'd shut out the world and be happy together in that white marble house among the cocoanut palms on the edge of the sea. They'd be rid of Mrs. Trollope and Jelly and the Baroness and the whole bloody lot. Inside that high wall she and Buck would have a life cut off from all the tiresome dreary world of the Taj Mahal and the race course. She and Buck would be like Adam and Eve in Paradise—Buck who was so honest and simple and good and clean. It would be like being born again.

As she reached her own door, the surge of happiness and freedom seemed to carry her away. Krishna, in his purple and gold, lay asleep on the stone floor. Carefully, she did not waken him. She was thinking, "Tomorrow I'll send back all that damned jewelry and then I'll be free."

Inside she closed the door and locked it against a possible second invasion by Mrs. Trollope. Then directly, swiftly she went to the cupboard and taking out her key, unlocked it to take down her jewel box. But the shelf where it always stood was empty.

For a moment she stood looking at the empty shelf in bewilderment. "It can't be gone," she thought, "I must have put it somewhere else. I must stop and think."

But thinking did no good. She always kept it there on the same shelf. There wasn't any other place. For five minutes she searched the room frantically. It was a bare room, furnished almost as simply as a jail cell; five minutes exhausted its possibilities.

Then she sat down, thinking, "I mustn't lose my head. I've got to think this out." It was a situation which a little while ago would have been simple enough. Now within a day or two it had become complicated and dangerous because out of it might come catastrophe in any one of a dozen forms.

Dazed, she sat on the edge of the bed, staring at the open door of the cupboard. All at once she was very tired, as if all the emotions of the day had piled up in one vast heap and suddenly toppled over to crush her.

She thought again, "I mustn't lose my head," and one by one the possibilities came to her—that Mrs. Trollope, desperate and broke, had taken the jewelry, that Botlivala had had it stolen to even his score, that even the Baroness might have had a finger in the pie. It occurred to her clearly for the first time how unsavory were all the people who surrounded her, how dangerous it was to take up thoughtlessly with any sort of person simply because he entertained you or you were too good-natured to do otherwise. They were all suspects when you came down to it, all these people with whom she had been living intimately—Mrs. Trollope, the Baroness, the Marchesa, Botlivala and all the others, even Jelly who had no sense of value of things but would always do you a dirty trick simply out of his liking for intrigue and melodrama.

But after all the jewelry might have ben stolen by any common thief. It wasn't as if she had kept it hidden; all Bombay knew of it. She had worn a good deal of it, even in the daytime, vulgarly Bill said, just because she liked the glitter of it.

"Nuts!" she thought ruefully, "Woolworth jewelry would have given me just as much pleasure." She knew now that she liked the jewelry only as a manifestation of her own health and exuberance.

And now what if Botlivala turned nasty and wanted back all he had spent for nothing save the pleasure of being seen about with her.

She looked down at her hands. Certainly it was her bad luck day. She wore only one large diamond, a wrist watch and a single bracelet. All the rest was gone and it wasn't even insured. She remembered suddenly having received a notice in Paris that the insurance had expired, a notice which she overlooked and then lost because she was too busy enjoying herself. But she couldn't have paid the insurance in any case. She was too broke. And then she remembered too that she had put on only the diamond, the wrist watch and the bracelet instead of a lot more because of Buck. When she was with him she was always ashamed of the diamonds, the rubies, the emeralds. She hadn't wanted to shock him, because she had wanted him to like her—the first time she had ever cared whether a man liked her or not.

Her head clearing a little under the shock of the loss, she thought, "Anyway, I was a fool to think of sending it back to Botlivala and Jelly's brother. They wouldn't even have missed it. I could have sold it for cash and that would have helped me out of the hole." She thought, "Something funny has happened to me! I must be getting screwy."

It was as if she were two persons—one shrewd but carefree and reckless, the other, careful, sober and sound. It was as if just now when she had been with Buck, a kind of hazy madness had claimed her. Everything she had thought, everything she had planned to do now seemed, in the stress of her uneasiness and fear, senseless and without reason. Always before she had been able to look out for herself, to manage in the face of any calamity. It seemed to her now that for several hours she had been another woman, a stranger to herself, emotional and unpredictable. The thought alarmed her. Everything she had done, even to "propositioning" Buck so boldly and shamelessly, now seemed unreal and alarming. She had, in the back of her mind, even considered the possibility of being his wife and going back to Jellapore with him to work side by side with him among all the miserable, poverty-stricken low caste people —all those people who had never before existed for her save as a vague, disturbing smell and noise on the edge of the India which entertained her.

For a moment she was frightened at the idea that somewhere inside her was a strange woman, who could emerge and go out into the world committing every sort of idiotic and romantic folly, wrecking her existence without her being able to prevent it. Because just now, as she sat on the edge of the bed knowing how many hundreds of thousands of rupees were gone out of that cupboard and how badly she needed them, even to pay her hotel bill, she was terrified. "Money," she thought, "makes you free and independent. It lets you tell the rest of the world to go to hell. That's its only value."

Now for the first time in her life she was not free. And she thought, "Maybe I'm getting fancy and developing a split personality." She wasn't quite sure what that was, but Bill had sometimes talked to her of such things. In the old days Bill had always told her that he loved her because she was simple and direct with no psychological complications. But she thought, "Easy now. Don't get into the intellectual stuff or you'll get out of your depths and become a horse's rear-end." It alarmed her too that she should be thinking, not "thinking out things," but thinking. "No, honey, Buck or no Buck, missionary or no missionary, you've got yourself to look after."

But thinking wasn't getting her anywhere. Her old spirit began to clamor suddenly for action. So she went to the door and opening it, prodded the prostrate Krishna quietly with her toe. The boy opened his eyes and with incredible agility sprang to his feet and salaamed. Bad conscience prodded him into extraordinary alertness.

"Krishna," she said, "who came into my room tonight?"

The boy made another elaborate salaam, "Memsahib Trollope and Sahib Wainwright."

"No one else? No other Memsahib?"

"No . . . missy. No Sahib. No Memsahib."

"Did you stay by the door all night?"

"Yes, Memsahib," with a fresh salaam. "All night." But when he straightened himself again, she caught a sudden shiftiness in his eyes. She was certain that he hadn't stayed there guarding the door all night. He had gone away, but once he had lied, she knew there was no hope of getting him to change his story.

"All right. Go to sleep again."

For a moment she almost envied him the coolness of the stone floor. The night outside was heavy and hot. Her room was like a steam bath. She didn't tell him about the jewelry. He would, she knew, in spite of anything she could do, of any promise of silence he might make, tell other boys, and before noon tomorrow everybody in Bombay would know of the theft. She was, she knew, already spectacular, even notorious. It didn't need the old-fashioned story of "actress robbed of jewels" to bring her to the attention of all Bombay.

She decided too not to tell the manager or the police until the morning. It was morning already, but it was still dark. The police wouldn't be very active at four in the morning and the manager wouldn't like to be hauled out of bed. And anyway there wasn't that much need for haste.

She went to the bathroom and there, behind the end of the bathtub, she found the jewel box. It wasn't even closed. One of the plush-lined drawers with the name "Ostertag, Place Vendome, Paris," lay on the floor beside it. Whoever had taken the jewelry had emptied the case and thrown it there in haste. Looking at it, she thought, "Maybe it was there all the time I was sitting in the other room talking to Mrs. Trollope. Maybe all the time she was talking to me she had all the jewelry shoved away inside her blouse."

Belowstairs, Buck lay awake for a long time. He heard the voices of Carol and Bill in the next room but he couldn't make out what they were saying. He made no effort. He even closed his ears against the blurred sound of the two voices because he had a dislike of eavesdropping and because he was afraid he might hear what he did not want to hear. Because a strange thought had come to him—that Carol was the girl Bill had married, that she was Bill's wife. He remembered hearing long ago that Bill had married and he remembered that on Moti's verandah Bill had said, "I got married but it didn't go very well. She was a nice girl. It wasn't anybody's fault." Beyond that Bill had told him nothing.

Lying there in the darkness, the idea had come to him, suddenly, out of nowhere, and immediately it seemed to explain everything. It explained the intimacy of their talk and feeling, of that curious half-realized "double talk" which he could never understand. It explained the curious things Bill had said of her as the two of them drove back from their shopping expedition, things which had seemed rotten and filled with implications, as if Bill were saying to him, "Who the hell are you to tell me about her?" It explained the curious "edginess" which had come between himself and Bill. Either she had been his wife or his mistress.

In his simplicity he saw that if they were divorced it was the same thing anyway. But it was fantastic that Bill had never explained anything.

Against the blurred murmur of their voices, his tired brain grew confused. Slowly a suspicion raised itself, a suspicion that he was being made a fool, just how or by whom he could not be certain, but it was, crudely, as if he were the country boy among city slickers. Maybe she wasn't what he thought her; maybe she was something quite different, terrifying and hard . . . and bad. In his unworldliness, he wasn't quite sure what he meant by "bad," but the thought that in his inexperience he might be only a sap, troubled him. Maybe Bill in the taxicab had been trying as a friend to warn him. Maybe Bill had seen what he himself had not known until tonight, that he was in love with her, and had tried to stop him.

But how in hell did you know what love was? Maybe he felt as he did only because he was ill and she had been kind to him. What did he know of her, really—except that there had been funny things in the past, the sort of things which were the only explanation of all the jewels he had found her showing to Tommy and Ali on the train. He really didn't know anything about things like that.

He knew now well enough that he had never been in love with his dead wife. She had been the only white woman within a hundred miles, and something, glands or simply being a healthy male, had made him endow her with all sorts of qualities which she did not possess—kindliness, understanding, intelligence, even beauty. He knew now—he had known for a long time—that outside the jungle, in the world where there were other women, he would never have looked at her twice. It had needed years of misery and unhappiness for him to discover the full depths of his folly, of how physiology and nature itself had betrayed him. It had needed years of struggle against hate to make him know the fool he had been. And now perhaps he was going to make a new kind of fool of himself. For all the time Carol had sat there on the edge of the bed talking to him, he had thought always of marriage. While he listened to her story of what she called Moti's "propositioning" he had taken for granted that marriage was what Moti meant. From the moment Hazel died, Moti had never stopped urging him to find a new and attractive wife.

But now suddenly, thinking things out alone in the darkness, it occurred to him that Moti hadn't meant marriage at all in relation to Carol—that perhaps she herself had never even thought of it. That was what that "double talk" word "propositioning" meant.

In the darkness he was glad he hadn't betrayed his ignorance to her. He flushed suddenly at the thought of his own innocence. "Country boy and city slickers." That's what it was. Just a sap.

He was aware presently that the murmur of voices in the next room had ceased and that at the same time, the door had opened. He felt the light against his tired eyes but he kept them closed, struggling between two desires—to pretend that he was asleep and avoid speaking to Bill, and to speak to him and ask him the things he had to know. Out of shyness and a weak and sudden desire to remain in ignorance, he would have gone on pretending he was asleep, but something about Bill's unsteady entrance took him back a long way to the time when as boys they had shared a room and Bill had come in again and again like this. Even then he had played the same trick of keeping his eyes closed, pretending, because Bill in this condition grew restless and filled with a desire to talk. Sometimes he would talk until daylight—and always it had been good talk and above all truthful talk, for about Bill, completely sober, there was a kind of steel band shutting away from others the innermost part of him, the part which was nicest, the part which few people save Buck himself ever knew. That was why Bill, sober, seemed always gay and superficial and entertaining —all that was a kind of disguise, a shield which hid the Bill inside.

And now Buck, knowing all this, thought, "If I open my eyes and speak to him now, perhaps we can get back again to the old life and the old intimacy. He'll talk honestly now." It was odd that he, who in his whole life had never once been drunk, should in one way love Bill most when he was tipsy. He knew that Bill was standing by the bed now, looking down at him. And so, still afraid of what he would hear, he opened his eyes and said, "Hello, Bill."

"How are you?"

"All right. . . . Better sit down. There's a chair just behind you."

"You don't have to tell me," said Bill, "I know when I'm drunk." Buck laughed weakly, "I didn't mean that."

Bill pulled out the chair and sat down. "Jesus," he said, "I thought you were going to die. You certainly can take it."

"I don't like it but what else can you do but take it?" Suddenly the thought occurred to him that Bill had run away and gotten

[253]

drunk because he could not bear the sight of his own suffering—and perhaps too because of Carol. That he would have to find out.

Bill said, "Did Carol help?"

"Yes. It's funny. It almost makes me believe in healers."

Bill laughed, "Carol a healer! Whee!" In his voice there was a shadow of bitterness. "Are you too tired to talk?"

"No," said Buck.

"I'm going away tomorrow. I've got the jitters."

"Why, Bill?"

"I don't know. Everything. I don't want to stay in India."

"I thought you liked it."

"I did . . . once."

Buck was thoughtful for a moment. "What's the matter now?"

"I don't know. It just seems a dirty, sordid place I want to get away from."

Buck laughed, "Temperamental, huh?"

"Maybe."

Bill, he knew, in spite of his being tipsy, wasn't being truthful. Something was holding him back, and Buck thought he knew what it was. Like a diver hesitating on the edge of a tank of cold water, he drew in his breath and plunged.

"Bill, I want to ask you something. You don't have to answer unless you want to."

"Okay."

"What was up between you and Carol in the past?"

In the dim light he saw Bill pull himself together and draw his sagging body straight. "Nothing," he said, "except that she was married to me."

"Oh . . . I thought that might be it."

"For God's sake, didn't you know it?"

"Nobody ever told me."

Bill's voice turned bitter again. "Nobody ever tells me anything," he mocked.

"Well . . . all I knew was that you had married somebody a long time ago. Tom Joyce told me when he went through here five years ago. I didn't know who it was."

"Well," said Bill, "it was Carol. We're not married now . . .

[254]

we haven't been married for six years . . . six years come this April."

"I thought you seemed to know each other pretty well. I can't pump people about things—I never could."

"Yeah, I know that." After a little silence as if talking to himself, "I guess I didn't know her well enough."

Then the conversation came to a dead end, perhaps because both of them were reluctant to carry it any further. Buck, his eyes closed, knew he had come against a wall and he knew now what the wall was. He knew what it was that had put sand in the bearings. He couldn't go any further. He couldn't bring himself to speak.

It was Bill, released by alcohol, who said suddenly, "Do you want to go to sleep?"

"No."

"Then there's something I want to ask you."

"Yes."

"It's about Carol. . . . Have you fallen for her in a big way?"

Buck didn't answer at once. Then he said, "I don't know. . . . I guess so."

"I guessed so too." Again the unwillingness to go further brought a silence. After a time Bill said, "There's something I've got to get off my chest."

Buck felt a sudden dread. Now he was going to hear it, all the truth which would show him up as a sap, the country boy among city slickers. "Go on," he said, "spill it."

Bill seemed suddenly sober. He sat bolt upright. The slight blurred quality was gone from his speech.

"It's not very easy. You've got to understand that I love you both very much, Buck. And you mustn't think I'm saying what I'm saying to get anything for myself. I guess there's no chance of that. I've given it up as much as a guy can ever give up a thing like that." He hesitated and Buck remained silent, his eyes closed. "It's no good, Buck. It's too late. Too much water has gone under the bridge. You're just a kid, you know, when it comes to things like this. You don't know what it's all about. You couldn't know. Carol is the swellest girl in the world . . . but she's been too many places and seen too many things."

[255]

Then Buck said, "She might change. People do change."

"Not much."

"I think we'd get on."

"You take her back to Jellapore with you. So what? She'd stand it about two weeks—living in a dusty Indian village . . . never seeing anybody but deadly women and dull men. And you can't quit your job and go away with her. What could you do? You couldn't change your whole life now. You couldn't give up what you've started even if you wanted to. It would mess up all the rest of your life. You'd get to hate each other."

He took out a cigarette and lighted it. With the click of the lighter, Buck without thinking why opened his eyes and by the glow from the lighter he saw Bill's face. He looked completely sober now, but his face looked drawn and tired, as if for the first time the years had begun to touch the friendly, gay, good-looking face that nothing had ever touched before. He closed the lighter and the face faded into shadow again, but the glimpse left Buck with an odd sensation of pity and the thought, "Bill had everything given him on a platter and he just threw it away, platter and all, the damned lovable fool."

Then Bill said, as he put away the lighter, "No, I've had my say. I won't ever mention it again. I wouldn't have opened my damned trap if I hadn't wanted to stop two people I care about from messing up their lives. It's done now. You can forget it if you want to."

In the window, the first signs of dawn were showing themselves. The sky above Elephanta far out in the bay had turned that lovely rose color which preceded the brazen heat of the Indian day. Buck through his closed eyes was aware of the light and he thought, "He's been on the level with me. We've gone almost the whole way. There's one more step." Opening his eyes he looked again at Bill. In the dim light his body was collapsed again as if what he had said had caused him an immense effort. His head was bent. He was staring at the end of his cigarette.

"Bill?"

"Yeah."

"Does 'proposition' mean what I think it does?"

He heard Bill's soft chuckle in the darkness. "Yes."

"Well, Moti propositioned her in my behalf . . . as a cure."

"That sounds like him. How did you know?"

"She told me."

"Oh!" Inside Bill was suddenly angry, no longer jealous at all, but only angry because for a second he thought that Carol had been up to her old tricks—of leading a man on to amuse herself. She couldn't do that to Buck. He wouldn't permit it. He'd bawl the hell out of her, the bitch! He didn't mind men like Botlivala and Jelly's brother and all the others in the long procession in London, Paris and New York. They asked for a drubbing and got what they deserved. But Buck was different. She couldn't hurt Buck. He wouldn't let her. Aloud he asked, "What did you say?"

"I said 'yes' but I wasn't sure what she meant. I sort of half thought that he might mean that I marry her."

Bill was silent for a time and then he said, "Well, I think Moti was right. It would be a lot better that way."

Buck, in the rising light, looked away from him and said, "But I don't want it that way." Bill did not answer him and still looking away out of the window toward the glow about Elephanta, Buck said, "Maybe I'm nuts. Maybe I'm a sap. Maybe I'm trying to make up for lost time. Maybe everything you say is true, Bill . . . but I've got a feeling that what I want to do is right. Maybe it'll help things turn out right for Carol as well."

Bill laughed. "The savior complex!" He was almost sober again and Buck knew that the old truthful Bill was withdrawing again inside the shell encrusted with doubts and bitterness and disillusionment, like a crustacean which, when hurt or alarmed, hides quickly away.

Buck thought, "There's nothing but to go ahead." Looking at Bill directly he said, "Bill, do you want to marry her again . . . because if you do, I'll clear out. Maybe it would be better if she stuck to you."

Again Bill laughed, "I want to marry her again but she won't have me. So don't let that stand in your way." He got up from the chair and said, "You'd better get some sleep and so had I." He sighed, "All talk is a waste of time anyway. All people ever do is go around in circles. I'll look in on you at noon."

It was finished, as if a steel curtain had come down abruptly.

Buck knew there wasn't anywhere to go. So he said, "Okay, about noon."

"I'm taking the Baroda Express tonight for Delhi." At the door he stopped for a moment and said, "Good luck."

He closed the door and inside his own room, he lay down on the bed without taking off his clothes. He had never been so tired in all his life but he could not sleep. The rising light was in his eyes and the heat that came up with the sun was already creeping into the room. But worse than the light and the heat were the thoughts which would give him no peace. Only one thing made him feel a little better—that for a little time he and Buck had got together again. He thought, "Maybe that's the best thing to keep—a friendship like that·between two men. Maybe that is the only thing which goes on forever."

For a little while he hated Carol who so brightly, so carelessly could go through life muddling the existence of other people. But presently, tossing in the heat, his head aching, he came to understand that she couldn't help being as she was. They had all begun the same way—Carol, Buck and himself—as Children of the Sun.

For Carol the whole of the next day had a quality of nightmarish unreality. She had fallen asleep at last out of simple physical exhaustion and was wakened by the heat with a hazy consciousness that something was wrong, disastrously wrong. And then she remembered the jewel case.

It was as if she awakened a different person, less soft than she had been the night before, less human. After a shower she became efficient, almost calculating and executive. One motive drove her. She thought, "I must get back the jewelry. Without it I am no longer independent. Without it I am meat for Botlivala, for the Baroness, even for Bill. If Mrs. Trollope took it, so much the worse. I'll get her off if I can but I've got to have it back." In some vague way which was not quite clear to her, the loss altered the quality of her relationship to Buck.

In the mood of activity, she thought again, "I must have been crazy last night."

First of all she sent Krishna for coffee and then she asked the manager to come up.

He was a suave little man with beady black eyes, a dark sallow skin and gray hair, tormented always by the exigencies of a clientele which was one of the oddest and perhaps the shadiest in the world, a clientele which drifted in and out, very often without money and sometimes disreputable. Always there was something happening. Being a respectable little man at heart, he was being perpetually startled and upset. He knew Carol as an old client who paid her bills and made no trouble, but he knew too everything about her and the strange company she sometimes kept, company which in the end could only add up to scandal and perhaps catastrophe. So when he heard her voice over the telephone asking if he could come up to her room for a few minutes to discuss a serious matter, he knew that what he felt was certain to come had happened. Sighing he left his desk and went upstairs.

In her room he listened quietly while she told him about the jewels. His tired worried face showed no astonishment until her answer as to what the jewelry was worth. Then his eyes narrowed and his black eyebrows came down.

"Who was in the room during the evening?" he asked.

"Mrs. Trollope and Mr. Wainwright."

"Do you suspect either of them?"

Quickly Carol answered, "I don't suspect anyone."

The manager began writing on a memorandum pad, not looking at her and said, "Oh, I see." And after a moment, "You didn't see Baroness Stefani?"

"No. Why do you ask that?"

Blandly he replied, "I was only trying to work out what possibly happened."

"No, I didn't see her after six o'clock. She has never been to my room."

"Was your boy here all evening?"

"He says so."

The manager made an inarticulate sound of doubt born out of a lifetime of experience with bearers.

"Is he an honest boy?"

She answered, without hesitation, "Absolutely."

He stopped writing, put away the pad and stood up, saying, "Of course you know we'll have to have the police."

"I suppose so."

"I should like it all kept as quiet as possible."

Quickly she said, "I would appreciate that. I won't speak of it to anyone. The quieter it is kept the better I'll like it." Again she saw what disaster the news would cause with Buck, with Bill, with the Baroness. And it would make her notorious in Bombay and make her seem incredibly silly . . . "Actress has jewels stolen"—like a broken-down fan-dancer seeking publicity to get a job in the cabaret at Green's Hotel. "No, for heaven's sake, let's keep it quiet."

"It would be very bad for the hotel." He asked one more question. "Were they insured?"

"No. That is, the insurance had run out."

His expression changed. The change was scarcely noticeable, no more than a faint shadow crossing the shriveled, worried countenance, but Carol knew what it meant. He was seeing her in a new way, as a girl on the way out. He was guessing a little of the truth . . . that very likely she was broke, that now, added to the worry about the robbery, he would have to worry about his hotel bill.

"Thank you," he said, wearily. "I'll let you know when the police come."

As he went out the door opened and in the doorway appeared another client whose account was beginning to worry him. It was Mrs. Trollope.

She had already, it seemed, been to the Army and Navy Stores and spent some of Bill's check, for she wore a whole new costume and hat, and the old worn handbag was replaced by a new white one. She looked smart in her undeveloped masculine way, and seemed brisk. Before she spoke, Carol was aware that the depression and hysteria of the night before were gone. She was bright and chipper, rather like a thin old bird.

She said, "Hello. What are you doing today?"

Carol thought, "She couldn't have done it. She couldn't be so brazen. She's only that way because she's got the money Bill gave her." And immediately even while she was speaking, she thought, "Maybe that's what a hand to mouth existence is like. Maybe it depends just on money—whether you've got a job or not. Maybe

[260]

that's what is ahead of me." It wasn't a very pleasant thought—that some day she'd be like Mrs. Trollope.

Aloud she said, remembering that she must keep quiet about what had happened, "Nothing much. Want to have lunch?"

"Love it." She sat on the bed, with an air of installing herself for a long stay.

"Oh, no," thought Carol, "oh, no, you don't." So she said, "I'll join you about noon in the bar."

"I thought I'd have a chat. I haven't anything to do."

Carol, nervous, turned firm, "I've got a lot of letters to write. I haven't got time to chat."

"I'll stay just while you dress."

"No, I've got a phobia about people being in the room while I dress."

Disappointment turned all the million lines of Mrs. Trollope's leathery face downward. She turned suddenly cold. She got up from the unmade bed. "Very well," she said, "I didn't mean to intrude."

"You're not intruding," said Carol, "only I'm peculiar—very peculiar. Bill says sometimes he thinks I'm crazy."

Mrs. Trollope ignored the remark, "All right. In the bar then about noon." And went out the door.

She went out the door, slamming it behind her, a trick that made Carol lose her temper. If Mrs. Trollope had been on the inside of the door she would very likely have been slapped.

On the other side, walking along the corridor, Mrs. Trollope was fairly happy. She didn't like being sent away, but otherwise life was going pretty well again. Carol had asked her to lunch. Bill had paid for her clothes and hotel. And the call on Carol had gone off very well, so well that it was probable Carol would have no suspicions.

Because it was Mrs. Trollope who had the jewelry. She had had it all the time stuffed inside her blouse while she sat there talking to Carol the night before. She had had it stuffed inside her blouse while she drank with Bill later in the bar downstairs. She had her plan all worked out. She would keep it hidden away until she got money from somewhere—by gambling or from Bill, to go to Australia. She would sell it there in Sydney or Melbourne, bit by bit, as she needed the money, taking it apart perhaps to sell stone by stone. Nobody would ever know anything about it.

The knowledge gave her a certain satisfaction. It was a kind of revenge for the way Carol treated her, but it confused her too, because deep inside she was all mixed up.

Then before Carol had dressed, the police arrived. When she was dressed and had her face made up and had thrown back the cover of the bed and tossed her clothing into the closet, she received them.

They were a tall middle-aged blond Englishman and a big Pathan whom she rather liked for his tough manner and hard exterior. When the Englishman introduced him as Captain Iftikar Baig, she thought, "Butch Baig! He looks like good company."

But her enthusiasm waned a little when they began questioning her. The questions were simple but the manner of asking them was rude and at times, almost insolent. Once she said, "You needn't act as if *I* stole my own jewelry."

"We hadn't meant to insinuate any such thing," said Captain Hollis, the Englishman. "We're merely trying to get at the truth."

"I'm telling you the truth. Please don't act as if I were not."

Their manner made her uneasy. It was as if she were a suspected person, and it made her afraid again, as if somewhere in the future all this lay before her—the lack of respect, the insolence, the suspicion. The thought chilled her, but when they began asking about her circle of acquaintances, she saw there was some reason for their thinking her a bad character. She thought, "I'm not really. I'm just too good-natured."

After all, it wasn't too pretty a procession—Mrs. Trollope, the Baroness, Jelly, with all his scandalous past and a possible assassination or two to his credit, the Marchesa, the Maharani, Stitch's sister, and all the odds and ends who went in and out of Jelly's house. She could see why they thought there was something fishy about the theft of the jewelry.

In their questioning they kept returning to the Baroness, as if they suspected her more than the others, almost as if they were seeking to fasten some crime, any crime, upon her.

"I hardly know her," Carol said. "She isn't a friend."

"We understand," said Captain Hollis, "that you had signed a contract to work for her."

She thought, "How in hell did that story get about?" and quickly she said, "There isn't any contract. There never was. The whole thing was a joke."

"Oh," said Captain Hollis, coldly. Then he rose and said, "If you don't mind we'll take the jewel box away with us for finger prints."

"Of course," said Carol. Again she said, "I'd like this kept as quiet as possible. I'd like it if nobody ever heard anything about it."

Captain Hollis, whose face was not very secretive, looked astonished, "You really mean that?"

"Of course, I do. I'm not looking for publicity. I'm not looking for a job."

"Oh!"

Then they went away. The Englishman went out the door first and as the big Pathan followed him, he turned, looked at her with a bold appraising stare and then suddenly grinned and winked. She turned her back at once, partly because the act of "Butch" Baig was insulting, but also because she could not help laughing. In the grin and wink of the big, good-looking Pathan there was something irresistible—a kind of lustiness, a kind of flattery, a kind of contempt for all women except for one thing, a kind of merry humor. Not given by nature to analysis, she did not try to discover why she laughed nor why it was she liked him. She only thought, still laughing, "The dirty dog!"

But the humor didn't endure for long. The visit had made her feel suddenly unclean, almost as if she were all the things the manner of the two men had implied. She thought, "That's what whores must have to endure—that, only a million times worse." And the chill came over her again, and with it a feeling of depression which settled there for good.

It wasn't helped any by the telephone call which came almost immediately. She went to the telephone with a feeling of dread and immediately she heard the voice of Mr. Botlivala. It was suave, too gentle, too plausible, too Oxford to be quite convincing.

He said, "Good morning, Carol. How are you?"

[263]

"All right." She tried to make her own voice sound casual, but something of the dread and depression crept into it.

"You sound tired."

"I'm not."

"I called up to ask if you'd have lunch with me?"

"I'm afraid I can't."

"I'm sorry. I wanted to talk over things. I'm sorry about yesterday."

It made her suspicious that he did not complain and reproach her with never being able to go out with him. She managed to say, "Don't worry about that."

"Can I see you later in the day?"

Her impulse was to say, "No, not today or any day. I never want to see you again. I'm sorry I ever heard of you." But her instinct told her to be cautious. It was different now that she no longer had the gifts to return to him. So she said, "Yes, about four o'clock . . . in the bar."

"There's racing today. We might go to the races."

"No, I don't want to go to the races." ("I don't want to be shown off any more like a two year old filly.")

"All right. At four o'clock then in the bar."

When she had left the telephone she sat on the bed for a time, staring in front of her, trying again to "think things out." Her suspicion of Mr. Botlivala increased. It was enough to make you suspicious that for once he had behaved as a gentleman. She thought, "Maybe he had the stuff stolen just to put the heat on me." And that thought made her angry. "He can go to hell! Nobody ever got me that way and nobody ever will." The whole thing was becoming incredible and melodramatic.

But she knew that sitting on the bed, thinking, would get her nowhere. By now, she thought, Buck might be awake, and she felt suddenly an overwhelming desire to see him. Near him she would find a sense of cleanness and security. In a way, his very presence would do for her what she had done for him the night before.

So when she had made up her face carefully, she went out the door to find that Krishna was not there. For a second she was angry and then she knew what had happened. The two policemen had taken him away to question him. But that too made her angry.

They might at least have shown her enough courtesy to ask her permission.

Bill wasn't in his room and that pleased her for at the moment at least she had no desire to see him. His room was still in disorder, the champagne bucket with the empty bottle still on the table; the bed, she saw, had been slept on but the covers had not been turned down. She thought, "He must have fallen asleep drunk." And that thought too depressed her as if in some way it was her fault.

She knocked on the door of Buck's room gently, lest she should waken him if he were asleep. But at once his voice answered the knock and she pushed open the door.

He was dressed, standing by the window and as he turned she saw that his face was yellow and drawn and old. At once she was aware of the new sense of intimacy between them, something which had been born during the night.

She said, "You shouldn't be up and dressed. Bed is the place for you."

"It's no good. I hate bed. It's like being chained down."

"Go back to bed and get up this evening. We can have dinner together."

A look of pleasure came into his tired eyes. "Could we?"

He sat down. "That'll be swell . . . because I think I ought to go back to Jellapore tomorrow."

For a second she felt faint. Quickly she said, "No, you can't do that."

"I've got to. Everything will go to hell while I'm away."

Quickly she said, "Moti says it would kill you."

"No, it won't. I'm tougher than that. It's no good soldiering on the job."

She suddenly saw Colonel Moti again, talking to her earnestly, telling her that only rest and care could save Buck's life. She knew that Moti wasn't lying. Moti was a doctor, a famous scientist. He knew what he was talking about.

She said, "You can't go, Buck. I won't let you."

He smiled, "You could go with me. There's a Methodist missionary in Jellapore—a parson—who could marry us."

Dizziness and confusion took possession of her. She managed to say, "Oh, Buck." She said it in a flat voice because in her confusion she felt nothing at all, and she divined suddenly that last night when she propositioned him, he had believed she was talking of marriage. She couldn't marry him. There were a thousand reasons why. She couldn't go away from Bombay until the menace of Botlivala was cleared up, until she was certain there would be no scandal about the theft. And there were so many things she would have to tell him, gently, quietly, hoping that he would understand. Bill was right. It would be insane to marry him now. It wasn't fair to him. Again suddenly he seemed to be very like his own son Tommy.

What she said was, "What about Ali? You can't leave him here."

"He'll be all right. He's happy with Indira Moti."

"He worships you."

"Yes."

"You said yourself that he was frightened."

He didn't answer this but said, "Don't you want to go?"

"I can't go away like that. There are a lot of things I must settle here."

He looked at her shrewdly, "Mr. Botlivala?"

She summoned her courage, "Yes, for one thing."

How much did he know? Who had been talking to him? There wasn't only Botlivala but there was Jelly's brother in Jellapore. She suddenly saw again that farewell party with the naked dancing boys and the subalterns in red coats kicking over the pots of orchids. She heard Moti saying again, "In Jellapore they know all about you—even the wild people in the jungle."

Abruptly she said, "Has Bill been talking to you?"

"Yes. He thinks we're both crazy. He thinks the 'proposition' is a better idea. I didn't know what that meant but he explained it to me." He smiled, "You see, I'm kind of dumb about things like that."

That was it. The whole thing was like taking candy from a baby. She couldn't do it. And he mustn't go back to Jellapore yet, not until he was well again. He couldn't die. The presence of Moti returned to her again. It was almost as if he were compelling her by hypnosis.

[266]

Buck was saying, "Bill was on the level about everything. You mustn't get me wrong about that."

"I know Bill."

"Does he often get drunk nowadays?"

"No. I never saw him like that before."

He was silent and presently she said, "Buck, I think we're crazy too. I know I am."

He grinned, "Maybe it's all right to be like that. Maybe we're lucky."

"Maybe we are, but I still think none of this makes any sense." He was looking more tired than when she came in. She said suddenly, "You're going back to bed now and try to sleep. You couldn't have slept much last night."

"I didn't."

"I'll come back for you about six o'clock. Then we can settle all this. Will you promise me?"

"Yes."

"I'll go away now. Have you got everything you want?"

"Yes."

"I'll try and look in again after lunch."

"It would be fine if you did."

"And don't be silly about going back to Jellapore."

"We can talk about that later on." He looked out of the window. "I hate it here," he said, "I'm like a fish out of water. Everybody makes me feel silly. I don't like Bombay. You ought never to have come here. Or me either."

"All right, honey, we'll try to straighten it out. But you've got to get some sleep."

She went away then, unwilling to trust herself any longer because she felt the old craziness stealing over her again. She might do something that she would regret forever, make some decision that would only harm Buck.

When she had gone, he sat looking at the door for a long time. Then slowly, wearily he undressed and went back to bed, but he did not sleep because the old doubts attacked him again, doubts about Mr. Botlivala and Jellapore and his brother, about all the weird people who surrounded her. And he thought, "I must be in love. There is nothing I can do about it. It's impossible for me to

[267]

live without her. I can't go away. I can't forget her. If I turn back now I will regret it all the rest of my life."

And he knew too in his simplicity that it was no longer a matter of choice. It was something over which he no longer had any control. He could not have gone back to Jellapore. He knew now he had only said he meant to go simply to make himself believe that he still possessed a will, that he could still control his own destiny. But even while he was speaking, he had known that he could not do it. And he had a strange presentiment that if he did go away he would die. His body told him that.

The lunch with Mrs. Trollope revealed nothing. She was in high spirits and although Carol watched every gesture and listened to every intonation she was able to discover nothing to increase her suspicions. Mrs. Trollope had been to see the fortuneteller after she left Carol's room and he had given her good news. The stars, she told Carol, were in a new position which augured for her a long period of prosperity and good luck. She was going to the races. Would Carol like to go with her?

No, Carol wouldn't, although she did not say that it was because she was having tea with Botlivala. She thought, "There goes the money Bill gave her for her hotel bill." She wanted to protest but she did not, and she thought, "Maybe I'm learning sense—not telling her anything, not butting into other people's business." But she didn't like having sense nor the price of the necessity. It was all very cramping—to calculate and count ten before you said or did anything.

Then the Marchesa joined them for coffee. She was leaving for Delhi in the evening, she said, to stay at the Viceroy's house.

"Bill's going too," said Carol.

"Meester Wainwright?" asked the Marchesa, her heavy lids heavier with sham innocence.

"Yes," said Carol. "Maybe he isn't taking the same train."

"There ees only one eefening train," said the Marchesa, and Carol thought, "I'll bet there is. If there were more you'd find the one he was on."

She was alarmed now and a little jealous. Bill was such an easygoing fool. She didn't want him mixed up with anything as obvious as the Marchesa. And she thought, "Staying at the Viceroy's house, my eye!" But Bill wasn't any longer her business either. The sooner he disappeared from Bombay and she forgot about him, the better. He'd tried to meddle between herself and Buck. To hell with him.

The Marchesa was saying that she thought him "charming—charming—and so good-looking—so nice—such a gentleman."

"Yes," thought Carol, "I know where she learned to talk like that."

She couldn't keep her mind on the conversation. It wasn't very interesting and she hated the company of women alone and her thoughts kept milling around and around to Buck, to Bill, to Mrs. Trollope, to Krishna and what had become of him, to Jelly and the Baroness. Once she even thought, "Maybe the best thing would be to take a night club job with the Baroness and clear out for Paris by the next boat."

The dull lunch was over at last and Carol with a headache born of worry and boredom, left the two women as quickly as possible. In the big hallway of the hotel she met the nervous little manager. He said, "I have news for you."

"Yes," said Carol quickly.

"It's not important. Except that your boy admitted he wasn't in front of your door all the evening. He was away for two hours. The hotel does its best to prevent things like this, but it can't be responsible for your servant."

"No, of course not." (Krishna, the little liar. Anyone might have gotten into the room while he was away.) "Thank you," she said to the manager.

Mr. Botlivala was waiting for her. As she came through the door she saw him rise from a table in the far corner of the room and come forward to meet her, and as she saw him she hated him, not now because she was contemptuous or thought him a nasty cad and brute, but because she was afraid of him.

They greeted each other and sat at the table without another word until he asked her what she wanted to drink. She ordered a gin sling and then he said, "I'm sorry about the scene I made. I didn't mean it."

"Don't begin to apologize all over again."

"I promise to behave now."

She smiled, "Oh, don't worry about that. It won't make any difference."

If only the jewelry hadn't been stolen, she could have given it back to him then and there and walked away without another word. She kept telling herself that she must go carefully and not lose her temper. Before now Mr. Botlivala had not been of any importance one way or another. She had been able to kick him around and make him like it. But now there was a difference. It wasn't only the lost jewelry; even that wouldn't have mattered. It was Buck. There was no use trying to kid herself. Since she had known Buck, Mr. Botlivala had become repulsive and evil to her, and the thought that she had ever permitted him to think that he was engaged to her revolted her.

She was aware that Mr. Botlivala was talking in his emotional, excitable way, pouring out excuses, making promises of good behavior, but because of the rush of thoughts, she did not hear what he was saying. She did not attempt to listen because she had heard it all before, many times. That was what had led her to say long ago, "Oh, be engaged to me if you like, if it'll make you happy." That was how she had come to let him give her the bracelet and rings—because she was sick of him and wanted to keep him quiet and because it made him in an odd way easier to handle.

She knew presently (after the waiter had served them) that he was crying like a woman and that he was saying that if she would marry him he would make her a settlement that would leave her independent of money for the rest of her life. She heard him even say that he would never come near her and ask no more of her than to live in his big ornate house and let the world believe she was his wife. And she thought, "A week ago I might have done that." And at the same time she was sickeningly ashamed not of herself but of that woman called Carol Halma who had gone about Bombay gayly, carelessly in this body which now sat opposite the whining Mr. Botlivala. At the same time she was aware of a dull astonishment that the vanity of any man could be so insane, for she knew that it was vanity and the fear of being jilted publicly before

[270]

all the people to whom he had boasted of her, which lay behind the pleading and hysteria.

She said suddenly, fiercely, "Stop behaving like a damned fool. People are looking at us." Near them sat two English people, a man and a woman, middle class, conventional, stupid and malicious. They were listening to everything that Botlivala said. The woman said something to the man and they both laughed, and again Carol thought, "That is what happens to whores," and, "I can't go on with this. Anything is better than this."

Mr. Botlivala was blowing his nose with a pale green silk handkerchief that matched his green necktie. She said, "I never meant to marry you, Botlivala, and you knew it."

"I believed you," he said, "I told all my friends and now you make me look like a fool. They'll all laugh at me the way they always have. You can't do that!"

She thought, "Good God! When am I going to be free of these self-pitiers—Botlivala and Mrs. Trollope and all the rest." Coldly she said, "I'm going to do it to you. And nothing is going to stop me." The spectacle of Mr. Botlivala sniveling became unendurable. "I don't want to see you again—ever. I don't even want to be seen out with you. For God's sake try to be a man just for a little time."

She saw the plump little body stiffen suddenly as if a poker had been rammed down its back. The eyes widened with astonishment until the yellowish whites were visible all around the pupils. And she was afraid again and her instinct told her quickly the truth about Mr. Botlivala. Without thinking, in anger, she had hit upon it. The truth was that Botlivala was *not* a man. For years, for all his life, he had tried to make others believe that he was a man. That was why he had clung to her so desperately, that was why he had spent all the money simply to be seen about with her, because she was beautiful and it made men envy him. That was why he could say he would ask nothing of her but to live in his house and make the world believe that she was his wife. She understood it all, quickly, in the passing of a second or two. At the same time, terrified, she saw him stand up and pick up his gloves. It was as if she were hypnotized and could do nothing.

[271]

Then as if in a slow motion picture she saw him take up his glass. Raising it he threw what remained of his drink full into her face, crying out, "Cheat! Whore!" and then in Hindustani he began to scream abuse, and pushing his way rudely between the tables he hurried out of the bar.

She did not see him go. She did not see anything at all—neither the waiters running to set right the overturned table, nor the crowding faces peering at her—faces brown and black and white. She simply sat there as if paralyzed until she felt a hand touch her shoulder and thought, "I suppose that's the police." But she heard a croaking voice behind the hand which she recognized at once.

"Come wit me," said the Baroness, "I'll ged you oud of here."

Like a child she obeyed. It was as if she no longer possessed any will. With the Baroness waddling in front of her like a fat tug pushing its way through the crowds of curious faces, she finally got out of the huge barroom. Now and then she heard the croaking voice in an extraordinary tone of command saying rudely, "Ged oud of de vay, you fool!" or "Move your chair and led me trough!" The Baroness required an extraordinary amount of room for passage for herself; it was easy to follow in her wake. In the hallway, the Baroness said, "Ve will go up by de stairs," and herself, puffing and blowing with the exertion, led the way.

It was only when Carol had climbed two long flights of stone steps that any sense of reality returned to her. Then suddenly the scene which had happened belowstairs reached the full proportions of its horror.

She had been humiliated in front of scores of people by a man who had one of the most evil reputations in a city where there were plenty of evil reputations—in a city divided in race where his color made the insult even worse. Now it was complete. There was no further to go.

Ahead of her the Baroness still led the way leaving in her wake the sound of puffing and the odor of perspiration and patchouli. Dimly it seemed to Carol that there was about her a sudden dignity and gallantry, and then suddenly she knew what it was. The Baroness, the Madam, had claimed her for her own. She had gone into the fray as she had perhaps gone many times into the battle for one of her girls.

[272]

Dully, a sickening thought came to Carol, "Maybe that's what I'm headed for. Maybe there isn't any use trying to beat it."

In her own room she flung herself down on the bed and began to cry. It was the first time she had cried in years and now it was as if all the weariness, the boredom, the dullness of months and years were pouring out. She gave way to her weeping luxuriously. She forgot the Baroness. She forgot the horror of the scene. Her mind went empty in the exquisite physical relief of hysteria, but through it she heard the voice of the Baroness, saying, "You must not mind. Men are horreeble animals." And after a little pause, "I know. Dey are my business."

Then Carol felt the bed sink beneath the dead weight of the old woman's body as she sat on it. She felt the touch of the hand covered with dirty diamonds and smelled again the odor of patchouli and perspiration and heard the croaking voice saying, "Don't vorry. You can gount on de Baroness." And suddenly the old woman became as horrible to her as poor Mr. Botlivala.

Trying to regain control of herself, she said, "Please go away now and leave me alone . . . please . . . just now I want to be alone."

The bed creaked as the weight of the Baroness released it and the old voice filled with timeless weariness, said, "I go avay now, but I come back. If you vant de Baroness telephone her." There was a little silence in which the Baroness did not go away and the voice again spoke, "If you vant, you can go back to Paris vit me."

Then the evil old woman went away, closing the door softly behind her.

It was dark when at last she stopped crying, thinking, "I'm no better than the rest—pitying myself." As she sat up, she saw in the dim light of the window the figure of a man standing in the open doorway.

It was Buck. He said, "I knocked but you didn't answer so I came in."

She didn't want to see him now. She only wanted to run away and see no one. Dully she said, "It's all right."

He closed the door and came over to her taking both her hands.

[273]

"I heard what happened. What do you want me to do? I'll do anything but I don't want to make it worse for you. I'll kill the son of a bitch if you want me to."

"There isn't anything to do that won't make it worse except to go away. I've got to get out of Bombay . . . any place."

Then he put his arms round her, shyly, in the friendliest way. It was the first time he had ever embraced her. He said, "We'll go to that place on the beach . . . tonight . . . if you want to."

"I guess it's the only thing to do . . . until a boat sails. I can't stay here. I can't be seen again in Bombay. I'll go on the first boat. I'll clear out."

He simply said, "We'll see about that."

Then she thought, "I've got to make sense. He's right. It's the only place to go." She kissed his cheek impulsively and said, "You're a swell guy, Buck." And then nervously freed herself from him. A strange thought came to her. "If I go there with him, we will have to live apart." But she said, "I must tell the Maharajah we want the place. The races are over. He's probably home now."

The old feeling of confidence returned to her. She said, "I'll telephone to him."

Buck didn't say anything. He only watched her, as if he were puzzled.

She got Joey on the wire. The Maharajah was gambling. He would see if he would come to the telephone. In a moment she heard Jelly's voice. "Yes, my dear. What can I do for you?" And she knew by his voice that he had already heard of what had happened in the bar.

She said, "I want to use the house at Juhu—Jai Mahal."

Mirth crept into his voice as he asked, "A second honeymoon?"

She said, "Yes," because there was nothing else to say.

"So Wainwright isn't going to Calcutta?"

Her tired brain worked quickly. If he thought it was Bill, let him go on thinking it. So much the better. For the moment it didn't matter. And he would find out. He always found out everything. "No," she said.

"There's a caretaker. I'll have Joey tell him you're coming and send out a cook and a couple of servants." He didn't ask her when she wanted to go. He knew that she wanted to go now, tonight—that she had to go.

Then she heard a chuckle over the telephone, and in a voice filled with insinuation, he asked, "What will Mrs. Trollope say?"

"I don't know and I don't give a damn. But thanks, Jelly. It helps me out of a hole."

She put down the telephone and stood for a moment looking out of the window. She saw nothing but she was aware of Buck's presence behind her. He made everything seem different. Then she turned and said, "It's all right. Everything will be ready."

"We can go tonight?"

"Yes."

Then she remembered the hotel bill. She might have enough cash to pay it. She might not. She knew that she dared not risk asking for it now. She thought quickly, knowing that she must not let Buck discover how broke she was, that she dared not risk a scene with the hotel manager. So she thought, "I'll only take one bag and leave the trunks. That will satisfy him. As long as Bill is in India he won't dun me."

She had never been like this before, at the end of her tether. Weary she suddenly cared no longer what happened. She only wanted to get away.

She said, "We'd better pack, Buck."

"Yes."

"I'm only taking a suitcase."

"Yes."

"We'd better go out by the harbor side." (On that side they would see no one.) "If you'll call a taxi and then come for me."

He put his arms suddenly about her and kissed her. Then in a quiet voice, he said, "We're going to be happy."

Fear went out of her suddenly. No other man she had ever known was like this. No man she had ever known had ever wanted to take care of her. Weakly she said, "Thanks, Buck. I hope so."

He went away and while she packed, she was happy again in a strange way with a happiness that was new to her. She had nearly finished when someone knocked at the door. She did not answer the knock. It was repeated and then Bill's voice said, "It's me, Bill. I just came to say good-bye."

She didn't want to see him but she said, "Come in."

He looked at the suitcase on the bed and she knew at once that he too had heard about the scene in the bar.

He said, "You're right to go away. Where are you going?"

"To Jelly's house at Juhu."

"Shall I beat up that greasy little bastard?"

"No. That would only bring in the police and the newspapers and make it worse."

"And Buck—did he accept your proposition?"

"Yes."

"It would have been better to go back to Europe. It is bad luck there isn't a boat. You just missed the *Rawalpindi*. There isn't another for two weeks."

"You were going to ship me?"

"Yes, I was going to stay over to do it."

"Thanks."

He lighted a cigarette and said, "There's just one thing."

"What?"

"You've got to give Buck a square deal. You've got to be honest with him."

"I mean to be—more honest than I've ever been with anybody—even you."

"Okay . . . because if you treat him badly I'll beat the hell out of you."

"All right, Bill."

"If you want money or anything, call on me. Just care of the company in Calcutta. Whatever is mine is yours and Buck's."

"You're a swell guy, Bill. I wish things weren't so complicated because I love you, too, but not the way I love Buck. That's never happened to me before. I can't do anything about it."

"Don't worry about me." He took her hand. "Well, good luck. You'll need it."

Then he went away and she sat down to write a note to the manager explaining that she had gone away and would return in a week or two. She knew it would not surprise him because it had happened before many times. In a little while Buck came carrying his own battered paper case. He looked happy and more than ever like Tommy.

"The taxi's waiting," he said.

Suddenly she felt excited and happy. Nothing else mattered but Buck. Nothing in the world. Whatever came now did not matter.

Outside the door there was no sign of Krishna. He should have returned long before now. But that did not matter either. She could write to the manager to tell Krishna to go back to Jellapore. But almost at once a shadow crossed her happiness. She knew what had happened. He had run away from her. Krishna, who had been her slave, who had adored her because she had given him a bicycle, had run away from her because a dissolute Parsee had thrown a glass of gin in her face in the crowded bar of the Taj Mahal.

An hour after they had left, Mrs. Trollope came along the jail-like corridor to Carol's door. The high spirits were gone now. In the dim light all the sagging lines had returned to the sallow face. Everything about her, even the new hat and the handbag, seemed to droop. She was again like a bedraggled sparrow.

Because the handbag was empty. The money Bill had given her for her hotel bill was gone, lost at the races. She had tried to find him to see whether she could not wangle more—only a thousand or two rupees to take to Jellapore's pleasure palace and build into solid money again. But Bill wasn't in his room and when she went to the desk she received a terrible bit of information. They said there that he had already left for Calcutta.

So there was no place to turn but to Carol, and now she was at Carol's door, knocking.

There was no answer. Wondering that Carol's bearer was not before the door, she knocked again, and when there was only silence she pushed open the door. The room was in darkness and when she switched on the lights, the trunks pushed in the corner, the bare dressing table told her the story. Carol had gone away. Very likely she had gone to Calcutta with Bill. Now there wasn't anyone to turn to.

For a time she stood staring at the desolate room, thinking furiously. She dared not risk selling any of the jewelry in Bombay and she could not get out of Bombay without money. And through her thoughts there emerged a hatred for Bill. She had been right;

he was the one who had destroyed her friendship with Carol. He had given her the money for her bills to be rid of her, and then taken Carol with him to Calcutta. He was the blond man the fortuneteller had talked about who would bring her bad luck. She had been right that day when she had quarreled with him in the taxi.

For a moment the whole world about her seemed to collapse. Wearily she sat down alone in the dreary room. Her head ached. She couldn't think. Everything seemed to whirl about inside her head—race horses, gambling tables, Carol, Bill, the Baroness, Jelly, her sister Nellie, the missionary. They whirled round and round, suffused by a brilliant light. She thought, "Maybe I'm going crazy." The sensation of madness lasted for a long time. When it faded, she lay back exhausted, the sweat streaming down her leathery face.

She thought, "There is only one place to go." That was to Jellapore's pleasure palace. Since the scene with Nellie she had not gone back because they had made it abundantly clear that she was not wanted. Well, she didn't mind that now. She was beyond minding a mere snubbing. If she could get Jellapore's ear, he might lend her money to play. Money meant nothing to him.

And so when she had had a couple of drinks in the bar, she took the new handbag, empty but for a couple of small rupee notes and a few anna pieces, and set out in a taxicab for Jelly's pavilion.

They were gambling, she knew, because the house was full of light and the row of vulture taxis stood outside. The old porter acknowledged her as she passed through the door with no more than a bird-like peck of a salaam—a salaam which said, "You're broke and down and out and unwelcome."

Inside it was no better. In the red and gold gambling room, Jelly sat wearily at the head of the table in his usual place, bored and a little tipsy. Joey was there and, thank God, Nellie wasn't. All the others, except a Portuguese, were strangers. Only a little while before, with Carol for her friend and money in her pocket, before the quarrel with Nellie, it had been very different. Now no one rose when she came in. No one took any notice of her. It needed desperation and all the hardness she could summon to enter the room and walk to Jellapore's side.

Fearing that she might lose her nerve, she went directly over to him and said, "May I speak to Your Highness, privately?"

He looked annoyed but rose and went with her into the room which had a view across the bay toward Elephanta. Then she told him everything—that she was broke and wanted to borrow money to gamble with in order to put herself back on her feet. The fortuneteller had promised her a run of luck so that the borrowed money would really be no more than an investment. She had counted on Bill and she had counted on Carol, but Bill had gone off to Calcutta taking her with him.

The Maharajah listened, bored, weighing all she said, indolently trying to find some new thread which might be woven into a full-sized intrigue.

When she had finished, he said perfectly coldly, "In the first place I never lend money. It is the one sure way of making people hate you. Besides, Carol has not gone to Calcutta with Bill Wainwright. I know where they are."

"Where?" asked Mrs. Trollope.

"I gave my word not to tell."

"Bill has gone to Calcutta. They told me so at the hotel."

He looked at her with a sudden swift glance of the opaque black eyes. "Are you sure of that?"

"Yes."

Then suddenly the light dawned. He smiled and said, "So it wasn't a second honeymoon—or it was, but with a different man."

"What are you talking about?"

"She told me a lie. She's with the missionary bloke. How very stupid of me. I should have guessed it. It wasn't very difficult to guess." Then he turned away, saying, "I must get back to the table. I'm sorry I can't do anything for you," and walked off leaving her standing alone in the middle of the big room.

Once again, for a shorter time, she experienced the sensation of her head blowing up. When it had passed and she was no longer dizzy, she hadn't the courage to go back again through the big room and past the porter. Quickly she went out through the garden, through the shrubbery, although she was terrified of snakes, past the old porter into the street where she took a taxi for the Taj Mahal.

[279]

There was one more chance and that she tried. She found the Baroness in the hall with the shabby, sinister little man who sometimes called on her. When he had gone, she told the Baroness that she needed money, that she would do anything for it.

But the green eyes of the Baroness turned to hard opals. "No," she said, "I haf only enuff money for myself."

A week ago she had considered giving Mrs. Trollope a job in the Paris house. There was something about her that would dress the place up. But that idea was past and gone. In the eyes of the Baroness, Mrs. Trollope had come to be merely a bringer of bad luck. When she had gone away, the Baroness turned toward the discouraged sagging back, raised two fingers and spat through them seven times. After that she felt better. It had never failed to work against the evil eye.

Bill dined alone at Green's Hotel, lonely and depressed. A voice kept saying to him, "You might as well get drunk. You won't sleep on that bloody train rocking and rolling about with the red dust in your eyes and teeth and hair." But he didn't get drunk because another voice said, "There's nothing in it. It doesn't lead anywhere. You wake up sober with a headache and you haven't forgotten anything. It all just begins over again." He had a couple of cocktails and some beer with his dinner and he kept wondering whether it was better to have the girl you loved go off with your best friend or with a heel you detested. That was a very fine-spun question. Maybe you felt just as sick one way as the other, except that it was different. Anyway, Buck would look after her. He wouldn't play her any dirty tricks.

The odd thing was that he wasn't worried about the girl he loved but only about his best friend. He was the one who would get hurt if anyone did; Carol would pick up and leave when she had had enough or if it didn't turn out well. In any case, he thought, it was all very complicated, so much more complicated than most people, caught by unhappiness, ever realized. Until lately he had been "most people" himself; what had happened to him hadn't hurt him or made him unhappy. It was only lately that he had begun to think about himself and what he was, and to discover that behind almost everything he did or thought or said

[280]

there were masses of complications. Take this mess—of his falling for Carol long after they had been married and divorced—just because he had come for some reason to be aware of her as a different person. And his feeling for Buck which he saw now in a new and different light. It would have been swell and easy if he could have hated Buck. The trouble was that you couldn't blame anybody for anything. The whole thing had just happened, and there wasn't anything to do to change it. But that didn't make it any easier to take, when you got to thinking of all the years and all the fun you would miss. It might be like an ache that went on forever tormenting you, or a hunger that would never be satisfied. It would be better to try and fail than never to know. Now he would never know whether he and Carol could have been happy and built up a good life together.

The porter from the Taj with his baggage interrupted the gloominess of his thoughts.

"You had better go, sir, if you're to catch the train."

So he went dully, not worrying about his luggage, whether it was all there or whether it arrived at the train. Usually he was a nervous traveler, but tonight his nerves were numb.

The station was hot and clamorous with the noise of trains and the curious eternally excited metallic voices of the coolies. He thought, "Why in hell does there always have to be so much noise about everything in India—the beating of gongs, the screaming and shouting which accompanies any conversation on a railway platform, the banging and thumping which accompanies every act of work." The heat seemed to rise from the bricks. Grimly he thought, "Well, tonight is a new low water mark for depression. I'll never feel any worse than I do now. That's something to be thankful for."

In the compartment he found that he was not alone. There was, sharing it with him, a beefy middle-aged Englishman and an Indian in European clothes, probably, thought Bill, a politician on his way to Delhi. They were already eying each other with suspicion and dislike. Bill said good-evening politely to both of them, thinking, "It's your quarrel, boys. Fight it out." He left them uncomfortably together and lighting a cigarette set out to walk up and down the platform until the train left.

[281]

He had barely made a turn of the platform before he heard a familiar voice, very lush, saying, "Good-eefening, Mr. Wainwright."

He knew the voice. It was the Marchesa. She was dressed all in white which emphasized the darkness of her overblown beauty.

"Hell!" thought Bill. "Good-evening," he said. "Are you going on this train?"

"As far as Delhi. I'm staying weeth the Viceroy."

"What a pleasant surprise," he said wearily.

"Would you like a drink?" she asked. "I have a quart of champagne on ice."

Well, there wouldn't be any harm in having a drink with her. His tongue was hanging out. The cocktails had begun to wear off, leaving him feeling hot and miserable. The idea of iced champagne was too much for him.

She had a whole compartment reserved for herself. The bed had been made up with sheets of pale pink silk with a pair of lacy pillows on top of the larger pillows covered with silk. A lacy dressing gown lay over the one chair. Above the odors of the station there was a scent of some thick heavy perfume. The champagne stood in a cooler from the Taj Mahal.

He thought, "A trollope's turn-down if ever I saw one." For a moment he thought of fleeing, but there seemed no way to do it politely. He had no taste for dark, lush, panting women. She started to open the champagne but he took it from her. As he opened it, he asked, "Is your maid traveling with you?"

"Of course. She has a compartment of her own."

It was good champagne, better champagne than he had believed it possible to find in Bombay. It was a man's champagne, dry and aromatic. The mere sight of it made him feel a good deal better. The taste raised his spirits.

She had taken out a very long Egyptian cigarette and was waiting for him to light it. The way she leaned forward a little, inviting his eye, creating a specious intimacy, told him volumes. It was an old technique, and it came from one place, the expensive kind of place.

"I always take champagne on a voyage," she said, and Bill thought, "Good Lord, she's a dull woman. She's so damned earnest over a seduction."

[282]

Outside the noises of an Indian departure began to fill the air, the sound of running feet, the shouts and cries of farewell, the peals of Hindu laughter. He finished his glass of champagne and said, "I'd better get back to my compartment before the train starts. Thanks for the drink."

"There's no hurry," she said, "we weell feenish the bottle togethair and you can get out at the first stop."

Another glass or two would be fine. He could play "dumb" and pretend not to know what was on the Marchesa's mind and get out at the first stop and still escape. In any case it was too late to change now for the train had begun to move. And then he thought, suddenly, tipsily, "I'm a damned fool. This is an express. The first stop is Baroda and that is eight hours away."

He wanted to laugh. "Country boy raped!" he thought. Well, there wasn't anything to be done now unless he pulled the emergency cord and called for the train crew to save him.

Outside the lights of the filthy Mill district had begun to rush past the window. What the hell difference did it make anyway, one way or another? He wasn't any virgin. He had no one to be faithful to. Carol, damn her, had gone off with Buck for good.

The Marchesa was saying, "You could spend the night here." And in her heavy, elaborate Levantine French, *"Cela m'est tout à fait égal."*

"Moi aussi," said Bill. "We'll have another glass." You might as well be gay about it.

"La vie," said the Marchesa, *"est si souvent tellement belle."*

"And how!" said Bill grimly. He took another drink and then asked, "You don't happen to have another bottle?"

"I have half a case."

"Better put another bottle on ice as a good start."

On the long ride to Juhu, past the lights of Malabar Hill and the rosy glow that illuminated the Jellapore pleasure palace, past the race course and the Willingdon Club and the open country beyond, the two of them rode in silence, both afraid. They sat, like adolescents, side by side, their hands clasped.

Carol was frightened because for the first time in her life she was running away. As the taxicab passed Jellapore's house (a little

[283]

before Mrs. Trollope arrived to beg for money) she closed her eyes, moved by a curious certainty that she would never again drive in past the vulture taxis under the jacquerandas to the doorstep where the old porter stood. Whatever happened, no matter what turn her life took it would never be back again on the old path. Even in the midst of her uneasiness, she experienced a regret or two, because inside Jelly's house she had laughed and had fun and won a great deal of money. She was afraid, too, because there was ahead of this adventure an end, and that was something she had never before experienced. Always before she had never known; one thing had led to another and presently when she had had enough of it, the adventure was finished. About this flight there was no adventure. There would come a day, suddenly, when it would be ended, and as the taxicab raced along past lights, through Indian smells and noises, she knew the end, no matter how it came, could not be happy.

She thought, "For God's sake, don't spoil it now by worrying about it." But the thought did no good. Once it occurred to her that the thing to do was to tell the wild taxi driver to stop, to get out and go away, leaving Buck before it was too late. But she did not do it.

And Buck, sitting there beside her, was afraid for reasons that were for him hazy and confused. In his simplicity and innocence he was afraid of boring her, afraid that to her he would always seem naïve and so in the end, after the novelty had worn off, he would become tiresome. Whatever trouble his conscience had caused him was gone now, for he had plunged and there was no turning back. He thought, "Maybe this is just giving her a push on down the way she is headed." And almost at once he thought, "Bill would laugh at you for having such a thought, and maybe he is right!" That was the disturbing thing—that perhaps after all Bill wasn't such a fool. And the thought of Bill brought up to him the picture of Bill's unhappiness. Bill was going off alone to Calcutta —Bill who was such a swell guy and wouldn't ever let you help him.

When they were nearly to Juhu Buck said suddenly, "It's a swell night." And out of the darkness in her corner, Carol said, "The combination of coconut palms and the Indian moon is always demoralizing." And then quickly she was sorry she had said it. It

[284]

had been a natural remark in the world she had just left, but to Buck it would seem only as if she were propositioning him again.

Jelly had been prompt. After two or three mistakes the driver found Jai Mahal. The coconut and betel palms behind the high wall were bathed in light from the house. Inside the gate there was every sign of activity. The servants were in sight, one of them sweeping the gravel paths with a broom of twigs, one scrubbing the marble steps, another sweeping hastily in a room overlooking the sea. A kind of steward in purple and gold came forward salaaming.

He addressed them in Hindustani and Buck, answering him, talked with him for a few moments and then said to Carol, "The Maharajah has sent out a cold supper. Tomorrow the cook will take charge."

"I'm not hungry. Thank him."

"Nor I."

The man took the two bags, Carol's elegant one and Buck's poor suitcase of shabby paper. And then Carol thought of something. She said to Buck, "Go outside and have a look at the garden. I'll join you in a moment."

Then she left him and went quickly up the winding stairway of white marble into the two French bedrooms. Quickly she set about her task.

It wasn't easy, for the bawdy French engravings were not simply hung on the walls but fastened by wire through the delicate filigree of the carved marble gratings which served as windows. When she had seen them on her first visit they had made her laugh, not only because they were funny but because of their frank Rabelaisian bawdiness. They weren't funny to her now, because she saw them in a new way. She didn't want them there while she and Buck were in the house. She didn't want him to see them. It wasn't that she disapproved of them, but because they were a false note which offended her sense of rightness. And Buck wouldn't understand why they were funny.

As her fingers worked quickly, unfastening the crude arrangement of wires, she thought, "After all these years I'm becoming a prude. That's a laugh if ever there was one." She swore quietly as

[285]

she broke one lacquered nail. She felt a kind of mild childish excitement. Bombay had become very remote, more distant than Paris, more distant than New York, or Minnesota, more distant than the stars. To hell with the jewelry and Mrs. Trollope and Botlivala. But all the same the thought of Botlivala made her face feel hot again and the old feeling of dread claimed her.

Finally she had all the bawdy pictures loosened and taken down and then came the question of where to hide them. She had no desire to carry them downstairs and perhaps encounter Buck with her arms filled with dirty pictures. The rooms abovestairs were part Indian and part European and bare of any spot in which to hide them with the certainty that he would not find them. She went through the four rooms searching without success. And at last, noticing the small stairway leading to the roof, she climbed it and pushed open the trap door at the top.

The whole of the roof was flat with two corded Indian beds bare in the moonlight and in the corner a great chest with a lid at the top which could be lifted up—a chest kept there possibly for the sheets and blankets when the beds were used. That was the place. Quickly she descended the stairs and carried up the obscene engravings in two loads. When she had placed them inside she closed the lid and went down again to the second floor. Then she sat down for a moment before the mirror of the elaborate French dressing table to do her hair and make up her face.

The reflection in the mirror wasn't flattering. The mirror wasn't new and like all mirrors in India it had suffered the ravages of damp during the monsoons and had turned blotched and green in spots. The face she saw reflected was tired and white, with great dark circles under the eyes. For a long time she studied it, thinking, "Well, honey, that's the first time in your life you ever looked like that." She did not blame the mirror, seeking in its murky depths excuses for an appearance which made her a stranger to herself. She thought, "You'd better pull up and get some rest. That puss never looked so hard and tired before. If he loves you with a face like that you must be pretty good."

Quickly, quietly, she repaired the ravages of the past twenty-four hours as best she could and when she had finished she studied the two adjoining bedrooms. They were neither attractive nor spiritual in appearance. They didn't even appear to be very clean. And the opulent red brocade coverings and gilded furniture had little relation to the intricate rather chill purity of the white marble walls and carved screens which served as windows. It was odd how Indian and Western things could never be brought together in the same room. The room was in a way like Jellapore himself—an odd, unhappy, tormenting mixture of West and East.

Looking at the incongruous mess an odd thought occurred to her —that she, a Swedish girl from Minnesota should find herself eloping to this strange and beautiful house with a missionary. But almost at once, she thought, "Maybe it isn't so funny after all. Maybe people do travel in circles. Because Buck is a lot like my mother and father—more like them than any man I've ever met." He was simple like them and full of faith in goodness and bewildered by anything that wasn't simple and good. The thought filled her with awe so that she was unnatural and shy when she at last went down the stairs to find him.

He wasn't in the house nor outside on the terrace with the little fountain. For a second, alarmed, she thought, "Maybe he's run away after all." But in the next moment she saw far down in the garden on the edge of the water, his tall figure in silhouette against the path of light made by the waning moon across the surface of the Bay. She did not go to him at once but stood there by the singing fountain, caught and made immobile by the beauty of the night and the scene and by that feeling which always welled up in her heart at sight of him. He was walking up and down the path, his hands clasped behind him. Twice he walked the full length of the long terrace and turned before she went down the steps toward him. Then she hurried, for she was afraid that pain had seized him again and that he was pacing up and down like an animal in a cage to fight it.

He did not see her until she said, "Are you all right, Buck?"

He turned quickly and came toward her, "Yes, honey. You were gone a long time."

"I was trying to make my face presentable."

"I wouldn't worry about that. It's a nice face."

"I thought you were sick again—walking up and down like that."

"No."

"What was the matter?" she asked, and almost at once regretted it. It was none of her business unless he chose to tell her. Was she going to be a fool like most women in love and try to take possession even of his mind and soul?

"I was just thinking."

She very nearly asked, "About what?" But checked herself.

He went on, "I was just thinking that maybe I was too darned conceited, thinking that I was indispensable—that maybe the villages couldn't get on without me. I've known fools like that."

She didn't say anything, for fear that what she said might be the wrong thing.

He went on, "I guess if I went away they'd soon find someone else to take my place."

So that was what he was thinking—that Moti was right, that he could never take her back to Jellapore with him because of what she had been. He was trying to persuade himself that everything he was, everything he lived for had no importance because of herself. Her instinct told her that she needed to be careful. Whatever she said now would be dangerous. It might be the small beginning which could wreck everything. In the moonlight she saw the extraordinary goodness in his face and was ashamed of herself.

Wisely she said, "Let's not talk about that now. Let's have a drink and lie in the chairs on the terrace and do nothing." (All that could be put off. It needn't be decided now. It was bad enough when it came.) She felt cold suddenly, shivering at the sound of the dry rattle of the moonlit coconut palms. "That was why we came here," she said, "To rest. We both need it."

The steward in elaborate purple livery, whose name turned out to be Ezekiel, brought them drinks. She said to Buck, "Tell him to go to bed and the other servants too. We won't need them."

"It's a good idea." He told Ezekiel to go away, and in a little while they saw him and the three other servants go down the path through the palms to the servants' quarters. In the garden now there was no sound but the singing of the little Mogul fountain like a thread of music against the accompaniment of the water pounding languidly on the beach at the foot of the garden. She

[288]

closed her eyes and said, "It's lovely here—it's like something out of the *Arabian Nights*."

She could say that to Buck. Bill would have laughed at her and told her she had a chorus girl's mind. But to hell with Bill. Would she never be free of him?

Buck said, "It's lovely. India is a lovely place." By his voice she knew how much he loved India, the India she did not know at all, the India her unseeing eyes had never known.

Then for a long time they lay there under the sky powdered with stars, happy and peaceful. The weariness slipped away from her and she fell into that state between sleep and consciousness when everything became simple and clear and stripped of all complications and falseness. And she knew that what was happening to her was good, better than anything that had ever happened to her before or ever would happen again. Lazily she lost all consciousness of time but presently she heard him saying, "You must be tired, honey."

"Yes."

"It's not too healthy—too much dew."

"No, I suppose not." She roused herself and stood up, looking out across the path of moonlight on the bay. It was odd how this could happen in Jellapore's house with its aura of corruption and evil. She said, "Buck, would you like to come to my room?"

She looked at him and saw his grin, "Yes, please."

Nothing else could have happened. It could never have been any other way since the moment she had turned and looked up from the jewelry she had been showing to Tommy and Ali and saw him standing in the doorway, that curious clear light in his blue eyes. It was beautiful, she knew suddenly, because it was inevitable.

He put his arm about her and for a long time they stood there beside the little Mogul fountain. The fear had gone out of both of them. There was no longer either time or space.

For fifteen days the world outside Jai Mahal and its garden no longer had any existence. It was a curious dream-like experience in which days and nights blended together and passed by, lost in a blur of time. Breakfast, lunch and dinner appeared and presently the remnants were carried away; the sun rose and set and the explosions of fantastic tropical color which accompanied them passed almost unnoticed, mere interludes in an unreal glow of happiness.

And through the curious haze of peace and fulfillment, there occurred the exciting adventure of two persons, a man and a woman, exploring new worlds of soul and spirit and personality. Because until they had come to Jai Mahal they had not known each other at all. Until then they had been simply two people reaching out through a mist toward what by instinct each of them knew was peace and fulfillment. It was the spectacle in time and space of two out of millions of individuals passing close to each other and being drawn together suddenly like two particles in the formation of a new world. They had not known each other at all except as symbols of something for which each of them had a need as strong as that of water for the thirsty and food for the hungry. It was that perhaps which Moti, in the cold detachment born of a fiery idealism, had seen as he sat among his microscopes and serums; for to him the two had been no more than two elements in a pattern which had to be fulfilled. That he loved Merrill and had come to have an odd rebellious liking for Carol did not prevent him from a determination to use them both for his own fanatic's dream of regenerating a whole people, a whole race. He, alone, the pure scientist, had understood what was happening and urged it on for his own ends.

So in the unreal isolation of the white marble house with its garden filled with cocoanut and betel palms, the two began to know each other, the countless small intimate things which, added together, made up that atom of humanity labeled Buck Merrill and that which made up a woman known preposterously as Carol Halma.

It happened during the night and at odd unexpected times during the day, moments when between them there occurred flashes of intimacy such as few people are ever permitted to know—times when Carol, timorous and alarmed by the thing which was happening to her would find him there, reassuring her, giving her kindness and strength, healing wounds of whose existence she had not even been aware until now, softening the calluses of the

[290]

spirit and soul which had grown about the woman known as Carol Halma. Now and then, in the midst of her happiness, she would think, "There can't be anyone as nice as Buck. What's happening is not true. It's all a dream from which I will wake up with a hang-over." Her heart told her that this wild and tenuous happiness was not enough, for there it had no foundation to give it solidity and endurance. It was something which seemed to exist in a void detached from all the sordidness of ordinary life.

For what astonished her was both his simplicity and his consideration—that when he touched her there was not the selfish, brutal desire of most of the men she had known, but only a solicitude for her, as if she were a child who had been hurt and frightened. It had been so different with Bill, tormented by the complications and mysteries of his own character. With Bill love had been a pleasant thing but a trivial one, which always left her woman's heart and body unsatisfied and hungry for a depth and beauty which her instinct told her must exist but which she had never touched. With Buck she discovered what tenderness could be, his own tenderness as well as the tenderness which in turn it summoned out of the depths of herself, the tenderness which had always been there, which made her kind to strangers like Mrs. Trollope and the Baroness and careless with dangerous fools like Botlivala—that tenderness which in the beginning had led her to help a stranger who was desperately ill in a railway carriage crossing the burning Deccan. But always she had kept it hidden for fear of being hurt, shielding it beneath an armor of laughter and good humor and triviality. And now there was no longer any necessity to hide away the feeling; it had fulfillment. It was as if a part of her, until now cramped and stifled, were suddenly freed and permitted to expand and flower.

And there was in Buck a kind of purity, perhaps that "cleanness" which both Bill and herself had always felt when they were with him; it enveloped everything, herself, the house, the garden, destroying the very aura of evil and lecherous memories that infected the place. It was the sense of purity and so of "rightness" which brought to her love for him that depth and richness which she had always sought for and, until now, never found. At times her heart cried out in triumph, "I was right. I knew it could be like this."

Timorously she had hoped for this purity (the hope lay behind the hiding away of the bawdy pictures). She had wanted the sense of purity not so much for herself as for Buck. She had said to herself, "For me it does not matter. I can take it. But for him it must be like that." And so it was—as simple, as good, as clean as nature itself.

Then when she was happiest, in those moments when she felt that it was impossible that life could be so rich and so beautiful, a small voice would cry out in her soul, "It can't last. It must end . . . and then what?" But quickly, consciously, she would stifle the small voice and flee from it back into that curious hazy world of happiness.

So in the fulfillment of things, her body became more beautiful. The weariness went out of it and the look of radiance returned. Even the servants felt a sense of change. As if they were aware of a remarkable spectacle which they had never witnessed before and might never see again, their voices grew softer and the tread of their feet lighter, until presently they came to be little more than dusky shadows in that blurred world of happiness. And as her beauty and her vitality returned, they came in their Indian way to believe, like the hill people back in Jellapore, that she must be a goddess walking on the earth. They worshipped her, as Krishna, who ran away, had once worshipped her. To them, as she moved during the day among the palms or along the terrace above the sea, she was no Swedish show-girl but the goddess Sita, only to them her dazzling blondeness more wonderful, more beautiful than the dark beauty of Rama's bride.

And for Buck these days possessed a triumphant and dazzling quality. It was as if he were born again, as if all the weariness, the disappointment, the illness had dropped away. For this was something he had never known or even suspected—that a woman could be so great a fulfillment of man, that any woman could be so tender; that the body of any woman could provide such delight and her spirit such peace. In his satisfaction, the doubts which had troubled him in the beginning withered and vanished in the brilliant light of what was happening to him. His happiness, both of

[292]

the body and of the spirit, was so great and so bewildering that everything, even the pangs of conscience over his desertion of the village people, vanished. The old doubts died quickly, for his instinct said, "No woman who is like this could be a bad woman. For whatever she has done, there must be a reason. Whatever she has done no longer is of any importance." For he too was dazzled.

To him it did not occur that one day the thing would have an ending. In his innocence and optimism it would go on like this forever since there was no reason why it should not. After a little while they would leave Jai Mahal and go directly back to Jellapore and there they would be married and would go on together for-ever till the end of time. He did not say this to her in so many words, but always he talked as if there were no dangers and no doubts. He talked of what they would do and of the beauty of the jungle and the trips made often enough in oxcarts between villages where there were no roads. He described the little house which was his headquarters, with its garden and broad steps running down to the river. She would like that, he thought. It was a lovely spot and in winter the climate was lovely too, because the house was in the hill country where the days were pleasantly warm and the nights cool.

And lying on the beach or on the terrace by the little marble fountain she would listen, never saying anything, wrapped in happiness and delight at the sound of his voice and the look in his clear blue eyes. It was a look which sometimes made her want to cry. She did not say to him that he was blinded by what had hap-pened to them and that it could not go on forever. She did not say that when he went back to Jellapore, he would go alone. She pushed the thought of those things from her, saying to herself, "It is enough that you are happy now." And there were moments when, enchanted by his love and his enthusiasm, she found herself believing in the story of their future which with such innocence and faith he was telling her. She even allowed herself to think, "Perhaps it could be like that. Why not? What is to prevent it?" Because in her health and happiness, there were moments when nothing seemed impossible to her, moments when she thought, "I am a different woman. If he is with me that is all I need. Nothing else will ever matter to me. I love him so much." She could not think what it would be like to waken, to go about streets, to listen to the birds, to feel the sunshine on her body, if he were not there too. And one day the thought came to her that in Jai Mahal they were like Adam and Eve in Paradise before there was sin in the world. "It must," she thought, "have been very like this. And it is Buck who makes it that way."

For him there was only one shadow which returned to him sometimes in the night when for a time a shadow of the old pain would waken him and keep him from sleep. It was the memory of his dead wife which moved him now, not so much to resentment, as to pity—that she had been as she was, that she had known so little, if indeed she had ever even suspected, the richness and beauty of what might have been. Because he saw now that she had died at last, narrow and starved and miserable, never having lived at all, never having known what it was to love even the small things like the song of a bird or the music of running water. She had never known what tenderness was, because she had always thrust it from her, willfully, almost with savagery.

There were times when in the darkness he reproached himself, knowing now that he had never brought her love but only the urging of his own healthy body, ignorant of what love could be. In the darkness a slow nausea and horror would come over him at the memory of the cold unhappy marriage, the physical horror of a sane healthy man at the monstrousness of some act of cold-blooded depravity. Yet out of it miraculously had come Tommy, somewhere now in the Mediterranean in the care of Dr. Snodgrass, the missionary. No, whatever happened, Tommy must never fall into the error which so nearly ruined his own life. When Tommy was a man, he must choose someone like Carol.

The dead wife returned again and again to him, grim and egotistical and pitiable, enveloped always in the aura of their mutual misery.

But the physical pain returned less often as the days passed and each time it returned, the savagery of the cruel ache was abated a little more. And now it did not matter, since Carol was always there by his side to drive it away by the touch of her hands. As the pain faded, his very body began to change, the muscles growing full again and rounded, losing that tense drawn knottedness which at times could be physically painful. He slept again for the first time in countless months, peacefully, knowing now not the sleep of utter exhaustion but of release and peace. And deep inside him he became aware of the old vitality beginning once more to burn with the old fire. And as it returned there came with it the old restlessness and hunger for work, slowly at first, showing itself in a desire for physical activity. He had to swim far down the beach in the muddy lukewarm water and go for long walks with Carol on the edge of the shore past the long row of fantastic houses which bordered the water. He understood for the first time the tyranny of the body itself—that its weakness and illness could destroy whatever you sought to accomplish, that its strength and health would permit you to move mountains and accomplish miracles. For he was no neurotic saint; his faith and strength were not born of illness and a distorted mind. He was a normal man, to whom physical weakness brought not visions but only despair.

As his spirit grew stronger he thought often of the funny little Moti and all his realistic theories. Perhaps Moti, the scientist, was right—that you must not abuse the body but give it what it desired in order to accomplish what the spirit sought to achieve. The body, Moti believed, was only a machine which must be made to serve you. Therefore it must be kept oiled and polished and shining as a well-kept machine should be treated.

And with returning strength, he began to be restless and to think again of the villages, worrying lest all that he had started on its way was being endangered by his absence. He knew his villagers well; he knew that if he was not there among them, they would begin to backslide, not from lack of desire but from the weakness of their skinny, malarial, half-starved bodies. He needed to be there to drive them on until the day came when they could stand on their own feet. That he knew could be accomplished, for he had seen it done. He had himself accomplished the miracle.

Carol, without ever speaking of it, saw the change in him. Day by day she noticed the yellow pallor fading and the color returning to the tired face. She saw his spirit rising and felt the current of his rising vitality. The spectacle delighted her, and at the same time filled her with alarm. She was accomplishing the cure but each day brought her nearer to the end, nearer to the moment when Colonel Moti would say that she was no longer needed but must go away. She felt at times like a condemned woman awaiting the horror of execution. And again, secretly, she would grow rebellious, thinking, "Why should I go away? Why should I give him up?" But all the time she knew in her heart that the fork in their paths was only a little way ahead coming nearer each day, each hour. The growing restlessness frightened her, the small things he sometimes said, showing where his thoughts were turning. There were even moments when savagely she was jealous of those remote poverty-stricken villagers whom if she had ever seen them, she had never noticed.

And then one morning he said, "I think we had better go and see what is happening to Ali."

Quickly she answered, "Yes, it's been a long time since you saw him." She was afraid suddenly, but she forced herself to go to Ezekiel and tell him that they must have a taxicab to drive to the Institute.

Summoning a taxi to Juhu was no easy business. A boy had to be sent all the way in to Bombay to fetch one. He left immediately on a bicycle, but before he had returned another boy appeared bringing a letter from the Institute addressed to Buck. With fear in her heart she watched him tear open the envelope and read it. She saw him smile and give the boy a rupee and heard him say something to the boy in Hindustani.

When the boy had gone he turned to her and said, "It's good news."

She said, "I'm glad," but she thought, "Good news! Perhaps for him but not for me."

He said, "They're taking the bandages off Ali's eyes this afternoon. He thinks Ali will want me there."

"You'll have to go."

"And he says that both Aligarh University and the Government are planning to confer honors on me for the work in the villages."

"That's wonderful, honey."

She tried to keep the fear out of her voice, but now he knew her too well to be deceived, and he put one arm about her shoulders and asked, "What's the matter?"

"Nothing's the matter. I'm glad, that's all—that they're taking notice of you. It's about time."

He handed her Moti's note, saying, "Read it, honey. Whatever is mine is yours."

She read it, her eyes rushing from line to line, until she discovered that there was more in it than he had told her. At the end there was a simple sentence or two:

The Dewan asked me to tell you that cholera has broken out among the villagers. It isn't bad as yet and his health department is doing everything that is necessary. He urges you to continue your holiday.

She looked at Buck and asked, "Why didn't you tell me that . . . about the cholera?"

"It isn't anything . . . there's always a certain amount of cholera from time to time."

"The Dewan wouldn't have written you if it wasn't serious."

"Never mind. If it gets worse we can go straight to Jellapore."

Then she made an excuse to leave him, saying she wanted to change her blouse before the taxi came. She left him because she had to "think things out" again, because a curious thought had come to her as she stood there reading Moti's letter—the letter which in itself was nothing and might be everything.

She was puzzled by two things—that he took the news of the cholera so lightly and that since they had been together he seemed to have forgotten about Ali and his blindness completely, as if the boy had been nothing to him. In her happiness she had scarcely noticed that he never seemed to remember Ali. Now with the news from the Dewan, the fact suddenly became important. Maybe it was going to be as Bill had hinted—that she would only end by destroying Buck, by changing him, leading him to forget all the things he was, simply through love of herself—not for always but until the day when, wakening, he would discover what had happened and blame her for the tragedy. Maybe this was just the small beginning of what was certain to follow. Maybe she ought to go away now and leave him, before it was too late and even the memory of beauty was spoiled.

But rebelliously she thought, "No, I can't! I won't do that! Why should I? I'll go back to Jellapore with him. I'll never see Jelly or his brother again. I'll stay in the villages and never go to the capital." That wouldn't be easy either, because to do that they would have to be married, and now with Moti's letter she understood what she had failed to understand clearly before—that Buck was, in his way, a public personage. If the British Government and a great Indian University were both recognizing his work, it meant that, in the world, he was somebody—a sort of prominent official and celebrity. It was important whom a man like that married.

It was all just as Colonel Moti had said that night when they sat talking in Bill's room beside the bucket of lukewarm champagne. It wasn't possible—no matter how much she loved Buck; it would only end in disaster and unhappiness. And Buck, the poor darling, in his innocence didn't see it at all—that when he went to Delhi he would have to go to the Viceroy's house and all the other official dinners alone because he couldn't take his wife who had been treated as a whore in the Taj Mahal bar by a depraved Parsee rounder.

In the muggy heat she suddenly shivered. Maybe it was all over now. Maybe they would never come back to Jai Mahal at all. Maybe Moti would believe the cure had been accomplished and send her away; and she would have to go because there was nothing else to do but to stay and ruin Buck and everything for which he had lived. She tried to make herself believe that all these fears were hysterical and that nothing mattered but their love for each other. But she had lived too long in too hard a world to deceive herself. Love she knew could destroy love when it became the end of everything, the only thing in life. It could make a woman's life but destroy the life of a man, especially a man like Buck.

She thought, "I must pull myself together and go downstairs or he'll notice something and grow suspicious." And suddenly she thought, "If only Bill were here." Bill, for all his nonsense, had a sense of proportion, born perhaps out of his own triviality and experience and cynicism. Bill would have helped her to see things sensibly; for she knew she was not being sensible. Neither her shrewdness nor her common sense any longer existed. She thought, "I'm the damndest fool in the world—a woman who is in love."

The taxi came presently, driven by a wild-eyed Sikh. Ezekiel came to the door with them and asked Buck in Hindustani when he should expect them back. Buck answered him and then turned to Carol, "I told him we'd be back this evening. Is that right?" "Yes." But in her heart she didn't believe it—she was afraid.

The boy, Ali, sat in the darkened room beside the room in which Indira Moti slept. All day he sat there, day after day, quietly, the young guinea pig nestling close against his bare brown leg.

A dozen times Moti's wife, moving quickly and silently as the night wind, came to the doorway to look at him, standing there for minutes at a time, speculating, trying to discover what went on inside the head and the heart of the small body. It puzzled her that she did not *know* at once as she nearly always knew about people. It was difficult, she knew, because he was an Asiatic and so, less transparent than any European; but more than that, there was between him and herself another barrier. He was Moslem, she herself was Bengali; and she knew out of long experience that few people in the world were further apart. It was the old story of the Athenian and the Spartan.

She knew there was pride inside the small body, pride born of the knowledge that he was one of the great Akbar's people, and there was stoicism which was so different a thing from the indifference and resignation of the Hindu. And there was a capacity for passionate affection which few Hindus knew—an affection and a loyalty so passionate that with his race it could overstep the limits of friendship between two men. She knew well enough that what the boy felt for Buck was an affection colored by this same passionate quality. That was why as day after day passed and Buck did not return to see him, the boy had grown more and more quiet, sitting perfectly still in the darkness which enveloped him, for hours at a time. It was as if something inside him, perhaps the childishness, were dying slowly.

And so she had been troubled, wondering how she could reach him; how she might explain so that if the hurt could not be cured, at least the pain might be softened. But for once in all her wise and sensitive life she did not know how to help the child. Childless herself, her whole instinct for children became concentrated upon him. She could not, she knew, make him understand what it was that was happening to his friend Buck. She would have had to explain to him so much that went before—the whole pinched Calvinistic background out of which Buck had come, the tragic mistake of his marriage barren of love and of passion. She would have to make the child see how incredible and even terrifying a thing was happening to his friend—a man who was suddenly becoming a man at last, with all the overwhelming emotion conceived in such a process. The gentle intuitive little woman was at times as much a scientist as her famous husband, but this did her little good when it came to making the small son of a mahout understand why his friend Buck had forgotten him. She could not talk to Ali about glands. She could not reconstruct for Ali a whole civilization so incredibly different from his own, which had produced Buck Merrill. You could not make a Moslem, even a Moslem boy, understand or believe that one woman could become for a man the beginning and end of everything.

She did her best to fill the long hours of the boy's darkness with distractions and happiness, but she was aware all the while that whatever she did or planned was futile. She knew that for the boy she, herself, and her blunt husband did not exist. There was only Buck who had taken him from the straw pile of the elephant *philkana* into his house, treating him as his own son, finding a great doctor to try to cure his blindness.

It was the "aloneness" of the child which frightened her, as if he had withdrawn inside himself and shut off all communication with the outside world, aware only of the hurt in his own heart. Day after day in the beginning he had asked, "When is Sahib Buck coming?" and then after a while he had ceased to ask, and merely to sit there waiting for what, for all he knew, might never come. And slowly, she knew, all his affection became centered on the small guinea pig which all day long lay quiet and snug against the bare brown leg.

So, desperately, to cheer him, she had said, "Sahib Buck will be coming back soon." It was, she knew, a pitiful crumb to throw him, but it was the best she could do, and in the vast wisdom which lay behind the great dark eyes, she knew that it was true. She knew that there would come a day when the intensity of what was happening to Buck would waver a little, and he would begin to remember again all the things he had been and done before the lovely blonde girl had changed his whole existence. There would come a day, she knew, when all the fury and beauty of his release would dim into that which was as usual as the sun rising and setting, and then he would become again the old Buck, for he would no longer be ill and baffled and unhappy.

A little after noon when the heat had become intolerable, the bearer returned from Jai Mahal with Buck's message, and as soon as she heard it Indira Moti went into the darkened room. She went softly, lightly, over to the boy and placed one hand on the small head.

"Ali," she said, "Sahib Buck is coming today."

The boy remained very still and after a little while he said, "When?"

"As soon as he can get here."

"Is he far away?"

"Not very far."

Beneath her hand she felt the small body shaking and she knew that Ali was crying, silently, without a tear, as the son of a mahout of one of Akbar's war elephants would have wept. At the same moment she fathomed the full depths of the boy's fear—that he had been frightened too because he had been left alone.

Quickly she withdrew her hand because she knew that he would be ashamed if she knew that he was sobbing.

"I will tell you the moment he comes," she said. "We will have a party to celebrate." And she went away, so that he might cry in peace like the child he was.

She did not tell him about taking off the bandages and that this afternoon he would know whether he was to see again or to live the rest of his life in darkness. She had not told him because she wanted it to be a casual affair, no more than the removing of a bandage from an injured toe. And now, if the operation had failed, it would not matter so much to the boy. At first it would not matter at all, because his Sahib Buck had come back to him.

On the long hot journey from Juhu to the Institute of Tropical Diseases Carol was bedeviled by the doubts which Moti's letter had raised. It was a battle against herself and the sickness she felt inside her, at the certainty that when they closed the gate at Jai Mahal,

[301]

they had left Paradise behind them, probably forever. A thing like that, she knew, couldn't go on forever and she thought, "I've been lucky to have known it even for so short a time. Most women never dream that such a thing could exist."

In the heat and dust she was bewildered now, not knowing what she meant to do next. If they did not go back to Jai Mahal—and even if they returned now they had left it, it would never be the same—there would be a part of Buck that remained outside. She would never again have him all to herself in the way women wanted forever to have men.

Sitting there beside him, trying to make small talk so that he would not notice her depression, she saw all the small things which told her that he was escaping back into the old world. You could see it by the new look in his eye—a look which had nothing to do with her—the change in the sound of his voice, the remarks he made now and then about the future and his work. He had already run away from her, far ahead, into a world in which she had no place. With returning health, energy was returning, and with energy all the passion for work and building up this thing which to him was nearly all his life. He wasn't regretting having closed the gate at Jai Mahal because he wasn't even thinking about it. Grimly she thought, "Probably all men who are worth anything are like that." And again, "Even if anything could come of it, I'd have to be just an old-fashioned girl." But the idea did not trouble her. After all, that was what she wanted. The thing that made her uneasy was that she did not know what lay ahead of her.

Then the taxi driver forced himself into her thoughts. He was a wild driver, worse than any of the wild drivers she had encountered in the East. The automobile, it seemed, always produced an astounding effect upon coolies in the East; it intoxicated their downtrodden, starved, beaten souls to feel beneath their bare toes an engine of great power, capable of immense speed, over which they held absolute power. Each coolie from the moment the wheels began to turn became a dictator, his soul released and drunk with power. This particular driver drove like a madman, at top speed, swerving around corners, charging through crowds, dashing in front of advancing cars at every crossroad. For a long time Carol man-

[302]

aged to keep silent but at last when she could bear it no longer, she cried out, "Buck, tell him to go slower. He'll kill someone."

Buck grinned, "He loves it," he said, "the speed frees his soul. Nothing else that he knows can do that." He leaned forward and in Hindustani admonished the driver who slowed from fifty to forty miles an hour through the swarming streets of the Mill district. But again and again, it was necessary to tell him to slow down. The nervous bare toes, it appeared, were beyond control even of the wild Sikh himself.

Indira was standing on the verandah when the taxi drove into the courtyard of the bungalow. She smiled at sight of them because she was glad to see them, but as she smiled the quick, dark eyes saw more than their mere bodies. They saw the whole story of what had happened to them; they saw the look of new life in Buck's eyes, the lightness of his step that she had not seen in years; they saw the happiness in Carol's eyes, and she felt a sudden pang in the knowledge that anyone so beautiful, so happy, should have to be hurt.

When she greeted them she said to Buck, "I told Ali you were coming. I didn't tell him about the bandage. I thought Moti could simply take it off and then if what we hope for didn't happen, he wouldn't mind so much because you would be there."

Then out of the darkness of the bungalow the Colonel himself appeared to greet them, and Carol though she dreaded seeing him because he was a symbol of what hung over her, felt a sudden pleasure, knowing again that she loved the man because he loved Buck and even more than Buck—truth and light. It was as if in a strange way, he was something to cling to; as if she knew that whatever happened these two Indians—Indira Moti and her husband—would always be there, rocks in the midst of everything. At the sight of them she felt again the curious sense of peace and certainty. Desperately she wanted them to love her as they loved Buck but even more she wanted them to respect her and believe in her. Moti, the way things were, should have been her enemy, but somehow he was not.

She saw too the look of delight in his eyes that Buck looked so well and so strong, but she knew that to Moti what happened to

[303]

her did not matter at all. Again she thought, "I should hate him, but I can't. He is better than any of us."

Moti thought they should go at once to Ali and so quietly they went into the darkness of the room where the boy sat, immobile, with the guinea pig nestling close to him. At sight of him Buck started to go to him but the Colonel raised his hand and said, "Wait." Then while they stood there watching, Moti went to the boy and spoke to him. He said, "We are going to take off the bandage, Ali. The doctor says it is time."

The boy turned his head toward him. He did not ask, "Will I be able to see?" He only asked, "Has Sahib Buck come?"

"He is on his way. He'll be here soon now."

Then quickly with his deft scientist's fingers, he unfastened the bandage and drew it aside. Carol, watching, held her breath, as if she were the boy himself. Now was the time. He would see a little now or he would be blind forever.

The room was nearly dark. The only light in it came through the shutters and the doorway which led to an inside room of the bungalow. None of them said anything. There was not even the sound of breathing in the room.

Ali, sitting cross-legged, stared for a moment uncertainly before him; then slowly, like an automaton, he turned his head to the right and then to the left as if he were seeking the light. Twice his head moved in the same fashion to right and to left as they waited, and Carol felt Buck's hand steal into hers and knew that he was trembling. Then as the boy's head turned slowly, the eyes came opposite the figure of Buck, silhouetted against the dim light in the doorway. The head stopped turning, the eyes stared and then slowly the crossed bare legs straightened out and the dark small face smiled. It was a smile such as Carol had never seen before, a smile of adoration, as if the son of the mahout had opened his eyes to find Allah standing before him.

She heard Colonel Moti's eager voice saying, "He sees! He sees!" and saw the boy slip down from the divan and run wildly across the bare room toward them. He ran straight to Buck and throwing his arms about him, pressed his face against Buck's lean stomach, saying in a funny, choked voice, "Sahib Buck! Sahib Buck!" She felt Buck's hand slipping out of her own and saw him kneel down and put his arms about the mahout's son, pulling him close against his own big body, pressing the dark face close to his. Then quickly she turned away, because she was crying—why, she did not know because it was for so many reasons: because of the small boy and the miracle which had happened to him, because of the strange abstract goodness of the Motis, but most of all because of Buck. She had never loved him so much. She loved him so much that now, in the dim light she could not look at him and risk having the others see what was in her heart. She thought, "I could never take him away, whatever happened. I could never take him away even from that small boy." She understood now all the fire and passion of Moti. It was as if the boy were a symbol of all the ill and suffering villagers of India who had such need of Buck because he understood and could help them.

She heard the boy's voice saying again, "Sahib Buck! Sahib Buck!" And then long quick eager sentences in Hindustani. She could not understand the words but she knew what he was saying —that they would be together again in Jellapore, that now he could learn to drive the Maharajah's elephant. And she heard Buck's voice saying, "He wants me to write to Tommy that he can see again and that when Tommy comes back, he'll be able to play with him again. He'll take Tommy to the *philkana* and teach him to drive an elephant."

Then suddenly the boy crossed the room, a little unsteadily this time and picked up the guinea pig which all the time had lain still and good on the divan. He brought it to Buck and held it up for him to see and admire.

"The guinea pig," said Mrs. Moti, "was his great friend while you were away."

Buck laughed, "We'll have to get a husband or wife, whichever it is, when we go back to Jellapore. We can't go against nature and defeat the purpose of the guinea pig."

Mrs. Moti said, "We could all do with a cup of tea. I'll tell them to bring it here and then Ali won't have to leave Buck, even for a minute. He oughtn't to go out into the bright light yet."

Then Buck sat on the divan with the boy standing between his knees, one arm placed childishly about the broad shoulders of his big friend. Now that he had Buck back again, the boy became interested in the miracle of his restored sight. He peered this way and that, the weak, tired eyes focusing on the smiling Moti, on Carol. For a long time he looked at Carol and then said something to Buck who laughed and answered him.

Buck said, "He wanted to know if you were the queen who had all the jewels. And then he said he knew you were beautiful but that you were more beautiful than he had imagined you. He said you were the most beautiful woman he had ever seen. I told him I thought so too."

Then the boy said something again and Buck answered him in Hindustani and then translated. "He said he knew it was bad manners but could he look at you for a long time. I said he would have plenty of time to look at you because you were going back to Jellapore State to live with us."

The speech startled her. She almost cried out, "Don't tell him that because it's not true. I can't go back to Jellapore!" But she said nothing and in the next moment she understood what lay behind the simple remark. He was not only telling her what he meant to do. It was not to her he had really addressed the remark but to Moti. He was telling Moti that he was not to dictate or interfere. She thought suddenly, "Why, Buck, you darling, you sweetheart. You know so much more than you let any of us even think you know." And she understood, with a sudden rush of joy, that Moti because he was famous and brilliant and great had always cowed her and made her feel that she was a little girl who must take orders from him and obey. She had thought that Buck felt the same way and so allowed Moti to bully both of them. She began to see how he got what he wanted, how he accomplished what he set out to do. Buck was no fool. Very likely he was wiser than any of them, wiser even than Moti, because he was kinder, though not perhaps so wise as Moti's wife.

Then the tea came and Moti said presently to Buck, "I've had another telegram from the Dewan. The cholera epidemic is worse than they thought at first. He urged me to tell you that if it spread any further they would need you."

"That's fine," said Buck, "I'd like to get back to work. Probably it's better if we go back at once."

Then when the tea was finished Indira Moti said suddenly to

[306]

Buck, "Could you come to my room for a minute? It's about some accounts that have to do with the Jellapore work." And Carol thought, "That's because Moti wants to speak to me alone. Now it's coming."

Buck spoke to Ali who climbed back again on the divan taking the guinea pig up in his arms. Then Buck and Mrs. Moti went out and Moti said, "It's fine about Buck, isn't it?"

"Yes," she said, not quite sure what he meant.

"He's always been a great man, but it's nice they recognize it—while he's still young. The University is giving him an honorary degree and the Government means to give him a title and probably a salary. That will be a help too. Do you think he is pleased?"

If she had spoken the truth she would have said, "I don't think he's thought about it twice." But she was still awed by Colonel Moti so she said, "I'm sure he is. Why shouldn't he be?"

"He seems very well."

"He doesn't have those awful attacks at all any more." She thought, "What is he driving at? Why doesn't he say what he is going to say?" She had a strange feeling of being paralyzed, as if she could not say what she wanted to say. Even her face felt frozen. The great burning dark eyes of the scientist were never turned away. It was as if he were watching an experiment. She was aware that Ali too, with the guinea pig in his arms, was watching her, with a look of adoration on his face.

"He's very changed," said Moti. "He's like the old Buck. He's like a man who has learned to walk again after being ill a long time. I personally am very grateful to you. All India would be grateful to you if it could know the story."

Bitterly she thought, "And now he's going to dismiss me with a good reference to take on the next job. But I won't be dismissed. I won't go."

"It would be a good thing," Moti was saying, "if you could keep him a little longer in Bombay—until he got a little more used to being well again, until he took it for granted, we might say."

"Or until," she thought, "he'd got used to me and wouldn't mind my going away." Aloud she said, "He's already talking about going back. This cholera business worries him."

Moti smiled, "That's not serious—at least not yet. It may become so." He lighted a cigarette and she still sat there, frozen, helpless, like a shy child. Then Moti asked abruptly, "What did he mean about going back to Jellapore State when he said 'we'?"

"I don't know. We have never talked about what was to happen when we left Jai Mahal. He always talks that way. He has from the beginning—as if there wasn't any doubt about anything."

The Colonel frowned, and Carol was suddenly aware of a feeling of comfort which came from the boy on the divan. Something about his adoration of her made her feel less lonely and afraid. Suddenly she went over and sat by him. The boy looked up at her and smiled showing all his white teeth. Then he put the guinea pig in her lap where it lay very still, the whiskers on its small nose twitching. Then he slipped his hand into hers.

Looking down at him and smiling, she said, "Thank you," knowing that he would not understand the words but would know what she meant.

Ali grinned and then very carefully he said, "T-h-a-n-k y-o-u."

"That's very good," said Carol.

Moti, she knew all the time, was watching everything that happened like a lazy cat.

He smiled and said, "Of course, Buck will be a kind of official now. He'll have to go to Government dinners and go to Delhi a couple of times a year."

"Yes," she said, dully, glad that Ali's hand was in hers.

"I have some news for you."

"Yes."

"The police were here this morning."

Her whole body stiffened suddenly, "What about?"

"About the jewelry," he smiled. "They thought your behavior was very odd—going away and taking no notice of the whole affair. It seemed the jewelry was worth a great deal of money. They discovered that I would probably know where you were. It's been in the papers that you disappeared."

"How? Why?"

"I don't think you realize what a figure you are in Bombay. Almost everybody knows about you. You're a kind of legendary person."

A feeling of sickness took possession of her. She wanted to cry

[308]

out. "Why can't they let me alone? If I don't care about the jewelry, why should the others care? Why can't they let me alone?" And then, all at once she knew how he was dismissing her. He had gone about it in this slow, roundabout way deliberately. He wasn't dismissing her. He was making her dismiss herself, making her see how impossible was the whole situation.

"And of course there's been a great deal about it in the papers."

"They promised me they would keep it quiet."

"I think they meant to. It was the Indian papers who got hold of it first. You see in Bombay there are a great many fanatic young Indians who snatch at anything to the discredit of Europeans. They work at making all Europeans seem disreputable. This was a fine story, especially as there were a lot of the people—pretty disreputable ones—involved as well, like your Mrs. Trollope and the Baroness what's-her-name and the dowager Maharani of Chandragar and Botlivala. These young political Indians hate other Indians like Botlivala because they ape the Europeans and toady to them."

"But I never harmed an Indian in my life. I like Indians and Buck is their friend."

Again he smiled quietly, "I don't suppose they have the faintest idea that any of this touches Buck in any way. As for yourself, you're just a means to an end. If they can discredit Europeans by ruining you, they will do it." He paused for a moment, thinking. Then he said, "It's not even as simple as that. Without knowing it, these seedy, ardent young men probably hate you—because each one of them would like to own you. You are blonde and beautiful, but you are European and for them unattainable. The human spirit is an odd thing."

She knew then that they had left Paradise forever. She had been a fool to think while she was happy in the garden at Jai Mahal with Buck that the world outside no longer existed, that its wheels had stopped turning just because she was in love and happy. Malice and scandal and rumor had been at work all the time. One at a time, slowly, bit by bit, all her follies were coming home to roost. It was as if she were shut into a room with the walls closing in on her.

"Of course," Moti was saying, "after the Indian papers published the story, the English papers had to go on with it." He lighted a cigarette, "And it didn't help any to have Botlivala sue you."

"Sue me?"

"Yes. Didn't you know?"

"No . . . for what?"

"To return the jewels he gave you. He claims you got them under false pretenses."

"Oh!"

For the only time in her life she felt that she was going to faint. She could no longer see Moti's face. The room itself seemed to spin around her. Wildly she thought, "The rat . . . the dirty little rat!" And then she heard the voice of the small boy beside her speaking —rapidly in a kind of childish anger, and she heard Moti's voice answering him. The dizziness passed and Moti's face appeared again out of the haze. He was smiling and she heard his voice saying, "Ali says that I am not to hurt you because Buck would not like it. I told him I was not trying to hurt you but that I only had to tell you news that was not good, but that it was better you should know. That's right, isn't it?"

"Yes. . . . I suppose so."

"You'd rather have me tell it to you alone, wouldn't you?"

"Yes . . . yes." (Oh, why had they ever left Jai Mahal? Why had they ever closed the gate behind them?)

"They've found the jewelry," said Moti.

"Where? Who stole it?"

"Your friend Mrs. Trollope."

"Oh!" (Then she had had it all the time, tucked away inside her blouse—all the time she sat there crying and talking in the bedroom.) "She's crazy," thought Carol. "She must be crazy."

"Apparently," said Moti, "she hadn't meant to try selling it in Bombay but she needed money desperately. They were going to throw her out of the Taj Mahal and seize her luggage and her sister refused to help her. So she tried selling a bracelet to one of the dealers in unset stones who come to the hotel. It was all very stupid and foolish, of course. The whole story was in the papers— about her being the sister of the Maharani of Chandragar and about her swindler husband in jail in England." He paused as if to give emphasis to what he meant to say. "The papers said that

she was a friend of yours and that you had been seen about to-gether constantly in Bombay—at the races, at the Taj, everywhere."
Then gently he said, "I didn't know about that."

"It's true and it isn't true. She was never a friend of mine. I felt sorry for her. Where is she now?"

"In jail."

"They mustn't send her to prison."

"I'm afraid they will."

"She's crazy—the poor thing."

Suddenly she had a wild thought, "What is your wife telling Buck?"

"Nothing about this. It is true . . . what she said. She is talking to him about the accounts. She's always raising funds for Buck's work. I asked her to take him away. I thought it was better that we should be alone when we talked about all this."

"That's right . . . thank you."

Then Buck wouldn't know any more than she had known. He had been shut up with her in their fool's paradise at Jai Mahal. He would have to find it out sometime. But now the less said, the better. He might never learn of the whole story, with all its sordid details.

"What do you mean to do?" asked Moti.

"I don't know."

"I think you had better go back to Bombay and see the police."

"I can't go back to the Taj—I can't!" (And have to face all those staring faces!)

Moti's voice went calmly on. "I gave the police my word that I would send you to them by evening. It's much the best thing to do. It's the only thing to do. Otherwise they might become very troublesome. It might start the newspapers all over again. I think the quieter we can keep the thing, the better."

For a long time she was silent. She had thought and thought but all her "thinking out" of things had come to nothing, worse than nothing. She was aware of the small hand still holding to her own. It was extraordinary how comforting it was. It was almost like having Buck there beside her.

Then suddenly her brain turned cold and very clear. It was no

[311]

time to be a sentimental fool. She said, "Will you telephone to the police?"

"Of course."

"What time is it now?"

Moti looked at his watch. "Four thirty-five."

"Say that I will be at the hotel in my room at six o'clock. They won't arrest me, will they? They won't want me to go to the police station?"

"They haven't anything to arrest you for. As to going to the station, I think I have influence enough to arrange that they'll come to the hotel."

"I think it's best to say nothing about it to Buck just now."

"As you like." A look of kindness came into the dark eyes of the Colonel. "Have you kept your room at the hotel?"

"No."

"Perhaps it would be better if my secretary telephoned to take a room. Then you could go in by the harbor side."

"Yes. That would be wonderful."

Colonel Moti got up from his chair. "I'll go then. I'll tell Buck you're waiting for him."

"No, not yet. Let him finish the business." She wanted to be alone for a little time. She had to be alone to pull herself together.

Moti went out and with his going she began to cry, not from self-pity but from despair and hysteria. At the sight of her tears the small hand grasped her own more tightly. Then the boy began to talk to her rapidly. She could understand nothing he said but she was aware that he meant to comfort her. Then in the rush of speech she recognized two words, "Sahib Buck." He was saying something about Buck and she thought, "He's right. I mustn't let Buck see me like this." And with a great effort of will she stopped crying, and freeing her hand from Ali's, she pressed his head against her for a second. Then she gave him back the guinea pig and going to the dim light at the window, she carefully made up her face.

When she turned back toward Ali, Buck was coming into the room, carrying a telegram in his hand. He said, "I've had another telegram from Jellapore. We'll have to leave for there tomorrow."

With her face in the shadow, the light behind her, she said

[312]

quietly, "I can't go that soon. I have business in Bombay that has to be settled before I go away."

"What business?"

"Legal business. Colonel Moti knows about it. We've just been talking. I could follow you in a couple of days."

She was thinking all the time, "That would give me time. If only he'd go away, maybe I could straighten things out. I can't do it with him in Bombay. Maybe that telegram will solve everything." And then for a second she felt wildly happy once more.

The light was on his face and in it she saw a look which she had never seen there before—a curious look of bewilderment and even suspicion. She knew suddenly that he was hurt because she was hiding something from him.

He asked, "What is this legal business?"

"It's nothing . . . just some boring details about some jewelry, but it has to be settled. Don't worry about it. You go on to Jellapore and I'll follow you there." She was eager to have him go because in his going lay her one chance to work things out. If the police returned her jewelry she could give everything back to Botlivala and Jellapore's brother, and he wouldn't need to know anything about it. She tried to keep the eagerness out of her voice lest it make him suspicious.

"No . . . I don't want to do that. I don't want to be separated from you even that long."

"It won't matter. It's for so short a time, only a day or two. And your going back right away will mean so much to all those poor people."

His face changed its expression. "I never asked you if you wanted to go to Jellapore. Maybe I was wrong. Maybe you don't want to go there. Maybe you'd hate it."

"That wouldn't matter, honey. I'd be happy with you. The only thing is that I mightn't be any good there."

"I'm not worrying about that."

She knew that Ali was watching them both. He could not understand anything they were saying but he sat, bending forward a little as if he were making a great effort.

"Anyway," she said, "I'll have to stay overnight in Bombay."

"You're not going back to the Taj?"

"It doesn't matter."

"Green's might be better."

She remembered what Moti had said about her being a legendary figure in Bombay—"the big blonde"—and said, "It doesn't matter. One place is as bad as another."

Then Colonel Moti came in and said, "I arranged for your room."

"We'd better go then," she said.

Mrs. Moti went over to Ali and saying something to the boy, quietly restored the bandage. Ali made no objection.

Mrs. Moti said, "He must keep the bandage on part of every day until his eyes are used to the light. That was part of Dr. Bliss' instructions."

The first sentence of the speech echoed in Carol's tired brain. *Keep the bandage on part of every day until his eyes are used to the light.* Maybe that was what was happening to her. Maybe it wasn't possible to have happiness and love like that in the garden of Jai Mahal all at once. Maybe it had to come gradually. Maybe you had to earn it.

On the long ride into Bombay, through the Mill district and the slums they rode nearly all the way in silence. It was as if her own body, her very emotions were numbed, the way people's bodies grew numb and indifferent when they were dying. She did not notice the heat, nor the smells. She did not even mind the mad driving of the wild Sikh. Her head ached and her brain was tired from so much "thinking out" of things; it wasn't used to thinking so much. She kept thinking over and over, "I must work this out. I must work this out. If I don't, I'm done for."

As if a barrier had suddenly come between them, they sat a little apart from each other. On his side of the wall, Buck was being tormented, not now by any such concrete thing as jealousy; it was that misty cloud of doubts returning about her past, about her reticence over the "legal business," about Carol herself. At Jai Mahal there had been no other world but theirs; there had been neither a past nor a future, but only the present which concerned the two of them alone. Now, suddenly, from the moment they had closed the gate of the garden, everything had been changed. In

[314]

some intangible fashion he could not understand she had slipped away from him. Why was she so eager for him to go at once back to Jellapore? Why had she been so evasive about her business? Then the most awful of doubts occurred to him—that perhaps she had never meant to marry him at all. Maybe she had merely meant all the time to go away with him and when it was over, leave him. But that couldn't be now. She could not leave him because without her he could not live. He would not want to live. What Bill had said to him echoed in his ears, the taunt that what he had done was the most dangerous thing a man could do—to discover about things when it was too late in life. He hadn't understood at the time what Bill meant; he understood it now. His own aching body and tormented brain told him.

He felt suddenly the touch of her hand and heard her voice, "You're not feeling sick again?"

"No, honey."

"Don't worry, baby. Leave it to me. All I want is a couple of days in Bombay. I promise you that. Only don't worry."

He took her hand. "Wherever you go, honey, whatever happens to you, I'm going with you."

She turned away and looked out of the window so that he would not see the tears in her eyes.

Then the taxi stopped with a jerk and through a mist she saw the Gateway of India and beyond it the bay with Elephanta dim in the mirage of heat above the water, and knew that she was back at the hotel.

They entered the hotel by the harbor side, encountering only an old woman who looked at them with mild curiosity and an unrecognizing stare and two Indian peddlers of jewels and silks. They climbed the cold stone stairs in silence as far as the floor where her room was. Then she said to Buck, "Don't worry about me. I'll be busy for a couple of hours. Go and get some sleep and I'll call you when it's time to eat."

He didn't say anything but simply stood looking at her with the same queer, puzzled expression which had come over his face at the Motis' bungalow. With anguish, she thought, "I'm hurting him and I love him better than I love life." Suddenly she said,

"Trust me, Buck. Please, trust me!" But the look didn't go away. He put his arms about her and kissed her.

Then softly she said, "I'll call you in a couple of hours," and hurried away from him, past the row of staring bearers to her old room. There, at the door, still in his purple and gold clothes, a little dirty and rumpled, she found Krishna. At sight of her, he rose and salaamed as if nothing had happened, as if he had not run away at all.

"That," she thought, "must be a good omen." For since she had gone to Jai Mahal she was beginning to have a vague belief in the powers of divination which most Indians have. She had meant to ask where he had been and why he had run away, but she knew the boy, in his Indian way, wanted to treat the whole episode as if it had never occurred at all. Maybe that wasn't a bad idea when unpleasant things occurred. Even if she did ask him, he would only lie to her and say that his mother was sick or his grandfather had died. He was solicitous and asked if she wanted a drink or her trunks unpacked.

"Yes," she said, "bring me a gin sling." That would help her to face the police. She was very tired. For the first time in her life she felt a desire to be cared for, protected and coddled.

When he had gone, she telephoned to the manager that she was back and that she would see the police when they arrived. His voice was tired, precise and cold.

Her trunks were all there against the wall in one corner of the room. There was no use opening them because whatever happened she would be leaving almost at once either for Jellapore or for Europe. Krishna brought the drink and went away, quiet, respectful, as much ashamed of himself as any bearer could ever be. She was hot and tired and the drink revived her a little. There was a knock at the door and when she said, "Come in," the door opened and the two policemen who had been there before came in—the tall pale Englishman and the dark, strapping Pathan. They were dreadfully punctual. "I suppose," she thought, "executioners are like this, punctual too."

The Englishman said, "Good afternoon, Miss Halma. We've come about the jewelry." The big Pathan bowed but said nothing save with his libidinous black eyes. She thought, "Whatever happens I must keep them in their place."

"Thank you. Won't you sit down?"

The Englishman sat on a chair, the big Pathan on a Vuitton trunk and she herself, holding the drink in her hand, sat down on the edge of the bed.

"Will you have a drink?" she asked.

Again the Englishman answered her, "No, thanks. I never drink in working hours and Captain Baig is a Moslem and does not drink at all." He paused for a moment, and then said, "We would have come sooner but we could not find you."

"Yes," said Carol, "I went away."

"It was a pity you went so mysteriously. It caused the department a great deal of trouble." His voice was cold and it was clear that he hated her. Why, she could not imagine. Simply causing a little trouble was no reason for the feeling she divined in him, something much deeper than mere annoyance.

"It is all a very unfortunate business," he continued. "I suppose you have heard who stole the jewelry?"

"Yes." She felt a hunch to use flattery, "It was very clever of you to discover it."

"Not very clever. It was simple. Mrs. Trollope is not a clever thief. She tried to sell the jewelry in Bombay to a jewel peddler. We know them all. He told us at once. When we checked on it, her finger prints were on the jewel case—hers and other prints which, I take it, were yours."

She finished the drink and wished desperately for another, but she knew that she must be on good behavior and not risk sending Krishna out for another. The manner of the Englishman annoyed her; he was like a precious Sunday School teacher.

He said, "I think you've been very unfortunate in the company you've chosen to frequent in Bombay."

"I knew about Mrs. Trollope. I knew she was hard-up, but I didn't think she would steal. I felt sorry for her. I think she's a little crazy. I don't want to make any complaint against her. If I get back the jewelry, that's all I want. Where is she now?"

"In jail. She asked to see you. You're the only person she asked for. She made no appeal to her sister."

That was bad. She didn't want to see Mrs. Trollope ever again. She was afraid to see her. It was Mrs. Trollope who had brought all the bad luck—Mrs. Trollope who had come so casually into her life.

"I'd rather not see her," she said. "It couldn't do any good."

"She seems to have an obsession that you bring her luck. However, that is a matter for you to decide. As to pressing the case against her, you need not. That again is entirely a matter for you to decide. Whether you can get her off or not, is another question. The hotel is involved, and the insurance companies—regardless of the fact that the insurance had expired—do not give us much latitude. It is their policy to press such cases. I'm afraid there isn't much that you can do about her. There have been a great many robberies, swindling cases and scandals in the Bombay Presidency during the past year—too many. The authorities are inclined to make an example of her."

What he was saying filled her with a slow horror. Mrs. Trollope as a person was a bore, but as a human being, God had not been kind to her. She was like a leathery unattractive little animal kicked about, abused, cowering, driven by her own unfortunate nature into every sort of folly.

"I'll go to see her," she heard herself saying suddenly. "I wish we could get her off altogether." Then she remembered the newspapers. "If I go," she asked, "the papers won't need to know about it, will they?"

A new look came into the face of the police officer. He glanced at Captain Baig, and said, "The attention given by the newspapers was regrettable, Miss Halma, but it was out of our control. The Indian politicians chose the case as a piece of propaganda. We will continue to do our best to keep it all as quiet as possible. Please believe me, we do not welcome the attention of the newspapers. They cause us a great deal of trouble."

Captain Baig was grinning now, showing his beautiful white teeth, and in the midst of all the worry, Carol thought again that he was a very attractive buck of a man, and very human beside the Englishman.

"You can recover your jewelry, Miss Halma," the officer was saying, "by coming to the police offices and identifying it."

[318]

"I should like to get it back as quickly as possible." (Then she could give back Botlivala his damned diamonds and put an end to all that business.)

"You may come tonight if you like. Perhaps the sooner the better."

"Tonight or tomorrow."

She had expected him to rise now that the business was over and to go away leaving her in peace. But he did not rise. He coughed and glanced at the yellow gloves he carried even in the heat. She waited, still aware of the big Pathan's ogling stare, and after a moment the police officer said, "I'm afraid there is one more thing I must go into. It's an unpleasant business."

She sat up very straight on the bed. What could it be now? Hadn't she suffered enough for all her folly?

"Yes," she said, "what is it?"

He coughed again and she saw Captain Baig sit up very straight on the trunk as if by an effort of will he had changed himself suddenly from a human man into a machine.

"The authorities would like to have you leave Bombay for Europe as quickly as possible. That was the real purpose of my coming here—to pass on the order."

For a second she could not believe what she was hearing. Then suddenly she was very angry.

"Do you mean that they are ordering me to leave Bombay?"

"I have tried to put it tactfully, but what it amounts to is an order of deportation. The *Rajputana* sails day after tomorrow. They would like you to leave on it. That will give you time to settle everything before leaving."

The blood rushed into her face. "Who is 'they'?" she asked.

"The Commissioner of Police . . . the Governor of the Bombay Presidency, two or three other high authorities. There have been so many annoyances lately created by transients of an undesirable sort, they have decided to take action. I'm very sorry I bring you the unpleasant news. I hope it doesn't upset your plans."

She tried to control herself. With her cheeks flaming, she said, "No, I meant to go in any case."

It was done now. There wasn't any choice left to her. She couldn't hope any longer that somehow, miraculously, everything

[319]

would turn out all right. She thought, "I've seen Buck already for the last time when he kissed me at the top of the stairs." She could never see him again now. He could not even be seen in the company of a woman who was being deported. Anguish swept through her and then left her suddenly cold. She thought, wildly, "Maybe if I were charming to them, they'd let me stay." But that was no good. Being charming to this Englishman would get her nothing. She knew Englishmen like him. If they had any emotions at all, they were not for her. Then she knew why it was that he disliked her, why he was enjoying the slow polite torment. Nothing she could do would affect him; he hated her because she was beautiful and a woman and men loved her.

And it was no good trying to charm Captain Baig. That would be only too easy, and anyway he would have no authority. The English would let him out on a string and pull him back when they saw fit. She looked wildly at him for help, but the Pathan was being "official." The animal look was still in his black eyes but he was sitting up straight as a ramrod.

Wildly she thought, "I'll fight. I won't be railroaded." And she said, "I've done nothing. I'm not guilty of anything. They can't send me away."

The Englishman said, "I'm afraid they have the power to send you away simply on the grounds that you are an undesirable person and that you keep bad company. You won't be sailing alone, Miss Halma. Most of your friends will be with you. The Baroness is going too and a Portuguese gentleman. Mrs. Trollope would be going except that she is being detained."

She saw that he was enjoying the torture. Fury took possession of her. She thought, "The Queen! The damned pansy!" She said, "I won't go. I'll fight the order."

Coldly he went on in his middle-class, suburban accent, "I think that would be unwise and perfectly futile. It wouldn't do you any good and if you dislike notoriety, it would only be asking for more."

She knew that he was right. There was nothing she could do. They had caught her. She stood up. "Thank you, gentlemen. I'll come to get my jewelry. I'm already packed. Am I supposed to buy my own passage?"

The two men stood up. "The Government will furnish you with a third-class ticket as far as Marseilles," said the Englishman. A look of satisfaction came into the cold blue eyes. "I apologize again for having to bring you unpleasant news."

She did not answer him, but held open the door for him to leave. Bowing a little the Englishman went first. As the big Pathan left, he smiled and showed his beautiful teeth. With his lips he said nothing, but the black eyes were bold and eloquent. They said, "Why don't you let me come to your room once before you leave. I am a man such as you'll never find again. It couldn't make much difference to *you*, and I would enjoy it immensely."

Then she heard Krishna saying, "A boy just brought letter for Memsahib." And she took the letter from him.

Closing the door behind her, she leaned against it for a moment with her eyes closed, and while she stood there the faint odor of patchouli came to her, telling her that the letter was from the Baroness.

It was almost dark now and without turning on the lights she walked to the window and read it by the glow from the wild and fiery sunset beyond Elephanta.

It read:

"Darling:

"I hear that you too are sailing on the *Rajputana*. What good luck to have company all the way back. I am going to Marseilles and not to Cairo. Ring me up when you come in. I am glad to get out of this Bombay. It is a filthy hole. I'll take care of everything here and in Paris. Don't worry. What luck to get back the jewels. She is an animal—that Mrs. Trollope.

"Affectionately your friend,
"Baroness Stefani"

Slowly she tore the letter into small pieces, thinking dully, "Well, why not?" Then she went to the door and said to Krishna, "Bring me a gin sling and tell a taxi to meet me on the other side of the hotel by the harbor." After that she sat at the washstand and wrote a note to Buck and when she had done that she took up the telephone and called the Baroness.

Bill's train came in at nine. For three days and two nights he had traveled across India from Calcutta to Bombay. He was hot, tired and covered with red dust. It was in his eyes, his hair, his ears, his mouth. At that moment as he walked along the noisy platform followed by Silas and the coolies bringing his luggage he wanted only a bath.

But in his heart there was a sense of relief, almost of happiness. His job was nearly finished and he had done it well. Twenty-four hours could take care of everything and day after tomorrow he would be aboard the *Rajputana* homeward bound, gone from India, perhaps forever. The old man had come across. He didn't have to stay in the East. He was going back to London.

On the way back to the hotel in the taxicab he wondered about Carol and Buck. Where were they? What had happened to them? It annoyed him a little that they had not sent him a message, not even so much as a postcard. But he thought, seeking excuses for them, "Maybe what has happened to them has made them forget everything else." For he knew that what had happened to them was no ordinary thing. There were even moments when he was envious because that sort of thing could never happen to him. Maybe nothing would ever happen to him that was any better or any more important than the adventure with the Marchesa. And again the problem of the Marchesa claimed him. Because that was what it had become. At this moment she was in another taxicab bound from the train to the hotel. She had been there, with him or shadowing him, since the moment the train had pulled out of the station in Bombay weeks ago, trapping him in her compartment with the champagne. The story of the visit to Delhi had all been bilge. She had never even stopped off at Delhi but gone straight on to Calcutta with him.

Now, grimly, he thought, "Why am I so God-damned attractive to women I don't want?"

Anyway he would be free of her for dinner, saying he had a business appointment; and with luck he'd get away on the *Rajputana* because he had told her he didn't mean to sail for another month. The very thought of her talking, talking, talking in her broken English, overwhelming him with endearments and attentions, made him feel sick.

At the hotel he went straight to the desk for his key, leaving

Silas to take care of the luggage. There was but one thing in his mind—a bath. It wasn't only the dust and heat of the trip; thinking about the Marchesa had made him feel physically dirty. For a moment he waited, swearing under his breath for the lift to descend. Then suddenly the door opened and three or four people came out and Buck was standing there in front of him.

It was a Buck whom he had never seen before. His hair was rumpled and in his blue eyes there was a wild look. He even stared at Bill for a moment without recognizing him, perhaps without seeing him at all.

Bill said, "Hello, I was wondering where you were."

Buck only took him by the arm and said, "Carol's run away."

"My God!" thought Bill. "It's worse even than I believed it was going to be." But he tried to behave as if the event were a casual incident.

"She'll probably come back."

"No, she won't. You've got to help me find her."

"All right! But stop acting like a lunatic in the hall. Come up to my room. I want a bath." Almost with violence he pushed Buck into the lift. The door closed and it began to climb. "Calm down, brother. It'll be all right," he started to say. "That's a girl I know. She probably just went out and forgot to tell you where she was going." And then thought better of it. Now wasn't the time to remind Buck that Carol had once been his.

The elevator stopped at Bill's floor and in silence they walked to Bill's room. Once inside with the door closed, Bill said, "Now tell me what it's all about."

Buck took a crumpled note out of his pocket and handed it to Bill. Smoothing it, Bill read in Carol's great scrawly writing:

"Darling:
It's all over. Don't try to find me. I won't come back. What we did was a crazy thing. I was a fool, and so were you. Just try to remember that it was fun while it lasted, and that it's finished. Think of me sometimes. Love,

Carol."

He read it through again, thinking, "Something has happened that I don't know about. Something worse than all the other

[323]

things." Then he looked at Buck and looking at him, knew that he had to be hard-boiled.

"Wait till I start a bath," he said, "and then tell me what's happened since I went away. It might be a help."

Inside he was boiling with anger. As he bent over the bath to turn the taps he thought, "The bitch has done it. She's had enough and now she's going to scram. God-damn her!" Probably she'd ruined Buck forever. He wanted to cry out to Buck, "I told you so," but that wasn't any good now. When he had gained control of himself, he went back into the room and said quietly, "Now tell me." He began to take off his clothes, listening with only part of his mind, the other part occupied with vengeful thoughts about Carol.

He was aware that Buck was trying to tell him shyly and incoherently about the thing that had happened to him at Jai Mahal. It wasn't necessary. You could see in Buck's anguished face what had happened. Maybe he would recover from it and maybe he wouldn't. He wasn't a boy who would forget it all and find another girl. He wasn't a rounder who could just go on to another woman. You couldn't say to him, "Tell her to go to hell and forget her." A little awed as he looked up at Buck, he thought, "This is something that has never happened to me and never will. This is something beyond my understanding. Good God, this is something frightening! It's like Tristan and Isolde."

And he heard Buck saying, "Something happened after we left Jai Mahal. I think it must have happened at Moti's. She was different after that. And when we got back here she told me she'd call me when she was ready to go to dinner. She didn't call and about eight o'clock I called her. Nobody answered so I went down to her room. The boy was there but he didn't know where she had gone. So I went in. One trunk was open. She wasn't there and I found this note." Then a look of horror came into Buck's eyes, "She couldn't have tried to kill herself . . . you don't think that?"

"No," said Bill. "I don't think that. She's too healthy. Healthy people don't kill themselves. Their bodies won't let 'em." He forgot all about the bath. Standing there in his dressing gown, he asked, "What do you think could have happened to her?"

"I don't know. But Moti might."

[324]

Bill thought quickly. He remembered what Buck had told him about Moti's talk with Carol. Very likely Moti did know something —a clue anyway. Bill knew about the whole business over the jewelry, but his instinct told him that if Carol had wanted to stay with Buck that wouldn't be enough to stop her. No, she'd probably had enough and was running away. The only thing to do would be to make it as easy as possible for Buck. If he could get Buck out of the way, he might himself be able to find her and try to straighten things out. That was the only thing to do.

Silas knocked at the door and came in with the baggage. Bill said to him, "Get downstairs quick and bring a bottle of whiskey, some Schweppes and a couple of glasses. Quick!" Then he went into the bathroom and turned off the water. When he came out again Buck was standing by the window looking out across the dark harbor. He was trembling as if he had a chill.

Bill said, "The malaria hasn't come back?"

Buck answered him without turning, "No, it isn't that." Then quickly he turned. "Wherever she's gone I'm going with her. She can't get rid of me as easy as that."

Bill didn't answer him at once but presently said, "I read in the papers that there was a bad outbreak of cholera in Jellapore."

"To hell with the cholera and Jellapore. It isn't only what's happening to me, Bill. It's what'll happen to her. Don't you see? I'm not thinking only about myself."

"I didn't think you were." Buck was right about what would happen to her. And when she went to the dogs, she'd go in her own way, wholly, completely, in a spectacular way. He thought, "Very likely there isn't anything either of us can do about her. There isn't anything anybody can do. She's been off the track for too long."

Silas came back with the whiskey and Bill poured Buck a stiff drink. "Take that," he said, "and then if I were you, I'd go out to see Moti. I'd even go to Jai Mahal if you don't find any clue at Moti's. She might have gone back there to hide. I'll search Bombay. There aren't many places for her to go . . . at least places that you'd know. She won't kill herself. She's not that kind."

Then Buck said a pathetic thing. "I'm afraid because she did

love me, Bill. I know she loves me. No woman could pretend a
thing like that."

"I'm sure she loves you, Buck, but she's a funny girl. She always
has been." But almost at once he thought, "I'm a fool to pretend
to know anything about her. I've never known anything like this."
He called Silas and sent him for a sandwich. He was hungry. He
had been looking forward to a long bath and a good dinner. Well,
all of that was shot now.

"What are you going to do?" he asked.

"I'll go and see Moti."

"I'll have a bath and then go out to look for her. What do you
want me to tell her?"

"That I'm never going to give her up. I'll beat hell out of her
but she's not going to get away." Buck took up his topee and then
put one arm about Bill's shoulders. "You're a swell guy, Bill."

"Oh, I'm all right," said Bill. "Get along with your job."

Then he went out, and Bill looking after him, was again filled
with awe because this was something beyond his understanding.
His thoughts slipped to the Marchesa and the thought of the Marchesa led to thoughts of a bath.

Bill found no trace of her in the hotel. No one had seen her go
out. He thought perhaps she had gone to Green's, but at Green's
there was no sign of her. Next he thought of the Willingdon Club
and called a taxicab and set out along the road by the sea. In
the heat he felt suddenly tired; as if all the weariness of the long
journey, all the boredom of business in Madras and Calcutta and
the dull depravity of the affair with the Marchesa, had caught up
with him. He felt depressed, thinking, "What the hell am I? Where
the hell am I going?" He had a strange sensation of marking time
in space, aimlessly.

The taxi passed Government House and the Temple of Parvati.
The air was filled with the smell of jasmine and incense and dust.
And then opening his eyes, he saw the lights of Jelly's little pleasure
palace and thought, "It's just possible that she might be there."
Leaning forward, he said to the driver, "Turn in at the house with
the lights."

It was the same as always, the line of vulture taxis waiting outside, the Rolls Royces inside the courtyard, the ancient porter at the door. He had thought he was never coming back here, and here he was.

He saw her almost at once.

She was sitting in the same spot where he had seen her on the night he had fallen in love with her for the first time. She was gambling and having luck for she had a great pile of chips in front of her. Botlivala was there, standing behind her and at the end of the table he recognized the Baroness in her preposterous gown of black sequins. Tonight she was wearing a red hibiscus flower in her hair. But he scarcely saw them. It was only Carol for whom he had eyes.

She was dressed in a white evening gown and was wearing a great deal of jewelry—the jewelry which had made all the trouble.

The moment he saw her he knew that something had happened to her, something very like what had happened to Buck. She looked more beautiful than she had ever been, but there was about her a look of fragility which she had never had before. She was thinner and there were dark circles beneath the blue eyes. She had been drinking and a glass of champagne stood beside her winnings. She was playing the bank and did not look up as he came in. She drew a card and won and Joey tipsily pushed the great heap of chips in the middle of the table toward her.

He did not wait but went round the end of the table and standing behind her leaned down and said, quietly, "Sell the bank. I want to talk to you."

She turned and gave him a frightened, startled look. Then quickly she said, "All right. Joey, sell the bank for me."

Rising, she took up her glass of champagne and came with him. Botlivala started to follow but Bill turned and said, "Keep out of this or I'll beat the hell out of you." Then as he turned he was aware of the Marchesa's great black eyes, watching them. He did not speak to her or make any sign of recognition.

They went into the small room overlooking the sea to a table in the corner just above the garden.

As they sat down, she asked, "Where did you come from? I thought you were in Calcutta."

"I came in tonight."

"Oh."

He saw at once by her manner that she meant to keep him at a distance, that there was something that she must not tell him. He would have to go slowly if he was to do what he had come meaning to do.

Quickly she said, "How was the Marchesa?"

The question startled him but he answered her, "Expert but too earnest. How did you know about that?"

"The Baroness told me. Anyway I could have guessed from the way the Marchesa treated me. You could have done better than that old hag."

"It's nothing to you in any case."

"Maybe not."

"What are you doing here? I should think you'd had enough of this."

"I wanted to make some money."

"You know what happened to Mrs. Trollope?"

She did not answer him and all the while he was thinking. "How am I going to begin. How am I going to break through? How am I going to manage it?" There was a sad, tired silence. She drank what was left in her glass and he thought, "She's had too much to drink. Seeing me shocked her out of it, for the time being."

Then he said, "I've seen Buck."

She looked away from him and then said, "Have you?"

"You ought to be ashamed of yourself. You're the worst woman I know."

"Worse than the Marchesa?"

"Yes. You know what you've done to Buck, don't you?"

"No."

"It would have been a lot better if you'd taken a gun and shot him."

She didn't answer him for a long time, and again Bill thought, "Where do we go from here? How am I going to get at her?" He had never seen her like this before. She was hard. She was dead. There wasn't any of the old spirit in her.

She said, "I want some more champagne."

"You're not going to have any more till we've finished talking."

[328]

She shrugged her shoulders.

"Why have you run away from him?"

"There wasn't anything else to do."

"What are you going to do now?"

"I'm sailing day after tomorrow on the *Rajputana*."

The news surprised him and for a second the hope that she would go back to him came to life again. But it died immediately in the knowledge that what had happened to her since he had last seen her only removed her farther from him.

"And then what?"

"I'm going to work for the Baroness in Paris. She's sailing too."

"Do you know what the Baroness is?"

"Vaguely. Don't worry about me. I've always been able to take care of myself."

"She's a procuress. She has a business spread all over Europe. The Marchesa told me all about her. The Marchesa began her career as one of her girls."

Carol smiled, and there was a trace of the old humorous malice in the smile. "Then my guess wasn't so bad. I guessed that the Marchesa came out of a beazle-hut."

"They're going to deport the Baroness. She's been trying to buy and ship Indian girls to Alexandria."

"The order has already gone through. That's why she's leaving."

"How do you know that?"

"From the police." Suddenly she said fiercely, "What do you want me to do? Do you think I want to leave Buck? Do you think I don't love him?"

"Then why are you going?"

She looked away from him. "How could I marry him," she said, "after everything that's been in the papers? Moti says I'm a notorious character in Bombay, even in Jellapore. And Buck is just on the edge of getting everything he's wanted all along—everything he's worked for all his life. The British Government is making his position official. A University is giving him a degree. He can't have a wife like me."

There were tears in her eyes, the first tears he had ever seen. He thought, "That's better. Now I can get somewhere. Maybe she does love him—maybe she loves him as much as he loves her."

[329]

"Running away won't do any good. He'll be ruined just the same. He said he'd go wherever you went and nothing could stop him. That's even worse."

"He only says that."

"In some ways, honey, I know Buck a lot better than you do. He means what he says."

A look of anguish came into her face. "But he can't do that, Bill. You mustn't let him do that."

"Have you ever tried to stop Buck from doing something he had set his mind on and thought right? I think whatever you try to do he'll be on the *Rajputana* with you and the Baroness. When I spoke to him about the cholera, he said, 'To hell with the cholera and the villages.' That's what you've done to him."

She rose suddenly and went over to the arched window where she stood for a long time. He watched, wondering again whether there was something she had not told him. He knew she was trying to pull herself together, so he waited, saying nothing. And while he waited the figure of the Marchesa appeared for a moment in the doorway. The plants standing in pots all about the table where he was sitting almost hid them from view. She looked for a moment at Carol and then went away again.

At the same time Carol turned and said, suddenly, "Bill, you could change it all. You could make it so that he'd stay here and go back to Jellapore."

"What could I do?"

"You could marry me again. Would you, Bill? Then he would *know* that everything is finished. He wouldn't try to break up something between you and me."

He answered her almost at once, because his answer was there, already in his heart. He had seen them both and he knew that his part in the story was finished. He knew suddenly how much he loved them both, more than he had ever imagined. Nevertheless, it took a great effort to say what his heart dictated.

"No, I won't. Because somehow you and Buck are going to come together again."

"No," she said. "It can't be. There's no use." She spoke in a voice that was dead, the kind of voice he never believed he would hear coming from her. "Please, Bill, marry me."

[330]

He smiled, "You don't mind ruining me. Now, do you?"

"I'll try not to ruin you, and besides, honey, you don't matter as much as Buck. Neither of us do. We're just nothing beside him—and it isn't only Buck. It's all the people he's helped."

Then quickly, on a hunch, he said, "There's something I don't know about. There's something you haven't told me."

She looked away from him and in the same dead voice, she said, "Yes, there is. I can't stay and he can't go with me because they're sending me away along with the Baroness."

For a moment he couldn't speak. Then he said, "Deporting you?" She said nothing and he asked, "Why? In God's name, why?"

"As an undesirable person."

He stood up and said, "You can fight them. I'll fight them with you."

"That's no good. It's bad enough already. If all that came out in the papers it would only make it worse. Buck couldn't marry a woman who had been threatened with deportation."

"Yes, that's true." He saw it all very clearly. There wasn't anything to do in that direction.

She was saying, "They're shipping me third class on the *Rajputana*. That's why I came here tonight—to make enough to pay for first class. I didn't want to borrow it from the Baroness."

"That's a lie," he said.

"Yes," she answered simply. "I came because I didn't give a damn and because I wanted to vamp Botlivala and hang on to the jewelry. I'll need it now."

He had been thinking fast and hard all the time she was talking. Now he said, "There's only one thing I could do. I could see the Governor himself and try to get the order rescinded."

She said, "He probably wouldn't even see you."

"He knows who I am. I've been to Government House." It was all very clear to him suddenly. He would see the young A.D.C. who met him on the boat in the shining white uniform. He would demand an interview with the Governor. He'd have to do it quickly because of the red tape . . . within twenty-four hours. Tonight was the time.

"Anyway I'm going to try it," he said. "Tonight."

She began to cry softly, "Bill . . . Bill."

He kissed her gently, quickly. Then he said, "Go back with me to the hotel."

"No, Buck will be there. If you couldn't do anything, I couldn't stand seeing him." She was silent for a moment. "I'll go back to the Maharani's. That's where I went from the hotel."

"Oh, my God!"

"I'll be all right there. Go and get my coat. Collect my money from Joey. I'll go through the garden. I don't want to go into that room ever again."

"All right. I'll meet you at the door."

She went out quickly, down the steps and he went back into the room where they were gambling.

While Joey paid off the chips, Mr. Botlivala stood glaring. Then the Marchesa turned over her cards, rose and came over to him. The sulky black eyes were clouded with jealousy and anger.

"Are you going away?" she asked.

"Yes."

"Weeth her?"

"Yes."

"She is sailing on the *Rajputana*."

"I don't know," he said.

"I am sure she is going."

He looked at her sharply, "Why are you sure?"

She smiled. An annoying smug smile it was. At sight of it a kind of hatred swept over him—hatred of her complacency and animalness, her dullness, her depravity.

"I theenk so," she said, "I theenk she's going because she must. Stay here weeth me and play. I need luck."

"Not a chance."

He turned his back quickly and heard Jelly's velvety voice, "What's the matter with Carol tonight?"

"I don't know," said Bill. Then because he could think of nothing better to say, he said, "I'm taking her home. I'll be back later."

"She was very lucky. She won a lot of money. Unlucky in love . . ." But Bill did not hear the rest of what he said.

He left her at the silly pink palace of the Maharani, thinking, "My God, what would have happened if I hadn't been there?" It

[332]

was terrifying how very small things in life could change the whole course of things. The taxi, its driver urged on by him, reeled and swerved between the flowering gardens of Malabar Hill down again into the city. It did not matter to him now how fast the driver went; it was not fast enough.

At the hotel Buck had not returned. He called Government House but the A.D.C. who answered said that Lieutenant Forsythe was not on duty. He only knew that he had gone to dinner at the Taj Mahal. Bill thanked him and hanging up quickly went to the dining room.

The party hadn't broken up yet. It was a large and rather pompous dinner of dullish people. It wasn't being a success. None of them were talking. Some of them were dancing. Those who remained at the table were watching the dancers. At the far end sat Lieutenant Forsythe.

He thought, "If we'd gone out with people like that instead of with the Baroness and Mrs. Trollope and Jelly, none of this would have happened. Maybe it would be worth being bored to death." Then quickly he summoned a waiter, wrote a note and directed him to take it at once to the blonde young man at the long table.

And almost at once he thought, "It's no use." He looked at his watch. It was already nearly eleven o'clock. The Governor would be asleep. Then Lieutenant Forsythe appeared and smiling, said "Hello."

"I'm sorry to have disturbed you. I wouldn't have if it hadn't been important."

"If there's anything I can do. . . ."

"Could you come to the bar for a few minutes and have a drink?"

The A.D.C. looked hesitant. "It's difficult to leave my party."

"It's a matter of life and death . . . or very nearly."

For a moment Forsythe hesitated. Then he said, "All right," and came along.

In the bar Bill took him to a corner of the noisy room and when they had ordered drinks, he thought, "I've sold a lot of things in my life, but I've got to be the top salesman of all time now." He said, "I wouldn't have annoyed you except that it's important. It's about Miss Halma. I wanted to speak to the Governor about her. I don't know whether you know what has happened."

[333]

The good-looking face of Lieutenant Forsythe went serious, and a little blank, with that maddening blankness which comes into the faces of officialdom.

"Yes," he said, "I know."

"She is a very good friend of mine. I want to help her."

"Does she mind going away quietly? There's no scandal about it."

"Yes. She does."

"Why? Has she any good reasons?"

"That's the whole story. It's something nobody in Bombay knows about."

The waiter brought the drinks and again Bill thought, "I've got to tell a swell story—a better story than I've ever told." It would have to be good to survive the noise, the lights, the music, the drinking all about him.

So he began, "Do you know a man called Homer Merrill?"

"Yes. Everybody in India knows him."

"He is a great friend of mine too. We went to school together."

In the bungalow at the Institute, the Colonel and Indira Moti sat on the verandah. The mosquitoes were not bad at this time of year and Mrs. Moti liked listening to the night noises. All her life, until she had married Moti, she had lived in a village in Bengal and she would have preferred living in the country instead of in this oasis in the hot slums of Bombay. In the evening in the villages you heard the soft, dry rustling of the bamboo and palm leaves and the chirp of fat crickets and the bellowing of the frogs in the village tank, the lowing of cattle and the sound of drums and flutes, and of birds moving about softly in the trees overhead. And you smelled the perfume of jasmine and night flowers and spices. Here there was only dust and soot and heat, and the shouts of quarreling men and women, of half-starved children crying outside the wall of the compound.

She was sewing on a sari which she meant to use in one of the dances which she herself had composed, outside the realm of the archaic, stiff, ritual figures of the Tanjore dances. The costume was of flame-colored stuff bordered and embroidered with silver. As she worked she thought, "I will be like a flame."

But she thought too of many other things. Her mind tonight

was relaxed and untidy. Moti, reading his scientific papers under the light on the opposite side of the verandah, was calm for once, not haranguing her or calling on her help for everything from the salvation of humanity to a lost *atchkan* button. From under her dark long lashes she looked at him, feeling tenderness and satisfaction because their marriage had been an understanding one. Marriages in India could be so many things. She had been lucky. . . . Sometimes, it was true, there were long periods when she felt lonely, the periods when for days at a time only his work existed, when he stayed all day and most of the night in the laboratory; but there were compensations, among them the fact that life with Moti was never dull. In his love-making he was as fiery, as passionate, as unexpected as in his mind. He was only tiresome when he behaved like God, and after all that wasn't a bad fault in a man. Other men had faults so much worse.

"No," she thought, "I have been very lucky. Before long I shall no longer be like a flame when I dance. I shall only be able to suggest a flame. But it won't matter. I shall always have that fiery Moti and I'll have my pupils."

The only sorrow was that they had no children, and even then it was not as bad as it might have been because Moti looked upon everybody as his children and so did not much notice having none of his own. And the thought of children led her to turn and look at Ali sitting on a rattan divan in the shadows where the strong light from Moti's lamp would not strike his eyes.

He was sitting cross-legged with the guinea pig between his knees, silently, saying nothing. She thought, "He too is thinking of the country and the elephant stables and the sounds of the jungle." After a moment he became aware that she was looking at him and turning his head a little he said, "Do you think it's true that Sahib Buck is going home tomorrow?"

"Yes, I think it's true."

"And is it true that he will take me too?"

"Yes. He'll take you too."

That, it seemed, was all he wanted to hear. He slipped back again into the silence of his thoughts.

One lone gong bird sounded its monotonous note twice in the darkness. The voice of a hawker selling sweetmeats came disturbingly across the walls. And then, quite close, in the courtyard at the side of the bungalow, Mrs. Moti heard the clanging of the Institute gate and the sound of a taxicab. She looked at Moti. In his absorption in what he was reading, he had heard nothing. So she rose quickly and went through the house to discover who the visitor might be and take care of the business so as not to disturb her husband.

On the rattan sofa, Ali too heard the sounds on the opposite side of the house and sat up very straight with the look of a listening gazelle in his great dark eyes. For a long time he sat thus and presently at the sound of footsteps from inside the house a look of pleasure came into his face, and putting down his guinea pig, he slipped from the divan and ran across to the door. He recognized the sound of the footsteps because for so long he had been "seeing" with his ears.

As he reached the door Buck and Indira Moti came through it. The boy threw his arms about Buck's waist and said, "Sahib Buck, are we going away tonight?"

At the sound of voices Moti at last came out of the depths of his concentration and looked up. The moment he saw Buck he, like Bill, knew something terrible had happened and felt a sudden shock of surprise that Buck could look as he did. He had never thought of Buck as emotional; he was so steady, so gentle, so lost in what he was doing. And Moti thought, "It has happened. She has told him she is going away." He did not divine that it was much worse than that.

Buck said to the boy, "Not tonight, Ali. I only came to talk to Colonel Moti." Then to Indira he said in English, "You'd better take him to bed. He understands much more than we think. I'll come and say good-night to him."

She spoke gently to the boy and reluctantly, he freed Buck and went away with her. Then Buck said quickly to Moti, "She's gone away. Do you know where she is?"

In Ali's bedroom, Indira Moti saw the boy into bed, went to fetch his guinea pig and brought him a glass of water. Then she reassured him, promising him that Buck would come in before he left.

[336]

But she wasn't thinking much about Ali. She was thinking of Buck's anguished face as she saw it for a moment in the dim light of the taxicab lamps and again as she quickly crossed the verandah to fetch the guinea pig. She understood what she saw there and thought, "Moti has played being God once too often."

Moti was a good man, she reflected, a brilliant man, a famous man, but there were times when he was not quite human. He understood equations and serums and social and political economy, but he understood people not at all. People were not mathematical equations; they were flesh and blood and glands and instincts. That was where her simple country training had taught her so much. Now, bending over the boy, she knew that she had known in the afternoon that there was tragedy ahead of them, that there was disappointment for Moti himself.

Now she wanted desperately to help, to do something. But she was unwilling to go to the verandah where the two men were. This was men's business, and an instinct thousands of years old told her to remain where she was. When things were bad enough they would both come to her; she had only to wait. She heard Buck's voice raised in argument, and although she had neither the intention nor the desire to eavesdrop she heard Buck shouting "You wanted this! Well, you've got it! To hell with you and India! I'm going to find her and I'm going with her wherever she goes!"

In an odd unconscious gesture, she drew her sari across her face in the darkness like a Hindu woman in mourning, thinking, "That can't happen. No, that can't happen because it would be the ruin of both of them." And in a clear flash of revelation she realized suddenly that she herself loved Buck and how deeply she loved him—not as Carol loved him but with a different kind of love, as if he were a son she had never had in whom she took great pride. And it was worse than that. In a world filled with disillusionment, with faithless and hard people, Buck was different. The world, her world of India in particular, had desperate need of his goodness and vision and faith. No, Buck could not be destroyed; he could not go away.

She went toward the door of the verandah, forgetting now that this was a man's business. As she reached the verandah, Moti and Buck were coming through the door. At the sight of Moti's face she wanted suddenly to laugh. There was in it a look she had never seen there before, a look of astonishment, almost of bewilderment on the familiar serious face.

Moti said, "We are going to Jai Mahal. I'm going with him."

From Moti's burning eyes she knew the story.

Quickly she said to Buck, "Don't forget Ali. He's keeping himself awake for you to say good-night."

Buck said, "Yes, of course," and went toward Ali's room. She knew that he wasn't thinking of Ali now.

To Moti she said quickly, "It's too late now. You must find her and make her go to Jellapore with him, whatever happens. You've played too often at being God. It never occurred to you that he was flesh and blood and a man."

Moti didn't answer her. He had the look in his eyes which came there when he had, after long and heartbreaking effort, made a new discovery in the laboratory.

In the noisy bar of the Taj, Lieutenant Forsythe was listening to Bill's story.

When Bill said, "You see now why something must be done. You do see, don't you?"

"It will have to be done tonight. The old man isn't easy. He has dyspepsia and he doesn't like to be disturbed late at night." The face of the good-looking A.D.C. had an odd expression. "I should tell you that the whole idea is impossible but I won't. But we ought to go right off. I'll go with you."

"What about your dinner party?"

"It can wait." He grinned, "They won't mind what I do, really—you see, I'm from Government House and they're in trade."

At that moment, over the shoulder of Lieutenant Forsythe, Bill caught a glimpse of Botlivala pushing his way between the tables. He thought, "Oh, my God! Here's more trouble!" There was no escaping Botlivala. Bill had deliberately taken Forsythe into a corner where they would be more or less alone. One more scandal and all chance of straightening things out would be gone forever. He thought, "I knew he was trouble from the first time I saw him. I've got to work fast."

Forsythe rose and started out, followed by Bill. Botlivala didn't notice Forsythe—probably didn't know him. Bill said, "Hello, Botlivala," in his friendliest manner.

But Botlivala was hysterical. The dark skin was gray and the yellowish whites of his eyes showed all around like the eyes of a hypnotist at work. He said, "Where is she? She's mine. Where did you take her?"

"Take it easy," said Bill. "I brought her back here. She wasn't feeling very well. Come out in the hall and we'll talk about it." He put one hand on Botlivala's shoulder. "There's no use getting excited about it."

"I want to know where she is, that's all. You made a fool of me once. It's not going to happen again."

Bill managed to steer Botlivala back to the hall. If he could get him to the harbor side of the hotel it wouldn't matter much what happened; no one would be there to see it.

Outside Forsythe was waiting. Bill said, "Excuse me a minute and I'll be with you."

Forsythe said, "Don't be long or the Governor will be in bed and then there won't be any chance."

"One minute." To Botlivala he said, "Come here and I'll talk to you," and led him round the corner behind the great stairs. The space there was empty. They were alone.

The rage of Botlivala seemed to have increased. It was the insane hatred of the impotent, ill-favored man for one who had everything. There were even little flecks of foam on his lips.

"I'm not going to stand it," Botlivala cried, and at the same time, out of his pocket, he brought a gun.

If he hadn't been in a hurry, Bill wouldn't have been so perturbed. He would have tried talking the dark little man into reason. It wasn't fear which frightened him now. He was in a hurry. He had to see the Governor, and quickly. There wasn't time to argue with Botlivala.

So it happened like lightning. He clipped the dark, insane face a little to the left of the plump chin. A look of astonishment came into the cloudy eyes. The head tilted back. The gun flew upwards and Mr. Botlivala fell against the wall in a sitting position, his head on his chest. He was out.

Bill picked up the gun, put it in his trousers pocket and a moment later he was saying to Forsythe, "Let's go."

"You got rid of him very quickly," said Forsythe as they stepped into a taxi. "He looked as if he wanted to kill you."

"He's always been a nuisance," said Bill, and let it go at that.

The aspect of Government House was not encouraging. It was in darkness save for three or four lights in the wing along the sea. At sight of the taxicab the tall Sikhs in red and gold, lowered their lances until they recognized Forsythe.

Inside the hallway, the A.D.C. said, "You'd better wait here while I talk to him. It will need some persuading."

So Bill, watched from the shadows by a waiting Indian servant, sat on a carved teakwood chair and waited.

It was the first time in a couple of hours that he had had time to think. For the moment she had looked at him and asked, "Bill, will you marry me?" he had known what he had to do. From then on he had acted not from thought or reflection but by impulse and instinct, as if he had been driven by something beyond either his control or his understanding. Now in the darkness, he thought, "Maybe I've been a sap again. Maybe if I had said 'Yes, we'll sail on the *Rajputana*' everything would have worked out well and Carol and I could have built up a good and happy life. Maybe sending her back to Buck will only end in disaster. Maybe I'm just Good-time Charlie again."

But he couldn't quite believe any of these things, because the same force which had driven him to act told him they were not true. What this fore-knowledge was or upon what it was based, he did not know, but the awareness of its power puzzled and awed him. He thought, "Maybe the Hindus are right. Maybe free will is an illusion. Maybe we are simply the victims of circumstances and our own characters." The thought came to him that perhaps Carol was back on the right path, now after all these years, on the other side of the world from where she had set out. Maybe that was where she belonged—this Swedish farm girl—working side by side with Buck among the remote villages. She was healthy and strong and she was not stupid and she was in love. In this life you needed direction, a somewhere to go. That was what had always been wrong with his own life—its aimlessness. Aimlessness was what had gotten Carol into all this trouble. Maybe she was headed back for the right track—if only he could put this through.

His memory of the Governor at lunch did not make him optimistic. He could see the little man with astonishing clarity, coming into the big dining room of this house—bored, cold, unsentimental, efficient and contemptuous.

Then the door opened and Forsythe came out. What could he ever do for Forsythe to recompense him? He must have acted out of pure kindness. There was no reason for him to intercede in behalf of two strangers like Carol and himself.

Forsythe said, "It's all right. He'll see you if you don't mind his receiving you in his dressing gown."

"It wouldn't matter to me if he was naked," said Bill. And then he did for him what was an extraordinary thing and a thing which the A.D.C. found disconcerting. He hugged Forsythe.

Forsythe led him along a passage and at the end held open a door for him. He said, "If you don't mind I'll go back to my dinner party. The rest of it is up to you."

"Thanks," said Bill, "I'll see you later."

The room was a library, small and rather cozy, which must have been the work of the Governor's wife. The Governor himself was sitting behind a desk. At sight of Bill he put down the detective story he was reading, took off his horn-rimmed spectacles and stood up. He was a small, thin, gray man—all gray. He wore a gray silk dressing-gown.

"Mr. Wainwright," he said.

"Yes," said Bill.

"Won't you sit down?" Then he said, "I remember you came to lunch one day weeks ago. My cousin Dorothy wrote me about you. It seems you're a very good friend of hers."

"Yes," said Bill, and to himself, "A very good friend."

"I'm very fond of Dorothy," said the Governor.

Bill thought, "That's good." It was odd how that lunch which had bored him and the letter which he had torn up and burned in the ashtray at Green's Hotel were now being of use.

The Governor was official and unsmiling. Bill had a sudden quick impression that there were no smiles in him. Then he said,

[341]

"Forsythe tells me that you want to intercede for Miss . . ." He hesitated and Bill said quickly, "Miss Carol Halma."

"Yes. That's it. An extraordinary name. Very difficult to remember."

"It is a professional name," said Bill. "She is of Swedish origin. Her real name is Olga Janssen."

"An actress, I believe."

"Yes," said Bill. The word "actress" sounded more dignified than "show-girl," so he allowed it to pass.

"You feel," said the Governor, "that the young woman is being treated unfairly."

"Yes," said Bill. "But it's more than that." As he spoke he had a sudden feeling that the Governor was interested.

"Suppose you tell me your story. Forsythe hinted at it. It didn't seem usual."

Bill thought, "Well, here goes."

He wasn't a storyteller, and he knew that this story must be well told because the whole thing depended upon how well he told it. There was so much too that would be difficult to explain, so much that was against Carol. He leaned forward a little in his chair and began. What he did not know was that the little Forsythe had told the Governor had whetted his appetite for more. The Governor liked reading novels as relaxation, but he liked still better hearing stories at first hand. The Governor's official life had always been a brilliant success. His life in relation to women had always been a notable failure. He laid his glasses on the desk and settled back in his chair to listen.

Although it was a re-telling, Bill told the story even better than he had told it to Forsythe. The force of which he had been aware in the dimly lighted hall came again to his aid. As if he were an actor, he kept one eye on his audience as he progressed. And he thought, although it was unusually difficult to read anything in the blank, cold face of the official, that he was achieving an effect. Even while he was talking, Bill thought, "I must tell him everything. I must stop at nothing. It has to interest him." So he even told of the part he played in Carol's life, that he loved her and that what he was doing now was for the sake of herself and Buck.

[342]

He talked for more than twenty minutes and the Governor still listened.

When he had finished, the little gray man behind the desk, shifted in his chair and said, "It is a very good story. I begin to understand why Forsythe was so affected." Then he was silent and thoughtful, picking up his spectacles and tapping the desk top with them. He did not mind awkward silences. Long ago, in his official capacity, he had learned their power and their disconcerting effect upon others. To Bill the silence seemed to last for years.

At last he said, "I understand why you feel as you do. After hearing the story, I feel inclined to make concessions. I have a great respect for Merrill. He is of the greatest value to us in India. I'm not sure she will be good for him."

"I felt the same way, sir. So did Colonel Moti. But both of us have changed our opinions. It will be worse for him if she is sent away, because he will follow her." He cheated a little in bringing in Moti's name. He did not know whether or not the Colonel had changed.

"The company she surrounded herself with," said the Governor, "is compromising, to say the least. We have had continuous trouble with Jellapore. This man Botlivala is a notorious rake. As for the Baroness and Mrs. Trollope. . . ."

Bill interrupted him, "I am afraid, sir, that a good deal of that is my fault. I introduced her both to the Baroness and Mrs. Trollope. They came out on the same boat with me. None of them are really what you might call 'friends.'"

"This Mrs. Trollope, it seems, has made great trouble for everyone. She is making great trouble for us now. Then we had it from a very good source that Miss Halma was working for the Baroness."

"That is untrue. The Baroness tried to engage her as a cabaret entertainer but she refused." Then he asked, "Is it possible to ask the source of the information? It might clarify matters."

"No," said the Governor, "I am not permitted to reveal names. I can only say that it came from a woman, highly placed, who knew of the Baroness' activities in Italy."

Bill sat up a little straighter in his chair. The single word "Italy" gave him the clue. It was like fitting a key in a lock. He saw it all now. The Marchesa! In her curious depraved passion for himself, she had wanted to get Carol out of the way because she knew all the time that she was a rival. This was a quick and easy way to do it. Denounce the Baroness, which was easy, and implicate Carol with her! That was how she knew Carol was being shipped on the *Rajputana*. He thought, "I must go carefully." Yet he felt that somehow he now held the key in his hand. Then suddenly he knew what to do. He had to act boldly.

He said, "I am afraid, sir, that the source is not very reliable."

"Why do you say that?"

"Because the Marchesa hates the Baroness. The Marchesa began her career as a girl in one of the Baroness' establishments."

Then for the first time the Governor showed signs of life. He leaned over the desk and asked, "How do you know that?"

"The Marchesa herself told me."

"Why would a woman so highly placed—the wife of an Italian General—reveal such a thing to a man?"

There was nothing for it. He had to jump. He said, "Because I happen to know her . . . intimately, *very* intimately, since I've been in India. She has just been with me in Calcutta and Madras. I think she was jealous of Miss Halma."

Then an extraordinary thing happened to the gray, stony face of the Governor. Little wrinkles appeared about the gray blue eyes. The lips curled at the corners with unsuspected humor. The Governor was breaking down.

He said, "I'm beginning to think that instead of sending Miss Halma away, I should take her under my wing to protect her from her friends."

Bill tried not to smile. He said, "I have told you everything, sir. I haven't held anything back."

Drily the Governor said, "There couldn't be much more, I should think."

But the Governor was thinking of something else and the something else delighted his Anglo-Saxon soul at that moment. It was the idea that a great Fascist leader had married a woman out of a brothel. The little wrinkles about the eyes and mouth increased in number. He said, "I have never been able to understand the Latin races."

[344]

Then his face grew serious. "But that has nothing to do with our problem," he said. "While you were talking, I've been thinking. I think we could make a compromise in the matter. It seems to me that there is a possibility that Miss Halma has been unfairly treated, and we certainly cannot afford to lose Merrill. He has peculiar gifts, tact and training which it would be very difficult to replace."

"Yes sir," said Bill, feeling rather like a boy who was being reprimanded.

"I suggest that we rescind the request for deportation—(Bill held his breath)—on the understanding that Miss Halma leaves for Jellapore with Merrill and that she marries him and gives her parole not to return to Bombay for a period of three years."

"I am sure," said Bill, "that she would not have the least objection to giving her parole. I doubt that she ever wants to see Bombay again."

"I've no objection to her going to Madras or Calcutta but I would advise her to keep clear of Delhi as well as Bombay for at least that amount of time."

Bill thought, "It's done! It's done!" But in the midst of his pride and triumph, there was a shade of sadness as well. The Governor had not finishing talking. He was saying, "People forget things easily. In three years they will have forgotten that Mrs. Merrill was ever Miss Halma. And after three years of life in the climate of the Jellapore villages I imagine that her looks will have changed so much that no one will remember her or trouble to look twice in her direction." He put on his glasses again. "Does that compromise seem satisfactory, Mr. Wainwright? It seems to me just, having considered all the circumstances."

The Governor's hand stole out toward his detective story. He said, "Allow me to say, Mr. Wainwright, that you tell a good story extraordinarily well."

Bill stood up and crossed to the desk. The Governor rose and held out his hand.

"Thank you, sir. I appreciate what you have done more than I can say."

"I have tried to be just and reasonable," said the Governor. "In Bombay it is sometimes very difficult to find the proper course.

Circumstances always seem to be very complex and confused. Good-night and when you see my cousin, give her my love."

"Good-night," said Bill.

He went out quickly, leaving the Governor to his detective story, and as he closed the door, he felt suddenly tired, more tired than he had ever been in all his life. He thought, "I hope there's a drink at the Maharani's."

In the taxicab on the way up Malabar Hill to the pink marble palace he went over the scene again in his mind, and presently he divined what it was that had won his victory. It wasn't the story he told. It was what he had said about the Marchesa. From the moment he had mentioned the Marchesa and her history, the little wrinkles about the eyes and mouth of the Governor had multiplied and with them his whole manner had changed.

"For once," thought Bill, "being a cad paid." But again he thought, "She asked for it, the bitch!"

It was odd that out of two affairs, that half-forgotten one in London with the Governor's own cousin and the boring, reluctant one in India with the Marchesa, had come all this good. The one had given him access to the Governor; the other had aroused the Governor and changed his humor.

In the darkness of the taxi, he laughed, "Maybe in the scheme of things, that's all I'm good for."

He found her in the small salon where the bullet from the Maharani's revolver had chipped the crystal chandelier. At the table just beneath the chandelier, sat the Maharani with three women playing mahjong. Beside them was a box of sweets and a bottle of champagne in a cooler. One of the women was Indian, the other two were European, rather dyed and made up and disreputable in appearance. Carol, dressed now in other clothes, sat watching them.

He said good-evening to the Maharani, acknowledged an introduction to the three women without hearing their names, and said quickly to Carol, "It's all right. I've come to take you back."

"All right," she said quietly, and got up like an obedient child to follow him. She said good-night to the Maharani and the three disreputable women, thanking the Maharani for having given her refuge.

"Good luck," said the Maharani.

Then Carol took up her jewel case and two packages done in white paper.

"I'll carry the case," said Bill.

"Okay."

In the taxicab outside Carol said, "Do you mean that you fixed it?"

"Yes," said Bill, and told her of the scene with the Governor. He told her everything, even about the Marchesa, sparing nothing. He told her quickly, because the reaction had come now. He felt excited. He wanted her to feel gay.

But his own gaiety did not touch her. When he had finished she was quiet for a long time. Presently, as they were passing the suburban railway station by the beach, she said, "It's funny how things get tangled up."

Bill laughed, "Yes, isn't it?"

"You're a swell guy, Bill."

"Oh, I'm not so bad."

Then suddenly she began to cry, quietly, making scarcely a sound. He only knew that she was crying by the sobs. He took her hand and said, "You mustn't do that. We're going to the hotel. You must pull yourself together."

"Let me alone, Bill. I was so frightened. I'm just crying out of relief."

"Are you going to be a good girl now?"

"Yes, honey. That's all I want."

"And not make trouble for Buck?"

"How can you ask that? Where is he? Will he be at the hotel?"

"I don't know. He went out to find you. He was going to see Moti and then to Jai Mahal."

"Oh, Bill. I love him so much. Nothing will happen to him, will it?"

"No . . . of course not. Tomorrow you'll be going to Jellapore." There was a silence and presently he asked, "Have you ever seen a cholera epidemic?"

"No."

"It's not very nice. In fact it's bloody awful."

"I don't care . . . not so long as I'm with him."

"I'm just preparing you. You're not going back to the Garden of Eden." And with a sensation of chill he remembered what the Governor had said of her beauty. After three years . . .

Then the taxicab slowed up at the harbor side of the hotel and they got out. Inside the hotel he stopped by the door. It was late and the hall was empty. Somebody must have found Botlivala or he had come round by himself and gone away. He felt the revolver in his trousers pocket and thought, "I wanted excitement, I sure found it." The whole thing was melodramatic, idiotic.

He said, "I'm not going upstairs."

"All right."

"I'm going to say good-night here and good-bye."

She looked at him in surprise. "Aren't you going to see Buck?"

"Yes . . . but I'd rather see him alone."

"I see." She held up the two paper parcels. "You've been swell, Bill. I hate to ask anything more, but I don't know what to do with these."

"What are they?"

"The jewelry—the big package is to go to Botlivala and the other to Jellapore's brother. They're marked. I don't know how to get them to them."

"I'll take care of it for you. I'll have the company's lawyer take care of it."

"Good-night, honey."

"Good-night." Then he said, "Buck doesn't need to know about the deportation business. Nobody needs to know."

"No. I'll never tell him."

"Write to me sometimes and tell me what's happening to you."

"Sure. You too."

"Good-night."

"Good-night."

Then she turned, awkwardly, and went away. He watched her until she turned a corner toward the lift and then waited to give her time to get out of the way.

Then he went to the desk and left orders to tell him when Mr. Merrill came in. After that he went straight to the bar and ordered

[348]

a gin sling. He wished he had somebody to drink with him—even Botlivala or the Marchesa. In that noisy, crowded room it was horribly lonely. It was going to be like that for the rest of his life.

It was nearly two o'clock when he saw Buck standing in the doorway, his hair still rumpled, the wild look of despair still in his eyes. Bill stood up and then Buck came quickly over to him.

"Did you find her?"

"Yes," said Bill. "It's all right. She's upstairs in her room. She's going to Jellapore with you tomorrow."

Buck sat down suddenly and turned very white.

"You'd better have a drink," said Bill.

"No, I'm going up to her."

"Finish my drink. It'll put you on your feet."

"Okay." Buck took the rest of the gin sling and finished it off. "You're a swell guy, Bill," he said.

"Skip it."

Then Buck stood up.

"Good-night," said Bill, "and good-bye."

"What do you mean . . . good-bye?"

"You're going away tomorrow. I'm leaving day after. It makes more sense to say good-bye now."

Then in a flash of the old understanding between them, Buck saw. "I see. I guess you're right. When will you be coming back?"

"I don't know. Some day. Write to me."

"I will. You write to me. Don't be like you were before."

"No."

"Good luck."

"Good luck."

Then Buck went away. Bill looked after him until he disappeared in the crowded doorway. Then he had another drink and the room became unbearable to him and he went to bed.

The smell of garlands of jasmine and marigold clung to the *Rajputana* long after she had left the pier crowded by farewell parties. The big ship had passed Elephanta on one side and Juhu on the other before the Goanese deck hands began gathering the bruised and trampled remnants of the flowers from beneath deck chairs and out of corners.

Bill stood at the stern alone at the rail, watching Bombay slip into a haze of heat. The Taj Mahal, the Readymoney Building, the Gateway to India wavered, trembled in the mirage and slowly vanished like the Fisherman's City in the *Thousand and One Nights.* A couple of Arabs and two or three Somalis in a *dhow* outward-bound for Africa waved as the great ship slipped past them.

Then Bill was aware of someone standing beside him and over and above the scent of crushed jasmine and marigold the sickly odor of patchouli came into his nostrils. He turned and the Baroness said, "Vell, dere she goes . . . dot feelthy city. I'm not sorry to be leaving."

"No. I've had enough."

"Fonny that ve should go back on de same boat."

"Yes," said Bill, "isn't it?"

There was a silence and the Baroness said, "You heard about Meesis Trollope?"

"No."

"She keeled herself."

The news shocked him out of his indifference.

"How? When?" he asked.

"Thees morning. Carol vent to see her, but it vas too late. She had already hunk herself in her cell."

Bill couldn't think of anything to say. Anyway Mrs. Trollope had solved the Governor's problem. She wouldn't be any more trouble to him. And she wouldn't be any more trouble to herself. It shocked him that he felt so little one way or another. The only emotion he felt was one of horror, because somehow she ought to be here standing at the rail beside himself and the Baroness. She belonged here, on her way somewhere else. She couldn't be dead. She was, in an odd way, eternal, like the Wandering Jew.

He heard the Baroness saying, "She vas a boring voman and a fool. She never knew vere she vas going. In de end dere vas no place for her to go."

Then he noticed that Elephanta with its temples was being swallowed up in the hot mist as the city had been. Its low hills and palms shivered and danced and then suddenly were gone. The water beneath the ship was changing color. The muddiness of the bay was fading, replaced by brilliant purple and aquamarine of the Indian Ocean. The smell of India—that strange smell compounded of jasmine and cow dung smoke, spices and dust—was fading. A little way from the ship three or four flying fish darted, now in, now out of the white-crested waves like pencils of light. For no reason at all he was aware of a swift feeling of relief and peace. It was over.

Suddenly he grinned, thinking, "Good-time Charlie is dead." But feeling a little sad, he said aloud, "Good-bye."

Beside him the Baroness asked, "Vat did you say?"

"Nothing. I was talking to myself."

FINIS